ROUGH & TUMBLE

RHENNA MORGAN

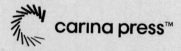

carina press™

ISBN-13: 978-1-335-01489-4

Rough & Tumble

This edition published by arrangement with Harlequin Books S.A.

® and TM are trademarks of the publisher. Trademarks indicated with ® are registered in the United States Patent and Trademark Office, the Canadian Intellectual Property Office and in other countries.

www.CarinaPress.com

Printed in U.S.A.

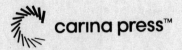
carina press™

Rough & Tumble
By Rhenna Morgan

**Live hard, f*ck harder and follow only their own rules.
Those are the cornerstones the six men of the Haven
Brotherhood live and bleed by, refusing to conform
to society's expectations, taking what they want and
always watching each other's backs.**

A self-made man with his fingers in a variety of success-
ful businesses, Jace Kennedy lives for the challenge and he
always gets what he wants. From the start, he sees Vivienne Moore's hidden wild side and knows she's his perfect
match, if only he can break it free. He will have her. One
way or another.

Vivienne's determined to ditch the rough lifestyle she
grew up in, even if that means hiding her true self behind
a bland socialite veneer. Dragging her party-hound sister
out of a club was *not* how she wanted to ring in the New
Year, but Viv knows the drill. Get in, get her sister and get
back to the safe, stable life she's built for herself as fast as
humanly possible. But Viv's plans are derailed when she
finds herself crashing into the club's clearly badass and
dangerously sexy owner.

Jace is everything Vivienne swore she never wanted, but
the more time she spends with him, the more she starts to
see that he loves just as fiercely as he fights. He can walk
society's walk and talk society's talk, but when he wants
something, he finds a way to get it. He's proud of who he
is and where he came from, and he'll be damned if he lets
Vivienne go before showing her the safest place of all is

in the arms of a dangerous man.

This book is approximately 105,000 words
Edited by Angela James

One-click with confidence. This title is part of the Carina Press Romance Promise: all the romance you're looking for with an HEA/HFN. It's a promise! Find out more at CarinaPress.com/RomancePromise

Dear Reader,

I'm practically cackling and rubbing my hands with glee at the amazing books we have in store for you this month. You're going to fall in love with the newest additions to the Carina Press author lineup while enjoying the very best of our returning authors. Forgive me for saying it but...whee! Read on for the goodness...

This month Lucy Parker brings us her much anticipated sequel to contemporary romance *Act Like It. Pretty Face* returns readers to the highly acclaimed world of the London stage with laugh-out-loud wit and plenty of drama. Iconic director Luc Savage is in for a surprise with his new show—not to mention a May-December romance with its feisty star!

New-to-Carina-Press author Rhenna Morgan kicks off her new super-sexy contemporary romance series with *Rough & Tumble*. With his badass don't-take-no-for-an-answer approach to life, Jace Kennedy is everything Vivienne Moore swore she never wanted in a man—especially after the rough lifestyle she grew up in. But Jace sees the hidden wild side in Vivienne, and he won't give up until he shows her the safest place is in the arms of a dangerous man. By the way, Jace might be a badass, but he's no alphahole. This is a guy every inch in love with his lady and willing to treat her like gold.

We return to Lauren Dane's Cascadia Wolves series with *Wolf Unbound*. We meet Tegan—a Pack Enforcer who, after the death of her mate, thought she'd be alone forever. Until she meets Ben, handsome, dominant...and human.

Amber Bardan returns with a stunning new stand-alone sultry contemporary romance in *King's Captive*. In Julius's world, on his island, he is King. Money and power mean he rules all around him—including her.

In fan-favorite A.M. Arthur's newest male/male romance, *As I Am*, scarred shut-in Taz finally braves the outside world for intensely shy Will, but secrets from both of their pasts could destroy their fragile new love.

Fans of Scott Hildreth's *The Gun Runner* be prepared! Michael Tripp is back and as bad as ever in *The Game Changer*. Tripp and Terra are moving toward their happily-ever-after, but first they have to overcome the secrets they're still keeping from each other—and her mafia family's inexorable determination to pull Tripp into *la famiglia*.

We're introducing three debut authors this month. First, Join Agents Irish & Whiskey in *Single Malt*, Layla Reyne's debut male/male romantic suspense. Widowed FBI agent and Irish ex-pat Aidan Talley falls hard for his handsome younger partner, Jameson "Whiskey" Walker, as they investigate cybercrimes and the murder of Aidan's late husband.

In *Mark of the Moon*, a hookup with a vampire goes wrong when Dana Markovitz is scratched by a jealous were-cat. You won't want to miss this sexy new urban fantasy series from debut author Beth Dranoff.

From debut author Sarah Hawthorne comes *Enforcer's Price*, book one in the Demon Horde series. In this romantic motorcycle club romance, Colt is just starting to trust again, but Krista is hiding something big. Can he still love her when she reveals sex and money go hand in hand for her?

Don't miss this amazing lineup of new and returning authors, and look for their next books in the upcoming months!

Next month: Don't miss Shannon Stacey's return to the world of everyone's favorite blue-collar family, the Kowalskis, with a heart-warming and funny all-new romance that also reunites you with all your favorite Kowalskis.

As always, until next month, my fellow book lovers, here's wishing you a wonderful month of books you love, remember and recommend.

Happy reading!
Angela James

Editorial Director, Carina Press

Dedication

For my readers—the lovers of happily-ever-afters and knights in tarnished armor. This world needs more romantics like us.

ONE

NOTHING LIKE A New Year's Eve drunk-sister-search-and-rescue to top off a chaos-laden twelve-hour workday. Vivienne dialed Shinedown's newest release from full blast to almost nothing and whipped her Honda hybrid into a pay-by-the-hour lot in the heart of Dallas's Deep Ellum. Five freaking weekends in a row Callie had pulled this crap, with way too many random SOS calls before her current streak.

At least this place was in a decent part of town. Across the street, men and women milled outside a new bar styled like an old-fashioned pub called The Den, with patrons dressed in everything from T-shirts and faded jeans, to leather riding gear and motorcycle boots. Not one of them looked like they were calling the party quits anytime soon.

Viv tucked her purse beneath the seat, stashed her key fob in her pocket, and strode into the humid January night. Her knockoff Jimmy Choos clicked against the aged blacktop, and cool fog misted her cheeks.

Off to one side, an appreciative whistle sounded between low, masculine voices.

She kept her head down, hustled through the dark double doors and into a cramped, black-walled foyer. A crazy-big bouncer with mocha skin and dreads leaned against the doorjamb between her and the main bar, his attention centered on a stunning brunette in a soft pink wifebeater, jeans, and stilettos.

The doors behind her clanged shut.

Pushing to full height, the bouncer warily scanned Viv head to toe. Hard to blame the guy. Outside of health inspectors and liquor licensing agents, they probably didn't get many suits in here, and she'd bet none of them showed in silk shirts.

"ID," he said.

"I'm not here to stay. I just need to find someone."

He smirked and crossed his arms. "Can't break the rules, momma. No ID, no party."

"I don't want a party, I want to pick up my sister and then I'm out. She said she'd be up front. About my height, light brown, curly hair and three sheets to the wind?"

"You must mean Callie," the brunette said. "She was up here about an hour ago mumbling something about *sissy*, so I'm guessing you're her." She leaned into Scary Bouncer Dude's formidable chest, grinned up at him, and stroked his biceps with an almost absentminded reverence. "May as well let her in. If you don't, Trev will spend closing time hearing his waitresses bitch about cleaning up puke."

Too bad Viv didn't have someone to bitch to about getting puke detail. Callie sure as heck never listened.

Bouncer dude stared Viv down and slid his mammoth hand far enough south he palmed the brunette's ass. He jerked his head toward the room beyond the opening. "Make it quick. You might be old enough, but the cops have been in three times tonight chomping to bust our balls on any write-up they can find."

Finally, something in her night that didn't require

extra time and trouble. Though if she'd been smart, she'd have grabbed her ID before she came in.

"Smart move, chief." The woman tagged him with a fast but none-too-innocent kiss, winked, and motioned for Viv to follow. "Come on. I'll show you where she is."

An even better break. The last search and rescue had taken over thirty minutes in a techno dance bar. She'd finally found Callie passed out under a set of stairs not far from the main speakers, but the ringing in Viv's ears had lasted for days. At least this time she'd have a tour guide and an extra pair of hands.

The place was as eclectic on the inside as it was out. Rock and movie collectibles hung on exposed brick walls and made the place look like it'd been around for years even though it reeked of new. Every table was packed. Waitresses navigated overflowing trays between the bustling crowd, and Five Finger Death Punch vibrated loud enough to make conversation a challenge.

The brunette smiled and semi-yelled over one shoulder, never breaking her hip-slinging stride. "Nice turnout for an opening week, yeah?"

Well, that explained the new smell. "I don't do crowds." At least not this kind. Signing her dad's Do Not Resuscitate after a barroom brawl had pretty much cured her of smoky, dark and wild. "It looks like a great place though."

The woman paused where the bar opened to a whole different area and scanned Viv's outfit. "From the looks of things, you could use a crowd to loosen up." She shrugged and motioned toward the rear of the room. "Corner booth. Last I saw your girl she was propped up between two airheads almost as hammered as she was. And don't mind Ivan. The cops are only hound-

ing the owner, not the customers. My name's Lily if
you need anything." And then she was gone, saunter-
ing off to a pack of women whooping it up at the opposite end of the club.

So much for an extra set of hands. At least this part
of the bar was less crowded, scattered sitting areas with
every kind of mismatched chair and sofa you could
think of making it a whole lot easier to case the place.

She wove her way across the stained black concrete
floors toward the randomly decorated booths along the
back. Overhead, high-end mini sparkle lights cast the
room in a muted, sexy glow. Great for ambience, but
horrid for picking drunk sisters out of a crowd. Still,
Viv loved the look. She'd try the same thing in her own
place if it wouldn't ruin the tasteful uptown vibe in her
new townhouse. Funky might be fun, but it wouldn't
help with resale.

Laughter and a choking cloud of smoke mushroomed
out from the corner booth.

The instant Viv reached the table, the chatter died.
Three guys, two girls and the stench of Acapulco Red—
but no sister. "You guys see Callie?"

A lanky man with messy curly blond hair eyed her
beneath thirty-pound eyelids and grinned, not even
bothering to hide the still smoldering joint. "'Sup."

The redhead cozied next to him smacked him on the
shoulder and glowered. "She's after Callie, Mac. Not
stopping in for a late-night chat." She reached across the
table and handed Viv an unpaid bar tab. "She headed
to the bathroom about ten minutes ago, but be sure you
take this with you. She stuck me with the bill last night."

Seventy-eight bucks. A light night for New Year's
Eve, which was a damn good thing considering Viv's

bank balance. She tucked the tab in her pocket. "Which way to the bathroom?"

The girl pointed toward a dark corridor. "Down that hall and on your left."

Viv strode that direction, not bothering with any follow-up niceties. Odds were good they wouldn't remember her in the morning, let alone five minutes from now.

Inside the hallway, the steady drone of music and laughter plunged to background noise. Two scowling women pranced past her headed back into the bar. One glanced over her shoulder and shook her head at Viv. "May as well head to the one up front. Someone's in that one and isn't coming out anytime soon from the sound of things."

Well, shit. This was going to be fun. She wiggled the knob. "Callie?"

God, she hoped it was her sister in there. Knowing her luck, she was interrupting a New Year's booty call. Although, if that were the case, they were doing it wrong because it was way too quiet. She tried the knob again and knocked on the door. "Callie, it's Viv. Open up."

Still no answer.

Oh, to hell with it. She banged on the door and gave it the good old pissed-off-sister yell. "Callie, for the love of God, open the damned door! I want to go home."

A not so promising groan sounded from inside a second before the door marked Office at her right swung wide. A tall Adonis in jeans and a club T-shirt emblazoned with The Den's edgy logo blocked the doorway, his sky blue eyes alert in a way that shouldn't be possible past 1:00 a.m.

Two men filled the space behind him, one shirtless

with arms braced on the top of a desk, and another leaning close, studying the shirtless guy's shoulder. No wait, he wasn't studying it, he was stitching it, which explained the seriously bloody shirt on the floor.

"Got more bathrooms up front. No need to break down the damned door." Adonis Man ambled toward her, zigzagging his attention between her and the bathroom. "There a problem?"

Dear God in heaven, now that the Adonis had moved out of the way, the shirtless guy was on full, mouthwatering display, and he was every book boyfriend and indecent fantasy rolled up into one. A wrestler's body, not too big and not too lean, but one hundred percent solid. A huge tattoo covered his back, a gnarled and aged tree with a compass worked into the gothic design. And his ass. Oh hell, that ass was worth every torturous hour in front of her tonight. The only thing better than seeing it in seriously faded Levi's would be seeing it naked.

"Hey," Adonis said. "You gonna ogle my brother all night, or tell me why you're banging down one of my doors?"

They were brothers? No way. Adonis was all…well, Adonis. The other guy was tall, dark and dirty.

Fantasy Man peered over his injured shoulder. Shrewd, almost angry eyes lasered on her, just as dark as his near-black hair. A chunk of the inky locks had escaped his ponytail and fell over his forehead. His closely cropped beard gave him a sinister and deadly edge that probably kept most people at a distance, but his lips could lull half the women in Texas through hell if it meant they'd get a taste.

Viv shook her head and coughed while her mind clambered its way up from Smuttville. "Um…" Her heart thrummed to the point she thought her head would float off her shoulders, and her tongue was so dry it wouldn't work right. "I think my sister's passed out in there. I just want to get her home."

Adonis knocked on the door and gave the knob a much firmer twist than Viv had. "Zeke, toss me the keys off the desk."

Before either of the men could move, the lock on the door popped and the door creaked open a few inches. "Vivie?" Callie's mascara-streaked face flashed a second before the door slipped shut again.

Months of training kicked in and Viv lurched forward, easing open the door and slipping inside. "I've got it now. Give me a minute to get her cleaned up and gather her stuff."

Adonis blocked the door with his foot. The black, fancy cowboy boots probably cost more than a month's mortgage payment, which seemed a shame considering it didn't look like she'd be able to pay her next one. "You sure you don't need help?"

"Nope." She snatched a few towels out of the dispenser and wetted them, keeping one eye on Callie where she semi-dozed against the wall. "We've done this before. I just need a few minutes and a clear path."

"All right. My name's Trevor if you need me. You know where we are if you change your mind." He eased his foot away, grinned and shook his head.

"Oh!" Viv caught the door before it could close all the way and pulled the bar tab out of her pocket. "My sister ran up a tab. Could you hold this at the bar for me and let me pay it after I get her out to the car? I need to grab my purse first."

He backtracked, eyeballed Callie behind her, and

crumpled the receipt. "I'd say you've already covered tonight." He turned for the office. "We'll call it even."

Fantasy Man was still locked in place and glaring over one shoulder, the power behind his gaze as potent as the crackle and hum after a nearby lightning strike.

She ducked back into the bathroom and locked the door, her heart jackrabbiting right back up where it had been the first time he'd looked at her. She seriously needed to get a grip on her taste in men. Suits and education were a much safer choice. Manners and meaningful conversation. Not bloody T-shirts, smoky bars and panty-melting grins.

Snatching Callie's purse off the counter, she let out a serrated breath, shook out the wadded wet towel, and started wiping the black streaks off her sister's cheek. A man like him wouldn't be interested in her anyway. At least, not the new and improved her. And the odds of them running into each other again in a city like Dallas were slim to none, so she may as well wrangle up her naughty thoughts and keep them in perspective.

On the bright side, she didn't have to worry about the tab. Plus, she had a fresh new imaginary star for her next late-night rendezvous with BOB.

DAMN IF THIS hadn't been the most problematic New Year's Eve in history. It wasn't Jace's first knife wound, but getting it while pulling apart two high-powered, hot-headed drug dealers promised future complications he didn't need. Add to that, two more customers arrested at his own club, Crossroads, in less than three days, and nonstop visits from the cops at The Den, and his New Year wasn't exactly top-notch.

Thank God his brother Zeke wasn't working trauma

tonight or he'd have had to have Trev stitch him up. That motherfucker would've hacked the shit out of his tat.

"You 'bout done?" Jace said.

Zeke layered one last strip of tape in place and tossed the roll to the desk. "I am now."

"Took you long enough." Jace straightened up, tucked the toothpick he'd had pinched between his fingers into his mouth and rolled his shoulder. It was tight and throbbing like a son of a bitch, but not bad enough to keep him from day-to-day shit—assuming he didn't have any more drug dealer run-ins.

"I don't know. Our straitlaced partygoer didn't seem to mind me taking my time." Zeke packed his supplies into one of the locked cabinets, the same triage kit they kept at every residence or business they owned. It might have been overkill, but it sure as hell beat emergency rooms and sketchy conversations with police. "Thought for a minute there the sweet little thing was going to combust."

"Sweet little thing my ass." Trevor dropped into his desk chair, propped his booted feet on the corner of his desk, and fisted the remote control for the security vids mounted on the wall. "I'd bet my new G6 that woman's got a titanium backbone and a mind that would whip both your asses into knots."

Jace snatched a fresh white club T-shirt from Trev's grand opening inventory and yanked it over his head, the wound in his shoulder screaming the whole time. "Based on what? Her courtroom getup or her uptight hairdo?"

"Like I judge by what people wear. You know me better than that." Trev punched a few buttons, paused long enough to eyeball the new bartender he'd just hired ringing in an order on the register, then dropped the remote on the desk. "You ask me, you're the one judging. Which is kind of the pot calling the kettle black."

The setback hit its mark, the Haven tags he wore weighting his neck a little heavier, a reminder of their brotherhood and the code they lived by.

It's not where a man comes from, or what he wears, that matters. It's what he does with his life that counts.

Twenty-seven years he and Axel had lived by that mantra, dragging themselves out of the trailer park and into a brotherhood nothing but death would breach.

"He's right," Zeke said. "You're letting Paul's campaign crawl up your ass and it's knockin' you off course."

Damn, but he hated it when his own mantras got tossed back at him. More so when he deserved it. He let out an exhausted huff and dropped down on the leather couch facing the string of monitors. "Play it again."

Trevor shook his head but navigated the menu on the center screen anyway.

"Not sure why you're doing this to yourself, man." Zeke pulled three Modelos out of the stainless minifridge under the wet bar and popped the tops faster than any bartender. God knew he'd gotten enough experience working as one through med school. "Paul's a politician with a grudge, nothing else. Watching this again is just self-inflicted pain. Focus on the real problem."

Jace took the beer Zeke offered as the ten o'clock news story flashed on the screen. The third-string reporter's too-bright smile and pageant hairdo screamed of a woman with zero experience but eager for a shot at a seat behind the anchor desk.

"*Dallas's popular club, Crossroads, is in the news*

again this New Year's Eve as two additional patrons were arrested on charges of drug possession with intent to distribute. Undercover police are withholding names at this time, but allege both are part of a ring lead by Hugo Moreno, a dealer notorious in many Northeast Texas counties for peddling some of the most dangerous products on the street."

"She's not wrong on that score." Zeke plopped on the other end of the couch and motioned to the screen with his bottle. "The number of ODs coming in at Baylor and Methodist the last six months have been through the roof. The guys from DPD swear most are tied to some designer shit coming out of Moreno's labs."

Trevor leaned in and planted his elbows on the desk, eyes to Jace. "You think Otter's going to hold out long enough to waylay Moreno?"

If Jace knew the answer to that one, he'd be a lot less jumpy and minus one slash to his shoulder. Pushing one pharmaceutical genius out of his club by strong-arming him with another was a risky move at best, but it sure as shit beat ousting Moreno on his own. "Otter's a good man with a calm head on his shoulders and a strong team. If he says he'll only let weed in the place and keep Hugo at bay, I'm gonna give him all the backing he needs. DPD's sure as hell not going to help. Not the ones in Paul's pockets, anyway."

"Paul doesn't have any pockets," Trev said. "Only his daddy does."

Right on cue, the camera cut to an interview with Paul Renner as reporters intercepted him leaving another political fundraiser.

"Councilman Renner, you've been very vocal in your run for U.S. Representative in supporting the

Dallas Police Department's efforts to crack down on drug crime, and have called out establishments such as Crossroads in midtown Dallas. Have you heard about the additional drug arrests there tonight, and do you have any comments?"

Renner frowned at the ground, a picture-perfect image of disappointment and concern. Like that dickhead hadn't been trying to screw people since his first foray from the cradle.

"I continue to grow more concerned with establishments like those run by Jace Kennedy and his counterparts," Renner said. *"It seems they continually skirt justice and keep their seedy establishments open for business. It's innocent citizens who end up paying the price, courted by heinous individuals peddling dangerous substances and amoral behavior. My primary goal, if elected to the House of Representatives, will be to promote legislation that makes it difficult for men like Mr. Kennedy and Mr. Moreno to escape justice."*

The toothpick between Jace's teeth snapped in half. He tossed it to the coffee table in front of him and pulled another one of many stashed in the pocket of his jacket.

"It's official, now." Trevor raised his beer in salute and tipped his head. "You're an amoral son of a bitch leading innocent citizens to ruin."

Motion registered in one of the smaller security screens, the bathroom door outside Trevor's office swinging open enough to let Little Miss and her seriously drunken sister ping-pong down the hallway. The two were about the same height, but you couldn't have dressed two women more differently. Next to Little Miss, her sister was best suited for a biker bar, all tits, ass and wobbling heels. Not that she was bad to look at. She just lacked the natural, earthy grace of the sober one.

Damn it, he needed to pace. Or get laid. Just looking at the ass on Little Miss in tailored pants made him want to rut like a madman. Never mind the puzzle she presented. Trev wasn't wrong—she had a shitload of backbone blazing through those doe-shaped eyes. The combination didn't jive with her image. Nothing like a paradox to get his head spinning.

"Guess we found one way to get his head off Renner." Zeke knocked back another gulp of his beer.

"What?" He back and forthed a glare between his brothers.

Trevor chuckled low and shifted the videos so Little Miss's trek to the front of the bar sat center stage. "Zeke said the only thing you've done amoral was that freak show you put on with Kat and Darcy at last month's barbecue."

"Fuck you, Trev."

"Fuck her, you mean," Trev said. "No shame there, brother. You didn't even see her up close. If you did, you sure as shit wouldn't be sitting here rerunning sound bites of asshole Renner."

"Hell, no," Jace said. "A woman that uptight is the last thing I need. Or did you miss her casing not just Zeke patching up my shoulder, but the bloody shirt on the floor, too? You'll be lucky if the cops don't show from an anonymous tip called in."

Little Miss and her sister stumbled into the front section of the bar, the sister's arm curled around Little Miss's neck in a way he'd bet would still hurt tomorrow morning.

Nope. Sweet hips, fiery eyes and a good dose of mystery or not, she was the last thing he needed right now.

Two men blocked Little Miss's path.

The women stopped, and the drunk sister swayed enough it was a wonder she didn't topple onto the table beside her.

One of the men palmed the back of Little Miss's neck, and she jerked away.

Jace surged to his feet, grabbing his leather jacket off the table. "I'm headed to Haven. You hear more from Axel at Crossroads or get any more grief from the cops, let me know."

Both men let out hardy guffaws and waved him off.

"Twenty bucks says our buttoned-up guest gets some help on the way out the door," Trev said.

Zeke chimed in behind him. "Yeah, let us know if Sweet Cheeks tastes as good as she looks."

Bastards. The sad thing was, Trev was about to score a twenty from Zeke, because Jace might not be willing to curl up with Little Miss, but he wasn't watching men paw her either.

TWO

Viv tightened her arm around Callie's waist and shook off the not-so-shy behemoth of a man gripping the back of her neck. His height alone was enough to make him intimidating, but paired with his shaved head and leathers, the scary vibe packed an extra punch. "I appreciate the offer, but we'll be fine."

"Ah, come on, darlin'." He stepped closer and shot a quick, conspiratorial grin at his cohort in crime, a much smaller guy who more than made up in the shaggy hair department what Cue Ball was missing. "Just trying to help out. Can't have a pretty thing like you out on the streets alone this time of night."

Stupid, stubborn men. One thing about guys who lived and breathed a hard life, they seemed to think the word *no* was a coy version of *maybe*. She feigned an innocent smile as best she could with Callie wrenching her neck. "Well, before I take you up on that, I should warn you, Callie's probably about five minutes from puking on anything or anyone within a twenty-foot radius. Seeing as how I'm right next to her, that would include me. You still up for helping?"

The mood killer worked even better than she expected, dousing the naughty gleam in both men's eyes faster than the people at the table behind them downed their shots. The big guy stepped back and waved her through without another word.

Viv half laughed and half scoffed, leaning into her first few steps to get some extra forward momentum.

Callie staggered closer and nuzzled next to Viv, her words coming out in a drunken, sleepy slur. "Thanks for coming to get me, Vivie." The scent of tequila and other things Viv didn't want to contemplate blasted across her nose and riled what little was left of the snack she'd pilfered at the New Year's Eve party. "You're a good sister. I can always count on you."

An uncomfortable pang rattled in her chest, memories of coming home to an empty apartment when Mom and Dad should've been there clanging together all at once. Family was supposed to be there for one another. To love each other and have their backs, not leave them to grapple with life all alone. "Yeah, Callie. I'm here. Always."

The bouncer who'd let her in took one look at her sister and stepped out of hurling range. "See you found your girl."

"I did, thanks." She shouldered the main door open and braced when Callie stumble-stepped down to the sidewalk. A little farther and she'd be home free, or at least in a place where she could battle the rest of the night barefoot in a comfy pair of sweats.

Behind her, the bar door chunked open, and a few of the people crowded in front of the bar called out goodnights and wishes for a happy new year to whoever had come out.

Viv stepped out onto Elm Street, Callie pinned to her hip.

Midstride, Callie lurched and waved to someone across the street. "Stephanie!" The unexpected happy dance knocked them both off center. Callie fisted Viv's hair in a last-ditch grasp to stay upright, but wrenched Viv's neck before she went sideways.

Viv stumbled, heels teetering on the blacktop and arms flailing for purchase.

Callie smacked her head on the curb.

Viv braced for her own impact, but strong arms caught her, her back connecting with a warm solid chest instead of the painful concrete she'd expected.

A deep, rumbling voice rang out behind her. "Get Zeke and Trevor out here. See if Danny's still around, too."

She clenched the leather-clad arms around her waist and fought to catch a steady breath.

The bouncer hurried into the street and kneeled beside Callie, gently lifting her so her head rested on his lap.

This fucking night. This horrid, embarrassing, fucking night. Behind her, murmurs and giggles from bystanders grew by the second. Her mind pushed for her to get up, deal with Callie, and get home where it was safe, but her body wouldn't move, mortification and the flood of adrenaline rooting her in place.

The man behind her tightened his hold as though he sensed her self-consciousness. "We got this, sugar." The tiny movement made the leather of his jacket groan. His scent permeated her haze, a sea-meets-sun combination that made her think of Mediterranean islands and lazy days on the beach, not at all what she'd expect from a man coming out of the dive behind her. He sifted his fingers through her freed hair, moving it to one side of her neck, and a stray bobby pin clattered to the asphalt. "Your neck all right? Your sister gave it a hell of a snap."

That voice. Every word radiated through her, grated

and deep like the rumbling bass of a stereo cranked up too loud.

He stroked her nape, the touch confident and not the least bit platonic.

Her senses leaped to attention, eager for more of the delicious contact. It was all she could do to hold back the moan lodged in the back of her throat. She swallowed and blew out a slow breath instead. "Yeah, I'm fine."

He lifted her upright, and the muscles in his arms and chest flexed around her, tangling what was left of her reasonable thoughts into a hopeless knot.

A man jogged up, hunkered down beside her sister, and opened up a leather duffel. Not just any man, the guy who'd stitched up the hottie in the office.

She surged forward to intervene, but firm hands gripped her shoulders and pulled her back. "Give Zeke a minute to check her out."

Viv twisted, ready to shout at whoever dared to hold her back—and froze. Her breath whooshed out of her like she'd hit the pavement after all.

Fantasy Man grinned down at her, a toothpick anchored at the corner of his mouth. His tan spoke of far more hours in the sun than the surgeon general recommended, and his almost black eyes burned with a wicked gleam that promised loads of trouble. And not necessarily the good kind, judging by the vicious scar marking the corner of one eye.

"Zeke's a trauma doc," he said. "Perks up like a bloodhound if anyone so much as stubs a toe."

Callie moaned, and Viv spun back around to find the doc prodding the back of her sister's neck.

"I know it hurts," Zeke said. "Can you tell me your name?"

"I don't feel so good," Callie said.

Zeke carefully moved Callie's head back and forth and side to side. "I imagine you don't. Still want to know your name though."

"Callie."

"That's a pretty name." Zeke dug into his duffel and pulled out a penlight. "You know what day it is, Callie?"

Callie's eyes stayed shut, but she smiled like a kid at Christmas and threw her arms out to the side, damn near whacking Trevor as he sat on the curb beside her. "Happy New Year!"

Trevor chuckled and shifted Callie away from the bouncer so she rested against his own chest. "I got her, Ivan. See if you can't find the crowd something else to gawk at."

"You know where you're at, Callie?" Zeke checked her sister's pupils for responsiveness.

As soon as Zeke pulled the light away, Callie blinked and focused on Viv. "I'm with Vivie."

Fantasy Man's voice resonated beside Viv's ear, the tone low enough it zinged from her neck to the base of her spine. "Vivie, huh?"

A shudder racked her and she crossed her arms to combat the goose bumps popping up under her suit jacket.

His arm slipped around her waist from behind and pulled her against his chest, his heat blasting straight through to her skin. "You okay?"

Hell, no she wasn't okay. Her sister was hurt and bystanders lined both sides of the street waiting to see what happened next, but all Viv could think about was how his voice would sound up close and in the dark. Preferably between heavy breaths with lots and lots of skin involved. She'd chalk it up to exhaustion, but her nonexistent sex life was probably the real culprit.

"I'm fine. Just tired." She forced herself to step away and faced him, holding out her hand. "And it's Vivienne. Vivienne Moore. Or Viv. Callie's the only one that calls me Vivie."

He studied her outstretched palm, scanning her with languid assessment, then clasped her hand in his and pierced her with a look that jolted straight between her legs. "Jace Kennedy."

Figured that Fantasy Man would have a fantasy name to match. It sounded familiar, too, though with all the pheromones jetting through her body she couldn't quite place where. Maybe wishful thinking or one too many romance novels. She tugged her hand free and stuffed her fists into her pockets. "Thanks for not letting me bust my ass in front of everyone."

He matched her posture and shuttled his toothpick from one side of his mouth to the other with his tongue. "Pretty sure I got the best end of the deal."

Zeke's voice cut in from behind her. "I think she's fine. Just a nasty goose egg and too much booze."

Viv turned in time to see the two men guide Callie to her feet. She weaved a little and looked like she'd fall asleep any second, but the pain seemed to have knocked off a little of her drunken haze. Her floral bohemian top was wrinkled and askew on her curvy frame, and her golden-brown hair was mussed like she'd just had monkey sex. Otherwise, she fit the rest of the crowd a whole lot better than Viv.

Pegging Zeke with a pointed look, Jace cupped the back of Viv's neck. "Check Little Miss out, too. Didn't like the angle her neck took when her girl went down."

He focused on Viv and held out his hand, palm up. "Keys."

"What?"

"Keys," he said. "Give 'em to me and we'll bring your car around."

"You don't need to do that." She pointed at the lot across the street. "I'm just over there, and Callie looks—"

"It's almost two in the morning, your sister's hammered, and you both took a fall. Fork over the keys, we'll get your car, pull it around and load your girl up."

Four unyielding stares locked onto her—Zeke, Trevor and Jace, plus a new guy with black hair and a ponytail nearly down to his ass. The way the new guy trimmed his goatee gave him a Ming the Merciless vibe. She shouldn't let any one of these guys near her, let alone surrender the keys to her car. "I think it's better if Callie and I handle it ourselves."

The muscle at the back of Jace's jaw twitched and his eyes darkened.

"I don't mean to sound ungrateful," Viv added. "I appreciate everyone jumping in to help. It's way more than you needed to do. I just don't know you guys. Have you watched the news lately?"

"That's fair." Trevor's focus was locked on Jace when he spoke, but then slid his gaze to Viv. "But this is my bar, your sister drank too much while she was in it, and hurt herself on the way out. It's in my best interest to make sure you make it home safe. Anything bad goes down between here and there, you could give me and my new business a whole lot of heartache I don't need, right?"

Trevor had a point.

"Give me the keys, sugar." Jace crooked the fingers on his outstretched hand. "You've done enough solo tonight."

She handed them over and Zeke stepped in, gently prodding the muscles along the back of her neck. "Any soreness?"

Viv shook her head as much as she could with Zeke's big hands wrapped around her throat.

Behind Zeke, Jace handed off the keys to Ivan. A second later, jogging boot heels rang against the asphalt followed by the chirp of a disengaging car alarm.

Zeke tested her movement side-to-side and front and back as he'd done for Callie and checked her pupils. "I doubt you'd feel it until tomorrow anyway. Probably wouldn't hurt to take a few ibuprofens before you go to bed." He jerked his head toward Callie, still swaying next to Trevor. "Same goes for her. You'll have a hard time keeping her awake and not puking with as much as she's had to drink, but if she starts to act confused, can't remember things, or complains of ringing in her ears, get her to an ER."

"You got anyone that can help you tonight?" Jace asked.

Trevor piped up. "I can ask one of the girls to stay with you if you want."

"No, I can handle it."

Zeke gave her a knowing look, pulled a card out of his billfold, and handed it over. "You need help, call. We'll get her where she needs to be."

As in to an ER, or a place that had a minimum thirty-day stay? God knew, she'd begged her sister to at least try an AA meeting, but Callie and their dad had cornered all the stubborn genes for the family.

Her hybrid hummed up beside them and Zeke stepped away. "Lay her down in the back, Trev."

The bouncer hopped out of the driver's seat and opened up the back door for Trevor, who'd given up steering Callie and opted for carrying her to the car.

Jace moved in close and lowered his voice. "She get like this a lot?"

The men situated her sister in the backseat.

"Yeah." God, she was tired of this routine. She'd give just about anything to surrender, curl up into a little ball and let someone else handle Callie's tricks for a day or two.

Jace splayed his hand along the small of her back and urged her forward as a big, mean-looking bike with even nastier sounding pipes rolled up behind her car. "Danny's gonna follow you home and help you get Sleeping Beauty settled in for the night."

"I don't think—"

"If your sister passes out, can you get her in the house on your own?"

"No."

"Then stop thinking and let us handle this," Jace said. "Danny so much as breathes funny, you call the number on Zeke's card and we'll deal with it."

Another good point. After everything they'd done for her tonight, the odds of any of them having bad intentions were pretty slim. And her dog would leave even a big guy like Danny a heaping bloody mess if Viv so much as snapped a finger.

He opened the car door and she slid behind the wheel, fastening her seat belt in a bit of a daze. "Thank you. For everything."

"Just doing what decent people do." He started to

shut her door and stopped. Leaning slightly into her space, he seemed to listen for something, glanced at the stereo display, then eased back. He studied her car, Callie curled up in the backseat, then Viv. His gaze lingered on her hair and he ran a few fingers through the curly strands. "Like it better down. Kinda wild."

Her heart tripped, and the last bit of logic left in her brain poofed to nothing. She clenched the steering wheel and swallowed, grateful to find her mouth wasn't hanging open.

He winked and stepped back. "Take care, sugar."

The car door thumped shut, muting out everything but the quiet strains of Shinedown and Callie's muffled snore.

She put the car in drive and forced her eyes to aim straight ahead. She wouldn't look back. He might've nudged her long-dead sex drive out of a coma, but he was bad news. Everything about him screamed danger and headstrong alpha, and she'd sworn she wouldn't have that kind of life for herself. One look in the backseat showed where that landed a person.

Still, making a right turn onto Highway 75 for her townhouse in Uptown instead of circling the block for another peek was tempting as hell.

THREE

ALONE IN THE compound's kitchen, Jace punched the brew button on his second pot of coffee, snatched his mug off the granite countertop, and stared out the massive window overlooking the pool. The sky had just started to lighten, only a slash of pink touching the horizon. If he'd used his fucking head last night, he'd be in his bed upstairs, passed out cold and resting up for a full day. Instead, he was nursing the dregs of two-hour-old coffee, counting down the minutes until he could kick last night's fuckup out of his bed without a guilty conscience, and twitching for an overdue phone call.

Man, bringing Lily Montrose home last night had been a serious mistake. Granted, he'd pulled his head out of his ass before he'd been stupid enough to actually fuck her, but he had a bad feeling he'd opened a door better left locked tight. Lily was nothing if not determined. She spent too much time around The Den not to know the perks that came with any tie to Haven, and landing a sugar daddy was high on her list of aspirations. Especially, one from the brotherhood.

On the dinette, his phone buzzed and lit up.

In less than three strides, Jace snagged it, barely pausing long enough to note Danny's name and 7:17 a.m. on the readout before he punched the talk button. He tucked the phone under his ear. "About time. I thought I told you to check in as soon as you were done."

"I did, Boss. Lily answered. Said you were in the head, and she'd let you know it all went fine."

"I tell you to give me an update that means you give it to me. Worst case it goes to another brother, not a bunny. Got me?"

"Why the hell do you think I'm calling you back?"

And that was why he figured Danny wasn't too much further from making it into their tight-knit group. The son of a bitch might have been hanging with a bad crowd and teetering with more than one bad habit a few years ago, but now that he'd got his legs underneath him and found something to be passionate about, he'd grabbed life by the short hairs and didn't back down from anything—not even Haven's leader.

Jace padded toward the main staircase, the sound of his bare feet barely registering against the hand-scraped wood floors. "Yeah, well, you've got me now. What happened?"

"Straightforward drop-off. The sister was out cold like Trev thought she'd be, so I lugged her upstairs and left Viv to it."

"Where's she live?"

"Few miles away. Uptown, on Clark Street in a swank three-story condo. Thinkin' my pipes woke a few of the uppity types."

Well, there went the theory Viv had just been dandied up for work. Between the rocker vibe Callie sported and Shinedown queued up on Viv's stereo, he'd kind of hoped Trevor was right in thinking there was more to her than what showed on the surface.

"Man, gotta tell you though..." Danny paused long enough to order a coffee, the rumble of voices and clanking dishes heavy in the background. "Sorry. Where was I?"

Jace ambled through his bedroom toward his adjoining office and frowned at Lily curled up in the center of his bed. Christ, even in sleep she had a pleased-with-herself smile tacked firmly in place. Definitely a monstrous fuckup.

"Getting a decent meal while all I've got lined up here is coffee, sounds like." He shut his door, settled in his desk chair and flipped open his laptop.

"Oh, the dog," Danny said. "She opened the door and the first thing I get is a fucking black Doberman with its ears back and a nasty-ass growl aimed my direction. Shit you not, man. She's got that beast trained to take down anyone who's out for harm. Coolest thing I've seen in a while. And guess what she named him?"

"Beats the hell out of me."

Danny chuckled the way men did before they got a good joke in on a friend. "Ruger."

"As in the gun?"

"As in. I'm tellin' ya, man, she's pretty laid-back."

"So, the buttoned-up lady's got a wild side?"

"Maybe. Hard to tell for sure. Weird thing was her house. All prim and proper except the room she had me put her sister in."

Jace drummed his thumb against the desk, those same instincts he'd felt before with Vivienne perking up and demanding attention. "What's so weird about that?"

"'Cause where the rest of the house is all straight lines and Snoozeville, the one room looks like a flower child got it on with a tattoo artist. Found one piece framed on the wall I wouldn't mind gettin' inked."

Interesting. "That Callie's room?"

"Nah. She said Callie had her own place." Danny's voice took on a chilly edge. "Shacked up with some dickhead, according to Viv."

"Almost sounds like you two sat down for a fireside chat." And didn't that idea piss him off.

"Nope. Minute we started talkin' about Callie's man, she shut down hard. Was pretty relaxed 'til then, though."

Another incongruous puzzle piece for the curvy lady with the wild-as-fuck hair. The strands had been so damned soft against his fingers, it'd taken all kinds of self-control to keep from fisting a chunk at the back of her head and kissing the dazed and exhausted look off her face. Shit, if he was honest, the only reason he'd considered hooking up with Lily last night was to take the edge off. An asinine attempt to dodge the pull he'd felt for Vivienne, but the second Lily had palmed his cock and tried to suck him off the truth had bitch slapped him with a hard dose of reality. He didn't want to just fuck. He wanted Vivienne. Hence, the blue balls and morning spent sucking back coffee.

Danny's voice sharpened. "You need anything else?"

Damn it, he'd totally zoned mooning over a woman's hair. Next thing he knew he'd be watching soaps and Oprah reruns. "Not a thing. Appreciate you helping out."

"Anytime, man."

Jace tossed his phone onto the desk, reclined back in his chair, and swiped the touchpad on his laptop. The Haven logo blazed bright on the black background, a tribal-styled tree with a masculine H encompassed by the tree's branches. Roots were everything. Where you came from formed you and gave you what you needed to live a strong life—if you let it.

So, what were Vivienne's roots? Tidy professional, or wild child like her sister? The more the pieces wouldn't fit, the more he wanted to nose around until he found the missing link.

Or maybe he just wanted another excuse to get his hands on Vivienne.

Muted footsteps sounded on the thick carpet behind him, and Lily's overpowering perfume wrapped around him two seconds before her hands slid around his chest. "Hey, baby."

God damn it. This was what he got for thinking with his dick. "You remember that talk we had last night?"

Lily nuzzled the side of his neck and purred. "I remember all kinds of things from last night."

"Let's focus on the very first thing." He typed in his password and navigated to his email. Not so much as a twitch of interest stirred beneath her touch. "As in what I asked you to repeat back to me before you settled behind me on my bike at The Den."

She froze, her lips still pressed to his neck even though they seemed to go ice-cold against his skin. "It's a onetime thing."

Jace sat up and snatched his phone. "Not trying to be an ass, but I want to make sure no more lines get crossed. Last night was last night. Today's a different day." He punched through his contacts and pulled up one of several stored cab companies. "I'll have a car downstairs for you in ten."

Lily straightened and sauntered into his line of sight. She was barely thirty and rocked an amazing body, everything about her natural and confident as hell. What turned him off was the way she used it. "Never pegged you as a cold son of a bitch."

Jace met her stare head-on. Okay, maybe he *was* being an ass, but better that than lead her on. "Not being cold, sweetheart. I'm giving you the God's truth. If I was cold, I'd have sent you home last night when I figured out I wasn't interested instead of giving you relief and letting you sleep the Scotch off alone in my bed. And, in case it missed your notice, you're the *only* one who got off, so I'm not gonna string you along and let you think we'll ever have anything else. If that makes me a cold son of a bitch, then so be it."

She pursed her lips and studied him, eyes lingering on his bare torso long enough he felt like a piece of meat. Funny how when Viv had done the same thing his cock had gone hard as a cinder block. She nodded. "The honesty's refreshing. Thanks for that."

It sounded like a chess move more than anything earnest.

She turned and sashayed back to the bedroom, her long dark hair swaying around her shoulder blades. Viv's was longer by at least two or three inches, wild with tight waves. Seeing the same view on Viv would be worth a whole hell of a lot more trouble than anything Lily could dish out.

He put in a call to the cab company and punched *Vivienne Moore, Dallas, Texas*, into a Google search.

Amaryllis Events flashed at the top of the results, an event planning business with a post office box for an address and a tasteful web design for broad audience appeal. A pretty passionate namesake for such a buttoned-up woman, considering its mythology ties.

He should walk away. His businesses needed attention, and chasing tail, no matter how fine it was, wouldn't make that happen. Hell, if he didn't get his shit together at Crossroads soon, he might be the next person who ended up in jail.

But the puzzle—damn it, he wanted the answers. And those lips. Christ, just thinking about how they'd feel on his cock made him want to stroke one off right now.

The simple black contact link on the corner of her web page practically screamed to click and feed his curiosity.

"Fuck it," he muttered, an idea already forming in his head. Axel was gonna kick his ass before everything was said and done, but he had a pretty good hunch it'd be worth it.

Low, GRUMBLING PIPES revved outside Viv's window and punched her from an uneasy sleep. Chipper sunshine streamed through the barely open plantation shutters across the bedroom and scattered the remnants of one seriously dirty dream. The damned thing had been so real, she half expected Jace to roll over from the other side of the bed, brace his muscular body over her, and pick up where her mind had left off.

Her soft blue-gray walls and white wood trim surrounded her, the peaceful hues at war with the buzz still humming through her. For crying out loud, she'd given herself two orgasms last night thinking it would take the edge off, but all she'd gotten out of the deal was an amped-up imagination. God, what time was it anyway?

She nudged Ruger far enough away so she could wiggle her arms out from under the covers and fumble for her phone.

10:14 a.m.

Great. A whopping six hours' sleep to start off her

new year. Between Callie's puking and her sex-starved mind, she was lucky she'd gotten even that much.

She wrestled her legs free and swung them over Ruger's head, no small feat considering the hundred-pound baby slept curled up at her hip, leaving her pinned beneath the sheets. "Come on, big boy. Let's see how our girl's doing."

Ruger jumped off her raised bed with its soft taupe and white shabby chic comforter. Aside from it and the ostentatious Cadiz Shell chandelier dangling above her bed, the girly bedspread was the only departure from the clean, tasteful lines throughout the rest of the house.

Well, unless you counted her safe room. She could remake the twenty by fifteen guest room in a weekend if she ever had to, but for now it was the one place she let her old self run free without anyone being the wiser. Just walking into the colorful, wild space lifted the weight of her tightly disciplined life.

She padded down the hallway and knocked on the guest room door. "Callie? You up?" Viv opened the door a crack.

Ruger nosed his way through. He nuzzled his wet nose against Callie's neck, giving her cheek a vigorous lick.

Her sister flipped on her side so her back was to the door and flailed her arm in Ruger's general direction. "G'way, ya dumb dog."

"You should be nice to him. He's the one who propped you up after round three with the porcelain god while I wiped dribble off your mouth."

Ruger groaned as if to say, *Yeah, what she said.*

Callie wiggled deeper into the covers and waggled

her fingers over her shoulder. "Just need a little more sleep, Vivie. My head's killing me."

"Gee, I wonder what caused that? The tequila, the weed, or some other fun substance from the gritty boys in the corner booth?" She trudged closer and settled on the side of the bed, gently moving Callie's hair aside to check the bump on her head. Like Zeke said, it didn't look too bad this morning, but it wouldn't hurt for her to take it easy today, not that she'd listen. "You want some more Tylenol?"

"Hu-uh. Just let me get a little more sleep."

Viv sighed and fisted her hands in her lap, so many retorts and arguments piling up at the back of her throat, she thought she'd be the next one kneeling at the porcelain throne. She stood and headed for the door. "Fine."

She snapped her fingers, waited until Ruger trotted into the hallway, and shut the door behind her. His nails tapped on the bamboo floors as he trailed her to the kitchen. "One of these days she'll figure it out." At least Viv hoped her sister would. Every time Viv picked up Callie, she seemed to be in even worse shape than the last, so much so Viv worried about *not* getting a call more than getting one.

A trip to the side yard for Ruger, a bagel, and a cup of coffee later, Viv jogged up to her office on the third floor. It was really more of a roughly finished-out attic with a fantastic picture window overlooking downtown Dallas, but it was quiet and gave her space to plan without needing to clean up her Post-its and marketing material.

Her whiteboard calendar hung on the far wall—empty. She scooted around her particleboard computer desk with its faux mahogany finish and rolled her desk chair into place. So what if she'd taken the über cheap route up here? She'd fitted out the rest of her home in quality stuff the way everyone said she should, but savings only went so far. Besides, her office decor à la Target had all the necessary drawers and cubby holes.

She snatched her bank statement off the desk and sipped her coffee, glaring at the balance like it might somehow make the numbers rearrange themselves. Yep, definitely a bad idea to go near any nonessential stores ever again.

Damn it, she couldn't go back to a normal job. Well, she could, but she'd probably commit murder by staple remover within two weeks. Desk jobs and corporate America rubbed her all kinds of silly, and finding another event company would be even worse. Once you'd been the queen of the castle, being demoted to grunt stunk.

No way was she giving up. She tossed the bank statement down and wiggled her mouse to wake up the screen.

Whoops.

She closed the internet session she'd had up and checked the doorway to make sure the coast was clear. Yeah, right. Like Callie would be up to see, let alone share, the naughty kink site she'd stumbled on last week. Besides, it was her house and she could do what she wanted.

Opening up her email, she sipped her coffee. She couldn't figure it out. All of her customers claimed they loved her work, but no matter what she tried, she couldn't generate repeat business. Maybe she needed to pick a specific industry and cultivate customers there. Health care might not be a bad idea. Hospitals were always working with charities and expanding their not-for-profit facilities. Plus, mingling with doctors would open up doors with spouses and social clubs.

Her email pinged and a slew of messages rippled onto the screen. Old Navy, The GAP, Groupon, Tribal Hollywood…ah damn, she'd have to bypass Victoria's Secret's end-of-the-year sale. That sucked.

She clicked delete, moved on to the next, and froze. *Customer Contact Request.*

Her heart jogged from first to third gear and she wiggled a mini happy dance. "Hazzah! Bring it, baby!" She opened the message and leaned in closer to the monitor.

Ms. Moore,

My name is Axel McKee, and I'm contacting you in regard to a sizable charity event being sponsored by my business, Crossroads. I received your name from a referral who insisted your work was high caliber and capable of handling intricate events with a wide range of clientele. My contact information is listed below. I'd like to talk with you and see if my event is something you're able to accommodate.

Sincerely,

Axel McKee

Well, hell. Talk about your double-edged opportunities. On one hand, Crossroads drew every imaginable crowd from rednecks to millionaires. Whoever it was that coined the phrase, "See and be seen," had probably been a regular. On the other, the club had been all over the news the last few months with reports of violence and drug busts. Maybe the charity event was a PR thing to bounce back from all the negative press.

She chewed her bottom lip and reread the message. She'd busted her ass to build a good reputation. To put the life she'd come from behind her and develop a clean, respectable image.

Her finger hovered over the delete key.

She glanced at the empty calendar and pulled her hand away. First quarter was going to be a bitch. No one threw parties until Valentine's Day at the earliest, and those were hard to snag if they weren't already booked. Budgets seldom got approved until late February or early March, which meant she'd have to make it until then before bookings picked up.

The bank statement sat innocently off to one side of her desk, but it may as well have been a neon light. No way would she make it to a March or April payday without some income, and this one sounded big.

Not all bars were bad. Jace and his friends might've been a little on the edgy side, but they'd handled things well. If she had a job to do, keeping her distance from all the partying should be a breeze. She hoped.

She picked up her phone and typed in her password. Desperate times and all that, right? Besides, a simple phone call to learn more wouldn't hurt.

FOUR

Eleven o'clock at night. What reasonable person did business at eleven o'clock at night, let alone on a Saturday? The last time Viv remembered doing anything remotely business oriented this late was her group cram session before the Leadership Development final in junior college.

She punched the lock on her car and triple-checked the deep V neckline on her wrap-around dress. The cut was a little more sultry than she'd normally wear to meet a client, but giving a sales pitch at one of Dallas's most popular clubs wasn't the norm either. The black color gave it a little more professional edge, but the trek across the stadium-sized parking lot made her rethink the wisdom in choosing black peekaboo pumps.

Ahead, the wide gray two-story building with the platinum-colored Crossroads marquee in the center thrummed with energy. Black and silver vertical accents were mounted at ten-foot increments with spotlights that shot upward behind them, acting as beacons to partygoers for at least five miles out. The circular drive teamed with hustling valets and every high-end car imaginable, and a line of seriously decked out patrons stretched at least fifty feet from the main door.

Guess that answered who did business at eleven o'clock at night.

She strode toward the four men working the open

doors, then hesitated about twenty feet out when a short-haired blonde at the front of the line aimed an, *Oh, no you don't,* sneer her direction.

"You Vivienne Moore?" one of the bouncers called out.

Viv tightened her sweaty grip on her briefcase and angled toward him, albeit with a far more hesitant gait. If it were her waiting in line, the last thing she'd want to see is someone sailing right to the front, even if Axel had told her to do exactly that. "I'm Vivienne."

The man nodded and flagged down a hustling waitress in the main foyer. "Candy, this one's for Axel." Four seconds later she was through the heavy metal doors and hustling to keep up with a seriously energetic redhead with black boy-shorts and a tight, might-as-well-be-see-through white V-neck T-shirt.

Music boomed and intoxicating color surrounded her. Blue neon rods shot up from long rectangle planter-type containers separating conversational areas made of red and gold leather couches. Crystal waterfall chandeliers dropped from the ceilings in between section after section of thick ebony pillars. Up ahead, laser lights spun in red, blue and green across a packed dance floor.

"First time here?" Candy stood at the foot of a black-carpeted spiral staircase with a hand on one hip.

Viv nodded and hurried to catch up. "Sorry, I didn't mean to gawk."

Candy waved her off and started up the steps. "Happens to everyone. I had the same slap-happy look on my face that first time, too. Now all I see are flashing lights and people waving me down every three-point-two seconds."

Viv could never get tired of this place. It was sensation nirvana, a bold mix of class and party all rolled up into one. She'd heard about how luxurious and over the top it was, had even caught a few pictures when some of her clients had shown party pics over the last year, but nothing could've prepared her for the real deal. The weirdest part was the club's neighborhood, clumped within the same square mile as a Chili's, two gentlemen's clubs and a church—sustenance, sin and redemption all conveniently located.

Candy unhooked a velvet rope with a VIP tag hanging in the center and motioned her forward. "This is our stop."

No. Freakin'. Way.

A black leather couch faced the dance floor below with matching chairs on either side, and a steel and glass—topped coffee table sat in the center. Talk about your bird's-eye view. From here, the only action a person would miss were the women staggering into or out of the bathrooms on the first floor.

Viv squared her shoulders and pasted on what she hoped was a businesslike smile. "Thank you very much. Will Axel be long?"

"Depends on the crowd. Some nights go smooth, and some nights get crazy fast. You want something to drink while you wait?"

"A Coke would be great."

Candy's head snapped as if she'd been shocked. "A Coke?"

Viv set her briefcase down on the floor and eased onto the sumptuous couch. "Trust me. Something stronger would be great, but on a business trip, that's not the best idea."

The waitress grinned and lifted an aha finger. "Gotcha. One non-mind-futzing Coke coming up."

Reclining against the plush cushions, Viv soaked it all in. The people, the music, the colors—it all came together for a tidal wave of passion and excitement that reached somewhere deep inside her and fired a wild buzz. God, what she wouldn't give to let go for a night or two and dance like the women below. To not care about the consequences and just be.

That wasn't what tonight was about though. She was here for business. Only business. Oddly, her instincts weren't firing all that well on this trip. Usually, she could get a pretty decent feel for people, even over the phone, but Axel had come off kind of strange. Like he couldn't decide if he wanted to laugh or choke her. The peculiar push and pull had almost made her decline the consultation, but then he'd mentioned their budget and she'd almost swallowed her tongue. The core event alone would float her well into second quarter, not to mention any side business the contacts generated. Assuming, of course, Crossroads's bad press didn't drag her down with it.

A little of the environment's shimmer faded, memories of her mom's shrill shouts reverberating louder than the beat rumbling from the dance floor.

"If you gave half as much focus to this family as you do for your next party, we wouldn't be in his hellhole."

The accusation had earned her mom a backhand from Viv's dad and a bruise that had lasted nearly a week.

The waitress sashayed through the section opening and set the drink on the table. "One innocent Coke. I let Axel know you're here. He said he'd be up as soon as he handled a small meeting of the minds."

"A what?"

"A meeting of the minds. You know, two testoster-one-overdosed idiots beating on their puffed-up chests for absolutely no good reason whatsoever?"

A shiver snaked down Viv's spine, past and present sparking a little too close for comfort. Just because two men got in each other's face didn't always mean some-one ended up in jail or dead. Viv grabbed her purse and dug for her wallet. "How much for the Coke?"

Candy grinned and shook her head. "You're in VIP. Drinks are covered here."

A shame she couldn't make better use of the privi-lege. A shot of tequila might make her nerves settle down. She handed a ten to Candy. "Well, then at least take this for getting me here in one piece."

The waitress took the ten and tucked it in her pocket. "Thanks. Axel shouldn't be too long, but I'll check on you in a few."

Crossing her legs, Viv white-knuckled her clutch in her lap and paced her breathing. The low, all-consuming beat from the dance floor vibrated through her in an al-most hypnotic pulse. The one-eighty span of nightlife shimmered with passion and excitement, hands down one of the classiest places she'd ever been to.

But it was still dangerous. The air practically snapped with it. One wrong move from a too messed-up patron and everything could go to hell in a blink.

It was just a job. One she needed really bad if she didn't want to go back to surfing a desk all day. All she needed was detachment. To focus on the work and not get sucked in by all the glorious lights and beautiful scenery.

"Ah, the lovely Vivienne Moore." The gravelly voice slashed through Viv's inner pep talk monologue and punched her heart back up to the stratosphere. A giant of a man stood just inside the velvet rope. His hair hung loose to his shoulders with enough waves to rival her own, and a beard that made her think of Scottish warlords. He'd pulled the top of his hair into a partial ponytail, but it didn't ease his rugged edge. In fact, the only things that made him look civilized were his tailored pants and a long-sleeved cashmere sweater.

"Heard a lot about you, but now that I'm getting an eyeful, I'm beginning to see why." He ambled closer and held out his hand. "I'm Axel McKee. Good to meet you."

The barely there brogue she'd picked up on the phone was harder to detect tonight, but the whole sophisticated Braveheart image was more than sufficient to jack with her head. "I'm…" *Shit, Viv. Think already.* She stood and shook his hand. "I'm Vivienne Moore."

His grin lifted to a full-bore smile, showcasing perfect white teeth. "Aye, that much I knew."

Well, duh. Great way to show off her razor-sharp mind. She smoothed her skirt and snatched her briefcase off the floor. "Sorry. You caught me off guard. This place is pretty spectacular."

"A place to let go and forget what waits outside, yeah?" He motioned her toward the ropes. "What's say we hunker down and see what you might do to help the bottom line."

Viv started forward, but Axel held up his hand. "Don't you want your drink?"

She glanced back at the table. "It's just a Coke. I don't like to drink while I'm working."

"Makes sense." He eyeballed the Coke then glanced at the long row of blackout windows opposite them. "Though I've got a funny feeling you'll be rethinkin' your order before the night's through."

SON OF A BITCH—Jace was gonna kick Axel's ass. Beyond the one-way glass lining the side of his office, over four hundred women gyrated and strutted, dressed for all manner of attention, but the one with Axel's hand on the small of her back was Viv. His fist hadn't come unwound since his best friend had clasped her hand in his a little too long then smirked at Jace over one shoulder.

Payback. An underhanded kick in the nuts for Jace pulling Axel into his schemes without talking to him first. The logical part of his brain acknowledged the action for what it was. Unfortunately, logic only seemed to take up five percent of his brain when Viv was the topic. Otherwise, he'd have never sent that email.

Axel and Viv strolled along the upper deck. Viv's body-hugging dress and killer curves drew repeated rubbernecks from the other VIPs, but she seemed oblivious, more interested in whatever Axel was saying and gaping at her surroundings.

Thirty minutes he'd watched her, on the cameras and through the glass. Every minute of it she'd been the same way. Open and transparent, enthralled with the sights and sounds.

Except for those few minutes right before Axel had shown.

Whatever had gone down with Candy had thrown a serious damper on her good mood. One minute she'd gently swayed in time with the music, and the next she'd gone rigid. Definitely something to swing by and have a little chat with Candy about before the night was over.

As soon as Axel guided Viv into the stairwell that led to their third-story offices, Jace turned and shut the door connecting his office to the conference room all but a few inches. The adjacent room was huge, with an oblong maple table big enough to seat twenty. The only entrances were from the hallway, Jace's office or Axel's on the opposite end. From here he'd be able to hear every word as it went down and watch the details through the security stream on his computer.

He settled behind his desk, snatched a toothpick from the dispenser near the corner, and popped it in his mouth.

Axel's booming laughter billowed down the hallway, Vivienne's light and happy chuckle right behind it. Yeah, having Axel pull front man to start with was a smart move. His easygoing attitude tended to set even the edgiest of people at ease, and Vivienne barely seemed capable of breathing around Jace, let alone laughter.

The main conference room door clicked open.

Vivienne strolled through ahead of Axel and settled her briefcase on the table. Her voice was breathless with the same husky quality that had plagued him since she'd fallen into his arms. "The lady who scheduled our appointment never mentioned who referred you to me, Mr. McKee."

"My da's long gone, lass, and callin' me Mr. McKee makes me jumpy." Axel strolled to the wet bar and set about pouring his favorite Scotch. "You up for something a little stronger than the Coke you were nursing downstairs?"

"No, thank you." Her posture stiffened and she rummaged through her bag the same way she had with Candy. She'd mentioned her sister tipped the bottle a little too often. Not too far of a leap for her to have a strong aversion to the stuff as a result. Or maybe she'd sworn off because she was just as bad.

Christ, he'd brought her here for answers, not more questions.

"Would it be horribly rude if I asked where you're from?" She tipped her head to one side. "You don't really have much of an accent, but the words you use… you're Scottish, right?"

"Indeed." Axel settled on one of the high-back conference chairs along the side of the table, just as casual as he would be chatting up a woman downstairs. "My ma followed a tourist here when she was nineteen, married him inside of two months, and had me nine months later. I've grown up a Texan, but Ma's brogue sets just as easy on my tongue." He paused for a beat, that fucking panty-dropping cadence he used to pick up women sliding out of nowhere. "I'll use it more if it does somethin' for ye, lass."

Vivienne laughed, unpacked a notepad from her briefcase, and sat on the edge of the chair next to Axel. "I thought you wanted to talk about business, not pick-up strategies."

"Well, now. That was before I met ye in person. Might be I've changed me mind."

"Yes, but I have bills to pay and you have an event to handle. Flirting, or anything beyond that, won't cover either of those."

Damn straight. Jace braced his elbows on his desk and the leather of his desk chair groaned loud enough to carry.

Axel's gaze shot to the camera mounted in the corner of the conference room, and the motherfucker grinned. At least he dropped the accent. "If I can't tempt you, then I guess we'd best get down to business."

"Please. You didn't give me much to go on beyond that you're hosting a charity event outside of your club venue."

"Not me, so much as a conglomerate of men I work with."

Conglomerate, huh? The rest of the brothers would get a kick out of that one. Though it did have a nice ring to it.

"Six different corporations come together every year for a bike rally. Proceeds go to Catherine's Kids."

Vivienne bobbed her head and scribbled details on her notepad. "I haven't heard of them."

"Not surprising. They're fairly small and don't get much in the way of press. They fund summer art programs for disadvantaged and financially strapped kids."

She popped her head up and swiveled for a better angle at Axel. "Who's Catherine?"

"Patron Saint of Artists, of course." He lifted his glass in salute and sipped his Scotch.

"And your event? What happens at the rally?"

"Been a disorganized cluster for the last few years, mostly friends of friends paying an up-front fee and chipping in for raffles and door prizes. The folks who run the charity are mostly volunteers, so we've a lot of hands to help. I thought if we brought in a professional, we might have better luck of makin' a difference and get better press out of the deal."

Viv stared at her notes and tapped her pen against her lower lip, then pegged Axel with a stern stare. "Would the need for improved press also have something to do with Crossroads getting negative press of late?"

Axel's killer smile whipped into place, the one that left most people wondering if they'd just won the lottery, or if they'd just signed their death sentence with a crazy man. "You're a smart one." He twisted his glass on the table and crossed one leg over the other. "Aye, Crossroads could use a shot of good. But the rally goes on no matter what. The kids come first. Always."

She jerked a sharp, approving nod. "Good. Now if you'll just run down the nature of the other participating companies, I'll see if I can line out some ideas for you."

And that was it. No more than a few minutes to assess the gig and the underlying benefits, and she was off, pinging Axel with rapid-fire questions that would make both their mothers proud. Even funnier was the way Axel fell right into it, lifting from his reclined pose and leaning in so he could follow her notes for himself. None of the details seemed to bother her. Not the huge crowd they'd drawn in years past, or the number of business reps to coordinate. Everything about her downshifted into a natural groove that exuded shrewd, sharp confidence, all kinds of creative ideas flowing easily past those sexy lips of hers.

And damned if it all didn't turn his dick to a cast-iron rod.

"Do you have a specific date lined out already, or do we have flexibility there?"

"We usually target late March, or early April. Makes

for nice riding weather, though so far this year any month would do. If we hire you, we'd set up regular payments based on milestones and dates, starting at the end of January. I'm thinkin' eight thousand a month would guarantee we get exclusive focus?"

"That sounds reasonable, though I'd ask for a booking retainer up front as well," she said. "I'm confident I can organize your event in a way that not only brings in more for Catherine's Kids, but also builds the positive attention Crossroads needs right now. Assuming you choose to use my company, of course."

Axel stood and ambled to the wet bar.

Jace pushed away from his desk, grabbed the historical file on the rally, and padded toward the door. Another complication was the last thing he needed right now. If he was smart, he'd walk away, give Viv the business and let Axel handle it all.

"Mr. McKee?"

This was it. Either Jace shut the door and let Axel know to do whatever he wanted about giving her the business, or he stepped in to handle the decision himself.

Fuck it. He'd never ignored his instincts before, and he'd be damned if he started now. Cursing himself seven different ways from Sunday, he pulled the door wide. "You should probably know a few more details on the event before you close the deal."

FIVE

Viv barely caught herself before she staggered back a step. Every logical business angle she'd queued up to close the deal fizzled to white space as the air whooshed out of her lungs.

Jace sauntered through the side conference room door in jeans so faded they had to be at least ten years old. A black T-shirt hugged his torso in a way she'd give a lot to trade places with. Unlike the ponytail he'd worn on New Year's Eve, his soft black hair hung straight and loose to his shoulders. Everything about him radiated energy, so much so her whole body felt as though someone had clamped jumper cables to her shoulders.

Okay, maybe not her shoulders. She white-knuckled the edge of the table and pasted on her best professional smile. "Jace—" She shook her head and tried again. "Mr. Kennedy, I wasn't aware you had involvement in this event."

"Hard not to since I'm one of the owners."

That's where she knew the name from. That up-and-coming politician had ranted on TV about Crossroads just a few nights ago after a nasty drug arrest.

Jace meandered next to Axel at the wet bar and poured himself a glass of the same thing Axel had. "What do you think of Ms. Moore's ideas?"

"Entertaining, that's for sure." Axel finished off his drink, keeping his gaze locked on Viv, then set it on the granite countertop and ambled to the door on the opposite end. "Gonna be interesting to see how it turns out."

The door clicked shut behind him and Viv spun back to Jace. "See how what turns out?"

Jace kept his silence and padded to the long conference table beside her. He tossed a worn folder down and laid out all kinds of spreadsheets and flyers from rallies years past. Despite his business demeanor, the air between them sparked with an almost dangerous vibration, his body so close to hers his heat radiated in an alluring wave.

"You mentioned culling volunteers we've used before and reaching out to customers of the businesses involved to expand participation." He shifted a few documents so she could better see them. "You'll find all the volunteer contact information here and business contacts on this one. The same docs are available in soft copy as well."

"You heard the whole thing." God, she was an idiot. She should have done her homework better. Or at least pulled her head out of her triple-X fantasies long enough to figure out where she'd heard of him before. She took a step back. "I'd like for you to explain what's going on."

Jace studied her, the toothpick at the corner of his mouth twisting and turning. Something about his gaze rooted her in place, like he didn't just look at her, but through her and into all her secrets. The corner of his mouth quirked and he lifted his tumbler for a drink. "You sure you don't want something besides a Coke?"

"There's a time and a place for alcohol. This isn't it. Particularly around a man like you."

His grin kicked up a notch, and the impact whacked

her chest as firm as a major leaguer at bat. The thing really should be illegal. "A man like me?"

She nodded.

"You think I'd hurt a woman?"

"I think you're the type to make a woman lose good sense."

He tossed his toothpick onto the conference table and closed the little distance she'd created. "Maybe you need a man capable of making you lose good sense."

Dear God, what was it about this guy? She'd never met a man who so thoroughly scrambled her thoughts and cranked her physical senses to overdrive. His scent was the same as before, all sunshine and beach, but with a darker undercurrent. A spice or woodsy edge she couldn't quite place. Power pulsed off him and almost dragged her forward. All she'd have to do is lean forward an inch or two and she'd not only get to see if his lips felt as good as they looked, but she'd finally learn if his beard was soft or scratchy.

"Are you going to explain how you heard everything?" she said so low it was almost a whisper.

He eased back, gaze roaming her face. "I was curious, so I looked you up. I have an event, and you have a company that handles them. Seemed a good way to get to know more about you and free some time up for me in the process."

"Free up time how?"

"I handled the logistics before, but it's no secret that's not my thing. I put together deals. Executing's best left to people like Axel." He sipped his drink, never breaking his unnerving stare. "Or you."

A shiver snaked down her spine, desire and self-preservation duking it out along every inch. Jace Kennedy was hands down the absolute prime candidate for who not to get involved with, no matter how much her body disagreed.

She shook her head to clear it and focused on the paperwork. "Yes, well, I prefer to keep my professional relationships without personal complications. It makes it too difficult to do my job effectively."

Jace leaned a hip on the table, retrieved his discarded toothpick, and laid it on his tongue. Smiling, he twirled the sliver of wood to the corner of his mouth, and a delicious ripple shuttled through her belly. What red-blooded woman wouldn't want to see that tongue put to much better use than playing with a toothpick? "So you're interested in the job then?"

The job. They were talking about the job. Not tongues, or skin, or hot and sweaty sex, but a job. Cash to pay the rent and keep her doing what she loved. Christ, maybe if she could catch a decent breath, her mind could function enough to process a coherent thought.

"I'd like a few days to check my schedule and see if I can't make accommodations for my other commitments." So what if her other commitments centered around networking luncheons and cold calls? He didn't need to know her calendar was empty, and a little time would give her a chance to think things through without him muddling her head. "This might be a full-time endeavor, but I don't want to burn bridges elsewhere."

"Sounds reasonable." He straightened to full height. "What's say we shake on it?"

God, she'd never make it through working with him. Just looking at his strong, outstretched hand shot her thoughts off into seriously dirty territory. His fingers were long and clearly no stranger to manual labor. If he played them with the same confidence he did everything else, there'd be no telling how fast he could get a woman off.

Their palms met and she barely stifled a groan, the heat and power behind his grip all too easy to imagine against her hips. "Should I contact you or Mr. McKee with my answer?"

She might've covered the groan, but there was no hiding the rasp in her voice.

Jace's gaze locked on her mouth and he gave his toothpick another twirl with his tongue. "Oh, definitely me. I tend to be a hands-on man."

She tugged her hand free and stepped back, nearly tripping on the edge of the chair behind her. Smoothing the front of her dress, she cleared her throat and started restacking the papers he'd laid out. "I'd like to keep these for reference, if it's alright with you?" Not waiting for an answer, she tucked the stack into the folder and snatched her purse. "I'll be in touch in a few days with my final answer. I appreciate your time and consideration."

Spinning for the door, her thigh smacked the armrest on the chair next to her and sent it spinning. He probably thought she was a bumbling idiot at this point, incapable of putting one steady foot in front of the other, but it was too hard to care anymore. So much adrenaline flooded her system that sweat lined the space between her shoulder blades, and her heart ached as though she'd sprinted up a forty-five degree incline.

She hurried out into the shadowed hallway and semi-jogged down the stairs. Who was she kidding? If she couldn't look Jace in the eye for more than five minutes without blubbering, then there was no way she could take this job. And passing on it was really for the best. She'd promised herself she'd stay distanced from this kind of lifestyle. With routine and respectable behavior came safety and reliability. She'd never find that in this kind of environment. Certainly not with a man like Jace.

The club's vibrant colors and thick crowds went by in a blur, the impact of her heels against the black industrial carpet vibrating up her legs. Cool January air drafted through the open metal doors ahead. Finally, she could breathe. A few more minutes and she'd be safe in her car, locked up tight, and headed back to her quiet world.

She stepped across the threshold and a big hand clamped down on her shoulder. "Ms. Moore, I'll have to ask you to hold up a minute."

Viv spun to find the big brute who'd hooked her up with Candy. "I'm leaving."

"Actually, you're staying," the brute said. "Got a problem, and need you to hold tight right here."

All around her, people in all manner of clothing and varied states of soberness strolled in varied directions. If there was a problem, she sure as hell didn't see one. "I think there's a misunderstanding. My meeting with Mr. Kennedy is over, and I'm headed back to my car."

Jace's voice sounded behind her, close enough his breath registered on the back of her neck. Her skin tingled with awareness. "Don't think you got everything."

The brute grinned and ambled back to his post.

Viv closed her eyes and dug for some semblance of disaffectedness. For crying out loud, she could fake it with the snootiest of people. Surely she could hold her own with a man who'd fit in at the trailer park back home. She steeled her spine, turned and couldn't help but giggle.

In Jace's hand was her briefcase. "Might need this when you get home."

"Thank you." She took the briefcase and tucked the folder inside. "I apologize for your having to trail after me. I shouldn't have hurried out the way I did."

"I upset you."

"Not you. I was just a little surprised—"

"Bullshit."

"Mr. Kennedy—"

"You keep calling me Mr. Kennedy, I'll have to paddle your ass." He guided her out of the streaming traffic and off to one side of the entrance, the clasp of his hand around her upper arm firm, but gentle.

"Okay, yes, you upset me." She tried to pull her arm free while struggling to keep up with his long strides. "I'm here for business. You can't say things like that and expect me not to get flustered."

Jace stopped and faced her, keeping his grip on her arm.

"You should go back to work. I'll think about your offer, but I'm not sure I'm the best person for this job."

He stepped closer. "I can't get back to work yet. I'm not done with you."

"I thought we covered everything."

"Not quite." His other hand came up and curled around the back of her neck, his thumb teasing the space just behind her ear.

She tried to step back, but the effort was half-hearted, every single nerve ending straining toward him with a magnetic pull. "Mr. Kennedy."

His fingers behind her neck tightened and he growled.

"Jace," she corrected, though it came out as more of a moan. "I told you, I don't like to mix personal affairs with business."

He lowered his head, and his fingers speared deep into her tightly bound hair. His lips whispered against hers a second before full contact. "I haven't hired you yet."

Oh, man. Those lips weren't as good as they looked, they were better. The kind a woman would give up a lot for. Firm and skilled, slanting against hers until she gave way and surrendered.

His tongue swept in, as bold and unforgiving as the man holding her in place, wiping away resistance and thought with each decadent thrust.

Giggles and the ever-present hum of music and excitement buzzed around her. A dim part of her tried to point out they were in public, but most of her just held on for the ride, savoring the hard, hot muscles beneath her palms and soaking up every sensation.

"I see my man's knife didn't put you down long."

Viv opened her eyes to spinning lights and colors, her body thrust behind Jace as four bouncers rushed to either side of Jace.

Jace's voice cut low and sharp through the crowd. "You've got a death wish comin' in here tonight, Hugo."

She might have thought Jace was intense before, but she was wrong. Horribly wrong. The cold glare he aimed at the man in the black suit across from him would send most people running, her included.

"Thought we'd made it clear," Jace said. "You're out. Otto's in."

Roughly thirty feet away, three burly men in riding

leathers and MC cuts stalked toward them with Axel leading the way.

Jace aimed a comment to the bouncer who'd stopped her on the way out. "Get Ms. Moore to her car."

The brute gripped her arm in a far less gentle clasp than Jace's and nearly dragged her to the entrance. Hugo's sinister chuckle trailed them on the way, cut short when the metal door slammed behind them. Only once she'd deactivated the alarm on her car and started to slide into the driver's seat did the brute relinquish his grip. Even then, he stood with arms crossed, waiting and watching until she backed out.

Her palms slipped against the leather steering wheel, and her throat was so dry she could barely swallow. She exited the parking lot and glanced in the rearview mirror.

The brute was still there, watching.

In the passenger seat, Jace's folder peeked from the top of her briefcase.

See? This was why she'd be an idiot to take this job. This life, Jace Kennedy, and everything that went with men like him was bad news. Exactly the kind of trouble she'd fought so hard to escape. There had to be another way to save her business. First thing in the morning, she'd start figuring out how.

SIX

MORNING SUNLIGHT HALOED the stretch of three-story townhouses in front of Jace. Slow but sure, the light burned away the lingering fog from another humid January night. He'd backed his pimped-out Midnight Edition Silverado into an empty covered parking spot behind Viv's alley, but the thing still stood out amid all the gold and silver foreign sedans. Not exactly his best choice for casing a residence.

Four days he'd waited for her to call and take the job. Four fucking days and his dick still got hard if she so much as registered as a blip in his head. Hell, he'd nearly drowned himself in Scotch the last three nights, trying to forget the way her taste had lingered on his tongue, and all that had done was drag his thoughts toward imagining how her pussy would taste.

His phone vibrated inside the pocket of his leather jacket.

Jace dug it out and punched the answer button beneath Knox's name and number. "Yeah."

The brotherhood's hacker and cyber genius sounded like he'd knocked back a whole lot more coffee than Jace. "Well, a chipper good morning to you, too."

"Didn't get out of Crossroads last night until 3:00 a.m. and I've been watching Viv's place since seven. Not a lot of room between the two to get as psyched as you."

"She gone yet?"

"Nope. Lights came on about an hour ago. I'm hoping she's out soon so I can get some shut-eye."

Muted, rapid-fire taps of Knox's fingers on the keyboard pattered in the background. "You sure you're up for this, old man? Been a long time since you swept a house."

Yeah, it'd been a long time. Like back when the brotherhood had just been him, Axel, their wits and a whole lot of balls. "Sure as hell not letting anyone else in Viv's place."

Quiet settled on the line, even Knox's lickety-split key taps falling silent. "Rules are rules, brother. We made a pact. Anyone close to the brotherhood's information gets a sweep. It's either that or risk exposure. You want this woman on the short list, then she gets a once-over like everyone else."

"Not balkin' on the rules." Actually, he was. He just wasn't saying it out loud. "I don't want a stranger in her house and their hands on her shit. Business or not, she's a woman, and we keep them safe."

"Mmm-hmm." Something thunked in the background, probably one of Knox's monster coffee cups he kept filled to the brim from 5:00 a.m. until noon. "Didn't see you volunteering when we brought Shelly in as office manager at Crossroads."

"Didn't care what you found in Shelly's house, or if you went through her panty drawer fifteen times."

"I didn't check fifteen times."

"No, but you did check, am I right?"

All Jace got in the way of an answer with a rumbling chuckle. "You ready to run this sweep or not?"

Not really. If it was strictly work, he could justify it like all the other jobs, but this one reeked of violation. He snatched his earpiece and slipped it into place. "Yeah. I'm going in without you live, though. I get into a situation, I'll call for backup."

On cue, Vivienne's garage door lifted and Jace edged a little deeper in his seat. Not that she'd be able to see him from his spot across the alley.

"So how deep are we going on background?" Knox said.

Jace tossed his mangled toothpick out the window and rummaged for a fresh one in his pocket. "Everything you can find out. She's got an event planning company called Amaryllis Events. Lives on Clark Street in Uptown. I wanna know where she came from, where she went to school, and anything from her history that stands out."

"So a B and E gives you the willies, but a background check you're good with, huh?"

"Anyone could run a background check."

Knox scoffed. "Not like I do."

On that point, he was absolutely right. How Knox tapped the sources he did still rocked Jace's head.

Viv hustled out the back door of her townhouse and around her cute little silver hybrid. Wherever she was headed, it was all business. Her hair was back up in that tight twist, and her dove-gray suit fit every curve in a way guaranteed to close whatever deal she'd set out to nab.

He clenched his fist, his palms burning with the need to slide his hands up and around those hips.

"Jace?"

"Yeah. She's just leaving. Listen, keep this shit tight, Knox. I get all the info first. When I want it out with everyone else, I'll share it at rally. If she even takes the job. We clear?"

Knox hesitated a beat, obviously uneasy keeping anything from the rest of the brothers. "Yeah, we're clear."

"Good. And the sooner I get the results the better."

"Patience never was your strong suit. Anything else?"

Backing out of the garage, Viv punched the garage control and the door hummed closed.

"Just keep your phone handy. I don't have a clue when she'll be back."

Knox chuckled low in his throat, muted clinks and running water in the background indicating he'd postponed any deeper dives until he got another java fix. "You're a crazy fuck. Aren't you the one who always says to make damned sure you know what you're getting into before you dive?"

"She's five-three and can't weigh more than a buck-thirty. I think I can handle it."

"Have fun. I'll call when I've got something." Knox clicked off and Jace thumbed through the rest of his contacts.

Three rings later, Danny picked up, his laid-back voice sounding like he'd been up all night. "Mornin', boss."

"You're sounding pretty slow."

"Just got off a thing for Beck. Overnight security for some bigwig I'd never heard of while Beck ran a different gig. You need something?"

Another benefit to Danny joining up with their group. Finding quality muscle for Beckett's security and investigations business was a bitch, and Danny was a bulldozer in any head-to-head.

"Just info." Jace snatched the bag of liver treats from the passenger's seat and started loading up his pocket. "The woman you helped on New Year's Eve, Vivienne Moore, you said she had a guard dog?"

"Yep. Called him Ruger. Great pup."

"How'd he react to you?"

"Great after she called him off."

Perfect. The one time he needed Danny to get chatty and the guy had to get tight-lipped. "Give me the commands. Plus any codes she used if she had a security system."

Quiet stretched through the connection.

"I know you, Danny. A man who made his living getting in and out of swanky houses the way you did before we found you marks those details whether they mean to use 'em or not. Now I need them."

"She's a really nice lady, boss."

Well, hell. Looked like Little Miss had more protectors than she realized. "Nothing's gonna happen to her. You've got my word. All I need is info, and I need inside to get it."

Another second or two of hesitation and a handful of gruff answers later, Jace was off the phone and strolling across the alley to Viv's garage. Breaking and entering in broad daylight was almost as stupid as him not tracking her movements for a day to two before, but he'd done worse. The nondescript gray sweats and baseball cap would do enough to throw most off his trail at least.

Everything around him was silent, folks out for a jog or walking their dogs long gone for work. So long as it all stayed that way for six seconds he'd be fine.

He wedged a plastic doorstop between the top of the garage door and the frame, slid a six-foot wire tool between the gap, snagged the garage door release, and the manual release snapped free. Five more seconds and he was inside with the garage shut behind him and the power door reengaged. Kinda like riding a bike.

Claws clicked on tile behind the door to the house followed by a happy whimper.

Might as well get the hard part over with. Given Danny said she didn't use her security system, he wouldn't have that hassle, but getting past the dog would be sheer fucking luck. He pinched a few liver treats from his pockets, held his ground by the door, and pushed the unlocked door open.

Ruger stood alert, ears sharp, legs braced and ready.

Damn. Danny had been right to be impressed. Jace loved dogs, and this one was a Class-A specimen with intelligent eyes and a shiny black coat. He also looked ready to sink his fangs into Jace if he moved a wrong toe.

Ruger scented the air, cocked his head and barked.

"*Leicht*, Ruger." Easy. Jace slowly lifted the treat between his fingers so the dog could see it. If he'd had more faith he wouldn't end up a man-size dog treat, he'd have laughed out loud at the situation. German commands—who'd have thought it? If he wasn't so pissed about how easy he'd gotten in the place, he'd say Viv was a genius. "*Sitzen.*" Sit.

Ruger eyeballed the treat, sniffed again, and eased to his butt.

"*Gut* boy." He eased forward, offering his empty hand first. "*Freund.*" Friend.

The dog responded just like Danny said he had on New Year's Eve, checking Jace over scentwise and then nuzzling his hand for attention.

Jace handed over the treat and scratched behind his ears. "Viv's got good taste, yeah, boy?"

Ruger wiggled his stub-tail behind so hard his whole body shook.

"All right then, you gonna help me check things out, or make me work for it?"

The dog shifted and nuzzled the pocket with the rest of the treats.

"Smart boy." He grabbed another treat and held it out. "What's say we get this done so I can bail before I'm in hot water."

He worked through the main floor as fast as he dared with Ruger on his heels. The downstairs held a simple layout, a contemporary kitchen with lots of stainless steel and neutral stonework. It opened to a vaulted living room with bamboo floors and tan walls. The furniture didn't vary much from the earth tone, straight-line vibe, and not one single thing was out of place. Hell, the space looked more like a showplace than an actual home.

At the top of the stairs, he found the master suite. It wasn't nearly as sterile as the main floor, though it was still mighty tame. Soft blue-gray walls and white trim gave the place an airy look, and the bedspread was one-hundred percent girl with frilly stuff lining the edges. The only thing that surprised him was the kick-ass chandelier hanging from the center of the room, tiny shells dangling at all different heights in a way that made him think of wind chimes.

He strolled into her walk-in closet. Neatly organized suits and shirts lined both sides, pants, jackets, shoes— everything in its proper spot. He turned to head back out and a splash of color caught his eye. Relegated to one small section were three or four pairs of well-worn jeans and colorful tanks and T-shirts. Nowhere near the kind of stuff her sister had worn, but still out of place among all the rest.

Her dresser boasted the same damned thing, everything nice, neat and drab except for one drawer at the bottom. He crouched down for a better look and fingered a red lacy thong. And here he'd given Knox a hard time about raiding Shelly's panty drawer. In the span of ten seconds, his mind conjured half a dozen scenarios of him pulling any one of the lacy confections off her luscious body.

Across the hall, he opened another door and almost staggered back a step. So, this was the flower child room. The walls were painted a deep purple and some kind of wispy fabric was draped around the double beam in the center for a gypsy tent look. Little white Christmas lights dangled in a haphazard pattern in one corner, and in the other was a makeshift table that hung from the ceiling with rattan rope. Christ, she even had a lava lamp.

Why? Over and over again, the simple question pounded him. If she liked color and bohemian styles so much, why keep it all contained and relegated to tiny corners of her life?

Outside a car door slammed and muted laughter registered through the closed windows.

Jace peeked through the plantation shutters but couldn't register anyone near either entrance. Beside him, Ruger happily waited, gaze locked on the pocket with the treats. If it'd been Vivienne, Ruger would've been long gone by now, treats or not.

He pulled the door to the flower child room shut. To his right was another set of stairs leading to a third story. To his left, the stairs down to the main floor. Twenty minutes he'd checked the place with not a thing to show for it except more questions.

Ah, to hell with it. He'd come this far, and she had to have a computer somewhere. He jogged up the stairs and found a tiny ten-by-ten alcove with a wide window overlooking downtown Dallas. The rest of the house might have been tidy, but up here it was chaos central. Colorful Post-its, papers, flyers. Every bit of it was out in the open. A simple computer desk sat in the center of the room with a big-screen computer in the middle.

Jace settled behind the desk and picked up the legal-sized form in the center.

Mortgage Refinance Application Form.

The date in the corner showed two days ago.

He wiggled the mouse and the monitor came to life and went straight to desktop, no password of any kind. A quick check of her calendar showed an appointment at nine o'clock this morning with her banker—and absolutely nothing else through the rest of the month.

Carefully rifling through the rest of the paperwork on her desk, he found a bank statement, the balance nowhere near where a woman with this kind of property in Uptown Dallas would need to keep from defaulting, which more than explained the refi paperwork. A quick check of her finance software and the rest of her calendar confirmed it—Vivienne Moore needed money and she needed it now.

Interesting. As sterile as most of it was, she obviously took pride in her home. Maybe if he found a way to fill her calendar outside of the Crossroads Rally, she'd be more receptive. Nothing said income better than a string of gigs to build the bank account. But he still didn't know what was holding her back.

He opened her internet history. Well, that might have something to do with it. Little Miss had been digging into not just him, but the club and Axel too, with extra time spent on news sites. Too bad she couldn't find his legit, white-collar stuff so easy. Then again, his investors always seemed to get a little jumpy when he mentioned being a more visible partner, which made it tough to close multimillion dollar deals.

Scrolling a little further down the history list, the subject matter shifted to everyday mundane sites. Target, Amazon, Yahoo, Google and—

Whoa. Now *that* was a good site. Jace clicked on the link and eased back in the desk chair, petting the top of Ruger's head. "Our girl's gotta kinky side, eh, Ruger?"

The dog nuzzled his pocket and Jace handed over another treat.

God damn it, he was insane to be chasing a woman who didn't seem to want anything to do with him, but everything in him screamed to make something between them happen. He'd have better luck making a compass point south than walk away at this point.

Sexy, kinky, smart, and mysterious to boot.

Yeah, one way or another, he was going to find a way into Vivienne Moore's world, even if he had to bribe her to do it.

SEVEN

VIVIENNE TOSSED HER latest paperback to the side of the bed and curled up on her side, staring out the open window. The gauzy fabric stretched across the ceiling fluttered in the breeze, and the crisp bite of winter filled the room with a clean, fresh scent. She tucked her toes under Ruger, sprawled at the foot of the bed.

Normally days like today, spent quietly in her room with a book, would level the worst stress life could throw her, but today nothing seemed to work. Not her favorite room, not her comfortable clothes, and most assuredly not her romance novels. Every time the author tried to paint an image of the hero, Viv kept superimposing Jace in his place, which only circled her back around to the issue at hand—take Jace's offer and buy herself some time, or tuck tail back to corporate America.

The refi wasn't really an option. Now that she'd seen the numbers in black and white, there was no way she could sign. Not only would she have zero equity left in her home with no guarantee her business would make it, but the rise in interest rates since she'd bought the place meant hardly any change in monthly payment. Other people might be able to swing such a huge risk, but Viv wasn't a fly-without-a-net kind of girl.

The strands of minilights in the corner clicked together on a sharper gust, and her makeshift swinging nightstand swayed beside the bed. The idea was one she'd copied off the internet. A simple eighteen-by-eighteen slab of honey-stained wood hung from rattan rope on each corner. Although, on windy days like this, using it to hold her hot chocolate probably wasn't her smartest move.

She sat up, grabbed her mug and put the novel in its place. No matter how bad she might want to ignore her decisions, it was time to up or duck on Jace's offer. Savoring her extra-sweet and semi-cooled drink, she padded closer to the window and leaned against the frame.

The view on this side of the street would have been a downer for most, but something about the old cemetery across the street gave her peace. The tall wrought iron fence with its fleur-de-lis post tops and the giant tombstones it protected seemed to anchor the rapidly changing area. A defiant nod to calmer times while everything around it jetted toward new-and-improved.

Which camp did she fall into? Her mother had harped on anyone in their family who would listen about the value of striving for more. Better income, better clothes, better people. There was always another rung to climb and something old to shake off. But here she was, being offered the chance for more from the very lifestyle she tried to distance herself from.

Surely she could manage the event and keep Jace at arm's length. It was a measly three months with a very non-measly and steady income. Three months would fly by in no time, and she probably wouldn't even see the guy very much.

I tend to be a hands-on man.

Okay, maybe that last part was a long shot. Knowing

how he'd acted so far, he'd likely check every fact and figure before he let her run with anything.

The memory of his kiss at Crossroads flared as bold as the sunshine outside, and her lips tingled. Lord, but that man could kiss. And he did it just like he did everything else, brazen and commanding, leveling any objections or obstacles before her mind even had a chance to fire.

Yeah, fighting that kind of temptation would be next to impossible. Although, he had enough negatives in his pros-and-cons chart to arm herself. The bad press, the arrests, the cops, and especially Hugo Moreno. Everything she'd read about the drug dealer was bad news, and he always seemed to sidestep authorities.

But if she pulled off the event and helped drag Crossroads out of its PR nightmare, it would be a serious coup. At this point, what did she have to lose?

She pushed away from the wall and patted her leg for Ruger to follow. She'd make the call to Jace, let him know she was in, and throw the rest to fate. Either she'd fight her way to success or go down in a blaze of glory.

Two steps toward her office, sharp knocks sounded on her front door.

Ruger peeled out and barreled down the stairs, his lean behind waggling like crazy.

It had to be neighborhood kids selling something. Somehow word must've gotten out she was a sucker for kids with fundraisers, because they were the only people who came to the front door.

Ruger was quite the fan of their tiny visitors, too. He ate up the kids' attention while she forked over money for stuff she didn't need.

"Just a second!" She snatched her purse off the

side table in the hall and nudged Ruger out of the way. Swinging the door wide, she pasted on a happy smile, and got an eyeful of hot damn and dirty dressed in a tight-fitting T-shirt and faded jeans. "Jace." She shook her head and gripped the edge of the door for dear life. "I mean, Mr. Kennedy."

Jace offered his hand to Ruger who unabashedly cozied up for a whole lot of love. Guess she wasn't the only one who got off on the guy's presence.

She snapped her fingers. "Ruger, *sitzen*."

The traitorous little fart obeyed, but not without a pitiful look over his shoulder.

"Sorry," she said. "Normally he's a lot more hesitant with new people." Well, more like a lot less friendly, as in bite first and ask questions later. So it was kind of weird he'd be so great with Jace.

"Maybe he's a good judge of character." Jace zeroed in on her purse then motioned toward the ground. "If you're headed somewhere, you might want to put on shoes first."

Ugh. She'd completely forgotten how she was dressed. Jeans and tanks were something she saved for home, and almost never went out in public with her hair loose. She tucked the purse under her arm and tried to smooth her wild curls away from her face. "I thought you were one of the neighborhood kids. I'm a sucker for a hardworking kid with a cute smile."

Jace perused her head to toe, slow and blatant. "A different look for you." He pinned her with a stare so heated it sizzled straight between her legs. "Looks good."

So much for easily distancing herself with everything wrong about the man. Right now she couldn't remember her middle name, let alone her pros and cons list. The government should bottle up the mojo he generated and use it as a scrambling mechanism, because it sure did a number on her common sense.

He braced his forearm on the door frame and leaned for a look into the hallway behind her. "You busy?"

Ah, damn. Unprofessional clothes and rude. The right thing would be to let him in and accept his offer like she'd planned, but a part of her didn't want him to see the place. He'd fit no better than a wild panther in a sterile office space and would be even less impressed.

Stepping back, she waved him in. "I was just about to call you, actually."

"That so?" Jace ambled passed her, his confident gait intimating he'd made his way through more than a few women's homes.

She hurried around him and angled for the kitchen. "Can I get you something to drink?"

"You have Scotch?"

"I was thinking more along the lines of a Coke or water. Wine is the only alcohol I keep in the house."

He paused in front of the canvas print she'd ordered off a discount online site and studied it. She still didn't care for the thing, but it worked well with the room. "I'll bring you a bottle you can keep on hand. For now, I'll pass."

"I doubt our working together would require you having a favorite liquor on hand at my home."

"So you've decided to take the job?"

Five minutes ago she had, but the second she'd opened the door, her libido had derailed all communications with her brain. She pressed her tumbler to the fridge's ice dispenser and corralled her common sense while the chunky cubes clattered into the glass. "I have, but I don't bring clients to my home." She paused midway through filling the glass with water. "How did you know where I lived?"

"Danny. Remember?" He faced her and looped his thumbs on the edges of his front pockets. "Is alcohol a problem for you, too? Or is it just your sister drinking until she can't see straight that makes you not keep it in your house?"

"I don't think that topic's relevant to our business together."

"It is if a substance gives you trouble and I'm the one putting you in close proximity to it. You might be the person who decides whether or not to tip one back, but that doesn't mean I shouldn't be aware of the issue and have a sensitivity to it."

Well, that was fair. And surprisingly refreshing. "You don't need to worry about me acting like Callie. I don't keep it in the house anymore because Callie thinks it's her mission to drink it."

"Figured as much." He sauntered toward the kitchen.

Viv shifted and stood so the kitchen island worked as a barrier between them. "Since we've got a limited amount of time to get things situated for the event, I'll start working out details first thing in the morning. Do I coordinate with you directly? Or will there be someone else I should work with?"

She hoped the latter, unless prolonged exposure somehow helped her develop a resistance.

He smirked at the abrupt change in topic and leaned into the countertop, arms crossed on the granite. "Have dinner with me."

What? She could barely keep an intelligent conversation with the guy in person, let alone navigate food safely between a plate and her mouth. Knowing her luck, she'd end up with stains on her clothes and lettuce stuck between her teeth. "I told you, business and pleasure don't mix. And even if I were willing to cross that line, I don't think the two of us would suit very well."

Liar.

He pushed away from the counter and prowled around it, coming up behind her. "We suited just fine three nights ago."

The low, delicious rumble of his voice tickled the nerve endings down her neck and spine. When his hands settled on her hips, a shudder too strong to hide rippled through her. "Still not good to mix pleasure with business." Nice words, but her tone was a cross between desperation and surrender.

Sweeping her hair from one side of her neck, Jace skimmed his lips along the sweet spot behind her ear. His warm breath fluttered against her skin, and the muscles at her core contracted. "No business to mix yet. All pleasure."

Oh, God. Never in her life had she wanted to let go with a man so badly. To lean into his strength and tuck reason and responsibility in some dark, impenetrable cell. Just to be and enjoy without worry for a little while.

She should move. Gain some distance and get them back on track. On business and planning. She shifted her weight to step away.

Jace's fingers tightened on her hips. "I'm also rethinking my offer."

Freezing water dumped over her head couldn't have straightened her spine any faster. She spun and faced him despite the limited room to move. "So, if I won't go out with you, you're retracting the job?"

"Not at all. Just changing the arrangement up a bit." He studied her for slow, unsettling seconds, resting on her lips for several heartbeats before he stepped back.

The second he was out of touching distance, her trance dissipated and she sucked in a lungful of air. A part of her wondered if he'd realized how fuddled her mind was and had given her the space on purpose.

"I met with Axel yesterday, along with a few of my other associates. We've got a full slate of marketing projects with event aspects that could use a woman like you handling the details." He strolled into the adjoining living room, resuming his perusal of her belongings with a crooked smile. "Between what we have and the connections you'll make along the way, I estimate your calendar for this year and part of the next will fill up pretty quickly."

He paused at the foot of the stairs, looked up to the second floor, and grinned like he'd just learned a naughty secret.

Shit. She'd left the door to her safe room open. Surely he couldn't see very much from there. "So you're offering additional work?"

The question drew his attention back on her and away from her secret place. "I am."

Twelve to eighteen months of solid work. With that kind of exposure and steady paychecks, she could not only rebuild the savings she'd blown staying afloat, but hopefully build some momentum. Assuming she could figure out what was causing her to lose referral business. "Then you'll understand our keeping a professional relationship is more important than ever."

He meandered toward her, stopping close enough her nerve endings perked up for a second Hallelujah chorus. "That's the biggest part I'm rethinking." He cupped the side of her neck, his fingers tangled in her hair. "I think you're a smart woman. One who wants more from life than punching in and out at eight and five. I appreciate that and want to help." He pulled her closer. "In exchange, I want two dates."

She planted a hand on his chest to keep her balance and angled for better eye contact. "Two dates?"

The devil couldn't have a more wicked smile. Between his pretty white teeth, full lips and dark beard, he could talk just about any woman out of her panties in under five seconds. "Two dates. The time and place of my choosing."

"Why?"

He loosened his grip on her neck enough to trace her lower lip with his thumb.

Her lips parted on instinct, and it was all she could do to keep her tongue from darting out for a taste.

"Why's not important. Just your agreement."

Was he kidding? He'd offered her a crazy chance to keep her dream alive and had every nerve ending pegged out at max wattage. Right now, she'd agree to robbery and might consider murder.

He leaned in, his lips so close hers tingled in response. "But know this, I expect your involvement. You will fully participate and not act like some cardboard cutout. You enjoy and have fun."

Warnings borne from years of self-preservation blasted fog-horn loud through her head, and she shoved free on instinct. "You mean have sex."

Jace let her go and laughed, the sound so full and

rich it echoed off the vaulted ceilings. "Sugar, I don't need to buy sex. Especially from a curvy little event planner who wears Levi's like they're custom-made for her delectable ass."

Well, didn't that make her feel like a knee-jerking idiot. "How else was I supposed to take, 'fully participate'?"

His laughter slowly eased, but his smile stayed locked in place. "Maybe I've a mind to show you business and pleasure can happily coexist." He tucked his hands in his front pockets, his hip anchored at a cocky angle. "Nothing's gonna happen on those two dates that you don't want. It's about letting go and having fun. That's it. Not much to ask for in exchange for you being able to grab your dream by the balls, now is it?"

The memory of a tropical vacation ad she'd seen years ago popped into her head. A woman stood at the top of a tall cliff and slowly leaned forward for the most beautiful swan dive toward the turquoise waters below. In this moment, the woman was her. Faced with an opportunity to let go and fall into the arms of something both terrifying and wonderful.

Two dates. Or, as Jace put it, two dates of letting go and having fun. Just enjoying without worry or responsibility. And after, she could put her tightly ordered life back in its neat little place. "You'll respect my limits?"

"Assuming you can put words around those limits, sure."

"What's that supposed to mean?"

"It means if you can clearly verbalize what's bothering you, or what you don't want, I'll respect every boundary you give. But if you're not sure, I'm going to push you to explore."

God, how nice would it be to let go just once? Her head bobbed an agreement before her conscience even figured out the internal debate was over. "Two dates."

Jace's brown eyes darkened to almost black and his smile slipped. In seconds, he'd shifted from playful devil to a hungry panther with an open cage door. He closed the distance between them and pulled her close. His lips barely brushed hers and his voice growled low and deep. "Good choice."

With that, he backed away and ambled for the entrance. "Saturday at noon." He opened the door, looked her up and down, and grinned. "And, for God's sake— wear those jeans again."

He winked and shut the door behind him, leaving her rooted to the same spot with her mind too scrambled for basic thought.

A year or more of steady work, and two dates with a man who made her wet with a look and kissed like the devil. What the hell had she just agreed to?

EIGHT

A FRIDAY NIGHT in a bar with more waitstaff than customers was never good. How his newest investor could label the place trendy was beyond Jace's comprehension. It had about as much personality as Viv's living room, and they'd tried to pass some kind of cheap Scotch off on him when he'd ordered Macallan. If that was the kind of service customers got, he could understand the empty seats.

His phone vibrated in his pants pocket, and the simmering burn he'd nursed since learning the last-minute change in venue jumped an extra notch. Axel's name registered on the display. "Where the hell are you?"

"Christ, you sound like my ma when she's just home from getting her hair done." Wind and the throaty rumble of Axel's Shelby Cobra droned in the background. "What's got your panties in a twist? Oh, wait. Let me guess. You actually peeled yourself out of those damned jeans and bothered to get gussied up to close your big deal, only it's rubbin' your delicate skin all wrong."

"Fuck you, McKee." Actually, Axel wasn't wrong on that score. While the black tailored pants and white button-down weren't uncomfortable, he always felt like an imposter dressed for the white-collar world.

"Got a bad feeling about this deal," Jace said. "Charlie's been hounding me for months to work a project he and his buddies could buy into, but the last two weeks he's gone radio silence. Only time I heard from him was today when he had me switch our meet from the club to some bar in Arlington that's nose-diving for bankruptcy."

"Stop bein' a fuckin' pessimist. I know how much this deal means to you, but Charlie's a good man. Worked his way up the same as us."

"He might've come from the same side of the tracks, but he's sure as hell distanced himself from it."

His pretty little elf of a waitress dared to look away from the muted rerun of one of those *Housewives* shows.

Jace motioned her over.

No sooner had she pushed away from the bar, Charlie strode through the door.

"Gotta go, our man's here," Jace said. "You gonna make it?"

"Need another twenty. Try not to fire that nasty temper you've been nursing the last few days on the poor man before I get there."

Jace ended the call, pried himself out of his too-stiff black leather chair, and tucked the phone in his pocket. He offered his hand to Charlie. "Thought you weren't going to make it."

"Yeah, been a crazy few weeks." He shook Jace's hand and darted glances over each shoulder.

Maybe Axel was right and Jace was imagining things. Charlie worked hard, and the pale blue button-down paired with gray pants made it look like he'd come straight from the office.

Jace waved Charlie into one of the two chairs next to him as the waitress sauntered up. "Charlie, what'll you have?"

"Just a vodka tonic for me."

Jace handed her the barely touched drink she'd brought him the first time around. "Let's give the Macallan another go, but this time I'd like the real deal instead of a well drink."

The waitress accepted the glass and shuttled a confused look between him and the bartender.

"Not your fault, sugar. Just tell them anyone who orders Macallan is gonna know the difference, and try to keep an eye on them when they pull that shit in the future. Management might earn an extra buck sneaking in cheap stuff, but you'll be the one who pays for it in tips." He laid a business card on her tray. "If this gig dries up, call Shelly at that number. She'll teach you the stuff they're not giving you here, so long as you're willing to learn."

The girl fingered the corner of the card a second, picked it up, and tucked it in her pocket. "Do I have to wait until this place dries up?"

Funny how telling her wording was. Even the waitress realized they were headed nowhere whether she'd consciously acknowledged it or not. "Whenever works for you."

She nearly skipped away, leaving the two men alone.

"Sorry for the last-minute change. I, uh—" Charlie leaned back and checked the window behind Jace. "I ran into a few problems."

"Thought the life of a stock trader was getting a little easier with the market headed up."

"The stocks are fine. It's the men involved with your venture I'm having problems with."

And Axel called him a pessimist. More like a businessman with a damned fine instinct. "What kind of problems?"

Charlie hesitated, scanning the club's main entrance. "We're getting a lot of pressure. Out of the five guys partnered for your investment, four of us have been told we'll lose big on other deals if we go through with yours."

Just breathe. Stay focused and keep your expression neutral. The rescheduled location at a no-name bar, Charlie's late arrival, the way he kept scouting the club—it all made sense.

Jace kept his fists unclenched. Barely. "I don't suppose this pressure's originating from one of Dallas's esteemed councilmen. Maybe one running for a House of Representatives seat?"

Charlie sat back in his chair, obviously stunned. "Did one of the other guys call you?"

"No need. Renner and I go way back. Went to school together at UNLV. Though we didn't exactly run in the same crowds."

"Well, he's got a pretty serious grudge where you're concerned. Enough he's pulling strings that'll hurt a lot of the men in this deal if you're anywhere on the contracts."

The waitress hustled back with their drinks, a whole different spring in her step the second time around. "Here you go. And I watched him this time like you said."

"Good girl." Jace handed her a twenty and she spun away with a sunshine grin.

"Look, Jace. I'm really sorry, but we just can't—"

"Do you want this deal?" Jace said.

"Of course, I want this deal. We all do. With the land you've got cornered, and the tenants already lined up, it's a slam dunk. But not at the cost of other business already in place."

Damn it to hell, he'd picked this group of men because they had fucking strong enough spines they'd be willing to do business with him publicly. Just once he'd like one of his non-entertainment ventures to have his name on it instead of one of the shell corps that hid his identity. Heaven forbid any upstanding citizens had their names tied to the redneck sin king.

"You don't have to lose the deal." Jace dug in his pocket for a toothpick and popped it in his mouth. "I've got a few shell corporations already set up. Spread the word around you broke the deal, give it a little time to settle, then we'll restart the venture with a whole new partner."

"What's to keep Renner from finding out the shell corp is yours?"

"You see me losin' money anywhere else?" Jace twisted the toothpick between his fingers. "Been getting around uptight assholes like Paul my whole life. He won't find this one any more than he's found the others."

Charlie sipped his vodka tonic then rested it on the armrest.

Jace leaned in and propped his elbows on his knees. "You don't like that son of a bitch any more than anyone else. Take the deal I'm offering you and know it'll make you a solid profit in the end. Not to mention you'll slide one past Renner in the process. That alone makes it worth it."

For long, quiet seconds, Charlie studied his cocktail. He tossed back what was left of the drink and set it on the brushed steel table. "Yeah, let's do it. I'll talk to the rest of the men and make sure they're on board, but I want this deal to go through, and I want it with you."

"All right then." Jace stood and held out his hand. "Now get the hell out of here before you're caught cavorting with the evil underbelly of society."

Charlie shook his hand. "It's not like that. Not with me."

"I know it's not or I never would have put this deal together with you. Renner's a dick. I know it better than most. I'm the last person who's gonna judge a guy for keeping his ledger in the black."

A few platitudes and five minutes later, Jace stared out the windowed wall at the taillights clogged up on the highway in the distance. Hard to tell what pissed him off more. Another failed attempt to have his name front and center on a profitable venture, or the self-imposed distance he'd kept from Vivienne the last two days.

Axel's boisterous voice echoed through the isolated corner of the bar. "He didn't show?"

Jace tossed his mangled toothpick to the tabletop and swirled his Scotch. "Already been here and gone."

"You're shittin' me. It's only been twenty minutes."

"Doesn't take long to share bad news."

Axel dropped into the seat Charlie had vacated, his standard pants and sweater combination paired with one of those messy knots on the top of his head the women loved to fawn over. "What happened?"

"Paul Renner. Seems he's put pressure on most of the men involved either directly or indirectly. If I'm involved, he'll pull strings elsewhere and hurt existing bottom lines."

"Fucking knobdobber. Charlie and his guys bail on the deal?"

"Almost. I told Charlie we'd switch to a shell corp so Paul can't track who's involved."

The flash of pity on Axel's face lanced straight through Jace's gut. "I'm sorry, brother. I know you wanted this one."

Jace shrugged and sipped his drink. "Business is business. Either way, I'll make a boatload." Though he'd have enjoyed the income a whole lot more if he could publicly lay his name to it. "What the hell took you so long?"

"Your dark-haired beauty. The woman's got a mind like a trap when it comes to logistics. I think my dick turned to stone when she started rattling off demands to your secretary."

"Your dick and Vivienne in the same sentence isn't improving my mood."

Axel dragged his forefinger back and forth through his beard. "You're awfully protective of this one. And throwing around an awful lot in the way of good deeds. Way more than needed for a piece of ass."

"That's because she's not a piece of ass." The retort snipped out harsher than he intended, fueled by the nearly nonstop beating he'd given himself ever since he'd left Vivienne's townhouse. The fact that she'd assumed he wanted sex in exchange for time with him still rubbed him all kinds of wrong. Hell, yeah, he wanted leverage where getting closer to her was concerned. But if she gave herself to him, he wanted it to happen because she was as on fire as he was, and damn sure not out of obligation.

"I like her spunk," Jace said when he'd finally wrangled his emotion. "She's got a dream but hasn't found a way to make it stick yet. I'm just giving her a boost and havin' her back. Everyone deserves a chance to prove themselves."

"You're treatin' her like a brother."

Jace froze with his drink halfway to his mouth. "Come again?"

"You heard me. If you didn't trust her, you'd have your bloody hands on every detail. Instead you're loadin' her up with every kind of opportunity and padding her sails. Same as you would a brother."

The Scotch burned down his throat. A proud, almost stubborn part of him demanded he put Axel in his place and deny any such thing. Another, far wiser, part of him sat stunned with realization.

"Remember our agreement," Axel said. "There's too much at risk for the brotherhood in bringin' any woman close who's not meant to be one of the clan. One wrong piece of information and she could unravel all we've built. Not to mention weaken our group." He leaned in, elbows on his knees and hands clasped between them. "Is she worthy of Haven?"

Was she? Hell, he couldn't even get past comprehending how deeply he'd gotten involved with Viv, let alone gauge the kind of longevity Axel suggested. Though if he was honest, there was definitely a protectiveness he'd never experienced with anyone outside of his and Axel's mothers. And even then, what he felt for Viv was unique. Almost instinctive and animalistic. "I don't know what she is to me."

"Then you might want to figure that out before you get much deeper. For her sake as well as yours." He motioned toward Jace's face with his glass. "I was with you when you got that pretty scar on your face, and I'll be with you 'til I'm not breathin' anymore, but the rest of the brothers won't take kindly to you putting their secrets at risk without their blessing."

"I'll figure it out. Then I'll tackle what needs to happen like I always do."

Axel smirked and chortled. "Mayhap you need to tackle the lass first and take the bloody edge off your temper. If you don't get relief soon, you're liable to do something stupid and land us a whole new mess of PR troubles."

Oh, he'd get relief. Just a little over twelve more hours and he'd be at Vivienne's front door and ready to teach the self-restrained minx how to relax. And maybe let his wild side out for a little fun, too.

NINE

WHAT THE HELL kind of shoes went with jeans, a tank and flannel shirt on a midsixty degree day in January? Viv traded her Toms for a worn pair of Sperry Top-Siders, then kicked those off just as fast as every other set she'd tried on. Her cute little combat boots with the zipper sides and lace-up fronts looked the best with the black and cobalt blue plaid, but given she had no clue where they were headed, they might set all the wrong look.

Pipes from yet another biker out taking advantage of the unseasonably warm weather rumbled down the street.

Ruger whined and took off downstairs.

Huffing at his abandonment, Viv made another pass through her closet. Shoes were something she held onto far longer than was healthy, so there had to be something that hit middle ground in at least one of the boxes. She sure as heck wasn't backtracking and changing her outfit. Just talking herself into wearing the jeans had taken thirty minutes.

Three sharp raps sounded on the front door, and Ruger answered with an earsplitting round of barks.

Leaving her shoe disaster behind, Viv hurried down the stairs, wedged her way past Ruger's waggling body, and opened the door.

Her over-exuberant dog darted past her and went

straight for Jace, who crouched down and greeted him like a long-lost friend.

It was the damnedest thing. She'd never seen Ruger take to a person so quickly, particularly not a man. "Sorry. He doesn't normally get this excited."

"Hope not. I'd rather he bite first and ask questions later where you're concerned." Jace gave Ruger one last scratch behind the ears and straightened, his leather jacket open to show a soft white T-shirt underneath. His hair was pulled back in a low ponytail, and his aviator shades made his tan even more pronounced than normal.

He slid the glasses off and took his time raking her with a slow, smoldering perusal and backing her out of the entry with a prowling gait. He shut the door behind him with barely a backward glance and laid another jacket on the hallway side table. "You wore the jeans."

"You asked me to."

Still stalking her, he nodded at her bare feet. "You're missing shoes again."

Out of hallway, Viv stopped and held her ground. "I wasn't sure what would be appropriate."

Jace wrapped her up, his big hands sliding between her flannel shirt and tank top until they splayed at the small of her back and shoulder blades. "Nothin' sexier than a curvy woman in a soft pair of jeans with bare feet." His lips hovered close to hers, the soft brush of his goatee making her mouth part on a sigh. "Makes a man want to get her in bed and kiss her to the point he can peel those jeans right off."

Man, he had killer lips. And with his hard body pressed against her and his fresh clean scent overtaking her lungs, it was a wonder she didn't just give in and taste them. "I'd planned to keep them on, so maybe it's better if you skip the kissing."

He smirked and pulled in a slow, sexy breath. "Postpone, maybe. If I kiss you now, we'll never leave, but no way in hell I'm skipping it." He stepped away, and every part of her from the neck down lined up to file a protest. "You got boots?"

Boots. Her mind scrambled, snatched his words from the recycle bin, and rewound. Footwear. She needed shoes. "Yes."

He grinned in a way that said he hadn't missed her mental lapse, and tucked a toothpick in his mouth. "Grab 'em and let's go."

Heart pounding, she jogged up the stairs with as much casual attitude as she could muster. A fine sweat coated the back of her neck, and she'd swear her cheeks were bright enough to give Rudolph's nose a run for its money. She'd need at least five minutes in front of a fan before she could face him again.

She stepped into her boots and zipped them up, then made one last stop in front of the mirror. There wouldn't be any fashion awards in her immediate future, but Jace wasn't exactly dressed to impress either.

Okay, that was a lie. He might not grace the cover of *GQ* anytime soon, but he impressed the hell out of her. Then again, he could probably do that naked.

The image of his bare torso and the tattoo she'd glimpsed at The Den flared in high definition in her mind. Oh, yeah. Dressed, or naked, he gave her body one heck of a wake-up call. A fact she'd be smart to remember and keep her wits alert. Going out today was one thing. Going beyond that wasn't such a great idea.

She'd go, have a good time and enjoy herself like she promised, but that was it.

Two steps outside her bedroom she halted.

The door to her special room stood open. Sprawled across the bed's rich eggplant-colored comforter, Jace had his hands tucked behind his head, eyes trained on the gauzy fabric overhead while his tongue worked his toothpick in a dizzying swirl. God, he looked good in there. Too good. Perfectly at home.

"The door was closed," Viv said.

Jace's gaze slid to her, that devious grin he seemed to specialize in making him look like a pleasure devil on a mission to torment. "Never could pass up a closed door. Makes me want to nose around until I learn what's inside." He scanned the random artwork hung in haphazard patterns on the far wall, mostly pencil sketches and tattoo designs she'd collected over the years. "It's a great room. Not sure why you isolate so much of yourself to one space."

"What makes you think this room has anything to do with me?"

"I don't think it, I know it." He pulled the toothpick out of his mouth and tucked it in his pocket. "The rest of the place is just a front. Part of the professional image you want everyone else to see, but this?" He scanned the room from one side to the other. "This is you."

She fidgeted with the doorknob, tucked her other hand in her back pocket, and studied her boots. "Are we ready to go?"

The mattress let out a soft creak and Jace's booted footsteps sounded on the bamboo floors a second later. He cupped the back of her neck and urged her face up to his. "I like this side of you."

She opened her mouth to protest, but Jace steered her from the room and closed the door behind him. In the hallway, he retrieved the leather jacket he'd set aside on the way in and held it up. "You'll need this."

"It's not that cold today. I'm fine like this."

He opened the front door and motioned to the black and chrome Harley parked right outside her front stoop. "Not when you're going forty to fifty on side streets. Then it feels a hell of a lot colder."

No wonder Ruger had darted to the front door the way he did. She padded to the bike and ran her hand along the leather seat. Memories of her father rattling off to her mom all the reasons why he needed this same bike all those years ago echoed in her head. "A CVO Softail Deluxe."

"I may have to rethink our plans."

Jace's grumbled voice punched through her thoughts and she whipped her head up to face him. "What?"

"You just nailed the model of Harley and stroked that seat the way a man wants a woman to touch his cock." He strolled forward and held up the jacket again. "Made my dick hard as stone and seriously makes me rethink leaving the house. You still want to tell me that room upstairs isn't you?"

She slid her arms in the jacket and shrugged. "I only know it because my dad wanted one."

Jace scrutinized her, a whole lot of confusion and suspicion narrowing his gaze until she looked away. "Get what you need and lock up. Time to ride."

An Uzi aimed at her feet couldn't have made her move any faster, his too-perceptive appraisal generating more adrenaline than her body knew what to do with.

She snatched her purse from inside, made sure Ruger was situated, then locked the front door behind her.

The bike's engine fired up before she'd even pulled the key from the lock. She dropped her purse in the saddlebag he held open for her. "Where are the helmets?"

Jace grinned that wicked smile and slid his aviators into place. "Never met a woman who needed wind in her hair more than you." He pinched the tail of her braid that had fallen over her shoulder and wiggled it. "And for the record, the bike's the only reason you're leaving the house with this in. It's comin' out as soon as we're parked."

"What if I don't want it loose?"

"Then I'll make it my mission to persuade you." He jerked his head to the back of the bike, flipped down a peg just above the top pipe, and tapped it. "Now hop on, sugar, and let's get this day started."

Her insides spun a whole string of cartwheels, clearly on board with his brand of persuasion despite her logic's damper. She could deal with that when the time came. Right now she had to figure out how to gracefully get herself situated on the altogether too small seat behind him.

With a little more wobble than she would've liked, she stepped on the footrest and swung her leg over the tiny backrest. She'd barely made contact with the leather when Jace revved the engine and eased the bike forward. She clutched his shoulders on instinct, but figured out quick the seat back wouldn't let her fall off the way she'd feared. By the time she'd unwound her death grip, they were out of the townhouse complex and rumbling through Turtle Creek. Vibrations scampered through her until she let out a delighted laugh.

The minute the sound slipped free, Jace released one hand from the bike and rubbed her knee. There was something different about the touch. An expression of pride and comfort more than anything sexual. A silent encouragement to let go and be in the moment. And damn it if a long-silenced part of her didn't perk up and pay attention.

He regripped the handlebar, but the heat from his touch remained.

She leaned a little closer to his torso to block the wind. He hadn't been wrong about the temperature. At a standstill, the weather and brilliant sunshine were ideal, but however fast they were going now made it seem closer to fifty. Her cheeks stung in a pleasant, just-conquered-the-mountain sensation, and tiny tendrils from her escaped braid whipped her temples and cheeks.

It was heaven. Liberating and joyful on one hand, and powerfully bold on the other. Scents overlapped and fought for supremacy—warmed asphalt, fresh-laid mulch from a nearby home, the algae from the park pond across the street, and more than one auto in need of a tune-up. A drive in the spring would be even better, the crisp edge of freshly cut grass and blooming trees overpowering every other scent.

Jace leaned heavy to the left and steered them into an older neighborhood in a super swank part of town. Homes architected in everything from baroque to contemporary styles lined the aged, yet well-kept streets, and mature cedar elms towered over the road on either side. She'd never bothered to do much research on this part of town when she'd bought her home, but one look at the real estate around her and it was easy to place them between one to twenty million each.

A tall wrought iron gate with beautiful swirls stood open with an ivory stucco wall shooting out on either side. Jace turned in and Viv's jaw dropped. The circular patchwork tile drive led to a stunning villa. Reaching at least fifty feet to either side of a tall center section, the stucco walls matched the outer wall, and wrought iron accents lined the old-world windows. Adobe slate tiles topped it off for a perfect mix of Italian and southwest influence.

Out of kilter and completely unexpected were the muscle cars lined along the outer drive. Four Harleys were backed in and parked in front of an open breezeway at the far side of the house, too.

A tiny chuckle wound through Jace's voice. "You can stop ogling and hop off, sugar."

Well, shoot. She probably did look like a Class-A gawker. She dismounted with a little more confidence and went back to soaking in all the lovely details while Jace backed his bike next to the others. Even in the early part of winter, the grass was spring green, and the scent of meat on a grill carried on the air. Laughter and the subtle bass of a rock tune drifted from the backyard.

Jace ambled toward her, her forgotten purse gripped in one hand. He handed the tiny cross-body to her. "You like it?"

"It's fantastic." She uncoiled the strap and anchored it on her shoulder. "Whose is it?"

The cocky smile he'd sported wavered for the briefest moment. He glanced at the ground, pulled out another one of those toothpicks he seemed so fond of, and looked back up, grin in place. "Doesn't matter whose name is on the deed. What matters is you stop wearing your shoulders for earrings and start enjoying your afternoon." He urged her forward with a hand at the small of her back. "Come on, Alice, I'll show you to the rabbit hole."

TEN

Now this was the good life. Springlike weather in January, severe clear skies, good friends and a tempting woman beside him. Jace had picked one of the oversize wicker chaises on purpose, pulling her down on his lap before she could protest, but she still sat ramrod straight on one edge, refusing to stretch out next to him.

Formed in a loose circle of lawn furniture and tables dragged in from all around the pool, Axel, Trev and Zeke chattered with their dates. Viv kept the conversation moving gracefully, always asking thoughtful questions and making sure everyone got equal airtime. He'd barely registered a tenth of the topics, his attention too focused on the animated hand gestures she used when she talked and wishing he could find a way to get her as relaxed when she was alone with him.

Jace slipped his hands beneath her flannel shirt and tank, and teased the soft skin along the waistband of her jeans. Nothing dirty, just a tempting touch to get her attention.

She straightened another inch and twisted. If it hadn't been for the soft surprise in her eyes and her slightly parted lips, he'd have thought she didn't like the contact.

"C'mere." He couched the request so it didn't carry far, but she still glanced back at his brothers and the women between them to see if they'd clued in. "You're not comfortable and today's about relaxing. Slide back here and put your feet up."

The look on her face was priceless. Big eyes with so much want and fear behind them, a stranger would've tagged him the big bad wolf offering a chocolate to a starving girl.

"Trust me," he said, even lower. "Just for a little bit. Relax."

She fisted her hand on her thigh.

He covered it with his free hand and soothed his thumb along her wrist. "Not gonna hurt you, sugar. You're safe."

The women guffawed in the background about God only knew what, and Zeke's date playfully slapped him on his shoulder.

Viv's stare never wavered from Jace. She unwound the leg she'd curled beneath the other and started to shift back.

Jace took over, easily sliding her onto his lap with a grip on her hips that lit all kinds of other images in his head.

Tucking her close, he kissed her temple and cupped the back of her neck. "Much better."

"You should have your boss call Viv then." Axel's voice rose from across the coffee table littered with everything from empty beer bottles and mixed drinks, to Viv's Coke. "Jace's dark-haired beauty's got a good head for parties. Though we've got her tied up pretty tight for the next few months."

Axel and his bad timing. The term "tied up" with Viv pressed against him and the memory of those kink sites on her computer were a deadly combination for a man trying to take things slow with a skittish woman.

The pretty little blonde pixie Trevor had brought as a date stirred some frozen concoction she'd worked up in the kitchen. "Trevor mentioned you have an event company. What's it called?"

"Amaryllis Events."

"That is so cool!" Zeke's long-haired brunette looked suspiciously like the stripper who'd given his brother a lap dance over a month ago. She wiggled to the end of her chair. "What's the biggest party you've done? Have you met anyone famous?"

And that was it. Three innocent questions and a whole lot of subsequent back and forth, and Viv finally unwound beside him. Even when he took a chance and slipped his fingers back under her tank, she stayed relaxed, enjoying the simple conversation with a sideways glance and a soft smile in between polite answers.

"I think it would be cool to manage a rock tour." Axel had introduced his leggy blonde date as a new associate, but Jace had a feeling she was a colleague of the pre-negotiated, hardcore-sex-after-the-picnic variety. "Just imagine all the crazy shit you'd have to break up… when…" The enthusiasm on her face died alongside her words, her gaze locked just beyond Vivienne's shoulder.

Before Jace could so much as question what was wrong, Lily Montrose strutted into view, her curves more than adequately displayed in a body-hugging white dress that was way over the top for a picnic. Her gaze lingered longer than necessary on Viv curled up on his lap. "Nice party, Jace."

"Yeah?" Jace said. "How'd you catch wind of it?"

"Ivan mentioned it. Thought I'd stop by and say hi." She smoothed her fingers over Jace's shoulder in a possessive glide. "Anyone need a drink?"

The touch was one thing, but paired with the whole lady-of-the-manor routine, Jace's temper ramped from nonexistent to borderline lethal. Not exactly a prime situation when he was trying to convince Little Miss he wasn't the big bad wolf.

He locked stares with Trevor and hoped like hell his brother got the message. "Nothing here that needs your attention."

Trev's gaze slid to Viv curled up against Jace and grinned. "How about you track down Ivan and see if he needs any extra help tonight? We've got a live band booked for the back room, and word has it they can be a handful. Wouldn't hurt to have an extra hand to keep 'em in line."

Every one of the girls averted their focus in one way or another, two fiddling with their drinks, and Axel's blonde snuggling up for a kiss. Viv, on the other hand, had all of her attention focused on Lily's hand on Jace's shoulder. If Lily wanted to parade herself around like a Saran-wrapped snowman, that was her prerogative, but fucking with Viv's head was something else altogether.

"Think it's in your best interest if you help Trev out and take that hand off my shoulder, Lily," Jace said.

"Sorry." Thank God, her nails weren't knives. The way they slid off him said her apology was mighty damned empty. She opened her mouth to say something else, zeroed in on Jace's death glare, and closed it. With a wiggle of her fingers toward Trevor, she spun for the sliding glass doors and the living room beyond. "I'll take care of the band, Trev."

"Appreciate it."

The second Lily was out of hearing distance, the tension in the tiny circle dissipated, and the girls kicked back in with their chatter. Well, all of them except Viv.

She spread her hand across his sternum, fingers idly tracing the outline of the dog tags under his T-shirt. "You okay?"

Christ, her touch was a benediction compared to Lily's. And simpleton that he seemed to be around her, his mind took note of her tiny fingers sliding against him and superimposed the image on his cock. Fuck, he'd be jacking off every other hour at this rate.

"I am now." Cupping the back of her head, his fingers tangled in her braid, and his calculating thoughts kicked out a fresh idea. "I could be better though."

For the first time since he'd met her, she gifted him with some of the saucy playfulness she'd aimed at the rest of the crowd, and cocked her eyebrow at a perky, but arrogant slant. Those kiss-tastic lips of hers puckered up in a cute pout. "Really?"

"Oh, yeah."

"And how would I do that?"

He loosely gripped her braid and let it slide through his fingers to the tip. He tugged the nondescript brown band holding it in place.

Viv pushed against his chest as though she meant to sit up, but Jace caught her with a hand at her shoulder. "You wanted to make it better."

"Getting you in a better mood and making me look like a wild woman are two different things."

"Sugar, you're a wild woman with or without the braid. You just don't let yourself out of the cage enough to enjoy her." He tugged on the band again. One more pull and he'd be home free. "Indulge me. Been dying to get my hands in your hair since New Year's Eve."

She shot him a disbelieving look.

Say yes. For the love of God, say yes and let go.

Her gaze drifted to his chest and she shrugged one shoulder.

Close enough. He pulled the band free and tossed it toward the table beside them. Fuck if he cared if it got lost. Between him and his brothers, they could come up with half a dozen more in a snap, but he'd rather her not have an excuse to knot it back up.

He worked his fingers through the sections, the slick and wavy texture a God damn thrill to touch. "Look at me, Viv."

She cocked her head a little, the tense press of her palm against his chest belying her careless facade. Slowly, her gaze drifted up to his. If she had any clue how sexy she was, or the impact she had on him, she sure as hell didn't show it. If anything, those pale gray eyes of hers screamed insecurity paired with a dangerous powder keg of passion.

He combed the heavy mass until it flowed loose, a dark chocolate that reached her shoulder blades. "I was wrong."

"Huh?"

His grin popped into place before he could catch it. Little Miss might not like leaving her hair down, but she sure shot to la-la land fast when someone played with it. He'd have to tuck that little nugget away for later. "Decided I'm still not feeling as good as I could be. Need a kiss to make it all better."

Viv tensed beneath his arm and glanced back at the rest of their crew.

Not for a second did he doubt Axel, Trev and Zeke knew every detail going down, but not a one of them showed it. Instead, they did their part to make sure the women kept the conversation flowing and stayed a long damned way from engaging Viv. Never underestimate a high-caliber wingman, let alone a trio.

He cupped her nape and urged her to face him. "Never mind them."

"It's kind of rude."

"According to who?"

"I don't know. Emily Post? Proper etiquette? PDA Anonymous?"

He couldn't help but chuckle. "Got a little smart-ass in there with the wild chick." He speared his fingers in her hair, cupping the back of her head. "Surely she's up for breaking the rules just this once."

Her gaze dropped to his mouth and her hand on his chest fisted.

A round of laughter fired behind them, but Viv stayed rock still, a few stubborn strands of her hair dancing on the light breeze.

He opened his mouth, ready to throw a dare down, but she leaned in and pressed her lips to his. Warm, wet, and parted just enough they meshed with his in a perfect glide. Her tongue slicked across his lower lip and her breath mingled with his. Her fingertips tickled the beard along his jawline.

Good God, if he died in the next five minutes he'd do it a happy man. He'd kissed her enough times he should've known what to expect, but something about this one rocked him. Vulnerable, innocent and hungry all rolled up into one.

No, it was more than that. This was freedom, and damn, it tasted fantastic on her lips.

She eased away. If he hadn't seen so much uncertainty behind her glazed eyes, he'd have swung her over his shoulder, locked them in his bedroom, and not come out for three days. Maybe more.

The quiet seemed to register with them both at the same time, and Viv twisted for a look behind her.

Oh, they had an audience alright. The women were a mix of playful and envy, but the men were more than a little smug. Shit, if they had any clue how Viv kissed, he'd have to fight them all off.

Viv pushed up and reached for her Coke, only to realize all she had left was ice.

Jace pulled the tumbler from her death grip and pried himself from the chaise. "I figure since you kissed me and made me all better, the least I can do is get you a refill. You want another Coke, or something else?"

Her gaze zeroed in on one of the girls' frozen drinks. "Coke's fine."

Gripping her chin, he urged her face to his. "What do you really want?"

She wrinkled her nose in way that guaranteed if he didn't have what she wanted, he'd buy the closest liquor store that did. "Do you have any wine?"

"Love the stuff when I'm in the mood. What kind?"

"Red?"

"Still kind of vague."

"Surprise me."

Hell, yeah, she had some smart-ass in her, and he fucking loved it. He leaned in and kissed that perky nose. "Good to see the wild child's finally lettin' loose."

He strutted off to the kitchen, the frustrated knot he'd lugged around since New Year's Eve finally easing up. He still had bubkes in the way of answers where she was concerned, but at least the puzzle pieces were almost on the table. Didn't hurt he felt about fifty feet tall at the moment either.

With a refreshed Macallan in hand and a wine opener in his pocket, he headed for the wine rack.

"Never thought I'd see you with a mousy thing like her." Lily's voice turned the Scotch easing down his throat to acid.

He slid a merlot free and meandered to the kitchen island. If Lily was stupid enough to go head to head with him, then she deserved a setback aimed her direction. Hell, with the way she'd acted on the patio, he was looking forward to it.

He set the bottle on the thick granite, and the heavy thunk echoed through the otherwise empty kitchen. Turning to face her, he leaned back on the counter and braced with a solid pull of Scotch. "You think she's mousy, huh?"

Lily big-mouthed the bait and sashayed closer. "Well, she's sure not your usual type."

"Yeah? What type is that?"

"Oh, come on, Jace. She's uptight and goody-two-shoes. Probably wouldn't know how to navigate your world, let alone keep your cock's attention."

Jesus, this woman was a piece of work.

She dragged one long fingernail down his sternum, then slowly toward his waist. "You really think her sweet and innocent is going to keep you interested long-term? I mean, she's either dressed for a boardroom or like one of the guys. You need someone a little more… comfortable being a woman."

"Someone like you."

"Exactly." She grinned, all devilish confidence and

forgone conclusion, and eased to her knees. "You'd never be bored with me."

And here he'd thought setting Lily straight for good was gonna be a tough, maybe even painful task. Seeing her make an ass out of herself where anyone could walk in turned it into a cake walk.

"Take a good look at yourself, Lily. That mousy thing out on the patio wouldn't get on her knees when just anyone could walk in, and she damned sure doesn't have to pour herself into a dress that shows more than it covers to make herself look good."

Lily's smile melted and her fingers tightened on his thighs.

"I was straight with you before we started, and I'm bein' straight with you now," Jace said. "What bores me is having to rerun how I was too disinterested in you to take what you offered. Hell, if I'm honest, I was bored with you before you got on my bike."

Oh, that one stung. Enough so, her wince almost made him regret saying it. Probably would have done something to ease the jab if her verbal slaps toward Viv weren't still rattling through his head.

He slid one hand in his pocket and sipped his drink instead. "Now are you gonna get up and keep yourself off my radar? Or do I need to make sure your Haven welcome is all dried up?"

Footsteps sounded from the living room a second before Viv's voice floated through the kitchen entry. "Hey, Jace. I changed my..."

Every damned time he saw her his insides took a punch, but right now with the flannel shirt gone and her hair draped around her shoulders, it was closer to a battering ram.

She froze not more than two steps in. "Oh." Her gaze darted between Jace and Lily kneeling at his feet, and her bright smile avalanched. "Sorry, I was just…" She ducked her head and rubbed her palms on her hips. "Yeah. I'm really sorry."

She spun before he could pull his head out of his ass and hightailed it toward the patio.

Lily took her sweet-ass time pushing to her feet, her scheming smile vile enough he damned near threw his drink across the room. "Oops?"

He plunked his glass to the granite and headed after Viv, but paused at the kitchen exit. "Want you out of the compound in five minutes. I don't want to see you. Don't even want to hear your name at any Haven business. I'm not keen to violence where women are concerned, but if I catch wind you so much as breathe anywhere near Viv, I'll make your life a fuckin' nightmare."

ELEVEN

STUPID, STUPID, STUPID. The internal chastising whipped through Viv's head almost as fast as her footsteps pounded against the stone decking. She kept her chin ducked tight to her chest, navigating toward her purse and shirt through the crowd around the grill. Her eyes watered and her knees shook as though they'd give out any minute.

God, she was an idiot. She'd known better than to open herself up to a man like Jace, but dumbass that she was, she'd dropped her guard. And look what it got her.

Marching to the chaise, she kept her eyes trained on her purse.

"You find him, Viv?" one of the girls said.

Oh, yeah. Found him knocking back a cocktail, with a hot brunette on her knees about to do things Viv had fantasized about. She wrestled her flannel shirt on and kept it to a simple, "Yeah."

Axel stood. "You okay, lass?"

She would be, as soon as she got the hell out of here and stopped fighting back tears. The sandstone patio wound around the far side of the house with a wide enough gap she hoped meant there was a side exit. "I'm fine. I just need to go." She lifted her focus only enough to skim the crowd and give what was probably the worst smile in history. "It was nice meeting everyone."

The other two men stood as well, but Viv strode away

before they could speak. Her throat tightened and a sob pushed up behind it. For just a little while, it had been so nice. Relaxing on a pretty day, flirting, being held by a man who made her want to snuggle deeper. Now the whole world felt like it was spinning out of control around her, the air in her lungs too thin to give her what she needed to survive.

A wrought iron gate sat only a few feet ahead. She plucked her phone from her purse and fired up the home screen. She'd call a cab, think about something mundane, and then have a huge pity party when she got home. Lots of wine, ice cream and anything else to dull the ache in her chest. She reached for the latch.

A firm arm wrapped around her waist and jerked her to stop.

Jace. Even without looking, she knew it was him, his clean, masculine scent coiling around her as stoutly as his arm.

She wiggled and shoved his arm.

It tightened another fraction and his calm, confident voice rumbled beside her ear. "Settle." Keeping their backs to the crowd on the patio, he wrapped his other arm around her chest, his hand curling around the front of her neck. "Put your phone away."

"I'm calling a cab."

"Only way you're getting home today is on the back of my bike or my truck, and you're not going yet. Not until we talk. After that, if you want to leave, we'll leave. No questions asked."

Cracks seemed to ripple through the heavy weight behind her sternum, and a tear slipped free. "I don't think I can trust you."

His fingers flinched around her neck. "Not asking

you to do anything more than listen. If you want, we'll do it right here where you've got plenty of audience. Me, I'd rather do it someplace quiet where I get your full attention."

God, this was torture. The hard press of his chest, his voice, his strength. How was she supposed to listen to anything he said and not replay what she'd seen in the kitchen over and over?

She nodded, the one quick jerk the best she could manage between her rigid muscles and his determined grip.

Slowly releasing his arms, he trailed one hand down her arm, grasped her hand, and led her back across the patio. If anyone had noticed their tense moment in the corner, they didn't show it, keeping to their tight huddles.

Everyone except Axel, Trevor and Zeke. The three of them stood, eyes to Jace, alert and ready for action.

Jace shook his head and kept walking, pulling her behind him.

They stepped into the living room with its soaring wood beam ceilings and distressed wood floors. The old-world ivory walls and honey-stained accents had calmed and comforted her on the way in. Now they just felt sterile and distant.

Across the vast living room, Lily strode through the entryway, her heels clacking on the intricate tiles. She sneered at Jace over one shoulder, threw the door open and stalked outside. The heavy door slammed shut behind her loud enough to rattle the walls.

Pausing only enough to check Lily's progress through the sidelights beside the front door, Jace started up the wide staircase with its intricate wrought iron spindles and hand-carved wood rails.

Viv jerked her hand free and held her ground. "Here's good." With a little luck, their talk would be quick and Lily would be long gone before her cab got here. She pulled up Google on her phone.

"I can work with that." Jace casually pulled the phone from her fingers, tucked it inside her purse, and tossed them to the hall table. For a guy who'd just been busted pre-kitchen blow job, he came off mighty calm, cool and collected. Definitely not apologetic. "I told you I'd take you home."

"And I'm a little more cautious than I was thirty minutes ago."

Jace grinned, though it was crooked and missing any kind of warmth. More like a goodhearted attempt to laugh in the face of something ugly. "I'll give you that play."

He crowded into her space and ran his hands up her arms. "You're jumping to conclusions." His touch ran deep like it always did, warming and uncoiling tension clear to her bones.

Unfortunately, it didn't turn off the snapshot of Lily on her knees and ready for action in her head. She stepped back. "That position's a bit hard to misinterpret."

Jace followed and gripped her hips, pulling her toward him so she had to brace her hands against his chest to keep from falling. "I didn't organize today so Lily could blow me in the kitchen, sugar. I did it so a curvy little kitten could let her hair down on a Saturday afternoon and show me the wild woman she's got buried inside."

"But she was—"

"I know what she was doing, and I was letting her hang herself so she could see how asinine she was acting. I'd laid it down and made it crystal clear what she was doing didn't just turn me off, but disgusted me, when you walked in the door."

Her mind flittered back to Lily on the patio and the way her hand lingered on Jace's shoulder. "But you've been with her."

Jace let out a tired huff and dropped his head. "I brought her here once, yeah." He raised it again and met her stare head-on. "Stupid fucking move on my part. I told her straight up she was just a one-night itch, but couldn't follow through with the scratch once things got started. I left her alone, drunk on Scotch in my bed until she slept it off, then told her the next day I wasn't interested. She apparently decided she didn't like that answer and made her play today, but she won't make that mistake again. Not after the ass chewing I just left her with."

Viv toyed with whatever the pendant was he wore beneath his T-shirt, smoothing the soft cotton enough the silver and black face showed through the fine fabric.

"Did I look like I was interested?"

For the first time since she'd stormed out of the kitchen, Viv consciously replayed the scene in her head, pushing past the shock and surprise. Lily's face had been blank. No, not blank. Calculating. And Jace had seemed about as interested as a homeowner with a door-to-door salesman. "No."

He cupped the back of Viv's head, his fingers working her hair as though he loved the feel of it. "Lily's surface deep in everything. She never thinks past her immediate needs and rarely ventures to the needs of someone else." The hand in her hair slid around, his thumb tracing the line of her jaw then on to skim her lower lip. "You've got layers. Lots of 'em. Passion and smarts and a sweet little heart. All of it wrapped up in curves that make a man want to touch. No contest there, sugar."

Outside the music jumped an extra notch. Through the wall of windows on the far side of the living room, she spied a handful of women dancing poolside. Only two hours they'd been here, but it was easy to forecast how things would be in another two or three. Wild and uninhibited without a care for what might happen. "I don't think I fit in here. I don't think I can."

Jace pulled her closer and wrapped her in an easy hug. His lips nuzzled near her ear and his hand stroked up and down her spine. "You ever thought about just being yourself and not worrying about where you should and shouldn't fit?"

A shiver ripped through her, the idea of letting all her worries and expectations go even for a little while the most profound temptation. A fresh fall breeze after the hottest, mostly stifling summer heat.

Everything he'd said and done since she'd known him darted through her thoughts. Making sure she'd made it home safe, all the business opportunities and contacts, the calm way he'd handled the run-in with Lily, the party he'd—

"You organized this for me?"

Jace smiled, this one bright and big enough that brilliant white teeth showed behind his devious lips. "Had to handle my own events before you came along." He smoothed her hair away from one side of her face. "You promised me, Viv. Two dates with you all in. You still have a mind to run after I told you what you thought you saw wasn't real?"

Lily sure hadn't looked happy when she'd stormed out the door. He'd also come clean on him and Lily having been involved, and had stayed scary calm through the whole altercation. So, odds were good he was telling the truth.

She swallowed and prayed she wasn't screwing up. Again. "I'll stay."

TWELVE

COOL, CRISP AIR gusted across the wide, manicured back-yard and up to Jace and Viv on the compound's balcony. The day might've felt like spring, but with the sun long gone, the temps had dropped to standard mid-January fare. Jace didn't mind it one damned bit. Not with Viv snuggled against his chest and staring out at the night.

She twisted and graced him with a happy smile, her hair still loose and whipping across her face. "It's a great view."

"Hell, yeah, it is." Not that he cared about the twinkling view of downtown. Viv's pink cheeks were way better, the absolute delight in her expression something he'd leap hurdles to create more often.

She faced forward again and studied the empty patio below. The only people still at the compound were his brothers and the women they'd brought, but they'd long since huddled in the warmth of the big entertainment room on the other side of the sliding glass door behind him.

He released his hold on the balcony rail and rested his hands on her hips. Whatever it was she used on her hair was crack for his lungs, something kind of exotic, but not overly girly either. A winter and fire combination he wouldn't mind lingering on his sheets and skin.

She finished off her wine and sighed, resting her head on his shoulder.

He held out his hand for the glass, barely brushing her breast with his arm in the process. "You want another?"

Handing it over, she shook her head.

Thank God for that. He might've insinuated he didn't mind her getting loopy when he'd poured her a second glass, but most of him was glad she was clearheaded. If they did end up in bed, he intended to make sure she remembered it in vivid detail and didn't need any booze muddying the water.

He stepped back, set the glass aside, and resumed his spot behind her. Fuck if he wasn't wound up tighter than a teenage boy on his first wave of testosterone. Every chance he'd had after their talk, he'd placed tiny, teasing touches wherever he could. After dinner, she'd sat on his lap and chatted with his brothers, squirming that fine ass against his dick until he'd considered bending her over right there.

Nuzzling the sweet spot behind her ear, he inhaled deep and slid one hand around her belly. "You remember that talk about limits?"

Her hands tightened on the iron rail and her muscles beneath his palm clenched. She nodded. "I remember."

"Good." He slipped his hands beneath the bottom of her tank and sampled the hot skin underneath. Slow and steady, he smoothed his palm over her abdominals and dragged his thumb along the bottom of her rib cage. Where she'd seemed content and engrossed in the view before, now her attention was squarely on him and his touch. He'd swear she wasn't breathing. "Relax, sugar. You want me to stop, I'll stop, but I've wanted my hands on you all day."

Her eyelids slid shut and she licked her lower lip.

Pressing his more than ready cock against her, he eased his hands higher, teasing the soft space beneath her bra line. "You with me?"

She sucked in a deep breath and lifted her chest in a slight, but distinct invitation for more.

"That's it." He skimmed his lips along her jawline and cupped her breasts. The thin, silky lace against his palms promised whatever she had on came from the good lingerie drawer he'd found while searching her house, and not the boring white and taupe top-drawer selection. Her nipples rasped against his hands and he groaned, playing the hard peaks with his thumbs. "Want these in my mouth."

With a single whimper, she ground her ass against him and let her head loll to one side, exposing her neck as her hands covered his above her tank.

He took what she offered, savoring the column with his tongue and teeth, and rolling her nipples between his fingers and thumbs. Her hips moved in a steady, needy rhythm so fucking erotic he could come just from watching.

Splaying one hand low enough to slip beneath the waistband of her jeans, he toyed with the edge of her panties and nipped her earlobe. "Don't expect anything from you. Don't want anything you aren't willing to give. But right now I want you naked, under me, and screaming the damned compound down."

She answered with a moan and a flex inward toward his hand.

God damn it, he wanted her clit under his fingers. To slip and slide through her wet pussy until she begged him for more. Hell, if half his brothers and their dates weren't so close, he'd finger her until she shouted out an orgasm to his uppity neighbors. "Look at me."

Her movements slowed and her eyelids drifted open as she peered over one shoulder.

Raw, uninhibited need flashed bold and beautiful, her eyes glazed and pupils so dilated only a thin ring of gray surrounded them.

"Not gonna screw up whatever's burnin' between us by giving you another reason to hightail it home. Turn all the way around so you can't hide your eyes."

Not breaking his stare, she turned in his arms, sliding her hands beneath his jacket and around his neck.

For weeks he'd tiptoed around this woman, biding his time like he'd never done with anyone else. He cupped the back of her head so she couldn't look away and blatantly palmed her breast with the other.

Her eyes started to shut, but Jace tightened his grip on her head, loosely fisting her hair the way he'd always wanted. "Eyes open." He rolled his thumb over her taut nipple. "Your call. You want this?"

As soon as the words came out of his mouth, he wished he could pull them back. If she said no, he wasn't sure an AK-carrying platoon could pry his hands off her. The vulnerability and hunger radiating from her alone was enough to make him want to beat his chest and pulverize anyone else who dared to touch her.

"I shouldn't."

Fuck. He growled before he could catch it and pulled her tighter against him.

Her gaze dropped to his mouth. Her pretty pink tongue peeked out and wetted her lower lip. Her voice shifted to something between sex kitten and confession. "But, yes. I want this."

Yes. Instinct took over, capturing her mouth and sealing her agreement before she could change her mind. Her lips were perfect. Soft and sweet, a trace of red wine on her tongue as it dueled with his. Her nails bit into the back of his neck, pulling him closer as though she needed what he gave her more than she needed air. Perfect. As wild and passionate as he'd sensed she'd be, mindless of where they were and the threat of an audience.

He pried his lips away, rested his forehead on hers, and sucked in a steadying breath. "You feel that?"

She bobbed her head, eyes dazed and lips swollen as her breath huffed against his face.

"Good. Remember it because as soon as I get you someplace private, I'm gonna ramp that up a notch or two." He snatched her hand and stormed toward the sliding doors, mindful of her shorter strides, but on a mission to get his mouth on the rest of her.

Two steps into the room, Trevor's pixie-blonde date perked up from the latest shooter PlayStation game, her focus darting back and forth between the fifty-five inch screen and Viv. "Hey, Viv! You ever play Call of Duty? Trev's got the new one. It's guys against girls."

Jace tightened his grip and kept walking. "She's busy."

Axel looked up from his nose-to-nose conversation with his own date, assessed Viv and Jace with a single glance and grinned. "'Bout damned time." He winked at Viv even as he curled his hand around his woman's neck, and out came his panty-dropping brogue. "Come find me if he lets ye down, lass. I've more than enough skill ta keep ye happy."

Laughter mingled with the game's rapid-fire shots,

but Jace kept going, drawing them deeper into the dark hallway toward the master suite at the end. Not until he opened the door and pulled her through the entrance did he dare let go of her hand.

The second he released her, Viv's steps slowed and her gaze shuttled across the oversize room. "Whose room is this?"

He shut the door and locked it. "Mine."

If his cock hadn't been hard enough to serve as a rock wall pillar, he'd have laughed at the expression on her face as she put it all together. "This is your house?"

"One of the names on the deed, yeah. Told you I put this together for you. Not going to do it at a stranger's house." He paced toward her.

She swallowed hard and took in the old-world elegance, dark woods and jewel-toned accents reminiscent of the law libraries he'd spent so much time at in college. Of course, this one had a King Kong—sized poster bed in the middle and was presently the center of her attention. "It doesn't look like you."

He came up behind her and pulled the leather jacket off her shoulders, taking her flannel shirt along with it. "Maybe you don't know as much about me as you think." Tossing them both aside, he made quick work of his own jacket.

She peeked over one shoulder, chin dipped so her gaze only hit him midchest. "I didn't mean it as an insult."

"And I didn't take it as one." He gripped her hips, his palms burning for skin-to-skin contact, and pulled in a fresh lungful of her addictive scent. "Just pointing out how there's usually more to people than we see on the surface." Gripping the hem of her tank, he eased it up and over her breasts. "Kind of like you."

Before she could argue, he pulled her shirt the rest of the way off and spun her around. If a man were capable of swallowing his tongue, her breasts lifted and framed in soft pink lace would do it. Not one decent word or compliment leaped to his lips. Only urges. Dark, dirty, primal urges that made his cock pound for freedom.

"There's not as much to me as you think," she said, but her face showed something else. Desperation, hunger, and so much longing it practically coiled around him. Fuck, but this woman needed touch. Touch and whole lot of release.

He backed her up, wisely keeping his hands from her chest until he got her situated. "Told you downstairs you've got loads of layers. You may not see 'em, but I do. It's going to be fun watching you learn them with me."

The back of her knees hit the foot of the bed and she sucked in a barely audible gasp.

Jace took advantage, urging her to sit and shucking her boots before her mind could get too far ahead and calculate consequences.

"I can do that," she said.

"Sure you can. But that might mean you'd start thinking, and my guess, that's not in my best interest." He tossed her last boot to the floor and peeled her socks off twice as fast. "You've got one job and one job only."

Her voice dropped to almost a whisper, a depth to it that reached between his legs and stroked his supremely frustrated dick. "What's that?"

Leaning in close, he ran his nose alongside hers

and teased her lips with his. "You feel. No worries, no agenda, no thinking, just letting go."

Her breath fluttered against his face, warm and fruity from the wine. "That's hard for me."

"Won't be tonight." He straightened and tugged off his own boots. "Now scoot that sweet ass back on my bed and focus on me. Only me."

For a second, he wasn't sure if she'd bolt, or oblige. If he hadn't divested her of her shirt to start with, it could've been a crapshoot either way.

The second she pushed toward the center of the bed, something in him shifted. Compulsion was too tame of a label. This was way more fundamental, primal even. A God damned animalistic urge that shoved every other priority beyond claiming her right out the door.

He crawled toward her, caging her with hands at either side of her head and knees on either side of hers. "You still with me?"

The same kind of look he'd expect on a first-time skydiver flashed across her face, but she lifted her hand and wrapped it around the back of his neck. "Yes."

"Thank God." He slanted his mouth across hers, a beastly side to him he'd never realized existed rearing up and taking over. Every ounce of control he'd mustered since the day he'd met her evaporated. The only things that mattered were getting more of her taste; her touch, and those little whimpers she made when he hit just the right spot.

Trailing kisses down her throat, he gave his hands free rein and cupped her full breasts. He scraped his thumbnail over one hard nipple and earned a low throaty groan from Viv. "You want my mouth instead, sugar?"

he said against the slope of her breast, licking and sucking the soft, creamy skin as he moved closer to the lace.

She answered with a pretty arch of her back and
fisted his hair at the back of his head. "Please."

He dragged one strap down and tugged the thin lace,
raking it across her nipple until the taut, rosy peak came
into view. His mouth watered, all thoughts of a slow,
decadent seduction scattering with a need to get her
naked and ready to take him deep.

He licked around the sensitive bud, fanning his hot
breath against the wet surface and teasing her delicate
skin with his beard.

"Jace." She coaxed him closer, one hand slipping beneath his shirt and digging into his back.

He sucked her deep, working the nipple as he rolled
its mate between his finger and thumb.

The whimper he'd wanted ripped up her throat and
her hips bucked against his. He'd never get enough of
that sound. Not even if he locked her up and devoted
the rest of his life to it, but damned if he wasn't willing to gorge on it now.

Sliding one hand beneath her, he angled for the bra's
fastener.

A sharp rap sounded at the door, and Jace froze.

The demanding knock came again, three in rapid
succession and definitely a man's knock. Considering
there were only five men in this world who'd dare in-
terrupt him right now, it had to be one his brothers. He
hoped for their sake the damned house was on fire.

He guided the lace cup back into place and pressed
a firm kiss to her lips. "Do. Not. Move."

Viv bit her lower lip and grinned, the flush spreading across her cheeks and chest giving her an innocent

look that made him consider killing whoever was at the door whether the house was burning down around them or not.

He stalked to the door and yanked it open. "What!"

Trevor stood with one hand on his hip and the other fisting Viv's purse. "The phone in this thing's been goin' off nonstop for the last fifteen minutes. Figured if they're calling that many times, it's important."

Jace snatched it from his outstretched hand and growled.

"Yeah, I figured you'd be thrilled." Trevor leaned around Jace enough to see past him. "Probably even more now, I'm thinking."

Behind him, Viv sat on the end of the bed and jammed her foot into one boot, her shirt and both socks already back on.

Jace gripped the doorknob hard enough his knuckles cracked. "You done?"

He had to give Trevor credit. He at least tried to cover his smile with a swipe of his chin as he walked off. "Looks like it."

Shutting the door none too gently, Jace stalked toward Viv. "Thought I told you not to move."

Viv laced her last boot and surged upright, hand outstretched. "It's Callie. Let me have it."

"How the hell could you know that?"

She snatched her purse and dug out her phone. "Because it's Saturday night, and it's after midnight. Everyone else I know thinks it's rude to call after ten." Despite her shaking hands, her thumbs navigated the screen in record time.

Damn it, he'd been so close. Not just to sex, but in getting through to her. Really seeing the woman underneath that uptight armor she hid behind. He fisted his hair on the top of his head and paced the length of the room.

"Callie, it's Viv. Where are you?" She sat back on the edge of the bed, her knees wide and elbows anchored on them. The way her head hung heavy spoke of way too much weariness and frustration. "I can't understand you. Who's with you?" A pause. "Where's that? Do you have an address?" Quiet. "Jesus, Callie, stay awake and focus. If you don't have an address, turn on that friend finder app I installed for you. I'll see if it works."

A fucking pick up call. He'd give Viv high marks for quick thinking with the app, but the fact that she'd had to plan for such a contingency said all too well how often this shit went down. At this rate, he'd be lucky if he could peel Viv's stress-ridden body off the ceiling, let alone get her naked.

With the phone away from her ear, she punched an app up on her screen, then zoomed and toggled like a pro. "Okay, I think I've got it. Near Love Field, right?"

Oh, hell no. He crammed on his own boots and mentally categorized all the shit neighborhoods in that part of town. Even Beck wouldn't head near that airport without backup or a loaded gun, and he was a mean son of a bitch.

He stalked into his walk-in closet, opened the gun safe, and loaded up with a shoulder holster and his Glock while Viv pried what she could from her sister.

"Well, do you know what the apartments are called?" Viv glared at the far wall, a pissed off expression he doubted she ever let her sister see. "Well, ask whoever lives there for a name. Or a number." She stood and marched to her jacket, splayed across the chair. "Okay, well ask them and text it to me. I'll be there as soon as I can. And whatever you do, stay awake."

Jace snatched his own jacket, intercepted her when she turned for the door, and got a good grip on her elbow. "We'll take my truck."

"Just take me home. I'll handle it."

"Not in that part of town you won't." He marched her toward the stairs, something between anger and outright terror she'd even consider going there alone rattling him in a way he hadn't felt since he was nine and earned his first scar.

"Jace—"

He spun her to face him at the top of the landing. "You ever been there?"

"Where?"

"Where your sister is. You ever been there before?"

"No."

"Right. So, let me paint a picture. Meth hotels. Assault. Burglaries. It's a nasty cornucopia for the DPD. Your sister shouldn't be there, and I'll lock your ass up in my bedroom before I let you go alone. Now are we good?"

She swallowed, a big, painful-looking gulp. "Yeah, we're good."

He nodded and guided her down the stairs. Hell, yeah, he was going with her. If not just to keep her safe, then to choke the living shit out of her sister.

THIRTEEN

VIVIENNE STARED OUT Jace's tinted passenger window, one hand fisted around the door handle of his truck, and the other tucked beneath her leg. The muscles in her torso were coiled so tight she wouldn't have to do crunches for a month, but it was either that or fidget, and she didn't want to give Jace any more reasons to scowl. She still couldn't figure out if he was pissed because of Callie's interruption, the part of town they were in, or a combination of both.

God, what a night. From boneless and close to spontaneous combustion, to rigid and ready to shatter in under thirty minutes. "You didn't have to bring me."

"We've been through this. Look out the window."

She couldn't. The glimpse of deserted, run-down streets and dilapidated houses she'd caught pulling into their current neighborhood had been enough to fire a cold sweat and turn her fingers to ice. With the height on Jace's truck, she got a bird's-eye view of every horrid detail.

Jace plucked her phone from the center console, checked the screen she'd set to constant display, and made a sharp left turn. "How often do you get these calls?"

Too often. Enough she couldn't remember her last uninterrupted weekend, though this had to be the worst. "Callie's a bit of a free spirit."

"This isn't a free spirit, this is stupid."

Viv bit her lip, all the denial she'd clung to in re-cent months flattening beneath Jace's simple statement. God, she was tired of this. Of the responsibility and the ugliness. All she wanted was to be home. Or back at Jace's house with nothing on her mind but pleasure. Not that he'd want much to do with her now. Talk about a mood killer.

"This shit," Jace said. "Her stupid stunts. This why you keep yourself so locked up?"

"I don't keep myself locked up."

Jace whipped into a drab gray apartment complex with boarded-up windows and a courtyard that looked like it had survived a nuclear attack. He slammed the gearshift into park, curled his hand around the back of her neck, and pulled her close so fast her breath left on a rush. His eyes were as dark as the night around them, the scar slashing across one eye almost sinister in the moonlight. "Sugar, you've got so much heat locked inside, you make Mount St. Helens look weak." He dragged his thumb across her lower lip, and her tongue darted out for a taste on instinct. His lips twitched as though she'd just proven his point. "I wanna be there when it goes off."

Warmth flooded her face and her thighs clenched, the muscles at her core fluttering so powerfully she al-most moaned. How did he do that? With their bodies separated by the console, he barely touched her, but with a few words and a look, he set her body on fire.

The splatter of breaking glass and drunken laughter filtered through the closed windows.

Viv jerked away and stashed her phone in her purse. "I need to hurry. She hasn't texted me in over fifteen minutes." Fumbling with the lever, she pushed open the door and jumped to the ground. At least Callie had texted an apartment number before she'd stopped answering.

Jace strode up beside her as her door slammed shut and gripped her upper arm as though braced to push or pull her to safety at a moment's notice. He steered her across the mostly dirt-covered courtyard with its random patches of dead grass. "What's the apartment number?"

"Twenty-seven." After staring at the screen and waiting for Callie to text something else, the number was practically burned into her retina.

They hurried through a breezeway, and a fierce gust slapped her square in the face, the scent it carried something straight from the bottom of a long-unattended litter box. "What's that smell?"

Jace paused and scanned the long row of apartments with their hit and miss functioning porch lights by each door. If it hadn't been for his tight grimace, she'd have thought the smell was her imagination. "My guess? Meth." He motioned to the building on her left. "That way, ground floor."

Meth? Was he kidding? She twisted as best she could for eye contact while still keeping pace with his too-long, agitated strides. Her breath huffed heavy with each step. "You mean cooking it? Or smoking it?"

"Does it matter?"

Good question. A better one was how he knew what it was to start with. Yeah, his club had earned some bad press because of some big-name drug dealer, but she'd never considered he might actually have enough experience with drugs to pinpoint a variety on smell alone. What was that guy's name? Something Moreno. Henry? Howard?

Ahead, the steady drone of cheap bass speakers rattled. They got to the unit marked twenty-seven in cheap tin numbers, and Viv raised her hand to knock.

Jace opened the door and pushed it wide before her knuckles made contact.

Hovel was too positive of a word for the dingy space. Sty might have been a good choice. A recliner that was probably olive green at one point in its life sat closest to the door and the beat-up TV, and a ratty couch from the seventies stretched along the far wall. Both housed passed out men with beer bellies and seriously dirty clothes.

Gripping her forearm, Jace pulled her behind him and murmured over his shoulder. "Stay close. I don't want you out of reaching distance, we clear?"

She pumped an enthusiastic nod, entirely on board with letting him take front and center.

In front of the couch was an old, cheap coffee table she could probably break with one sharp kick. On top of it were a few small pipes and several twisted cellophane bags with some kind of off-white, almost tan powder inside.

She grabbed Jace's shoulder, pulled him closer and whispered. "Is that meth?"

He shook his head, but he was clearly distracted, his attention darting in all directions for anyone else in the apartment. "I'd guess H." He jerked his head to the sleeping men in the living room. "If it was meth, they wouldn't be sleeping."

He crept down the dark hallway. At the end were three closed doors, one dead ahead and two on either side.

Muffled grunts issued from behind one door.

Jace eased it open then jerked back, pulling the door shut with him and shielding Viv from the view.

"What's going on? Who was it?" Viv said.

"Nothing you're gonna see, but it's definitely not Callie."

Before she could analyze his deadpan retort, he opened the second bedroom door and flipped on the light. The dirty bulb flickered to life over three women passed out on a bare mattress, none of them Callie.

"I don't know them," Viv said. "Maybe we've got the wrong place."

"Maybe." Jace turned off the light and closed the door, aiming for the last one. "We're about to find out."

The door met resistance at only a foot wide. A dirty linoleum floor showed through the gap along with a vanity covered in everything from beer cans to uncapped toothpaste. The mirror looked like it'd never seen a bottle of Windex in its life. Near the edge of the tub were a pair of tan boots with turquoise inlay, and they were attached to someone sprawled near the toilet.

Viv's boots. The ones she'd loaned her sister over a month ago. "Callie."

She tried to shove past Jace, but he held her back. "Hold up." He maneuvered the door open enough to squeeze by and leaned over to pull Callie's torso out of the way. "Jesus."

Viv slipped in behind him a second later and nearly retched at the acidic stench. "Oh my God." On the downside, Callie had puked her brains out and mostly missed the toilet. On the upside, she'd passed out away from the mess and kept most of it off herself.

Before Viv could do more than hunch down beside

Callie and smooth her hair away from her face, Jace shrugged out of his jacket and lifted her up to wrap her in it.

Viv gripped Callie at both shoulders to hold her steady while Jace worked—and froze. "Is that a gun?"

Jace finished the job without stopping and draped one of Callie's limp arms around his neck. "It ain't a toothpick. Wished like hell it was." He cradled Callie in his arms and stood. "Go."

She couldn't take her eyes off of the gun. Even with Callie's dead weight in his arms, the butt of the big, black weapon showed big as Texas.

"Viv, go."

Right. Bad time to freak out. She lurched upright and darted out of the horrid bathroom without a backward look. All the details she'd noted on the way in swished by in a hurried blur, Jace's heavy footsteps tight behind her. She needed air. Cool, crisp, untainted air, and she needed it now.

A gun. Yeah, this was clearly a good part of town to have one in, but he'd known to bring one with him. So, what did that say about him?

Slinging Callie's weight to mostly one shoulder, he jerked the back cab door open on Viv's side of the truck and heaved himself up. He laid Callie out along the bench seat like she weighed no more than a three-year-old, hopped down beside Viv, and slammed the door shut with way too much force.

His nearly black eyes sparked with enough anger Viv inched backward.

Jace noted the reaction, gaze shifting as though he measured the newly gained distance. The muscles at the back of his jaws twitched. He opened her door nice and slow. "Get in."

Her mouth ran dry, and all the analytical thoughts in her head scattered. Part of her wanted to run, or maybe sprint, to safety. Someplace neat and tidy that fit her quiet, well-organized life. Something else held her still, the need to comfort and soothe whatever it was that had him so damned angry as tangible as a tether knotted around her waist.

She ducked her head instead and stepped up on the running board, checking Callie over the seat back before she settled in her seat.

You got a death wish comin' in here tonight, Hugo.

Jace's altercation with the guy in the suit that first night she'd been to Crossroads flashed bold and bright in her memory. That was the drug dealer's name she'd heard referenced on television. Hugo Moreno.

Thought we'd made it clear. You're out. Otto's in.

What the hell had he meant? More importantly, what kind of man had one-on-one, first-name-basis conversations with drug dealers? Although, that went a long way to explaining his ability to identify drugs by scent. Not to mention a comfort level with guns that scared the shit out of her. Was that how he managed to afford such a huge house in an elite part of Dallas?

The truck's engine roared to life, vibrating the floorboards beneath her frozen feet. Outside her window, the scenery slowly shifted from dark and ominous, to bright and well-populated. The colorful signs along Lemmon Avenue and late-night partiers filtered through her shell-shocked psyche until she could finally draw in a steady breath.

Behind her, Callie moaned and rolled to her back, slinging one arm over her forehead.

Viv swallowed as much as her fear-coated tongue would allow. "All those drugs...should we take her somewhere? Make sure she's okay?"

Jace made a sharp turn onto Turtle Creek and checked his rearview mirror. "If that's what you want." The words were right, but they felt more for show than anything.

"What do you think?"

He kept his eyes straight ahead for long, drawn-out seconds before he slid his gaze to her. "I think your sister's straying into territory she won't live long playing in." He stared back out at the road. "But for tonight, I think she's fine sleepin' it off."

There it was again. More knowledge of this lifestyle than made her comfortable. Yet some underlying current warned she wasn't getting the whole picture. Did she really want this kind of person in her life? Out of all the men she'd ever met, she'd never had such a connection like what she had with Jace. Someone who made her come alive not just physically, but mentally. Not once had she been bored with him, her mind nimble beside his as they'd lazed away the afternoon. Back and forth, the thoughts pummeled her emotions, the tug-of-war leaving her insides taut and shaky.

Jace pulled in front of her townhouse stoop, and Viv hopped out, key in hand. Just like New Year's Eve, a big man with long hair and a black leather jacket was hauling her unconscious sister up the stairs. Although this time, Callie got far more detailed treatment. Before Viv could get her own jacket off and let Ruger out in the side yard, Jace had already pulled off Callie's boots, the jacket he'd wrapped her in and tucked her under the covers.

Viv sat beside her and smoothed her hair off her face. A flush dotted Callie's cheeks and her breath came in sharp, shallow pants. Whatever Jace might be into, he'd taken care of Callie tonight. Of both of them. "Thank you."

"You want to thank me, you swear to me you'll never go off to someplace like that alone."

She nodded, agreement all too easy after everything she'd seen. "I had no idea. I've never seen her this bad before. Never been anyplace like that."

He curled his hand around her arm and pulled her to her feet. "You don't belong there. No woman does."

An odd statement, one that counterbalanced all the negative evidence she'd seen tonight.

Pulling her out into the hallway, he shut the door behind them and faced her, backing her against the opposite wall. He scrutinized her, his eyes locked in such an unrelenting and shrewd stare she swore he was categorizing all the warring thoughts shuttling through her mind. "You gonna be able to deal with her?"

She nodded. "Just another night. I've got the routine down."

His mouth tightened in a way that said he didn't care for her answer. "You got a clear head?"

"Trust me. The last trace of wine left my system the minute we pulled into that parking lot."

"Good. Then you'll be clear on this. Our next date is Friday night at eight o'clock. It'll be a long night, so make sure Callie understands you're not on call. If you're smart, you'll leave time to recover on Saturday."

She'd never make it through another date. No matter what she'd agreed to before, tonight she'd almost stepped across a very dangerous line. One she wasn't sure she'd ever be able to come back from.

His eyes locked onto her lips for long, tense seconds before he stepped back and jogged down the stairs.

"Jace."

He stopped at the landing and looked back, the scowl on his face intense enough to stop the devil in his tracks.

"I don't think another date's—"

"Next Friday, Viv. Eight o'clock. Non-negotiable. You made a deal, you'll pay it." He turned for the door and pulled it wide, but glanced back before he left. "Trust me. You need this."

FOURTEEN

VIV TOSSED THE new event flyer she'd printed on top of
all the others and buried her fingers in her loose hair, elbows braced on the desk. Midmorning sunlight slanted
over her desk in the office Axel had set up for her at
Crossroads, a second-story corner space with probably
the only window to the outside world. Every other place
in the club was dark, dark and darker.

Four days since her carefree Saturday afternoon had
gone to hell and not once had she heard from Jace. Her
hair tickled her cheek, a taunting reminder of how she'd
stupidly left it down in some twisted maneuver to prove
herself. At least that was the bullshit line she was feeding herself, even if deep down a part of her wished he'd
see her and be pleased with the effort.

*Why do you care? He's dangerous. Clearly, he's into
bad things and bad people.*

*Yeah, but he also is thoughtful, smart and has a pro-
tective streak a mile wide.*

Sounds like an ax murderer to me.

*He might be an ax murderer, but he kisses like a
God.*

She fisted her hands on the desk and shook her head,
so tired of the nonstop back and forth bickering in her
head, she thought she'd scream.

"Did they say somethin' nasty to you, lass?"

Axel's voice cut into her thoughts and she whipped

upright, tidying the disarrayed stack of draft printouts. "What?"

He motioned to her desk. "The papers. You look like you're ready to commit murder, so I thought sure they'd somehow broken you."

God, it was hard not to be happy around Axel. He had such a carefree way to him, as if he lived one hundred percent in the moment and never dared venture any further for fear he'd miss something. "I'm fine." She set her tidied stack aside and pulled her calendar up on the monitor. "Just a little out of it today."

"You sure? I've got a shredder and I'm not afraid to use it."

She giggled despite her off-kilter mood.

"Jace got you busy?"

That was an understatement. "I'm booked for the next six months, and I've still got a dozen or more emails he sent me yesterday to go through."

Surprisingly, none were like the Crossroads gig. The rest were all corporate engagements, ranging from software development to real estate, and the people were fantastic to work with. Not stodgy like the people who normally hired her. She should be thrilled and working every angle to the max, but her usual drive just wouldn't engage.

Axel leaned one hip on the desk and towered over her, his big, burly physique and wild hair well inside her personal space. It'd driven her nuts the first few days, but she'd quickly learned that was the norm for him. "I think the sensitive man thing here is to ask if you want to talk about it."

Another laugh slipped out, though it sounded as tired as she felt. Reasonable given how light her sleep had been lately. Even Ruger looked like he was ready to find a new bed partner. "Sensitive? Are we talking about you, Axel?"

"Ah." He pressed his hand above his heart and closed his eyes. "Ye wound me, lass. Never has a more compassionate man walked the Earth." He winked and crossed his arms, scootching back until he half sat on the desktop. His voice dropped to a dirty rumble. "Now tell Uncle Axel what's got you so vexed."

God, she'd read this man wrong at the start. All she'd seen was the long hair, the gruff exterior and the sin haven where he worked. In reality, he was all heart with so much more beyond the surface.

Just like Jace.

"Where are you from?" The question jumped out on the heels of her realization. Her heart pumped with the first decent inspiration she'd had in days.

His lighthearted smile slipped and a bone-chilling scrutiny swept in. "You askin' where I'm from, or Jace?"

Her cheeks fired hot, and for once she wished she didn't have a window spotlighting her embarrassment. So much for the subtle approach.

"We both grew up in Dallas," he said before she could come up with a lame excuse. "But if you want to know about the man, I suggest you ask him." He leaned in, a mix of troublemaker and flirt coloring his expression. "Gets a man all caveman when a woman starts wantin' to dig deep. When it's a woman he's after, anyway."

He sat upright again and slid one of the flyers she'd tidied where he could better see it.

Viv cleared her throat and fiddled with her pen.

As nonchalance went, it was a total bust, but she'd be damned if she didn't protect her pride at least a little. "Is he after me?"

Axel's gaze shifted, not enough to make him lift his head from his perusal of the flier, but enough to register his wariness. "I'm thinking that's another thing you'll need to ask him."

Tossing the pen to the desk, Viv plunked against the seat back and crossed her arms. "I couldn't ask him if I wanted. He's never here."

"You want that?"

Wasn't that the million-dollar question of the week. One she'd agonized over nearly nonstop since he'd walked out her front door Saturday night. A shaky certainty settled in the bottom of her gut. "I'd like to at least talk to him. To know him a little more." And wouldn't a shrink have a heyday with that statement?

Axel's devious chuckle rumbled through the room and he pushed away from the desk. "Got a funny feeling you'll get what you wish for…whether you like it or not." He ambled toward the door. "Make sure you leave the afternoon open. Misty from Transcendental Software will be here at two."

The parting shot thwacked her upside the head and sent her scrambling for her calendar. "Their party's not until May. I haven't even scanned the details yet."

Axel paused in the doorway, his big paw wrapped around the doorjamb and an ornery smile spread wide. "No work, darlin'. Just pleasure."

ONE SHORT RAP on his office door was the only warning Jace got before his brother Knox ambled in.

"Man, I really need to reevaluate my involvement in

the entertainment biz." Unlike most of the men flocking the bar downstairs, Knox had stuck to his standard graphic tee, jeans and his go-to brown bomber boots. A nondescript manila folder about an inch thick dangled from one hand, and a drink was clutched in the other. "Swear to God, I just saw two women on the dance floor lip-locked and wearing dresses so tight they may as well be naked. Software and hacking's not nearly this fun."

"Jackie and Matilda." Jace might've been planted behind his desk and far away from the one-way wall of windows overlooking the dance floor, but there was no doubting which two women Knox referred to. They loved attention and weren't afraid to cross the line in getting it.

"You say that like the shit doesn't get you hot."

"Any man with a functioning dick would think it's hot—the first twenty times they saw it. Now it's just a rerun." Not to mention it had no heart. Now, Viv in the center of his bed, cheeks flushed, back arched and nipples hard for his mouth, that he'd take on a third world country to see. "You got the report?"

Knox sank down into the scarred leather couch along the back wall and tossed his file on the granite-topped coffee table. "Not the most exciting name I've tracked."

Boring was good. Hell, it was a fucking relief. "What's in it?"

Kicking one foot up on the coffee table, Knox shook his tumbler enough that the ice swimming in the amber liquid jingled. "Grew up not too far from here. Tulsa. Comes from a low-income family. Dad bit it with a gunshot wound in a bar fight gone bad thirteen years ago. One sister, Callista Moore, who made it out of high school and made a few tries at junior college for health care, but got the boot for bad grades and poor attendance. Vivienne went to junior college too, but aced everything. Got an associates in Hospitality Management then started schlepping the corporate scene with a job here in Dallas."

"And the mom?"

Knox rubbed his chin. "Best I can tell, Mom cut out and filed for divorce before your girl got out of high school. The split shows going final before Viv graduated. Mom's sitting pretty now, though. Married a sugar daddy up in Nashville not three months after the ink on the divorce decree was dry. She's been licking up the good life ever since."

Maybe not so boring of a history after all. Jace pushed away from his desk and meandered to the window overlooking the crowd below, sipping his Scotch. The turnout was better than normal for a Wednesday, businessmen with rolled-up shirtsleeves and women in their corporate skirts and tailored pants snatching some midweek relief in the form of booze and music. "Anything else?"

"Squeaky clean. Pays her taxes like clockwork, and not so much as a parking ticket."

The abject fear on Viv's face when she'd laid eyes on his gun flashed vivid in his memory. A reasonable response for someone who'd lost her dad to a bullet, but the rest still didn't add up. How did a woman like Viv fit with a bar-brawling dad and a party-chasing sister? Unless she'd learned from Mom and was walking the uppity life in search of a well-heeled keeper.

He took another drink. "How'd the bit at Nieman's go?"

Knox groaned and dropped his head back on the

couch. "It went well enough that you're setting a bad example for the rest of us. My secretary's already spread the gossip far and wide how she got carte blanche with your credit card for the sole purpose of dollin' up your new squeeze for some big shindig."

God, he wished he could've been there for that. Viv's place might not be finished out with everything top of the line, but she had an eye for quality. Just the idea of spoiling her for a day and letting her have whatever she wanted made him feel about three feet taller. He knew better than to get near her yet, though. He had a point to make. One he wanted to drive home crystal clear. "As long as she kept the details under wraps with Viv, I don't care if she sends out a global email."

"Didn't drop a word. Just got her measurements, picked out the frills and paid for the tab. Your girl nearly drove Misty nuts with the questions though." Knox drained his drink and thunked it on the coffee table like it was made of stone instead of crystal. "You need anything else? Or am I free to broaden my entertainment background?"

Jace grinned, the wicked smirk reflecting back at him through the glass. "I'll give you ten percent ownership in Crossroads if you can get between Jackie and Matilda before they head home for the night."

"I'll take that bet." Knox surged upright and stretched his neck as though bracing for a fight. "Too much macho biker and businessman bullshit down there. They need a man with a mind."

"Gonna wow 'em with your hacker skills?"

"Hell, yeah. We always find a backdoor." Knox waggled his eyebrows and shut the door behind him on the way out.

The poor bastard didn't have a chance. True, his hot nerd routine usually worked on most women, but Jackie and Mattie were man-haters to the core. If his brother did end up between them, he'd have earned every damned percentage.

He turned back to the crowd below in time to catch Knox's intended targets slide into a corner booth. Too bad he couldn't figure Viv out as easy as he did those two women. The bit about her mother rubbed him the wrong way, his real-world experience warning Viv could be a junior gold digger in the works.

His gut said otherwise. Something had to have happened. Something that put a stopper on all that passion she kept bottled up and made her tuck certain parts of herself in a self-imposed prison.

Soon enough, he'd find out. Friday night was just around the corner.

FIFTEEN

TWELVE YEARS PAST high school and Vivienne was finally going to the prom. She smoothed her hand over one scarlet, velvet-covered hip, luxuriating in the slick-soft feel against her palm. The body-hugging gown accentuated her curves, and the halter bodice with its plunging cowl neckline screamed sensuality without coming off cheap. A perfect selection for a grown-up fairy-tale evening.

Okay, so maybe tonight wasn't the same as prom night. In truth, she still had no idea where she and Jace were headed, but considering she'd wanted an occasion to dress up like this since her junior year, it was close enough. It would've been nice if Misty had slipped up at least once during their shopping trip, but the woman had stayed frustratingly tight-lipped, playing the giddy, high-drama secretive operative all too well. Viv's only clue the night would lean toward something formal were the strappy matching heels she'd tried on, but this was even more formal than she'd imagined.

On the bathroom countertop, Jace's note lay inside the tissue-lined box, his message scrawled in bold, confident strokes in the center. *Wear your hair up. I dare you.*

The sneaky bastard. The front of her gown might be classically elegant, but the back was pure daredevil. Every inch from her neck to the softly draped fabric just above her ass was exposed. If she wore it up, she'd have no way to cover herself, save the nearly sheer wrap he'd included. If she wore it down, she'd feel less exposed, but he'd get her hair loose and wild the way he always claimed to want it. Either way, he couldn't lose.

I dare you.

She snatched the box of bobby pins from her hair drawer and gathered the wild mass at the back. She'd take that dare, if for nothing else, than to tease and torment him the way he always tempted her.

The last pin in place, she stepped back and studied the final product. She'd started to try a heavier hand with her makeup, but somehow it always looked cheap on her, so she went with her usual approach. Even with a light hand on the blush, her cheeks were flushed, and her eyes sparkled from the excitement prickling through her veins.

What are you doing, Viv?

I'm living. It's one more date with a man who's shown me nothing but decency.

Decent to you maybe, but what's he up to when you're not around?

"Stop it," she said to herself in the mirror, a little of her enthusiasm ebbing beneath the internal debate that kept popping up at the worst damned times. She'd listened to that shrewish, pessimistic voice the night they'd picked up Callie and treated Jace abysmally as a result. Until he gave her concrete evidence to go on, he deserved at least the benefit of the doubt. Maybe even an apology for the cold treatment she'd given him, assuming she could gather the courage to give one.

Three sharp knocks clattered up from the front door,

and Ruger peeled out of her room and bounded down the stairs, his claws clickity-clacking along the way.

Viv trailed more slowly behind him, her stomach spinning in a mix of emotions she didn't dare give too much focus.

Ruger waited for her at the door, his whole body wagging in lieu of his snipped tail and his tongue hanging out, ready for a thorough greeting.

Traitor dog. Though she kind of understood his enthusiasm. She might be slow to admit it, but something inside her trusted Jace instinctively, despite his gruff outward appearance. Not to mention the impact he had on her libido.

She opened the door and her breath caught in her throat. Common courtesy banged on the locked-up processor in her head, ordering her to step back and let him in, but somehow the command short-circuited on the way to her feet.

His hands were anchored in his pockets, the crisp, clean lines of his tuxedo accenting his powerful frame. She'd seen him with his hair pulled back in a ponytail a few times, but this time it looked different. More polished and *GQ* than disheveled. Mixed with his tidied-up goatee, he'd give any male model a run for his money.

"Hi." A lame attempt at a sophisticated greeting, but at least she'd managed something. So what if it was only one syllable?

He stalked toward her, those dark, sinful eyes of his trailing up and down her body in a slow, sensual glide.

Her feet finally got on board and made a tiny retreat, though not nearly enough to make up for the distance he'd gained.

Nudging the door shut behind him, he grinned and

grazed his thumb down the line of her neck. "You took the dare."

One touch and all the thoughts and plans she'd had for apologies and meaningful conversation disintegrated, her mind as empty as a well shaken Etch A Sketch. Tangible contact was the only thing that counted. The only thing that mattered.

"Turn around."

Such a simple request, but it slithered through her as potent as an erotic command, a lick of compulsion that pooled low in her belly. She turned, keeping him in her sight over one shoulder.

He cupped her shoulders, and the heat from his palms soothed away her tension. His lips pressed at the curve where her neck and shoulders met, and his warm breath fluttered across the fine hairs at her nape. "I'll take it down later."

A glimmer of wit surged free of her dumbfounded thrall and the retort she'd used on their last date leaped to her tongue. "What if I don't want it loose?"

His lips curved against her skin. "Then I'll make it my mission to persuade you."

"You said that last time."

"Did it work?"

A shiver snaked down her spine and his hands tightened on her shoulders, telling her he hadn't missed it. "I'm beginning to think you could charm panties from a nun."

His low chuckle vibrated through her and his warm knuckles trailed slow and sensuous down her spine. "Why have a nun's panties when I could have yours?" His fingers splayed at the small of her back and dipped beneath the soft fabric, skimming low enough to tease the bare flesh underneath. "Although, it feels like they're already missing tonight."

"You knew damned well I'd never manage anything under this dress without it showing."

"So I'm charming and smart?"

"Charming and devious."

He gripped her hip, a possessive edge to the clasp that made her suck in a quick breath. His beard tickled the shell of her ear and his voice rolled through her in a slow, mesmerizing wave. "I'll show you devious when I get you out of this dress and my tongue on your pussy."

Oh. My. God.

A pulse she might as well have called a mini orgasm rippled through her core, and her heart punched from languid to frantic. What was she doing? They hadn't even made it out of the house and she was entertaining the one act guaranteed to push their relationship from safe to highly unprofessional. And they were in her freaking entryway. The absurdity of it shook a tiny laugh out of her.

He eased her around, the heat in his gaze still bright, but curiosity burning alongside it. "Something funny?"

Tapping her temple, she stepped back and thanked the universe for the break in tension. "My hamsters. They're busy tonight."

He cocked his head and gave her a lopsided grin. "Can't have that. Get your wrap, and we'll see what we can do to shut them up for the night."

A quick snack for Ruger and a last-minute check of her makeup, and Jace guided her over the threshold with his hand at the small of her back. She halted two steps out. Parked in Jace's usual spot was a gleaming black 911. "Where's the truck?"

"At Haven." He opened the door and held out his hand, palm up. "Didn't figure you'd appreciate climbing in the truck with that dress, and the Porsche is a hell of a lot more fun to drive."

If he had any idea how tricky it was navigating into the equivalent of a cockpit in a tight-fitting dress, he might have chosen otherwise, but she was awfully glad he didn't. Black leather surrounded her, broken only by the sleek silver accents and the soft white backlight of the gauges.

Despite his size, Jace slid into his seat with the ease of a man well accustomed to such luxury.

The engine roared to life and Viv buckled up. "What's Haven?"

"Exactly what it sounds like."

"Another club?"

Jace gripped the stick shift, his eyes thoughtful as he stared out the front windshield. "It's family." With that, he put the gear in first and steered them out of the complex.

Emotion resonated thick through the car's interior. The depth layered within his simple response rattled pieces of herself she'd thought safely tucked away. The closest she'd ever come to such powerful feelings where family was concerned was in keeping Callie safe, saving her from the perilous lifestyle that had already robbed them both of too much. But Jace uttered it with reverence. "Do you have a big family?"

"By my definition of family? Yes."

"How do you define it?"

He glanced at her, no more than a second with his eyes off the road, but enough to expose his uncertainty. Gripping the steering wheel tighter, he pursed his mouth as though missing his ever-present toothpick. "I have one living relative who shares my blood—my mother. But I have five brothers I'd give my life for in a heartbeat. They're my family."

"They're adopted?"

Headlights from the car behind them spotlighted his quick smile. "Not in the normal sense, no. There's the family you're given by birth, and there's the family you choose for yourself. My brothers are family by choice."

"Axel." The connections flared quick and sure in her head. "Zeke and Trevor. Who else?"

"Beckett and Knox."

"What about Danny?" He'd helped Vivienne on New Year's Eve and had been at the party last Saturday, though nowhere near as close as the others.

Jace's lips twitched as he guided the car to the exit ramp. "Not yet. We'll see."

Downtown Dallas's tall buildings and bright lights surrounded them, everything from modern architecture with space-age silver siding to painted murals on concrete walls whizzing past as Jace navigated the intricately laid out streets. "Am I allowed to ask where we're headed?"

"A fundraiser in the Dallas Arts District. A charity I work with for troubled male teens."

"You work with a charity?"

His smile slipped and a cold, emotionless mask dropped into place. All the warmth and easy rapport they'd built in their quiet moments alone turned brittle.

Shit. And here she'd been learning so much about him, finally prying beneath the surface. She rubbed her hand along her velvet-clad leg, the need to fidget in the tiny space so strong she nearly choked on it. "I didn't mean that the way—"

"Doesn't matter." He smiled at her, but it lacked his usual fondness and said in big bold letters he'd had enough heart-to-heart.

To hell with that. Jace wasn't the only person who could get what he wanted. "Tell me something else."

"I think you've already got a clear picture in your head."

"I've got an outline. I want you to color it in for me."

The light ahead of them turned red.

He twisted enough to pin her with a throat-choking stare, a combination of danger and dare burning in his gaze. "What do you want to know?"

Everything. To get behind the bearish exterior and find out what made him tick. Not that his glare indicated he'd buy it if she told him so. "Something besides what you show everyone else."

Quiet pressed heavy all around them, even the engine's purr disappearing in the moment. "Most people see what they want no matter what you show them."

"And sometimes we judge how people will react before we give them a chance. Show me. Color in the outline."

The light flipped to green and the two limousines in either lane ahead of them inched forward.

Jace shifted into first and checked his rearview. For the barest flicker, vulnerability shined in his dark, passionate eyes, there and gone so quickly she almost missed it. "I've got a law degree from UNLV. Went on a full scholarship."

"You?"

He shook his head, his self-deprecating smile driving home how her shocked response had easily proven his point. "Like I said, people see what they want, no matter what's really there."

She reached across the console and gripped his thigh, the powerful muscle beneath coiled tight. "Jace, I—"

"Doesn't matter. I know what I'm capable of, even if others don't. And I'm usually capable of a hell of a lot more than they are."

"No, that's not it at all. I just…" *Never gave you a chance to fill that space. Never looked beyond the surface.* But there was more to it, too. Something he didn't realize either. "The thought of you in a quiet library poring over legal documents is a little incongruent. You seem so much bolder than that. Larger than life."

He glanced at her, one scrutinizing pass before he downshifted and whipped the car into the valet line beneath the white lights and boldly colored banners. Pulling in a slow breath, he threw the stick in neutral and yanked the brake.

The valet opened her car door, letting the crowd's animated rumble whisk away the silence.

Viv shifted to swing her legs over the car's low clearance, but Jace's hand clamped on her thigh.

"What's fair is fair, sugar. You owe me an equal revelation." He released her only to grip the back of her neck and whisper against her lips. "Think on that."

THE LAST BITE of chocolate torte melted on Viv's tongue, a hint of mint making the dessert that much more decadent. She stifled an appreciative moan, gingerly set her fork on the plate, and relaxed into the padded chair back with its silver silk cover.

Jace leaned in, one arm casually draped behind her

while his calloused fingertips traced idle designs on her shoulder. His low, raspy voice hummed through her, amplifying her already sugar-induced high. "You could do this in your sleep."

"Eat like a frat boy?"

His sinful chuckled drew an envious glance from the woman beside her. "Coordinate an event like this."

Heat flooded her cheeks and her chest drew tight, the simple pleasure that came from his belief in her building the same kind of pride she'd felt the first time she'd ridden a bike with her dad running alongside her. Only this was more heady and potent. "You haven't seen my work yet. Not really."

"Don't think so?"

She shook her head.

He lifted his chin toward the plate. "What kind of china is that?"

"Wedgwood."

Pursing his mouth, he looked around the room. "How many people do you think they have staffed?"

"I'd estimate thirty up front and half that in the kitchen. But don't forget the bartenders during cocktail hour. That probably adds another ten."

"How do you think the auction went?"

"The paintings went exceptionally well, and the sports memorabilia did great with the men, but the spa packages were a little too lean to draw good attention from the women."

"Care to tell me how much this meal ran the charity per plate?"

"At five courses with three entree choices and the size of the waitstaff, it probably ran two-fifty to three hundred a plate, though a little higher wouldn't surprise me with a well-known caterer."

He leaned so close, his warm breath fluttered against her face. "Still think I haven't seen your work?"

Tingles fanned out across her shoulders and her breath thinned to the point she was surprised she didn't pass out. "Oh."

"Oh." He grinned at that and sat back in his chair, crossing one leg over the other. If she hadn't seen him in faded Levi's and a leather jacket, she'd have easily placed him as the careless debonair sort. "Don't forget I've heard an earful from Axel. The man's half in love with you and your plans."

Finally, an opening. After the tension in the car on the ride over, she'd begun to think she wouldn't have another. "Why am I working with Axel?"

He deliberated for tense seconds, his thumb swiping along the soft blue tablecloth in an absent rhythm. "Because I'm not afraid to mix pleasure with my business, but I want to make sure you're grounded in how much value you bring to the table before I show you how it's done."

Oh, boy. Her stomach loopty-looped in an amusement park spin, and her pulse skittered in a way that couldn't be good for her bloodstream. He really wanted something between them. Enough he was willing to take his time and build her up in the process. Wasn't that what she'd always wanted? A partner to go along with the chemistry?

A middle-aged brunette with a classic chin-length bob to Jace's left touched his sleeve and motioned to the man on the other side of her. "Jace, have you met Mr. Downing?"

Jace transitioned smoothly to introductions as he had throughout the night, standing and confidently shaking the man's hand before settling back in his seat with pleasantries and easygoing smiles. The way he interacted with those around him was astonishing, his poise putting others at ease even though his presence stood head and shoulders above the rest. He was like a panther padding through a herd of thoroughbreds. They might be well-to-do, but she got the sense he could take them all down in a heartbeat if he were so inclined.

The thought jettisoned a shiver through her.

Jace noticed the tremor and turned away from the woman beside him midsentence. "You all right?"

Smoothing her napkin atop her lap, she coughed to hide her fluster. "Just making observations."

The nod he gave her was nearly as unconvincing as her answer had been, but he didn't push it, instead gesturing to her wine. "You want another?"

Given she'd managed to nurse her last one for over an hour, she figured another couldn't hurt. "Why not?"

The smile he graced her with left her stunned, her mind tuning out everything but his powerful form and confident strides as he prowled across the room.

"He's larger than life, isn't he?" The society woman seated at Jace's left studied him as he wove through mingling crowd. Her expression spoke of lost days and way too many regrets until she beamed a shy smile at Vivienne. "If half our donors knew what he did to help our youth, they'd be ashamed of their own meager efforts."

"Jace?"

She nodded and forked a small bite of otherwise untouched torte. "Yes. He insists on keeping his involvement anonymous, though I guess I can understand why. If other charitable organizations found out he was willing to provide full college scholarships for their organizations, they'd be banging on his door nonstop. We're very lucky to have snagged him first." She hesitated midbite. "Oh, my. I hope I didn't share something I shouldn't have. I just assumed—"

"No, no. You're fine. Jace and I haven't talked about charitable donations, but we chat about all kinds of other things. I promise, your secret's safe with me." Full scholarships? As in plural? How much money did nightclubs generate?

The Negative Nelly side of her conscience poked and prodded from the bowels of her jail cell.

Setting her napkin aside, Viv held out her hand. "I'm Vivienne Moore. I work with Jace and some of his colleagues on several promotional events."

"Very nice to meet you, Vivienne." She returned Viv's shake with an unusually firm grip for a woman so petite, a pleasant surprise compared to what she usually encountered from Dallas's elite. "My name's Evelyn Frank. I'm in charge of donor relations and social events for our foundation."

"Well, you've certainly outdone yourself with this event. It's moving wonderfully."

"Oh, sweetheart." She waved her hand in a dismissive flip and dabbed her lips with her napkin. "Much as I'd love to claim this work as my own, I only do the hiring. Our event planner's got a great imagination. Though, I wish her personal life had a few less bumps. But what she lacks in stability, she makes up for in creativity."

"Creativity is half the battle in this business," Viv said. "That and connections."

Evelyn set her napkin aside and angled more toward Vivienne, hands folded politely in her lap. "So, tell me about your business. Do you do formal events, or more fun and flashy arrangements for the entertainment world?"

"Actually, the entertainment realm is new to me. For the last few years, I've been focused on professional engagements or charitable events like this one."

"If you have a card, I'd be happy to pass it on to some of my contacts. Or maybe keep it for myself. One never knows when an event will develop an unexpected wrinkle."

"Of course." Viv dug in her handbag, grateful she'd caved to the shameless preparation beforehand. She handed several over. "I have references for all kinds of events you can contact as well. Just email me at the address listed."

A cultured, masculine voice sounded behind Vivienne. "Excuse me, ladies."

Viv twisted in her chair.

A familiar face she'd seen much of in the past few months on television beamed a megawatt smile at both of them. His hair was an unremarkable brown, but probably maintained by a hairstylist who charged more per cut than her car payment, and his skin tone was just a little too off to be anything other than bottled.

"So much lovely art to take in at this event and yet I haven't spoken to one of the loveliest creatures in attendance." He held out his hand and shined a picture-perfect, yet empty smile. On the outside he was the ideal image of what she'd always thought she needed in a man. Cultured, affluent, well-mannered and career-driven. And yet the last thing she wanted was to touch him.

Two years of schmoozing and politicking her way through uncomfortable social situations pushed Viv to her feet. "You're very kind. I'm Vivienne Moore. And you are?"

She knew damned well who he was, but if she'd learned nothing else in her line of work, it was that people like this man enjoyed beating their chests a bit in the get-to-know-you phase.

Sure enough, his smile inched wider, and he smoothed the front of his tuxedo jacket. "My name is Paul Renner."

SIXTEEN

JACE PAID THE bartender and wound through the crowd, a Scotch for him and a Merlot for Viv in each hand. His tux jacket hung heavy on his shoulders, restricting his movement, and the ever-present weight of his bowtie gripped like a waiting noose. One more hour tops and he'd have Viv back at her place and be able to shuck them both.

Pain in the ass or not, the getup had been worth it. One look from Viv as he'd stood on the stoop and his confidence had soared high enough he could've given every last Marvel character a run for their money.

Sliding between two women caught up their latest gossip, he angled for Viv and nearly tripped.

Paul Renner stood at Jace's five-thousand-dollar table with his hand on Jace's woman. How the hell neither glass shattered between his fingers was a fucking miracle.

Jace stalked closer.

Viv laughed at something Paul said, her head tilted at an inquisitive angle and her body language utterly at ease. Nowhere near the skittish colt she seemed to be with Jace.

Logic told him to beat feet the other direction and leave her to the asshole with his upstanding citizen bullshit, but his instincts overrode the idea and throttled his temper, ready for confrontation.

Viv glanced up and caught his approach. Her smile burned a little too bright and polished, a classic client smile to charm and lure someone in. Was it for him, or the politicking bootlicker?

Didn't matter. One way or another, he'd put some heat on her cheeks and make damned sure that son of a bitch kept his distance.

"Jace, you won't believe who I've met." Viv reached out for the wine Jace offered and motioned toward Paul. "Paul, this is Jace Kennedy, a contributor to the organization we're all here for tonight."

A contributor, not her date. An interesting way to put it. He clunked his Scotch on the table behind them and eased Viv away from Paul, her bare back pressed against his front and his fingers curled possessively at her waist. "Paul knows who I am."

Vivienne stiffened against him, nothing Paul would see, but enough to show she caught the danger in his voice.

"Indeed, we've known each other since college." Paul peered at Viv, his face pinched with barely concealed concern. "Well, I don't want to mar your evening. It was good to meet you, Vivienne." He flicked a none-too-subtle glance at Jace then refocused on her. "I hope you'll have a safe evening. Perhaps we'll meet again under more relaxed circumstances."

That no good son of a bitch.

Sure as Paul had intended, Viv frowned and watched his retreat. "What's he mean by that?"

"He means he wants to be a pain in my ass the same as he's always been." One of these days, he'd stop taking the high road and show that fucker just how dirty Jace could get. For now, he'd wait. Timing was everything.

"That sounds like an interesting story."

Sharing was tempting. Waaay tempting. But a part of him didn't want her swayed by history. She'd be much better off if she ferreted out the kind of man Paul was on her own.

Viv twisted to better see his face. "Jace?"

"Another time." Christ, waiting for Viv to come around was killing him. He'd never bided his time with a woman as much as he had with Vivienne, and Paul sure as shit wouldn't have been able to goad him with anyone else either.

Maybe diluting who he was with her was part of the problem. If she couldn't take him the way he was, no amount of padding would ease the landing later. He turned her to face him, one arm looped around the small of her back. He palmed the back of her neck and inhaled the sexy perfume that had teased him all damned night, a scent that made him think of desert flowers and spice. "On a scale of one to ten, where do auctions rank for you?"

"Rank how?"

"Excitementwise. They do anything for you?"

God, that quirky thing she did with her mouth gave him all kinds of dirty thoughts. Like a naughty schoolgirl, hiding a smile. Although on Viv, it actually came across innocent. And didn't that just make him want to teach her every debauched thing he knew. "Unless I've got money in the game, I would say I'd rank them at a two."

Oh, yeah. Lots and lots of debauched things. He traced the exposed skin just above her ass. "Have you got your fill of the event planning underbelly?"

Her gaze drifted across the room, but he'd swear it

was to buy time more than any real perusal. Not once did she lock on to a particular item, or form that studious frown she always got when she was picking apart details. By the time she met his stare, her cheeks were pink. "I think so."

One small miracle down, a taste of heaven to go. He tugged the wineglass from her hand, set it on the table, and snatched her wrap from the back of her chair. Holding it wide, he settled it around her shoulders and stepped close enough her hair tickled his cheek. "Then I'm taking you home and finding at least ten different ways to make you scream my name."

THE PORSCHE'S STEADY purr filled the car's otherwise silent interior, and the soft white streetlights above Highway 75 zoomed past. Viv dragged in another too-shallow breath. Three more miles and she'd have to make a decision. Clearly, her body was ready for an Olympic swan dive, but her mind couldn't stop churning. Her belly and thighs clamped even tighter, straining to hold what she hoped was a relaxed exterior.

Jace downshifted and slid to the far right lane. If he felt a tenth of the tension radiating off her, he didn't show it, his movements confident and effortless. He reached across the console and captured her wrist, stroking her pulse point with his thumb in a raspy glide she couldn't help but imagine somewhere else. "Breathe, sugar."

Her pulse leaped to an all new high, the feverish rhythm of his strokes making her light-headed and more than a little flushed. Guess that answered whether or not he was picking up on her jumpiness, though if he meant to calm her, touching her and talking in that sexy, low grumble was the wrong approach.

"I don't know what this is, what's going on with us." The statement shot out before her better judgment could shut it down, but with it came relief, her attention zeroed in and craving his answer.

"What do you want it to be?"

"I don't know, but it feels…" Huge. Limitless. Scary as hell. "Big."

He chuckled and took the exit to her house. "In my book, big is worth the risk and the ride." The headlights from a car behind them reflected off the rearview mirror and spotlighted his dark eyes as they slid to her. "But then I'm not a fan of regret."

And there it was. The lure that tempted her to jump, no matter the cost. She'd felt something similar before she'd quit her desk job, but this was on an entirely different scale. Money and work she could recover from, but a gamble like Jace could rip open old wounds and leave a few new scars alongside them.

The two blocks to her house raced by, and Jace slipped the Porsche into the reserved spot outside her townhouse. The engine quieted with a subtle protest, and the soft leather seat groaned as Jace unwound himself from the driver's seat. He shut the door behind him, and the muted chunk resonated firm as a gavel.

What *did* she want? If two days, or two weeks from now she looked back on tonight and didn't take the risk, could she live with the regret?

Her door opened and cool air whooshed in along with it, caressing her fevered skin. She fisted her purse in her lap.

"Look at me, Vivienne." Not a request, but a command, softly wrapped and dripping in sin. He stood close, his hand outstretched. "Give me your hand."

So steady. No quiver and no hesitation, just an unapologetic confidence that dared her to fall and let him catch her.

She slid her hand in his.

He guided her to her feet, his warm, calloused palm scraping against hers, a world apart from the soft, well-manicured touch of the politician at the event.

Soft, comforting certainty settled over her, no different than spring's first warmth after a long, cold winter. No one knew what tomorrow would bring, or any day after that, but she had right now. In this moment, all she wanted was Jace and everything that went with him.

Striding to the stoop on shaky legs, she dug her keys from her clutch.

Jace's hand settled hot and possessive at the small of her back. God, she loved that touch. The mix of protective and possessive that tempted her to let go and trust. Adrenaline coursed through her so strongly she fumbled with the lock three times before the key finally slid home.

The door had opened no more than three inches when Ruger's cold, wet nose found her sweat-slick palm and nudged her for attention. She tossed her purse to the side table and gave him what he wanted, the strength of his happy greeting and the familiar setting easing her nervousness to breathable levels.

Ruger sat, lowered his ears and whimpered, his gaze trained on the door behind her.

She twisted, expecting to find Jace behind her. Instead he stood on the stoop, hands anchored in his pockets. A deceptively casual pose from a distance, maybe, but the way his chin dipped and his intense stare locked on her painted a pure predator ready to pounce. "Jace?"

"Invite me in."

A sweet, fluttering pleasure speared straight between her thighs. He might as well have said *I'll fuck you until you can't breathe anymore if I step inside, but you have to ask for it.* God knew, that's how her body interpreted it.

An idea she'd toyed with through the charity event glimmered back to life. "You said you wanted an equal revelation."

He lifted an eyebrow.

Oh, damn. Was she really going to do this? Clearly her libido had staged a coup and taken over with priorities. "There's something I can show you. Something I've never shown anyone else. Will you come inside?"

His lips curved in a lascivious grin that made it crystal clear just how literally he'd translated her invitation. He prowled across the threshold and shut the door behind him, never breaking eye contact even as he threw the bolt. "No one?"

Ruger padded beside Jace as he advanced, ready for attention and none too happy he wasn't getting it.

"Well, Callie and…" Shoot. She wasn't ready for this just yet. "One other person, but no one else."

He kept coming until only inches stretched between them. "Show me."

She licked her lip, her mouth too dry to speak and her mind too focused on his lips so close to kissing distance. She'd never get the admission out at this rate. She swallowed and stepped back, snapping her fingers for Ruger to follow. "Can I get you something to drink? All I have is wine."

"I'm good." Behind her, Jace's easy footsteps clipped against the wood floors.

She snatched a wineglass and the bottle of red she'd started last night, and poured herself way more than anything she'd get in a restaurant. What the hell had she been thinking offering to show him her secret? A guy like him would laugh at such a silly revelation. Of course, if things went as far as they sounded like they were headed, she wouldn't be able to keep it a secret anyway.

She turned from the back counter in time to catch him tossing his jacket across the arm of her couch.

He ambled toward her and rolled up his shirtsleeves. Not only had he ditched his ponytail, but his tie hung loose around his neck and the first few shirt buttons were opened, displaying the tanned skin beneath. Lifting his chin toward the drink in her hand, he pulled the backless barstool out from underneath her center island, sat and hooked his heel on the lowest rung. "Must be a hell of a secret."

"Not really. Not for a man like you."

He cocked his head and rubbed his chin. If someone from *GQ* saw him in that moment, elbow propped on the black granite countertop with one foot braced on the floor, they'd sign him in a second. Especially with his black hair free and wavy to his shoulders, and the bad boy gleam in his eyes. "A man like me?"

"Don't even go there again. You'll see what I mean and think I'm silly." She sipped her drink and paced toward the open living room, giving a wide berth to where he sat. Pausing beside the couch she trailed her fingers along the lapel of the jacket he'd tossed aside. How funny that he'd dressed up to show her another side of himself, and now she was about to give a glimpse of herself that was entirely the opposite.

She turned, leaned one hip against the couch, and took another fortifying drink. The rich, fruity wine lingered on her tongue and flowed smooth down her throat. Ah, hell, she should just blurt it out and be done with it. The worst that would happen is he'd get a good chuckle and leave. "I have a tattoo."

One heartbeat. Then two. Then three.

His gaze slide down her body, slow and assessing, then back up. "Where?"

Okay, not laughing, so that was good. "My hip."

Like a rock, his focus dropped and latched onto her hips. If Superman had swooped in and done the red-eye-laser thing on the same spot, she couldn't have felt the impact more.

"And who's seen it?"

"Like I said, Callie and the guy who did it."

Jace stood. "And it's how old?"

She gripped the couch cushion beside her, the soft olive chenille not nearly sturdy enough for the support she needed under his penetrating scrutiny. "I got it about two years ago."

He stalked toward her, a wolfish expression to match each unhurried step. "Then how is it another man's never seen it before?"

Jesus. She hadn't even thought to prep for that angle, and the answer showed just how lame her life really was. She took another drink, for all the good it did her Sahara-dry mouth. "I've only been with someone once since then. We kept the lights off."

He stopped in front of her, pried the wineglass from her hand, and set it on the end table. "So, what I just heard is you've been with someone once in two years, not with one person several times. That right?"

"Well, I—"

"Simple question, sugar. Yes, or no." He turned her so her back was to him and carefully worked his fingers through her bound hair, feeling for pins and pulling the first one free.

"Yes." It was closer to a whisper than a true answer, but his brief hesitation as he worked said he'd caught it.

His fingertips slid against her scalp, confirming he'd found all the pins. Slowly, he worked through the strands until her hair was a wild mess around her shoulders. He pushed the mass aside and bared her neck.

Instinctively, she angled to give him better access, craving the feel of his lips on the vulnerable skin. His warm breath whispered against her neck. "Vivienne?"

"Hmm?"

His hands circled her waist. His thumbs grazed the undersides of her breasts in a teasing, hypnotic stroke. Low and tempting, his voice rumbled through her. "Tonight the lights will be on."

SEVENTEEN

VIVIENNE TRAILED ONE step behind Jace on the way to her room. Their steps were hushed and unhurried, but his big hand encompassed hers in the take-charge hold of a man too long denied. Even with the arm span between them, his presence burned and crackled with tension, a hungry, impatient animal.

At the top of the stairs, he twisted the knob to her special room, but Viv tugged him back. "My room's the other one."

He opened the door anyway and pulled her along with him, flipping the light switch along the way. The sparkle lights and small bedside lamp with its purple shade flickered to life. "I know which room is yours." He released her hand another few steps in and toed off his dress shoes. "That one's got a touch of you in it, but this one's the real deal."

"I like my room."

"It's a pretty room. Lots of girly touches and a whole lot of *Better Homes and Gardens*, but it's about as much you as a tux is on me." Perched on the edge of the bed, he peeled off his socks, tossed them aside, and scooted back on the bed so he reclined against the headboard. His smoldering gaze cruised languid and sultry up and down her body. "The first time I take you, it'll be in a place that fits the real you, not the one you want me to see."

A slow, ragged breath slipped past her parted lips, and her skin prickled as though she already stood naked before him. "I have my reasons."

"I don't doubt it, and I want to hear every damned one of them. Later. As in, after we've both come and you're naked next to me so I can focus." He grinned and settled deeper on the bed. "Ready to see that tat, sugar."

Cocky bastard. The way he was splayed across her bed, one leg up with his strong forearm propped on it, and the other crooked to one side, he looked entirely too sure of himself.

Fine. If he wanted to see her tattoo, she'd show him. Maybe she'd show him how swimming in a flood of pheromones felt in the process. She walked her fingers along one thigh, bunching the soft velvet beneath her fingers and slowly lifting the hem with it.

His grin grew, a panther who'd just realized its prey wanted to play. "What are you doin'?"

The velvet inched past her knee. "Showing you my tattoo like you asked."

"Stop."

She froze, her fingers jumping to obey the quiet, but unyielding command before her mind even registered the word's meaning. "I thought you wanted to see?"

"You invited me through that front door, sugar. You want to change your mind, that's one thing. But if you're still in, then I want to see your secret *and* the canvas that goes with it."

The velvet slipped from her fingers and her breasts grew heavy behind the tight halter of her dress. Just the idea of standing naked in front of Jace rippled goose bumps in all directions. How she'd manage it in reality she couldn't fathom, but if it gave her one tenth the thrill coursing through her right now, it would be worth it.

She ducked her chin and felt for the clasp behind her neck. The two simple loops slipped free and she caught the two sides before they cleared her collarbone. Her heartbeat smacked an unmerciful rhythm, and her focus went hazy, everything but the tips of her toes peeking from beneath her gown's hem falling away.

Shit. Her shoes. She'd forgotten her shoes. She'd never get the strappy heels off gracefully and maintain the grip on her dress.

"Vivienne." Jace's voice registered, firm and comforting through the fog. "Look at me, sugar."

Swallowing around the tight lump in her throat, she lifted her gaze and nearly staggered beneath his sweltering stare. The space between them sparked, charged and potent with a dangerous edge.

"Let go."

Of everything. Her dress, her inhibitions and her fears. He didn't say as much, but he didn't have to. Not with the heated challenge on his face. Her palms grew damp and her body sung with feminine power. So what if she still had on the shoes? They were three inches high and sexy as hell, perfect for stepping into the moment.

Inhaling deep, she lifted her chin higher and let the fabric fall. The silk lining slicked against her heightened skin and clung to her hips a fraction longer than the rest before pooling at her feet.

Jace shifted on the bed, gripping his cock through his pants and growling low and guttural as he leisurely perused every inch of her. His gaze locked onto the tattoo at her hip and the hand on his cock tightened. "A dragon."

"I'm not sure if that's a compliment, or you think I've got bad taste in artwork."

"I think my eyesight's not as good as it used to be. Come a little closer."

She stepped from the velvet circle around her feet and sidled closer, luxuriating in the feel of her hips as they swayed. The power she'd felt under his gaze before was nothing compared to the absolute dominion she felt now, the pride and lust as he watched her amplifying every sensation without so much as a touch.

He smoothed his hand up and over her hip, his thumb reaching out to touch the dragon's tail where it circled the outside of her hip bone. "Still not close enough."

"You're less than two feet away."

"You know what they say about jackin' off making you go blind. I've sure as shit done my share the last two weeks waiting for tonight."

The image of Jace in bed at the compound, naked and stroking his cock, flashed bold and beautiful in her mind, and sent a shudder coursing through her.

Jace chuckled and tightened his grip on her hip. "My naughty girl's got a good imagination."

"What makes you think I'm naughty?"

"Caught that shiver, sugar. Not to mention you've got some damn nice ink of a wicked dragon with his head aimed straight at your pussy. Now, crawl the fuck up here and let me look, then I'll show you how I spent my nights thinking about you."

"He's not aimed that way."

Jace grinned, the tilt so hungry and dirty it was a wonder she didn't come right then. "He's lookin' straight at it. Wants it as bad as I do. Now are you gonna straddle me and let me pay homage? Or do I need to pin you on your back to do it?"

Jesus, the man had a mouth on him. If he could get her this wet without touching her, God only knew what he'd do with actual contact. She slipped the back straps off her heels and kicked them to the side.

"Damn shame those had to go. Was looking forward to enjoying those, too."

She crawled onto the bed and straddled his hips. "You're greedy."

"Fuckin' A." He gripped her waist and urged her toward his shoulders as he inched lower on the bed, his mouth close enough his beard tickled her skin. "But I give as good as I get."

Oh. Holy. Hell.

With one hand holding her firm against his mouth, he traced the dragon's tail with his tongue, nipping and sucking a fiery trail toward the dragon's head. The other hand ghosted up her inner thigh, his work-roughened thumb working devious circles closer and closer to her core.

"Jace." She squeezed his shoulders and hung on for dear life.

"Yeah, sugar." He kept his focus, his voice distracted as he left behind her tattoo and blazed a sensual path low across her belly.

"Shouldn't we..."

His thumb bypassed her slick folds and moved across the tightly trimmed curls on her mound. "Shouldn't we what?"

"You're still dressed." Her hips flexed, willing him to

slide his thumb lower and give her the touch she craved. "Shouldn't we slow down?"

He hummed against her and lifted his head. "I don't know." He slicked a finger through her folds and circled her entrance. "Feels to me like we're right on schedule."

His finger slipped inside, and Viv's head dropped back, her knees parting for more of his wicked touch.

"Christ, that's hot." He worked her in a slow, steady rhythm, sliding a second finger inside as he drew decadent circles around her clit. "That's it, sweetheart. Ride my fingers."

She lifted her head, her unbound hair tickling her shoulders and back as she opened her eyes to find Jace's gaze riveted to her undulating hips.

"Gonna take you just like this. Feel your pussy glide up and down my cock until you suck it dry."

The muscles around his fingers fluttered and her thighs clenched tight.

"Yeah, right on schedule." He pulled her against his mouth, replacing his thumb on her clit with the hot press of his mouth. He licked the hard nub once, twice, then sucked it deep.

"Jace!" Her pussy clamped around his fingers, contracting over and over, unrelenting ripples feathering out to the arches of her feet. Dozens of times she'd pleasured herself to some astounding orgasms, but this was huge. A violent storm and easy mist all at once, uncoiling tension she hadn't even known existed.

His fingers slowed, still moving in a steady rhythm, but guiding her down from the peak in smooth, easy strokes. His tongue circled her clit and lower, his appreciative moans vibrating through her swollen folds as he feasted on her release. His sex-weighted eyelids lifted and his gaze locked on to hers, a devilish gleam burning in the dark depths. Sliding his fingers free, he licked one last pass and pressed a lingering kiss atop her mound. "That's one."

Then I'm taking you home and finding at least ten different ways to make you scream my name.

His words from the charity event blasted through her mind. "You can't be serious."

He walked himself back on his elbows and started unbuttoning his shirt. "Sugar, I might be rough as hell around the edges, but my follow-through's just fine." He dug into his pants pocket and tossed two condoms to the bed. "Now help me get the rest of the way out of this outfit so I can get back to enjoying myself."

Any lingering arguments died on her tongue, the opportunity to replace her imaginary fantasies with a real-life visual sending her fingers to the fastener at his waist. She splayed the opening wide and tugged his pants down his hips as he shucked his shirt to one side of the bed.

The pendant she'd always felt beneath his shirts rested against his sternum on a wicked platinum chain. Dog tags, though way more high-end than anything service issued, with an edgy H surrounded by a tribal tree and etched atop a black background. Those and his black boxer shorts were all that stood between her and over six feet of tanned, muscled male.

She licked her lips and let out a shaky exhale. She traced a nasty scar that cut across one shoulder, down across the tattoo over his chest. It matched the emblem on his pendant, but had far more details, knotted roots woven and tangled together as though binding it to his heart. Slowly, she worked her way further, reveling in the roped indentions defining every delectable muscle. Beneath the black cotton covering his hips, his fierce erection stretched the fabric taut.

Jace cupped the hard length and stroked. "Love the way you're staring at my dick, babe, but I'd like it a lot better without these briefs."

"Yeah." Whether she answered out loud, or only inside her head was a bit of a toss-up, her focus too intent on peeling the tight waistband down until his perfect cock sprang free. Long and thick, it stretched nearly to his belly button, a heavy weight against his stomach. She swallowed and licked her lower lip, leaving him to kick his briefs the rest of the way off. She straddled his thighs and ran her finger along a prominent vein running from the base to the ridge beneath the flared head.

Her hair fell around her on either side as she leaned in, blocking out the light, but she didn't need it. Her lips skimmed the rigid length on feel alone, her lungs reveling in the woodsy musk of his sex.

Jace hissed and swept her hair up in two hands. He fisted it against the back of her head, flexing his hips against her questing mouth. "Fuck, that's beautiful."

She licked the deep ridge beneath the head, circled his glans, and closed her lips around him. His salty precome coated her tongue, and a low, animalistic growl rang in her ears a second before he gripped her beneath her arms and pulled her astride his hips.

The condom package was already open and Jace was sheathing his thick rod before she'd even caught her bearings. "One of these days, I'm going to indulge the hell out of that fantasy, but the first time I come it'll be buried deep in your pussy." With one hand gripping her firmly at the hip, he eased her up and over his shaft and slicked his cock's flared head through her wet folds. His hot, heavy breath fanned across her face. "You want this?"

Was he insane? The house could be on fire and a nuclear bomb headed straight for Dallas and she'd want this. "Do I look like I'm running?"

"Nah, sugar. You look like you're ready to be well and truly fucked." He nudged just past her entrance, promising without giving. "You want it, then take it."

Damn right she would. She braced her hands on his pecs and sank deep, the dark stretch of his cock ripping a long, gritty moan past her lips.

Perfect. Steel wrapped in softness, each ridge and ripple raking her channel with exquisite sensations. Over and over, she took him, her heavy breasts swaying with each punch of his hips against hers.

He urged her closer with a hand behind her shoulder blades and sucked one nipple deep, his big hand molding and holding her in place for his devious mouth while the other anchored at her hip. His thrusts took over, pounding up and into her in a tumultuous rhythm.

She widened her knees farther, taking what he gave her. Surrendering to the hedonistic bliss, every raw and dirty sensation she'd always craved.

He suckled the other nipple and worked the one he'd left with a pinch and pull.

"Jace."

"Fuckin' love my name on your lips." He grazed the sensitized peak with his teeth and flayed it with his tongue. "Say it again."

"Jace."

A guttural rumble vibrated from his chest and up

her forearms. He clenched both of her hips and stabbed deeper, pounding to the root. "Again."

"Jace."

"That's right." He dipped his thumb between them and circled her clit. "Find it, sugar. Come on my cock and give me my name, one more time."

So close. Her belly clenched and her thighs shook, release so close it hovered just a breath away. "Please."

"Oh, baby, I'll make you beg. Next time. I'll spank that pretty ass until it's bright red and please is the only word you know."

Fuck. Her pussy seized, a relentless grip that fisted his shaft in heart-stopping contractions and sent colors blazing behind her clenched eyelids.

"Son of a—" Jace punched upward, once, twice, and ground himself against her, his cock jerking inside her as his fingers dug into her ass. His short pants huffed against her neck and his beard tickled her collarbone, his hips grinding in slow, deep circles that rubbed her clit just right and drew out the torturous pulses from her climax.

That image. Her, bent over Jace's lap and vulnerable to whatever he wanted, had burned a perma-space inside her mind, her core still fluttering with the promise of actual fulfillment. She nuzzled into the crook of his neck, pulling his strong, manly scent deeper into her lungs and riding the lingering aftershocks.

She'd never bared her fantasies before. Wouldn't have dared with the staid, professional types she'd dated the last few years. But Jace…she'd bet he'd be all over them. And what did the fact that she'd consider sharing them with him say about the direction her feelings were headed?

Splaying one hand at the small of her back, he rolled them over, his cock still buried inside her. He braced one elbow by her head and speared the fingers of his free hand through her hair. His hips softly undulated against hers. His eyelids were heavy with release and his grin reeked of well-satisfied male. "Think I've made an executive decision. We're never leaving the house."

A little more of the barricade she'd erected to keep her safe the last many years crumbled, and a tight burn started at the base of her throat. "Yeah?" She bit her lip to hold back the emotion and glanced at the one remaining condom on the bed. "I don't think you came prepared for that kind of a lock-in."

"Good point. We'll leave, get provisions, then barricade ourselves after." He slipped free and sat back on his heels. "Gonna take care of this condom, sugar. You stay put."

"Bossy."

He studied her for long, tense seconds then smiled in a sexy-sweet lopsided grin that made her breath catch. "Felt good, didn't it?" He smacked her hip and shifted off the bed. "Don't move." He ambled to the small connecting bathroom, the tight muscles in his ass flexing in a way that made it evident where the bulk of those amazing thrusts had come from.

A languid glow drifted through her, lulling her toward something she couldn't quite describe. Heck, she wasn't even sure she wanted to know what it was, let alone describe it. It felt too dangerous. Too risky. But it was tempting, too. The promise of belonging mingled with a roller-coaster-worthy thrill.

The water in the bathroom shut off, and he padded into the room, the light behind him perfectly outlining his strong body. He paused beside the bed, looking his fill at her stretched out on her side with one hand tucked beneath her cheek and a knee cocked in front of her. The rumbling bass of his voice was even deeper than usual, rich and sated. "I got it wrong."

"Got what wrong?"

He tugged the sheets out from underneath her, slid in beside her, and tucked her inside the crook of his arm. "Tried to imagine what you'd look like after. Your hair down, that sleepy, well-fucked look on your face, and a little smile on your lips." He swept her hair off her back and ghosted his fingertips slowly up and down her spine. "I didn't do you justice."

God, she was so screwed. The space behind her sternum tightened, and tears muddled her vision, years of stuffed emotion bubbling up no matter how hard she gritted her teeth. So damned long she'd fought to better herself and build a safe life, and yet, here she was, tangled up and perched on the edge of falling for a man her instincts insisted was dangerous. Everything about him drew her in. His intensity. His intelligence. His presence. Never mind the bad press and him being on a first name basis with drug dealers. If things went sideways with Jace, he could destroy her heart far worse than her mom and dad ever did.

And she still wanted him. On every level.

He smoothed his hand over her ass, gentle and yet possessive. "You okay?"

No. Not even close. She'd never felt so gloriously exposed in her life. So alive and terrified in the same breath. For the life of her, she couldn't figure out how to balance the two. Not with him this close, his scent lingering on her skin and his warmth seeping to her bones. She let out a slow breath through quaking lips and fought for a light, playful tone. "I don't think anything that's happened in the last hour can be categorized as okay."

"Nope. Exceptional, maybe. Stellar's probably better." He rolled, propped himself on one elbow beside her, and stared down at her with the most heart-stopping concern she'd ever seen on a man. "Doesn't explain why you're trembling next to me though."

A tear slipped down her temple before she could choke it back. "I'm a girl. Great sex makes us emotional."

One side of his mouth crooked in a funny grin. "Thought we agreed on stellar."

"You picked stellar. I was leaning toward phenomenal."

Downstairs, Jace's mobile rang.

She toyed with the chain around his neck and focused on the intricate design etched on the platinum tags. "Go answer your phone. I'll be fine. I just need a minute to level out, that's all."

He studied her, slowly tracing her jawline with his thumb. "You get from now until I finish that call. Then we're talking."

Not if she could help it. It was too soon and everything too close to the surface to do more than simply enjoy. Her voice wobbled a bit, more husky and broken than she'd hoped for. "Talking's overrated. Go get your phone and come back to bed."

He smirked, kissed her cheek and whispered low in her ear. "Nice try, sugar. But we're still talking."

He crawled off the bed, tugged his pants on, and stalked down the stairs. In less than a minute, one side

RHENNA MORGAN
191

of a heated conversation and a whole string of profanities filtered up the staircase, followed by a clipped ending and Jace's heavy footsteps.

Not long enough. Not nearly long enough for her to plug up all the emotions swarming her.

Carelessly tossing his mobile to a chair in the corner of the room, he crawled across the bed and straddled her, turning her so she couldn't hide her face. He swiped his thumb along her cheek. His lips were pressed in a harsh line that said he wasn't giving up until he got to the bottom of whatever troubled her. "Talk."

What could she say? That he'd stomped in, upended her tidy life and pried open her eyes to everything she'd been missing? "I'm scared."

His eyes narrowed. "I scare you?"

A half laugh, half sob huffed out and she swiped the back of her hand across a new tear. "Yes, I'm scared. Of you, of this, of us. It's not safe."

He flinched and leaned back on his heels. "And you need safe. Like Paul."

Her sob shifted to more of a self-deprecating chuckle. "Paul is definitely safe. You are not."

His eyes widened and, for the briefest moment, the confidence that always surrounded him like a living, breathing shield fell away, revealing the raw and vulnerable man underneath. Just as quickly, his expression hardened, his lips pressed into an unforgiving line and his brow furrowed. He rolled off the bed and snatched his shirt.

Viv scrambled to the edge of the bed, instincts tripping into damage control. She'd seen all kinds of moods with Jace in the two weeks she'd known him, but never had she seen him as abrupt and closed off as he was now. "Where are you going?"

He left his shirt unbuttoned, sat in the side chair and started on his socks. "Work."

"Work? Now? It's after one o'clock."

"Crowd's gotten out of hand and the press is out for a story." He practically stomped into his shoes, crammed his phone in his pocket, and glared down at her. "Clothes and pedigree don't make a man, nor do they make a man safe. You want some tame, soft-touch jackass who'll screw you and toss you aside when it suits him, then Paul's your man." His gaze slid to the tattoo on her hip. "The sooner you figure out who the hell you are on the inside, the happier you'll be."

Before her mind could process his entire rant, he was at the front door, slamming it shut behind him.

What. The. Hell.

She dropped down to the bed, pulling the covers over her and fisting her hair on the top of her head. Being an emotional mess was *her* job. And she'd been doing a damned fine job of it, too. What kind of man gave a woman two mind-blowing orgasms and then flipped out like a hair-trigger teenage girl?

The twinkle lights she'd rearranged to match what she'd seen at The Den glowed back at her, not one single answer cascading down no matter how long she stared. Everything had been fine. He'd even been sensitive in his own he-man kind of way with the whole "talk" thing.

And then you told him he wasn't safe.

She'd compared him to Paul. A man who'd looked down on Jace with disdain and disgust. She might not know the story between them, but it didn't take a rocket scientist to see it was ugly.

Most people see what they want, no matter what you show them.

Oh, shit. He wasn't mad, he was hurt. Badly. Flayed wide open by words she'd intended an entirely different way.

She lurched from the bed. 1:30 a.m. glowed a soft white from the bedside clock, only thirty minutes until closing time. If she hurried she could catch him before he headed out to God knew where and fix it. Or at least try.

She hustled to her bedroom and her walk-in closet, and stood in front of the long row of suits pants and skirts she usually wore. In the back corner of the closet, her favorite white tank and jeans were folded up on the shelf.

Maybe Jace was right. Maybe she had been hiding, stifling who she was and what she enjoyed beneath her twisted childhood fears. She snatched the well-worn clothes off the shelf and suited up. Well, she could fix it. Both her path forward and the damage she'd done tonight. Assuming she could find and corner him long enough to listen.

EIGHTEEN

WORK LIGHTS FLICKERED to life over the dance floor, and the last of the Saturday night crowd staggered toward the exits. Most nights Jace nursed the promise of an overflowing bottom line while he watched the bar empty, but tonight he just wanted everyone to get out. The sooner folks were gone, the sooner he could get to Haven. Away from work. Away from people.

Away from Viv.

He knocked back another slug of his Scotch and hissed around the burn as it slid down his throat. *Safe.* Hell no, he wasn't safe, and didn't want to be. If Viv wanted to stuff all that passion she had bottled up and waste it on a coattail-riding, pretty boy like Paul, then so be it.

The door to his office opened and Axel sauntered in, his unruly Scot's hair tied back in a tidy tail and a drink fisted in one hand. "Cops are gone." He shut the door behind him and dropped onto the leather sofa. "Sorry they bugged you during your thing with Viv. The office chicks didn't know I was on call."

Below him, the bouncers started their sweep from the back to the front, checking for passed out patrons and any other nasty surprises. "Doesn't matter. You got it handled, and I needed an out."

"Odd since the only thing you've thought of lately was how to get in."

Jace fisted his hand in his pants pocket, pride and mangy stubbornness refusing to meet Axel's steady gaze in the window's reflection. "Misjudged this one."

"You sure?"

He wasn't sure what he thought anymore. He couldn't remember the last time his gut had called it so wrong, but she'd stated her fears about as blunt as a sledgehammer. "Girls up front said the DPD hit us three times tonight."

Axel shook his head, clearly not buying Jace's diversion tactic. "Crowd was crazy. Soon as we broke up one brawl, someone else started another. Cops said they're getting customer call-ins."

Fan-fucking-tastic. Although, maybe now that Viv was out the picture, he'd pull his head out of his ass and figure out how to navigate his club from the PR Bermuda Triangle.

"Head to Haven, Jace. Take some time, nurse a few pours of Scotch, and chill tomorrow. I can take the clubs for another night."

Twenty-four solid hours at home and offline from his businesses? His mom and Axel's mom, Sylvie, would be in hog heaven. Much as he hated Axel having to cover the properties another night, digging in with his roots would be smart. To surround himself with where he came from and what he did all this for. "I'll help you shut down first."

"That's the spirit." Axel stood and clapped Jace on the shoulder. "You check the North and East bar, and I'll meet you in the office in thirty. We'll have you home in no time."

Jace powered off his computer and tossed back the last of his Scotch. Three-thousand acres and nothing but quiet and killing time how he pleased. Normally, the idea of heading to their place out north of Allen sent his brain offline, but tonight it felt a little off.

Combing the North bar and checking out the bartenders took all of ten minutes. That section of the bar catered more to rough men craving low-key, high-quality liquor and zero bullshit. They might not be the tidiest bastards, but they held their liquor a hell of a lot better than the yuppies did, and they almost always used cash.

He dropped off the register drawers with Shelly at the office and headed back out for the East bar. A smoky cigarette haze hung high over the lobby, paired with sweat and an overpowering clash of colognes and perfumes. He'd have to talk to the guys on floor duty about cracking down on the smoking, or he'd just be waving another red flag for the city to nail him with.

"Damn it, let me through. I want to see Jace."

Jace halted at the sound of Viv's irate voice slicing from the entrance.

He turned in time to catch his bouncer, Bruce, block the partially open entry and rumble something in return. Viv wasn't visible, but the flashes of movement and heavy chatter from outside said his closing crowd wasn't in too big of a hurry to head home.

"Don't give me that shit," Viv bit back loud and clear. "I've been in and out of here every day for the last two weeks. You know I've got business here. Now get out of my way."

Sounded like Little Miss had worked into a hell of a snit. He ambled closer, staying out of her line of sight. He had to give Bruce credit. Not once did he lose his cool. Viv, on the other hand, was livid. He'd never heard her this forceful, not even when she'd screamed his name and come around his cock.

He shouldn't engage. Should just finish out the East bar, get this place locked down and get the heck out. He tapped Bruce on the shoulder and motioned him to move away. "I got this."

Viv's rant dried up the second she laid eyes on him.

Damned if his mouth didn't dry up, too. Her hair was wild and loose, still tangled and well-fucked the way it'd been when he left. Those sexy gray eyes of hers were sharper in color than normal, and her cheeks were flushed a pretty pink. But not a bit of that compared to the rest of her, the jeans he loved and a plain white tank paired with the leather jacket he'd gotten her. "You're acting pretty bold for a woman who wants nothing to do with a dangerous man."

She planted her hands on her hips, and Jace nearly swallowed his tongue. His little firecracker was out and about without a bra, the rigid points of those sweet nipples he'd sucked on pressed against the tight fabric and a hint of their dusky color showing through the white. "You misunderstood."

For a second, one hopeful, disconcerted second, he second-guessed what he'd heard out of her mouth. The memory of how she'd looked at Paul at the charity dinner streaked in behind the hesitation. She'd been relaxed. Poised and interested. Nowhere near the terrified expression she'd nailed him with when he'd crawled back into bed and curled up beside her. "Hard to misunderstand when a woman tells a man she's afraid of him. I think that pretty much summed your stance up nice and tight." How he managed such a hard line, he'd never know, but he was going to pat himself on the back with a whole fifth of Macallan when he got to Haven. One thing was for sure. He couldn't do this. Not here. Not now. Not with his gut stinging like she'd flayed him inside out.

He latched onto her shoulder and guided her through the lingering crowd toward the parking lot. "If you're here about the job, it's solid, but I think you'd be best to head home."

She jerked her shoulder free and snatched his wrist before he could step out of range. "Please. Just listen."

He aimed a none-too-subtle glare at her grip then lifted a you-really-wanna-try-that-with-me eyebrow.

Dropping the connection, she stuffed her hands in her back pockets and nailed him with another un-abashed view of her tits.

Christ, a man could only take so much. He fisted his own hands in his pants pockets and forced his eyes to stay on hers. "Talk."

She hesitated a second, studying her boots long enough he thought she'd changed her mind. Then she met his eyes head-on. "When I said Paul was safe, I meant he was *safe*. As in, not the least bit frightening. And before you get your hackles up and start snarling about goody-two-shoes assholes, I mean that as in he doesn't affect me."

The crowd hummed and pulsed around him, but everything inside him froze. He wasn't sure what the hell he'd expected, but it wasn't that. Hell, not even close.

"I don't see him as safe because of what he wears," she said, "what part of town he lives in, or who his family is. I mean he's safe because he can't shake everything inside me with a single look. His hand on my arm barely registered, but yours I register everywhere. So, yeah, he's safe. You?" She huffed out a borderline hysterical laugh and shook her head, her wild curls dancing around her cheeks and shoulders. "You scare the hell out of me because you make me feel. You make me reevaluate everything I'd thought to be true and dare me to throw safe straight out the window."

You make me feel.

The simple statement orbited his head so fast not much else could get past it. Hell, even if he could move, he wasn't sure he wanted to for fear he'd shatter the moment.

"Say something." Her chest heaved like she'd sprinted a mile instead of unloading a one-ton truck of surprise on his gut. Tears pooled in her eyes. "Please."

There had to be a catch, some pitfall he wasn't seeing. But damn it, he couldn't just let her stand there and think what she'd said didn't matter. He stepped sideways to steer her inside. He'd take her to the office and buy his head some time to catch up.

Viv matched his move, as though to block him from leaving, and gripped his shoulder. "Wait."

A gunshot rang out.

Viv jerked and fell against him as the crowd scattered, Bruce and the rest of his team jumping into the fray while screams and pounding footsteps rang against the asphalt.

Shielding Viv, Jace wrapped her up and backed her into the shelter of the club, throwing the door shut behind him.

She trembled against him, her forehead on his chest and her own cry broken and filled with pain.

"Vivienne." He tugged her away from him by both shoulders and her sob turned into a shriek. "Sugar—"

He froze.

Blood bubbled from a puckered hole between her shoulder and her neck, a crimson trail staining the front of her white tank. "Shit."

Axel shouted from across the lobby. "What the fuck is going on?"

"Gunshot. Let the guys handle it. Need you with me." He swept Viv up and stormed deeper into the bar, weaving through the blur of patrons rushing the opposite direction. Barked orders from the bouncers up front and feminine shrieks pelted against his ears as harsh as shrapnel, and his heart thrashed in an angry assault.

You make me feel.

Christ, he was an idiot. A hot-headed, knuckle-fucking-dragging idiot.

Axel's heavy footsteps pounded behind him.

Laying Viv out on the nearest booth, he eased her leather jacket aside with too-unsteady hands and bit back a curse. The wound was high enough it couldn't have hit anything life threatening, but it bled like a son of a bitch. "They got Viv," he said to Axel as he hurried closer. "Get me a towel from the bar."

"You sure ye don't want the kit?"

"No time. I want her out of here before the cops show." He smoothed her hair away from her face and leaned in close. A piercing weight pressed against his chest, the same unyielding rage he'd felt the night a man had dared to hurt his mother all those years ago.

Her eyes locked on his, wide and glassy, and her shaky breaths fluttered across his face. "Hurts."

"Take a deep breath, babe," he said. "It might hurt like hell, but it's superficial. Zeke will fix you up and you'll be fine."

Nice fucking words. She'd shown up, laid herself bare, and he'd gotten her shot.

Axel handed him a clean, white bar towel and stacked two more beside Viv. "How do you wanna play it?"

His temples throbbed from the strain of his clenched jaw, the need to choke whoever'd dared to hurt her drawing his fists up just as tight. "Get Knox on the security tapes. I don't want one scrap of her being here on any of 'em. Lose the whole damned night if you have to. Until I know what the hell this is about, no one but brothers know she was here. And make sure Bruce keeps his shit tight."

"You think this was aimed at her?"

"Moreno saw her with me at the club. Not a stretch for that fucker to target her to get to me. Until I know for sure, she's protected."

"How you plannin' to do that?"

"I'm taking her to Haven."

"Come again?"

"You heard me." Jace braced the towel over the wound and Vivienne whimpered. He lifted her up as carefully as he could.

Sirens sounded in the distance.

"The brothers aren't gonna like that," Axel said. "You sure you're ready to cross that line?"

Jace stalked toward the back entrance. "The line you need to be worried about is what happens when I find the motherfucker who pulled that trigger."

Viv tucked her chin to her chest and held her breath, every one of Jace's powerful strides resonating from the painful epicenter near her shoulder. The mix of blowtorch burn and pounding throb churned her stomach, but she didn't dare retch for fear she'd wrench the pain even higher.

Jace punched the steel door at the back of the club open and the sudden motion jarred her shoulder.

Her ragged cry ripped across the deserted alley.

Brushing a kiss against her forehead, he stalked toward his Porsche. "Sorry, sugar. Just hang tight while I get us out of here." He settled her in the front seat and punched her seat belt in place. Thank God for that, because she wasn't too sure she'd be able to stay upright without it.

The cool January night air slid across her clammy skin, and a shiver rattled down her spine. The Porsche's engine growled to life and the car shot forward.

She pried her eyelids open and the world beyond her passenger window did a Tilt-A-Whirl spin. "You said it was a gunshot."

Jace jammed the gearshift into the next gear so hard she'd have winced if her body wasn't already shaking. "From the parking lot. Don't know who, but Axel's working it."

"Guns and booze. A bad mix. Trust me, I know." In the back of her mind, a warning tripped on her warbled statement. *Too much information. Shut it down and keep quiet.* But why? She'd made up her mind to lay everything on the line with Jace. Not much of a better way to explain the way she was than reality. Her gaze locked onto the blood smeared across his once crisp white shirt, and a fresh wave of nausea bubbled up.

Jace curled his hand around the back of her neck, his fingers smoothing across her hairline in a comforting stroke. "Just breathe through it, sugar. Gonna get you fixed up."

She let her eyes slide shut and her head loll forward, focused on his touch. Fixed up would be good, preferably with lots and lots of pain meds. "Presbyterian's on my insurance. Does Zeke work there?"

"Not takin' you to a hospital."

Viv jerked her head upright and shrieked at the sudden movement. Surely she hadn't heard that right.

Jace tucked his phone under one ear before she could get clarification and barked at someone on the other end. "Got a problem. Had a shooter at the club and they hit Viv near her left shoulder. Looks superficial, but she's bleeding like hell."

God, she was tired. And cold and hot at the same time. What the hell did he mean he wasn't taking her to the hospital?

"Not going that route," he said into the phone. "Meet us at Haven."

The highway lights sped by so fast they all seemed to run together, almost as fast as her heartbeat.

"God damn it, I said Haven, not the compound. Just be there." He punched the end button and tossed it to the console. "Need you to hang on for another twenty, Viv. Got plenty to make you feel better at home."

"Jace, I need a doctor. And medicine, and—"

"Got everything you need at Haven and Zeke's on his way. Trauma's his thing and yours isn't critical. Until I know you're not a target, I want you somewhere I know I can keep you safe."

Moreno saw her with me at the club. Not a stretch for that fucker to target her to get to me. Until I know for sure, she's protected.

The statement he'd made to Axel hadn't made sense at the time, blistering pain overriding the need for analyzing subtext, but now it rewound loud and clear. Mixed with all the violence they'd had in recent weeks and the concern Axel never bothered to hide, she wasn't sure how to process it all. "It was just an accident."

He veered onto the highway and jostled her head to one side.

For once the pain barely registered, the desperate need to close her eyes and surrender sweeping over everything else. Her breath came shallow and quick, her fingers and toes so cold, she'd give anything for an electric blanket.

Jace swept his thumb over one cheek, cold air stinging against the wetness in its wake.

Jesus, she was crying?

"Going to take care of you, Viv. You've got to trust me on this."

She forced her eyes open.

His gaze was locked on the road, his expression defiant and scary, a promise of violence she wouldn't wish on her worst enemy. She should be fighting, demanding he let her out of the car, or take her to a hospital, but the fight just wasn't in her. Her body had all but taken over and focused on the simple task of not bleeding to death in his nice car.

No, there was more than that. There was trust. Instinct that said to uncoil her cramped and tired fingers from the illusion of control she'd clung to, and surrender. Her eyelids slipped shut and darkness closed in. God help her, she hoped that instinct didn't get her killed.

NINETEEN

LOW, MASCULINE VOICES nudged Vivienne from an un-
natural sleep, the conversation's intense rumble pricking
her sluggish consciousness. Talk about relaxed. Every
inch of her from crown to toenails seemed weighted by
at least an extra twenty pounds, and her eyelids felt as
though they'd been soldered shut. A slow, aching throb
pulsed between her neck and shoulder.

The gunshot.

Piece by piece, her memory came back online. The
harsh, almost terrifying expression on Jace's face before
she'd blacked out. The fear as the shrieks and pande-
monium exploded around her. The sharp, searing tear
as the bullet ripped through her flesh.

And still her heart slogged along at tortoise pace.

The voices stopped and heavy, muted footsteps
sounded against carpet, coming up on one side of her.
Papers rustled and the punctuated scratch of pen on
paper followed.

Warm, firm fingers pressed against the inside of her
wrist and Viv flinched, her eyelids finally getting on
board with the whole awake concept.

Zeke eyeballed his watch. "Didn't mean to scare
you." He held his fingers at her pulse for another ten
or so seconds, and plucked the penlight from the neckline of his scrubs. Sitting on the edge of the bed, he held
one eyelid open and checked her pupils.

The light pierced straight to the base of her skull and made her stomach lurch.

"Shitty way to wake up, huh?"

"Yeah." Her voice rasped in a grated whisper and her tongue nearly stuck to the roof of her mouth. She licked her lips but didn't get much in the way of relief.

Zeke checked the other eye then snatched the folder he'd tossed beside her. "The cotton mouth is normal with morphine. Jace went to grab you some water, but you probably want to ease into it at first."

Now that the reflection from the penlight had died off a little, the dim environment registered. A big bedroom, with dark woods and a very old-world feel, virile elegance similar to Jace's room at the compound, but on a much more elaborate scale. This was home. His real home.

Zeke scribbled on the paper on top of the folder, the sharp, powerful strokes that of a man either highly pissed off, or in a very big hurry. With two bold underlines, he tucked the paper in the folder, crossed his arms over the bloodstains halfway down his shirt, and nailed her with a shuttered, watchful stare. "How's the pain?"

She swallowed as best she could with her dry mouth. "Still there, but I don't seem to care."

That, at least, tipped one corner of his mouth, a little of the playful Zeke she'd come to know peeking through. "Opiates are good that way." As fast as it came, the grin faded. "We'll back you off to Lortab from here out. By midweek you won't need more than acetaminophen and ibuprofen."

"How bad's my shoulder?"

He leaned over and ghosted his finger over the wide bandage taped into place. "Hit your supraspinatus muscle, just above your shoulder blade. Thirty-two caliber. Your jacket did a lot to help. Three to four inches lower would have been a game changer. With this, you're just not doing push-ups for about a month."

Her tank from last night was gone, replaced with a similar one that had to be Jace's considering how loose it was. The hem tickled just below her hips, and if her nerve endings weren't playing a trick on her, the wife-beater was the only thing between her and the sheets.

Zeke ambled to a brown attaché made of soft, worn leather and tucked the folder away.

"Is Jace okay?" The last half of her question snagged on a catch her throat.

Zeke hesitated a second, flipped the messenger-styled flap closed, and faced her. "What's Jace to you?"

Her thoughts whirled with about as much grace as a rear-wheel drive in an ice storm, the mix of the unexpected question and the intensity on Zeke's face compelling answers before she found traction. "I'm trying to figure that out."

"Then I suggest you get clear, because Jace is already there."

"He told you?"

"He didn't have to." He jerked his head, indicating the room around her. "You're here. That says enough."

"What's that supposed to mean?"

Zeke's head snapped back. "He hasn't told you?"

Hopped up on painkillers or not, there was no missing it was more of an accusation than a question. "Told me what?"

Jace's voice shot across the room. "She good?"

Whoa, boy. She'd thought Zeke's attitude was extreme, but it didn't come close to the power radiating off of Jace. He prowled barefoot across the room in Levi's and a black Led Zeppelin shirt. Both looked like they'd been around since the band's heyday, and were faded and tight in all the right places.

"She's solid." Zeke glanced between her and Jace, pensive. "Has lots of questions, though."

Jace strolled to her opposite side and set two bottles of water on the nightstand. "Those are mine to answer, not yours."

The starefest between the two made her want to slink down under the covers, or even better, disappear entirely.

Zeke shook his head and stepped away, whatever nonverbal man-speak had gone down between them ending in either surrender, or disbelief. "I'll bunk down here until next shift if you need me. After that, I'll want to see her wound every twenty-four for a few days." He grabbed his briefcase and headed out of the room.

"Hit the door on your way," Jace said to Zeke, his gaze on her. He eased onto the armchair beside the bed and braced his elbows on his wide knees.

The door snicked shut.

Adrenaline surged past the morphine's weight and sent her heart off at a gallop. Whatever was going on in that shrewd head of his took on a nearly tangible aura, hot as the sun's surface, and yet shadow dark. Part of her insisted now was the time to hightail it for home no matter how little she had on, but another, far more instinctive part of her considered wrapping herself in his dark heat.

His raw voice rasped between them. "How's your pain?"

Even with a bullet hole in her shoulder and a healthy

dose of narcotics swimming through her system, she responded to the gravelly sound, the same as when he'd demanded his name from her the night before.

She licked her lips and his gaze zeroed in on it. "Better than before. Steady, but dull."

He snatched the water bottle from the nightstand, unscrewed the lid and handed it to her. "How much do you remember?"

Sweat lined the ice-cold bottle, and the frigid liquid forged a relieving path down her throat. "I remember enough." Like the fact that he'd never responded after she'd laid everything out for him. That he'd been about to step away when the bullet had ripped into her shoulder. Nothing like a gunshot to complicate a man's exit strategy. "I'm pretty clear up until you took the exit off 75."

"Your head clear now?"

"Well, I probably shouldn't sign any legal documents, if that's what you're after." She coupled it with a chuckle, but it came out too nervous to be genuine.

Jace stared back at her, deadpan.

Her laughter died off, and she took another drink.

He cupped one fisted hand with the other, his gaze forceful enough to lock her in place. "You clear enough you're going to remember what I have to say to you?"

Seriously? A gunshot wound wasn't enough for one night, and now he wanted to add the old heave-ho? Well, to hell with him. "Yeah. I'm good. Listen, if you'll just give me my phone, I'll call someone to come get me."

"You're not going anywhere."

"Really, you don't have to do this." She motioned with the bottle in her hand around the room. "I know you only brought me here to keep a low profile with the cops. Axel told me how they've been harassing everyone at the club. It was probably a freak deal. I won't say anything. Just let me get out of your hair. You don't have to say anything else."

Jace surged upright, snatched the bottle from her and plunked it on the nightstand. "You had your say. Now you're going to give me mine." He sat back down, poised on the edge of the chair.

"Jace—"

"I don't live between lines set by lawmakers and politicians. I piss more people off than I care to count and cross boundaries some people wouldn't approve of. I do what I think's right based on my sense of discipline and honor. I take care of what's mine and I do it with a vengeance." He smoothed his thumb down her forearm and rolled her arm so her inner wrist was exposed. Coaxing her fisted fingers open, he circled his roughened thumb against her palm. "Something you need to deal with, sugar, is you're mine. That means I'll find whoever hurt you and make sure he never puts you at risk again."

Her mind tripped and floundered, so flustered by *you're mine* roaring in her head, she couldn't pull coherent thoughts together, let alone talk.

His touch shifted, drifting in a hypnotizing, back-and-forth rhythm against her pulse point. "That also means I'm with you until you figure out you can live your life like you really are and quit hiding it."

"I don't hide—"

"I know where you came from."

Panic kicked and clawed behind her sternum, the flush of his possessive caveman comments shifting to a cold sweat.

"I know about your mom leaving and your dad's drinking. I've already seen Callie in action."

"How do you know all that?"

"How doesn't matter. What does is I'm not gonna let you color how you view me, or my life, with your past. I'm my own man, with my own history, and I damn sure won't let it own me the way it's owned you."

"My past doesn't own me."

"It doesn't?" The edge in his voice clamped tender teeth on her anger. "Then tell me why you keep that one, wild room of yours tucked away where no one can see it? Why you wear tailored everything in public, but slide those fucking sinful jeans on the minute you're out of everyone's sight?" He lifted her wrist and brushed his lips against the sensitive skin. "Why you pore through those erotic books and dirty sites on your computer."

Viv ripped her hand away, and a sharp stab pierced her wound. She whimpered and held her breath until the pain ebbed. "You went through my things?"

"The brotherhood's got a lot of businesses. You working for us puts you in close contact with the information that goes with it. Anyone in that kind of proximity gets a sweep, no exceptions. That's not normally something I do, but yours wasn't a job I was willing to delegate." He grinned, not at all repentant. "The dirty sites were just a bonus."

"Jesus, Jace. Have you ever heard of a background check? Or just asking what you wanted to know?"

"Background checks aren't for shit. You want to know something about a person, you look where they live. And besides that, you weren't exactly talkative at the time."

"That doesn't give you the right to break into my place and dig up my history."

"I told you, sugar. I've got my own code, and part of it's keeping my family safe. Mine and Axel's moms, my brothers…" He circled the wrist she'd yanked away, a loose contact that banded like a snug cuff, but sent the most primal comfort coursing through her veins. "And now you."

Family.

The simple word gonged so forcefully through her head, it was a wonder any other sound penetrated. All her life she'd wanted the kind of closeness Jace hinted of. Loyalty and protectiveness. A safe haven she could run to when life threw its curveballs. "You called this place Haven."

"That's what family is."

"Not always."

He shifted off the bed and sat beside her, careful not to jar her shoulder, and smoothed his thumb along her jawline. "In this one, it is."

A slow burn pressed against the bridge of her nose and tears threatened. This was so whacked. A smart woman would be throwing anything within reaching distance at his head and scrambling for the door, not shivering like some lost waif with a piece of chocolate dangling in front of her. She lowered her voice. "What you did was wrong. How am I supposed to trust you?"

"I've got no problem earning back what I've lost, but you barely let me close enough to win it the first time. You pushed me away and kept the ruffian at a distance."

Her cheeks heated and she smoothed the blanket across her lap to keep from looking at him. "I told you what I meant by that."

"You did. Owned your shit and was proud of you for it." He lifted her chin with his finger. "Now I'm gonna own mine."

He studied her for so long she thought he wouldn't say anything else. "I was an ass. Covered up my hurt with temper and got you hurt as a result. I should have stopped and asked what you meant before I stormed off and, swear to Christ, you've got my vow—that shit will not happen again. I'll check it. I'll listen and I will not run. Not with you."

Holy wow. As apologies went he'd danced around the words *I'm sorry* in every way imaginable, but the message settled on her heart more deeply than the most reverent kiss.

"Been sitting there while you were out," he said, "replayin' the way your blood looked on my hands. That second when you passed out in my car and I wasn't sure you were breathing. The truth of the matter is, life goes fast. A drunk driver could've killed you tonight as easy as a bullet at my club. You got to live life full throttle so there are no regrets when it's time to cash in."

"I'm sure it was just an accident. Someone drunk who did something stupid."

"Maybe." He curled his hand around the side of her neck. "But I'm not going to lie to you, Viv. From now on, there aren't any secrets between us, and straight up, in my world I deal with some nasty bastards. So, I'm going to find who did it and make sure there's no risk of it happening again." He leaned closer, so slow and deliberate her heart accelerated until her chest ached. He whispered against her lips. "And then I'm going to tempt you out of that shell and teach you how to live."

"You could hurt me," she whispered back.

He grinned, still teasing her mouth with his barely-there touch. "Won't ever be with intent, and if I do, I'll bust my ass to fix it. Not sure you get it yet, but you will eventually. You're mine."

His lips sealed against hers, gentle and still so rife with meaning and purpose it rattled to her toes. He pulled away and stroked the line of her hip through the blanket, apparently not the least bit concerned he'd just upended her world.

"I'm not yours." It seemed the right thing to say out loud, but inside she nestled against the claim as cozy as a kitten in a windowsill.

"Yeah, you are. I knew it the night I met you. The same as when I met my brothers. I just couldn't admit it until I saw your blood on my hands. You might not want to concede it yet, but something deep inside you knows it, too." His hand on her hip stilled and tightened. "The same part of you that's got you fired up for me even though you've got a nice little hole in your shoulder."

"That's the morphine."

He laughed, a strong, masculine bark that filled and brightened the room despite the dim lights. His gaze dropped to her lips and his chuckles subsided. "One other thing. That easygoing routine I've been servin' up to keep from spooking you? It's done. You'd be wise to batten down the hatches and heal up quick because you're about to find out what it's like to belong to a man like me."

Jace eased off the bed beside Vivienne and tried like hell not to chuckle at her shell-shocked expression. While he wasn't all that keen on drugs, he had to admit a loopy Vivienne was pretty cute. Particularly when it swiped all those damned barriers off to the side and let her emotions have center stage.

He ambled to the connecting bathroom and flipped on the vanity light with a little more force than necessary. The bit about dropping the tap dancing routine was the absolute truth, but actually carrying it out scared him more than any of Hugo's thugs. Couching who he was, or his behavior, to mingle with people who'd help his bottom line was one thing, but he couldn't remember the last time he'd altered his behavior with someone close. For all he knew, he'd yank off the subtle veneer, and she'd hightail it to the nearest bunker before he could say, "Excuse me."

Well, if that happened, then he'd deal with it. From here forward, she got him the way he was with no lies between them. He swiped the bottle of antibiotics Zeke had left for her off the counter and tapped her night-time dosage into his palm. He had a whole host of other problems to deal with first. Five of them to be exact. The brothers were already lighting up his phone and demanding answers as to why he'd broken one of their most fundamental agreements and brought an outsider to Haven. And not just any outsider, but a woman.

He ambled out of the bathroom and slowed at the sight of Viv in his bed. Her head was tilted to one side and her eyes were closed, that wild hair of hers splayed on his pillow. She might have built a pretty good buzz and been startled by a few of his admissions, but the narcotics were doing an adequate job of keeping her in his bed where she belonged.

Snatching the water bottle off the nightstand, he unscrewed the lid and sat beside her. "You need your meds. You good on the morphine, or do you want me to have Zeke give you some more?"

Viv pried her eyes open and took a few seconds to assimilate everything he'd said. "No. I think I'm fine for now."

"You change your mind, you let me know, and we'll get you fixed up. There's a time to tough this shit out, but now isn't one of them." He handed over the medicine, waited for her to get it down, and set the bottle back beside her. "You need anything else? More pillows? Less? Zeke said the pull on your shoulder would hurt more laying flat, but I can't sleep worth a damn propped up."

"I think he's right. And honestly, I could probably sleep through a train wreck and not care." She lifted her head and studied the room, eyes landing on the bathroom before she flipped the covers aside. "Although, I think I'd be smart to hit the bathroom before I pass out again."

Jace halted her with a careful touch at her shoulder. "Hold up. I'll carry you."

He bent to pick her up and she shied away. "You can't take me to the bathroom."

The hell I can't leaped to his lips, but he stifled it at the last second. Damn it, this was exactly the kind of censoring BS he needed to stop with her. Although a soft touch considering the circumstance wouldn't hurt either. "You've got a hole in your shoulder, and you earned it at my club after saying some of the sweetest words I've ever heard. So humor your old man and let him make sure you don't bust your ass while the room goes Tilt-A-Whirl."

Before she could answer, he gently slid his arms

under her knees and cradled her with her uninjured side against his chest. He navigated them through the bathroom door and toward the toilet, letting her feet slide slowly to the floor. He guided her backward.

Viv dug in her heels and pushed back, bracing her good arm against the door to the private enclosure. "Oh, no you're not. Not this. That's too much."

Stubborn Little Miss. Though he liked seeing her get fired up. Once she finally let go and figured out he was solid, they'd probably have some knock-down, drag-out fights. He couldn't wait.

He kept one arm banded around her waist, but pinned her chin with his fingers and thumb so she couldn't look away. "I'm gonna give you this because it's my fault you're in this damned position. Plus, I get you're not used to this kind of thing. But I need you to understand something. When I say nothing else between us, I mean nothing. Anything that's a part of you is worth my attention and care. We clear?"

Her lips firmed up good and tight, and her face turned a pretty pink, but she nodded her head. "If it means you let me pee in peace, I'll agree. For now."

Peace the likes of which he hadn't felt in a very long time, if ever, spread through him, and a low chuckle shook his chest. Oh, yeah, they were going to have a tussle, or two, but neither one of them would ever be bored. He kissed the top of her head. "Glad I could persuade you."

She staggered back and shut the door in his face.

The process of her doing her business and getting her hands cleaned up after took a fair amount of time, but once he got her back in bed, his worry leveled out. He turned off the bedside light, shucked his clothes, and climbed in beside her on her good side.

Viv sighed and rested her temple on his shoulder, her soft curls tickling his skin in a tempting, luscious stroke.

He lifted his arm and let her burrow closer, whatever kind of exotic shampoo she used filling his lungs with spice and something flowery. As soon as he found out what it was, he was stocking Haven with a year's supply of the stuff.

She fisted her hand on his chest. The room's shadows were heavy, but with the one light in the bathroom he'd left on, her face was barely visible, her eyes opened and aimed at the wall.

For a second, doubt crept in and prodded his steamroller, cards-on-the-table approach. "You're an honest woman, Viv. Fear from your past aside, tell me you don't want this and I'll step away."

She kept her silence, her unfocused gaze steady for long, tense seconds before she uncurled her fingers and splayed them over his heart. Laying a soft kiss as best she could without turning, she nestled closer.

Not the most resounding vote for moving forward, but one he'd take with both hands and not look back. He caressed her shoulder and sucked in a deep breath. "Then let go, Viv. Let go and let me give you what you need."

TWENTY

VIVIENNE SHUT THE bathtub faucet off with her toe and sank into the warm water until the level landed just above her breasts. The master bath was just like everything else in Jace's suite, top of the line and gracefully done, but the colors here were light and bright compared to the bedroom's masculine hues, sand, cream and taupe seamlessly blending for a peaceful, spa-like environment.

More than anything, she'd like to sink the rest of the way under the warm pool and give her hair a good scrub, but Zeke had been adamant about her sticking to showers for the next week. Plus, Jace nearly went into orbit anytime she tried to do anything upright.

The change in him still knocked her off her feet. Not that he was all that much different than before, just that he was *more*. More intense. More direct and protective. A gruff, macho man version of touchy feely that tug-of-warred her between overwhelmed and surrender.

Letting her head loll back against the rolled up towel behind her neck, she let her eyes drift closed and floated on the dregs of her Lortab haze. Drugs weren't something she'd ever felt comfortable with, especially with her family's background, but considering everything she'd been through, they probably helped a whole lot more than they hurt.

A click and quick footsteps sounded from the bedroom, followed by Jace's stern voice. "*Leicht*." Easy.

A second later, the footsteps kicked higher, a trotting pattern mixed with the jingle of Ruger's name tag against his collar. Her big baby rounded the bathroom corner so fast his back legs nearly spun out on the huge ceramic tiles. He plunked his paws up on the ledge and leaned in so fast, she halfway feared he'd jump in with her.

"*Sitzen*," Jace said before Ruger could so much as get in a decent lick.

The dog obeyed, but aimed a wounded look at Jace and whimpered for good measure.

"Poor thing." Vivienne held out her hand and let him nuzzle and lick her palm. "I wondered where you'd run off to," she said to Jace.

"Wouldn't be right to leave him there much longer without a break. He needs to be with you, anyway."

Totally sweet. Most guys she'd gone out with only registered Ruger so far as the threat he posed. Jace actually cared enough to think about him without having to be asked. "Yeah, but I need to go home."

"You're not going anywhere until I know you're safe and you're in better shape."

She sighed and let her head drop back against the towel. "You can't keep me here."

"You hear what I told you last night?"

"Which part? Where you said the life I've been living was a complete lie? Or where you confessed to breaking into my house and violating my privacy?"

He edged Ruger away enough to sit on the edge of the tub. "I never said your life was a lie. I just said you were covering up the best parts of you. The rest was me coming clean on the shit I'd done so we don't have walls between us. Now, back to the topic. You're staying here because I know you're safe here."

"You're overreacting. That shot was probably nothing more than a drunk in the parking lot grandstanding for a woman with the safety off. You said yourself things have been bad there lately."

"And if it wasn't?"

Yeah, that was the other common sense shaker in the whole scenario. Jace might not have gone into detail the night before, but he'd made it clear he dealt with some nasty people in his world. Drug dealers like Hugo Moreno and other people who might have a penchant for guns. It was too much to process. Logic tugged and prodded on one side of her, and emotion stomped and pouted on the other. At this rate, she'd need a solid week of peace and quiet to figure things out.

She sat up and gripped the side to push herself upright.

Before she could so much as get her legs underneath her, Jace was there, carefully lifting her up and out of the tub without the least consideration for his clothes. He eased her to her feet on the big cream rug. He'd barely unwound his arm from her waist when he wrapped a bath sheet around her shoulders.

"You don't have to do all this," she said.

"Not doing it because I have to." He gently smoothed the soft, thick towel up and down her arms and hips. "I'm doing it because I want to."

She stilled him with a hand on his forearm. "Jace—"

"I've never brought a woman to Haven." He tightened the towel around her and stepped in close. "I'm the first of my brothers to do it. I get you don't understand what that means yet, but it means a hell of a lot to me. Is it such a hardship to let your man take care of you for a day or two and leave behind your nice and tidy world while you heal?"

A quiver jangled through her, more from his words than her damp skin. She'd never thought herself territorial before, but the idea no other woman had been with him in this special place ticked the balance in her logic versus emotions debate. Not that she'd share that with him just yet. The uncensored Jace Kennedy she'd witnessed in the last twelve hours seemed cable of stretching inches into megamiles. "I'd planned to work tonight."

"Got a big office you can use."

"You'll tell me what you learn about the shooting?"

He studied her, mouth pursed as though gauging his words. "Unless it might put you in a spot, yeah. I'll share."

The knotted chaos in her gut surged forward and lodged in the base of her throat, confusion, fear and longing stinging her eyes with the promise of fresh tears. She looked away and tried to grab the towel so she could get dressed.

Jace pulled her back against him, stroking her spine with one hand and cupping the side of her face with the other so she couldn't avoid his gaze. "You said I made you feel. Said I made you want to throw safe out the window. But here's the deal, sugar. You need an updated definition of what safe means. If it meant Emily Post and High Tea at four, then the road you were on might be the right one. But from my view, safe means knowing someone's got your back. That they think ahead and anticipate what you need before you even realize you need it. It means knowing someone else will put you first even when it might hurt the giver. Under that definition, you stick with me, you'll never be safer."

Such beautiful words. Rich with so much depth and passion she couldn't process it all at once. "Jace." His whispered name slipped from her mouth as tears trailed down her cheeks, the chasm of doubt and worry she'd created between them near to overflowing with hope. So many years she'd wanted to have someone say sweet things to her, to care about what she wanted and see to her needs instead of the other way around. But to have that alongside such intellect and conviction? Never in her wildest fantasies had she ever thought she'd be this blessed.

She raised herself up on her tiptoes, clenched his T-shirt the best she could with her arms trapped between them, and pulled him closer.

He skimmed his lips across hers, coaxing them apart with a tempting back and forth that sent her thoughts and concerns skittering in all directions. His tongue swept inside, his taste as bold and confident as everything else about him, taking what he wanted while still focused on her pleasure.

She moaned into his mouth and tried to wrestle her good arm free to pull him tighter.

"Ahem." The awkward intrusion came coupled with two sharp raps on the bathroom door.

Viv jerked her head away in time to glimpse Zeke grinning from the doorway just before Jace shifted and blocked Vivienne from view.

"I see our patient's feeling better." Even without the visual, Zeke's voice rang with wry amusement.

Viv ducked her chin and rested her forehead on Jace's

chest, her cheeks on fire from the intimate exposure and his lingering kiss.

Jace caressed the back of her neck. "You better have a damned good reason why you're still standing in that doorway."

"Well, you kind of changed the rules on us, big guy. Never had to second-guess coming into a brother's room before, now did I?" If Zeke was even the least bit put off by Jace's brusque response, his taunting retort hid it well. "The guys are ready for rally and the girls have dinner on the table."

Jace jerked a nod at Zeke over his shoulder and sucked in a deep breath. Waiting until the bathroom door clicked shut, he stepped away and urged her into the bedroom. "Come on. I picked up some clothes from your house."

She made it two steps before Zeke's comment registered and stopped in her tracks. "I thought you didn't bring other women here."

He backtracked and tugged her forward with a much firmer grip, but his lips twitched as though he fought back a grin. "Rein that fire in, sugar. You wanna find out who the girls are, you're going to need to get changed and get your curvy butt down to chow like everyone else." He pulled a fresh pair of jeans and a pale pink cotton tank out of a duffel, and tossed them on the bed.

She snatched the duffel instead, hoping he'd packed a decent set of underwear, but flinched at the exaggerated movement.

"Easy. Your temper's only going to get the pain fired up again." He pulled a simple pair of gray cotton hipster panties with two tiny hot-pink bows from the bag, but stuffed the matching bra back inside. The fact that he'd picked the exact set she'd hoped to find only fanned her aggravation.

She fisted the towel around her chest and shook her head. "Sorry. I don't know what's wrong with me. I'm never this short-tempered. I just—"

"Got shot? Been up and down on painkillers and are cooped up in a place you don't know?" He pried her hands away from the towel so it dropped to the floor and guided her until she sat on the edge of the bed. "I'm thinking you've earned a tantrum or two."

"What are you doing?"

He crouched and held the panties up near her feet. "I'm trying to help you get dressed so you can get downstairs and put that curiosity of yours to rest."

"Hmm." She stepped into them and marveled at the sight of him bent to his task, the big, unstoppable Jace Kennedy at her feet, humbly helping her dress. If it wasn't so heart-stoppingly sweet, she'd have overdosed on the power rush. "Well, you can't blame me for asking. You're usually trying to get me out of them."

The devil grinned up at her, shimmied the soft cotton up and over her hips, and cupped her ass, pulling her against him. "Keep talkin' that sass, sugar, and I'll take my dinner between your thighs." He smacked her butt and grabbed the tank top, maneuvering her into it and the rest of her clothes without another word.

"Zeke seemed angry I was here."

He paused in fastening the last button on her jeans then shook his head and finished. "Not with you, with me."

"Why?"

"Because we agreed Haven is safe ground. No one

but family comes here. Ever. And I didn't stop long enough to clue them in you fit that criteria." He laced her fingers in his and led her into the hallway. Cream walls and dark-stained trim lined either side. A thick, crimson runner stretched over distressed wood floors, soft as cotton beneath her bare feet. "Truth of the matter is, I broke that rule, too. We don't bring anyone into the family without a vote by the brotherhood."

"What's the brotherhood?"

He paused at the top of a grand staircase that had to be at least nine feet wide with wrought iron balusters and more of the bloodred carpet. He tucked a wayward strand of hair behind her ear, and graced her with a lopsided, but oh-so-tender smile. "You already know who they are. It started with me and Axel after an ugly deal went down with my mom. We made a vow we'd do whatever it took to get our moms out of the dirt. We hit the books at school, went from C's and D's to straight A's, then earned scholarships to college. I got another free ride to UNLV for law school. Along the way, we found other men like us, smart and willing, but stuck in a dead end. We invested time and money in them and helped them find their feet."

"But why so secret? What you're doing is a great thing."

"It might be great for us, but you gotta remember, we come from the streets. The way we do business, a whole lot of folks would frown on if they found out. So, we keep it close. Family only, especially here at Haven. It's the one place we never have to couch our words or pretend to be someone we're not." He grinned. "Kinda like your special room."

He started down the stairs, guiding her alongside him.

"When you say 'frowned on,'" she said, "are we talking illegal?"

He slanted her a sideways look and ambled toward the rumbling, masculine voices emanating from the end of the hall. "That all depends."

"On what?"

He paused just outside a huge arched stonework opening she'd have expected in an old English hunting lodge. A very polished and expensive hunting lodge. "There's what the brotherhood deems right and wrong, and what the law deems right and wrong. Sometimes the two meet and sometimes they don't, but we always go with the brotherhood's vote."

"That's a dangerous game, Jace."

"Life's dangerous. We don't do stupid shit, sugar. And I damn sure won't ever tangle you up in it, but I told you I'd be honest. Now you're getting that honesty."

He tried to tug her past the opening, but Viv dug in her heels and yanked him back. "I don't suppose you could give me an example of how big a gap we're talking when the law and the brotherhood's votes don't mix."

For long seconds, he stared at her, pensive. He edged in close enough his heat radiated along her bare arms and shoulders. "Yeah, I'll give you one. The bastard who shot you? There's legal justice and brotherhood justice, and you can pretty well count those sides will be extremely far apart."

"Jace—"

"That's enough for now." He pulled her beside him and wrapped his arm around her waist. "You let those questions simmer and we'll hit 'em harder later. Right now you need to meet the girls."

Before she could argue, the whole crew came into view—Trevor, Zeke and Axel, plus two other men she didn't recognize. Gathered round a granite-covered island that could easily seat ten and looked like it'd been imported straight out of a gentlemen's club, they turned to her and ceased all conversation.

Instinct screamed to turn tail and run hell-for-leather back to the bedroom. Maybe all the way back home. Pride put her back up instead. "Um. Hi."

"You know Trev, Zeke and Axel," Jace said. "Beckett's the muscle man near the fridge and Knox is our resident nerd."

Said nerd closed his laptop and flipped Jace the bird. "You're just pissed you didn't know me before you actually had to work your way through college." Knox stood and ambled toward her with his hand outstretched. If he was really as much of a geek as Jace indicated, he sure blew textbook descriptions out the window. His hair was only down to his chin, but it was dirty blond and tousled in a sexy *GQ* kind of way. One look at his gray eyes and anyone would know he'd give Einstein a run for his money. "I'm Knox Torren."

Viv shook his hand and tried not to pay too much attention to the other four stares aimed her direction. "Vivienne Moore." She glanced at Jace beside her. "But I'm guessing you already knew that."

"And then some," he said.

Jace smacked his brother on the shoulder. "Don't freak her out, asshole." He pulled Vivienne toward the huge guy with the crazy-big muscles and the closely cropped, dark brown hair. Ushering her in front of him, he motioned to the last of the brothers. "Beck, this is Viv."

Beckett dipped his head, slow and cautious, but didn't say a word. His loose tank and workout shorts put his impressive muscles on full display. The damp edges around his hairline and the sharp veins prominent at his forearms and shoulders made it clear the exercise gear wasn't just for show.

A Southern-sweet, but deadly firm feminine voice cracked across the room. "Beckett Tate, when a woman's introduced to you, you answer proper."

Viv spun toward the voice along with everyone else.

Two older women meandered in via a different entrance, one with long hair in an auburn hue that couldn't be natural, and the other with platinum hair almost as riotous as Viv's and well below her shoulders.

The redhead smirked and aimed for the kitchen.

The other aimed a well-honed mother-glare at Beckett. Her face was a classic oval shape that matched Jace's, but her coloring was the exact opposite, creamy skin, blue eyes and bright to Jace's dark.

"Yes, ma'am." Beckett shifted into Viv's line of sight and held out his hand. "I shouldn't have been so rude. Heard a lot about you from Jace. Nice to put a face to the name."

Viv shook the hand offered and plastered on the best smile she could with the woman's stare weighting her shoulders. "It's nice to meet you, too."

"Much better," the woman said. "Now, Jace, introduce us to your girl so we can eat."

A boyish grin she'd never seen Jace wear before crept into place as he led Vivienne forward. He motioned to the redhead washing her hands at the kitchen sink. "Viv, that's Sylvie McKee, Axel's mom."

Well, she should have put those two together on her

own. One solid gander at the twinkle in Sylvie's eyes and you couldn't help but catch the resemblance. Sylvie wiggled her fingers in a playful greeting and grinned the same ornery smile as Axel.

Viv had barely nodded her head in answer before Jace stopped her right in front of the blonde. "And this is my mother, Ninette."

TWENTY-ONE

JACE RESTED HIS arm along the back of Viv's chair and reclined in his own, tipping his beer up for another swig. Just under ten years he'd owned this property and not once had the dinner conversation been this uncomfortable. He toyed with a strand of Vivienne's hair, her posture about as unrelenting as the awkward tension in the room. They'd exhausted talk of weather and sports about halfway through the meal, and now his brothers seemed content to feed their faces while his mom and Sylvie made small talk with Viv.

"Man, I'm stuffed." Beck shoved his plate away and dropped against the back of his chair hard enough the legs scratched against the tile floors. "Sylvie, for a Scottish chick, you do good Texas."

"Bah, fried chicken's nothin' ta fish 'n' chips." Sylvie slid a nearly empty bowl of mashed potatoes Vivienne's direction. "Do ye want more potatoes, lass? Ye've hardly enough ta keep yer legs in a stiff wind."

Giving up on shoving her corn around on her plate, Viv set her fork down and wiped her mouth. "I think it's the medicine. I'm not very hungry."

"We'll knock it back a touch if the pain's tolerable," Zeke said. "You can take the stronger dose at night."

Viv smiled and nodded, but it lacked her normal conviction. If Jace could pry her head open, he'd probably find she had ten different escape plans charted by now.

Probably best he put them all out of their misery and got on with the pissed off elephant in the room. "Everyone done?"

Nods and varied grunts of agreement circled the table.

"Then let's rally." He stood and carried his and Viv's plate to the kitchen, the clicks and clanks of flatware and scooting chairs behind him saying his brothers weren't far behind.

One by one, they dutifully rinsed and loaded up the dishwasher while his mom oversaw the last odds and ends being carried to the kitchen.

Jace ambled back to Viv, doing her best to wipe down the table while keeping her shoulder stable. He wrapped an arm around her waist and pulled her back against his chest. "You don't have to do that," he said low enough only she could hear it.

"I don't like standing around and doing nothing."

More like there wasn't a snowball's chance in hell she'd show disrespect to his mother by not making an effort, which only went to show how well the two of them would get along. It might take a few hours of Ninette grilling Viv twenty ways to Sunday to get there, but they'd suit just fine in the end.

The men meandered toward the back staircase that led to the basement, but paused at the top.

"You coming?" Trevor said.

"Yeah." Jace turned Vivienne in his arms and lowered his voice. "Need to talk business with the guys. Just hang with the girls and relax, all right?"

Her volley back to him was just as quiet, but held a whole lot more heat. "You realize you introduced me to your mom with messy hair, barefoot and with no bra."

"You give my mom time to share and you'll figure out

none of those things mean shit to her." He kissed her forehead and slipped away, giving his mom a pointed look on his way to his brothers. "Take care of my girl for me."

"Mmm-hmm." Ninette sealed up a tub of leftovers and yanked open the refrigerator door. "Because we gentle creatures can't take care of ourselves." She winked to lighten the barb, but he took it how she meant it. *Butt the hell out and let me handle this the way I want.* As if any living being had a chance of telling Ninette Kennedy how to run her life.

With one last peek at Vivienne, he followed the guys down the hardwood steps to the basement. He might have put his penchant for dark woods and old-world decor to work in the rest of the house, but down here it was Man Cave 101. Stonework walls and dark wood ceiling beams were the only traces it even belonged in the same house. Aside from the two sixty-five-inch TVs mounted side by side on the far wall, the pool table, and the pinball machine, every piece of furniture came courtesy of one of the brother's pasts. Zeke's worn couch, Axel's haggard recliners and Trevor's milk crates holding up an oversize door he'd used as a coffee table back when Axel and Jace had first found him.

They filed around the first conference table Jace had bought right after he'd closed on his first club. The maple wood was scarred and didn't have a single matching chair around it, but it held some damned fine memories. He sat at the end seat he always took, Axel taking up the other. "Knox, you get anything on the tapes?"

"Got a shot of the shooter from the parking lot cameras. Definitely male. Might be good enough to get facial recognition somewhere else, but he did a good job covering up what he could. Hat, hoodie, glasses, bulky clothes, the whole bit. Shot out of the parking lot in a silver Taurus old enough my grandma's sewing machine could outrun it. No plates."

"Can't imagine that shot was for Viv," Trevor said. "If she hadn't sidestepped exactly when she did, that bullet would have nailed you square in the chest."

Axel plunked his beer to the tabletop. "Had to be Hugo. No one else pissed and ballsy enough to make that kind of move."

"I'm not buying it." Beck pushed the gray wool slipper chair he'd picked up at an auction far enough away he could prop his size fourteen Adidas on the edge. "Moreno might be pissed, but he's not an idiot. The kind of money he's losing ain't enough to risk a run-in with cops. If he wanted to hurt you, it wouldn't have been with a parking lot full of potential witnesses, either."

"What if he was trying to get to me by targeting Viv?" Jace said.

Beck laced his hands behind his head. "Makes more sense the shooter wanted you. And I still don't think the one pulling the shots was Moreno. Had to be someone else."

Zeke leaned in and planted his elbows on the table, those too shrewd eyes of his zeroed in on Jace. "Then Vivienne's safe and can go home."

"She's not going anywhere."

Every man stared him down. Trev, Beck and Knox managed neutral expressions, but Axel and Zeke both looked like they were up for one hell of a debate.

Axel rubbed his thumb through his beard. "What's to keep her here if there's no harm for the lass?"

Fuck. Of all his brothers, he'd expected Axel to back

his play. Not be the first to throw up an obstacle. "The only way she's leaving is if it's what she wants."

"We had an agreement," Beckett said. "No women at Haven without buy-in from the rest of us. This is our safe ground. Lots of information laying around for someone we're not all on board with. Hell, man. You heard what dinner was like. Everyone's afraid to talk for fear we'll let slip something we shouldn't."

"You're using Haven resources for her too," Knox said. "Using Misty for that shopping trip, background checks, security coverage—"

"Hookin' her up with our clients and havin' me run interference," Axel added.

Jace fisted his hand on the armrest. "You got a point to make, brother, then quit shimmying up to it and get it out there."

Axel shook his head. "Not one man in this room that's got a problem throwin' down for someone who's yours, but you haven't claimed her. Not with us."

The urge to fidget crawled up his spine, and he'd have given at least a grand for a decent Scotch and a toothpick. Admitting to Viv how he felt had been a no-brainer, an instinctive move he couldn't have avoided any more than he could stop breathing. But this...

Every man sat motionless, their easy posture belying the tension in their eyes. Accepting the risk Viv represented for him personally was one thing, but putting his brothers' lives and businesses in jeopardy was something else altogether. He didn't even know if Viv would stay. How would they look at him in days or weeks from now if she bolted after they lowered their guards?

They'd hold you up and keep you strong the way family should.

Clean as a freshly honed blade, the thought sheared straight to the heart of the matter. They'd cross that bridge when they got to it, and they'd do it together.

He met each man's gaze one at a time. "If you'd do these things for me, you do 'em for her." He ended with a nod to Axel, the one brother who'd been with him from the time he was three. "She's mine."

ON THE SCALE of most awkward moments, contributing to dinner cleanup with only one arm and two women she didn't know had to rank as one of Viv's top contenders. She swept the last of the table crumbs into the palm on her injured side, and bit back a curse at the stabbing pain in her shoulder.

"You ever spend time with Jace when he's in a foul mood?" Ninette said from behind the sink.

Vivienne shuffled to the trashcan and shook the crumbs free. "Once or twice. My sister in particular seems to prod his nasty side to the surface."

"Then you know it's not a side of him that's fun to be around. So, why don't you sit and keep me and Sylvie company instead of prodding that shoulder of yours. Rally shouldn't take too long tonight."

"I can't—"

"You take advantage a week or more from now and act like a princess, that's one thing, but no one's gonna think bad of you if you take care of yourself right now. For God's sake, you got shot. When else can you take a load off?"

Sylvie took the pan Ninette handed over to dry. "Childbirth, that's when. Ye ask me, any woman who cares for a child, born or adopted, needs at least three weeks' hazard pay per year."

The two women whooped and high-fived with an easy camaraderie that could only come from years in each other's presence.

Funny, Viv couldn't remember her mother ever hanging out with other women like that. Gossiping and meddling in other people's business when she shouldn't, yes. But any easy, lighthearted friendships? No.

Viv finished straightening the chairs around the huge table and eased into one along the side near the wall. "What's rally?"

Ninette's laughter died off. "My boy brings you out to Haven but doesn't share the business he and his brothers do down there?"

"I'm not sure I'm too clear on the whole Haven business either."

Ninette slanted a sideways look at Sylvie and dried her hands on a towel. "What has he told you?"

"I know it's special. Only family. You and Sylvie, and his brothers."

Ninette opened a side drawer from the built-in planner desk and pulled out a pack of cigarettes. She tapped one free and anchored it between her lips. "He tell you anything about how he grew up? How he got that nasty scar?"

If Viv could've curled up into an inconspicuous ball and just rolled into a dark corner, now would've been a fantastic time to do it. Between the slow throb in her shoulder and the after-haze of her pain meds, she was already maxed out on discomfort. Ninette's questions ratcheted things up to a level she wasn't prepared to handle. "I figured when he was ready to tell me he would."

"He was nine when he got it. Grew up overnight because of things I wished he'd never been exposed to. Though I gotta say, it made him a hell of a man. He knows what he wants, goes after it and does it with honor. Might not be the way other people would do it, or the way it's supposed to be done, but he does it all the same." She flicked an ash in the ashtray and blew out a slow stream of smoke. "What is he to you?"

"I'm sorry?"

"Jace. The boys say you're not the usual type he gravitates to. Say he's dancing to a different tune because of you."

A warm buzz fanned out beneath Viv's skin and her face went hot. "I can appreciate you worrying about your son, but I'm pretty sure he's fully grown and more than capable of figuring out who he wants to dance with and how."

Sylvie chuckled with the same devilish belly laugh Axel favored, even if it was on a much higher octave. She hung her dishtowel on the oven handle and sauntered toward the kitchen table. "Uptight or not, our girl's got a wee bit of fire underneath."

Viv straightened in her chair. "Uptight? You have no idea who I am or where I came from."

Just like Jace, Ninette cocked one perfectly arched eyebrow high and grinned as wicked as a cat after a canary appetizer. "Don't I?"

All the fight in her whooshed out as sure as she'd been whacked in the gut, and a sharp pinch started up at her temple to match the pain in her shoulder. "He told you?"

Ninette blew out a hard puff of smoke and her eyes twinkled. "Nope. Sylvie sweet-talked Knox."

She found this conversation funny? Viv could barely call up enough memories to smile about, let alone laugh.

"And just so you know," Ninette added, "Jace'll wreak havoc on Knox for spilling. So, unless you have a strong dislike for Knox, you might not want to share that tidbit."

"And Knox knows because…"

"He's the one who did the digging," Sylvie finished. "Always does. Either him or Beck."

Great. If Knox and the moms knew, then odds were good everyone did.

The table's smooth, matte finish filled her vision. The urge to run, bolt and bar herself inside her townhouse, or maybe even tuck tail and scurry back to Oklahoma, practically burned the soles of her feet. A lot of good that would do with a fuzzy head and no car, though.

Sylvie sidled up beside her, tilted Viv's face toward her with a grip on her chin, and cupped her cheek. The soft, gentle smile on the woman's face was the picture-perfect version Viv had imagined growing up, patient and attentive. "No one here without a past, lass." She stepped away and tapped Ninette on the shoulder as she headed to the big, arched exit. "I'm headed upstairs. Bring Viv if she's up for it. And some popcorn. I need a snack ta go with my Charlie Hunnam fix. But ye'd best find a way ta get our girl's foot off the gas before Jace gets back. Way she's lookin', we're bound ta end up a car short and Jace a loose cannon."

Our girl. It was the second time she'd used that expression, and Viv still couldn't figure out how to process it.

Ninette pulled another long drag from her cigarette and let it out slow. She propped her elbow on the kitchen table and rolled the pad of her thumb along one fingertip, not the least bit concerned how close the smoldering tip of her cigarette hovered near her perfect blond hair. "You gonna let loose with the questions? Or are you gonna keep poor Sylvie from her *Sons of Anarchy* fix?"

"What questions?"

"The ones burning behind those pretty gray eyes of yours."

Viv blinked and ducked her head. "A person's past should be up to the individual to share. They're just details without the context."

"Is that really what's bothering you? That we all know you grew up rough?"

Was it? Between her financial strain, Callie's spiraling behavior and getting shot, it was a wonder anything about her past even fazed her at this point. Sure, she wasn't proud of her past, but it was something she should have been given the opportunity to offer when she wanted. "Jace broke my trust the way he went about getting it. He could've asked."

"I told you, Jace sees what he wants and goes after it. Does whatever it takes to make it happen."

"At the expense of what's right?"

Ninette snuffed her cigarette in the crystal ashtray and huffed out a laugh. "Who defines what's right? Did he hurt you? Use what he learned against you? Have you even stopped long enough to consider why he did it?"

"He said they sweep any person's home that works close to them, but that he didn't want the men in my house."

"That's right. He could've handed the job off to someone who wouldn't have cared, but he didn't. There's not a single thing he learned that anyone holds against you." She leaned into the table, arms crossed across the top and studied Viv. "What Sylvie said is right. We don't judge. We don't have the room to." Her gaze slid to the side and a wry smirk twisted her lips before she looked back at Viv. "Jace was nine years old when he found out I was a prostitute. That was the same night he killed a man to keep a john from killing me."

Reality stopped. Even Viv's breath and heartbeat seemed to trip while her mind scrambled to process the full impact of Ninette's blunt statement. "I don't…" What could she say? Nowhere on her list of polite responses did she have anything close to adequate. "Nine?"

"Nine." Ninette shook her head and stared down at the table. "I didn't have protection. I figured it was better to play it safe with higher-end clients and not share my earnings with anyone. More money to sock away so Jace could have a good life. An education. One of those clients liked me a little too much and followed me home one night. Long story short, he got a little crazy and pulled a knife. Jace got it away, but earned those scars in the process. It ended with Jace burying that knife in the man's throat. I've tried for years to get him to spend some of the money he's earned to fix the scars, but he says it's a reminder—to protect the people he loves, and to remember where he came from."

She stood, taking the ashtray with her, and strolled back to the kitchen island. "Lots of different ways to move through this life. You gotta decide what kind of man you want with you on the way." She set the ashtray down and ambled toward the same exit Sylvie had taken. "The popcorn's in the pantry, middle shelf, but hurry up. Soon as those boys are out of rally, Jace'll sweep you back into isolation and you're bound to miss a great Hunnam butt shot."

TWENTY-TWO

BRIGHT LIGHTS DANCED behind Viv's eyelids and nudged her foggy mind up from sleep. Licking her parched lips, she lifted her head to get her bearings and flinched at the sharp reprimand from her shoulder. She braced for another tweak and forced the recliner's backrest up a little higher anyway.

Beside her, Ruger lifted his head, ears perked and ready for a command.

"Not yet, buddy. Give me a minute to reboot my brain and I'll smuggle you outside for a break."

He huffed and rested his head back on the makeshift bed Jace had made out of old blankets. She couldn't really blame him for being bored. As napping spots went, Jace's office had proven a dark and comfortable oasis when he'd first headed off to work on Monday, but after nearly two full days of nonstop sleeping, she was just about ready to swear off pain pills and solitude forever.

Oh, who was she kidding. She hadn't just been sleeping, she'd been hiding. No matter how much she wanted to tell herself otherwise, her conscience had been ramping up its internal lashings for the last twenty-four hours. She wasn't normally a wimp when it came to getting to know other people, but for some reason she just hadn't been able to force herself out of her pity party long enough to muster the courage to face Jace's mom again.

Mindful of her shoulder this time around, she shifted the soft chenille blanket to one side of the recliner, reached for the button to lower the power footrest, and froze.

She hadn't had a blanket when she'd fallen asleep. And her laptop was closed and plugged up to the charger across the room instead of in her lap where it had been the last she remembered.

Late-afternoon sun slanted through the barely cracked plantation shutters along the far wall, the dark chestnut stain reflecting the bold rays up onto the vaulted ceiling. Standing, she snatched her cell phone off Jace's massive desk.

4:14 p.m.

Jace had said he wouldn't be home until 5:30 or 6:00 at the earliest, but he'd said something similar the last two days and always ended up home early, both times loaded up with her favorite takeout and a ridiculous number of desserts.

Outside the window, Haven's picturesque entrance stretched at least the length of a football field. Even with the grass dulled to a soft winter brown, it could easily have graced a postcard, especially with the house's tall peaks, chocolate facing, and tumbled stonework. She still hadn't been able to decide if it was more of a rustic ranch style, or a mountain chateau. Maybe a little of both.

The wide circle drive sat empty and the only cars parked outside the main four-car garage were Sylvie and Ninette's.

So much for Jace coming home early. That meant either Sylvie or Ninette had been the one to cover her up, and didn't that make her feel like even more of an ass.

Well, enough was enough. Sure the *Sons of Anarchy* watching had been as comfortable as watching a love scene in front of your parents, but if they could show her kindness, the least she could do was crawl out of her cave and show some gratitude.

Smoothing her sleep-mangled hair into place as best she could with one hand, she motioned for Ruger to follow and meandered through the quiet house. It was always this way during the day, only hints of feminine voices or lilting laughter drifting up to the wing where Jace and Axel's suites were located. The scents were different, though. Like the first night she'd met Sylvie and Ninette, the air hinted at something cooking on the stove. Something spicy and rich that made her stomach send out a rumbling reminder that she hadn't had anything more than the bagels Jace had brought up this morning.

As soon as she reached the arched stone opening to the kitchen, Ruger galloped to Ninette and Sylvie paired up at the counter, leaned into Ninette's thigh, and waggled his whole backside in happy greeting.

"Well, hello, handsome." Ninette set the spoon she'd been using to stir beside the big pot on the stove and scratched the top of his head. "You need to go out?"

"I've got him."

Viv's presence was clearly unexpected, because both of them spun at once, jaws slack and eyebrows high.

"It's good ta see ya up and around, lass." Sylvie set her chef's knife aside and snatched a towel off the counter. "Do ye need something?"

A swift kick in the booty most likely. Now that she was standing here, both women aiming patient gazes her direction, she felt twice the fool as before. She cleared her throat and dragged her courage up from the mental swamp she'd wallowed in. "I think what I need most is to lay off the pain pills and reconnect with the real world for a while."

Ninette leaned one hip against the counter and smiled. "Well, if you want to reconnect, then you picked the right night to do it. The boys are all due here by six tonight for family night."

Ruger padded to the sliding glass door that led out to the ranch's vast acreage and let out a pathetic wine.

Vivienne hurried to let him out. "Family night?"

Turning back to the counter, Sylvie lined up a halved onion and attacked it like a veteran sous chef. "Ye know. Dinner. Fun. Relaxing. The usual things families do when they get together."

No, she didn't have a clue. About the only times her family ate together were holidays, and that was more of a well-orchestrated miracle where dinner was ready at the same time and everyone was under the same roof. "It sounds nice."

Something in Ninette's expression shifted, a spark of cognition that left Viv wanting to fidget. The look was gone just as fast, smoothed over with the same determination she'd glanced on Jace's face countless times since she'd met him. Knowledge gained one second, and a plan lined out in the next. She motioned to the massive kitchen table nestled in front of the equally sizable picture window. "Why don't you have a seat and keep us company while we cook."

It was tempting. Seated at the table, she'd be able to keep some distance and not have to address the nagging thoughts that had plagued her for the last few days. "Actually, I'd like to help if I can. I'm not the fanciest cook in the world, but I can pull off the basics."

"How are ye with sweets?" Sylvia said.

"I inhale them so fast my conscience can barely get a word in edgewise."

Both women chuckled, but Sylvie set aside her work to gather up some ingredients in the pantry. "If ye can work from a recipe, I'm runnin' behind on desserts. Since we're leanin' toward junk food for the main course, I thought we'd keep it simple and do sugar cookies to finish. No point in puttin' anything fancy in our gullets after a schoolroom cafeteria entree."

Viv meandered closer and peeked in the big pot. Nearly browned ground beef simmered in the bottom. To the right of the stove was a huge can of tomato sauce and three different types of seasonings. "Chili?"

"That's part of it," Ninette said. "It was Knox's turn to pick dinner and he's stuck on childhood favorites. So tonight it's conies and Frito Chili Pie."

"Really?" Her stomach rumbled its approval and her mouth watered. "I haven't had Frito Chili Pie in…well, since middle school."

"Exactly." Sylvie bustled to the kitchen island, her arms loaded up with everything from sugar to a bottle of vanilla big enough to be stocked in a professional bakery. "At least we're not eating fish sticks again. Sometimes I think the lad is just tryin' to yank our chains and see how far he can push us."

Ingredients unloaded, she plucked a thick three-ring binder from a shelf built into the end of the island and thumbed through the pages. Every entry was handwritten in neat cursive on pages that ranged from pristine white to aged yellow. "Here we go." She spun the binder around and pointed to the recipe on the right. "That's me ma's recipe. Easy as pie and perfect every time."

And that was it. No more than five minutes since she'd been in the room and they'd accepted her as easily as they had the first night they'd met. No questions or judgments as to why she'd kept her distance, only open acceptance. One small hurdle over and one much more sensitive one to go.

The next half hour moved at an easy pace, both Sylvie and Ninette peppering her with light questions about her business and the corporate jobs she'd had after junior college. Oddly, she hadn't had to ask a thing. In addition to their own queries, they'd offered up a few funny stories about Jace and Axel growing up together, the funniest one surrounding a pinch on a convenience store gone bad.

"Swear to Christ, I dinnae know what the two o' them were thinkin'," Sylvie said, her eyes full of tears from laughter. "They truly thought they'd pulled off some dastardly heist, only to learn they'd be earnin' service time at a homeless shelter for the grand sum of five dollars' worth of bubble gum."

Vivienne smiled, spooned out another dollop of dough, and dropped it on the greased cookie sheet. "How old were they?"

"Seven." Ninette laid out the hot dog buns on her own cookie sheet in preparation for the warming drawer under the oven. "Sylvie and I were at a hair salon next door and the two of them refused to wait inside with us. At the time, Jace swore they had a plan to resell the gum at school and pay the store manager back with interest, but the truth of it was, they didn't know a dollar from a fiver back then."

Yeah, that sounded like Jace, especially the paying back part. On the surface he might look dangerous, but if there was one thing she'd learned about him in the last several weeks, he had the honor of an old-world knight.

Sylvie turned off the water, settled her washed chopping block in the drying rack, and wiped her hands on a faded green kitchen towel. "I need ta run up and change before the boys get here. Vivienne, do you need anything?"

Her nerves perked up and bristled on a fresh wave of adrenaline. The last time she'd been alone with Ninette she'd had a hard-core dose of reality dropped over her head. Still, better to tackle the challenge she'd set for herself one-on-one than with an audience. "No, I'm good. Thank you."

With a sweet smile and a saucy wink, she hustled out of the kitchen, leaving Viv alone with Ninette and her swirling thoughts.

The timer for the top oven pinged and Viv grabbed the oven mitt off the counter beside it.

"Here, let me get the top one." Ninette bustled up beside her and held out her hand for the glove. "Jace would rail me up one side and down the other if you got hurt on my watch."

Vivienne handed the mitt over and picked up the tray she'd just finished lining with fresh dough. As soon as Ninette had the baked cookies on the cooling rack, Viv slid the fresh tray in with her good arm. She set the timer for eight minutes, paused for a second to bolster her courage, and turned. "What you have here is really special."

Ninette stopped wiping down the counter around

the stove top and twisted enough to meet Viv's gaze. "Come again?"

"Jace. Haven. Your family. All the brothers. It's special."

Her face softened. "It is special. Took us to hell and back a few times to get here, but I wouldn't trade a minute of it."

Vivienne hugged her arm tight to her side, her wound throbbing as fast and furious as her labored heart. "My life wasn't anywhere near as rough as yours. I was never hungry. I never faced the realities Jace did, and my parents never sacrificed for me or Callie like you did for him, but seeing all of you together, I think I'd choose your world over mine."

For several seconds, Ninette didn't move. Just studied her with a scrutiny Viv felt clear to her toes. Her face softened and she tossed the sponge into the sink. "All kinds of rough in this world, sweetheart. Rough in the real world or rough in the heart, it's all hard on the soul." She padded closer and carefully wrapped Vivienne up in a hug. "When I said we didn't judge, that included feelings, too. They are what they are. The trick is owning them so you can move on and find your happy."

Viv's breath hitched. She circled her good arm around Ninette's waist, the movement as shaky and uncertain as the fragile hope fluttering beneath her skin. Countless times she'd craved such a connection from her own mother. A simple touch. A kind word. But it was Ninette who'd given it to her. A woman who'd faced real harshness in her life and still found it in her to share comfort and compassion.

The sliding glass door whooshed open and Ruger

galloped into the room, his nails clicking against the tumbled marble floors.

Axel ambled in right behind him, his playful bellow resounding through the kitchen. "Someone start pouring the whisky. The menfolk have arrived."

Ninette relinquished her hold on Vivienne and patted her good shoulder, but not before Jace spied them from the entrance. Without missing a beat, she slid in between Vivienne and the men and opened her arms, demanding her greeting without a word and buying Viv precious time to gather her wits.

Axel tugged Ninette in for a sound smack on the cheek, then laid a far more tender one to Vivienne's temple. "I see someone's found her feet again. Good to see you up and around, lass."

Vivienne grinned and sidled back up to the island and the cookie mess she'd left behind. "Being lazy for a day or two was nice, but a girl can only take so much."

Jace followed Axel's pattern almost identically, wrapping his mom up in a bear hug and gifting her with a kiss on the cheek as well. "Everything okay in here?"

"Perfect." Ninette cupped Jace's cheek the same way she probably had when he was little then sashayed back to her cleanup job near the sink. "I was just thanking Vivienne for assuring me my new jeans, in fact, did not make my ass look fat. Which is a good thing considering what's on tonight's menu."

Axel pulled a bottle of Scotch from the built-in bar and scoffed. "Like every one of us haven't told you the same, but you never hug us for it."

"That's because when a man says it, he's avoiding trouble. When a woman says it, it counts double." She turned enough to catch Viv's eye and gave a conspiratorial wink.

Jace slid in behind Viv, wrapped her up at the waist and nuzzled her neck, inhaling in that sexy way that always gave her goose bumps. "How you feelin', sugar?"

Sweet champagne-bubble tingles danced low in her belly, their effervescence so powerful she could have floated to the ceiling had it not been for his anchoring presence. "I'm good," she muttered, though how she managed even a modicum of volume was an utter miracle.

"Yeah?" He swept her hair away from her neck and nipped her earlobe. "You gonna turn around and give me a welcome home kiss, or do I have to take it?"

Her lips tingled and her cheeks fired hot, her senses all too aware of the other people in the room and their polite attempts to ignore the PDA via polite chit-chat. "I don't think that's a good idea."

"Been thinking all day about the sweet woman I left curled up in my bed at 6:00 a.m. You ask me, I think it's a damned fine idea."

She gripped his wrists and squeezed, trying unsuccessfully to fight the shiver that shuttled down her spine. "But your mom," she whispered.

Jace froze, only the tickle of his beard and his warm breath stirring against her. His voice resonated low and steely. "Turn around, Viv."

Behind her, Ninette prattled on about some new escapade between her and Sylvie at the mall, but Vivienne would swear she felt Axel's gaze aimed directly on her and Jace. In that second, she didn't care. Couldn't. For three days she'd stolen nothing more than soft kisses and gentle touches from Jace. She could have no more ignored his command in that moment than an addict in withdrawal could have walked away from a token fix.

She turned and lifted her gaze to his, the impact of his enigmatic dark eyes sending shockwaves straight to her core.

"You want to kiss me?"

She licked her suddenly parched lips. "Yes."

"You're mine. You're in my home. Surrounded by family. Safe." His thumbs shuttled along the sensitive space just above her hip bones, the contact as powerful as skin-to-skin even through the soft cotton of her pajama bottoms. "Take what you want."

No judgment. No rules. Ninette had promised her as much, the same as Jace. Mustering her courage, she rolled up on her toes and pressed her lips to his.

He groaned and palmed the back of her head, the perfect mesh of their mouths void of the heated sensuality they'd shared before the shooting, but wrought with awe and emotion in its simplicity.

Too fast, he pulled away only enough to meet her eyes. Pride blazed bright in his gaze, radiating through her in a pleasant hum. "Wasn't so hard, was it?"

Maybe not for him. She'd barely shared school progress or friendly gossip in front of her parents growing up, let alone kiss someone in their presence. As fast as her heart thrummed, she may as well have streaked through Times Square. "More than you know."

He smirked and kissed her forehead. "It'll get easier."

He'd just turned and tucked her into the crook of his arm, his mouth opening to speak when Sylvie bustled into the room. "What did I miss?"

Axel grinned and saluted Jace with his Scotch.

"Someone's gettin' a much finer welcome home than the rest of us, that's what."

"Jealous?" Not waiting for a response, Jace shuttled his attention to Ninette. "What's for dinner?"

Ninette frowned and lifted the lid on the pot full of simmering chili. "It was Knox's choice tonight."

"Christ," Axel grumbled. "Knox's taste in food is as bad as his wardrobe."

"Hey, I heard that." Knox and Beckett strolled through the stone archway coming from the house's main entrance, Knox in a similar getup to the first night she'd met him, only tonight's graphic tee sporting the Avengers instead of some smart-ass comment. "And don't knock the tees. Chicks love my wit."

Beckett made his way from Sylvie to Ninette, kissing each of their cheeks the same way Jace and Axel had upon entering. "What I overhead heard last night, it wasn't your wit she was begging for."

Ninette scoffed and went back to stirring the chili, not the least bit put off by Beckett's suggestive comment.

Beckett sauntered her direction. "Hey, Viv."

She tried to take a step back, but with Jace snuggled up tight beside her, couldn't gain any leverage.

Beckett swooped down and mirrored the kiss-to-cheek routine with her. "You feeling better?"

She blinked. Then did it again, and again, waiting for reality to come back into focus. No matter how many times she repeated the process, the move still registered the same in her memory. "Um….yes. Thank you."

He shot her one of those *man, girls are weird* grins, shook his head, and moseyed to the counter with the still cooling cookies. "Axel did you see these? Dinner's not a total loss. Sylvie made cookies."

Sylvie glanced up from the pulling the hot dog buns out of the warming drawer. "Not me, lad. Vivienne made those."

Beckett's expression blanked. His gaze shot to Viv, then up to Jace, and he shook his head. "She's hot and she bakes. You're fucking lucky."

Snickering, Knox hefted a towering stack of plates from Sylvie and headed for the dining room. "Quit sucking up and help me set the table."

In a blink, it was over, the ebb and flow of everyone moving around the kitchen, making drinks and carting things to the table, washing away her fears and breathing new hope into her soul. She peeked up at Jace behind her. "What just happened?"

He chuckled, pulled her into his arms and kissed the top of her head. "Beck's more of a doer than a talker. I'd say you just got his nonverbal version of *welcome to the family.*"

A tug issued behind her chest, a foreign but pleasant sensation that left her out of sorts and flailing for solid mental ground.

"Vivienne, get a move on," Ninette urged from behind her. "You don't get a chair and a plate loaded up before the boys do, you'll end up with only a handful of Fritos and a spoonful of chili."

"She's got that right." Jace guided her toward the dining room with a hand low on her back. "Rule one of big families. Every man for himself at chow time."

The next hour shuttled past in a happy blur. Zeke and Trevor's arrival, passing plates and trading small talk. By the time her plate was half empty, she was gorged on more than food. The sheer energy bouncing between those gathered around the table was enough to fuel her spirits for months. Just watching them was a revelation. A completely different experience than what she'd had that first night. Zeke and Knox constantly traded playful barbs and neither seemed comfortable with sitting still. More reserved with their words, Trevor and Beckett stuck to sports commentary and new business ideas, while Axel and Jace coached and critiqued the concepts offered.

And Sylvie and Ninette silently lorded over it all, their wise gazes soaking up each moment with smiles that spoke of years rich with memories.

Jace wiped his mouth and tossed his napkin to the side of his plate. "All right, whose pick is it tonight?"

"Mine." Ninette reclined back in her chair and sipped her tea.

Vivienne leaned closed to Jace and whispered, "Pick for what?"

He beamed and twirled the toothpick he'd stuck between his lips with his tongue. "Game night. Every Wednesday we eat and we play. Everyone gets a turn picking, one for food and one for the game."

Trevor inched his chair away from the table and rubbed his stomach. "Thank God, I'm up next week. Between Knox's junk food this week and Sylvie's cranachan last week, I'm gonna be dead before I'm fifty."

Zeke planted his elbows on the table and rubbed his hands together. "What am I beating you at tonight, *mamãe*?"

She mock scowled at him, the barest smile lifting the corners of her mouth. "Genius IQ or not, I can still take you in whatever I pick, Zeke Dugan."

"Hey." Knox dropped his hands to his hips and frowned. "I'm the genius, he's just good with textbooks."

"And blood and guts," Axel added. "Let's not forget the good parts."

Jesus, they were all insane. Gloriously and perfectly insane. She'd never been more entertained in her life.

On Ninette's other side, Beckett nudged her with his elbow. "You pick poker, I'll help you team up against him. We'll take him down in thirty minutes."

"God, not that," Zeke said. "I can't sit still that long."

She narrowed her eyes at him, scanned the rest of the table, and cocked her head when she got to Viv. "You ever play Monopoly?"

Everything inside her froze, the happy buzz beneath her skin going ice-cold in a second. "Um…" She swallowed and peeked at Jace.

He stared down at her, his patient demeanor as rock solid as the granite tabletop.

You're in my home. Surrounded by family. Safe.

Keeping the arm on her injured side cradled close to her side, she shifted enough to lean into Jace, splayed her hand on his thigh, and focused on Ninette. "We never had game night at my house." Well, her dad had a time or two, but those playing had been reserved for his friends, and had centered more on whisky than cards.

"You've never played Monopoly?" Knox sagged against his seat back, clearly stunned. "How's that possible?"

Axel chuckled and shuttled his gaze to hers. "Wouldn't matter if you'd played before or not. Not the way we play it. Brotherhood rules only."

Jace dropped the arm he'd stretched out on the back

of her chair to her shoulders. His warmth cocooned and encouraged her, fanning the blossoming comfort his family had built throughout dinner. "You up for it, or you want to rest?"

The out he offered was tempting. A chance to hide, recalibrate and process everything she'd seen and felt.

Jace's thumb shuttled back and forth against her skin, a silent comfort in the face of her rioting emotions.

It was just game night. She didn't have to make anything more of it than that. Could keep the concept of family tucked tight in the corner of her mind and view it as a fun chance to get to know new people. Nothing more, nothing less. She drew in a steadying breath and forced a brave smile. "If you're willing to teach me, I'm willing to give it a try."

His mom was a genius. Jace didn't have a clue what had spurred her to pick Monopoly tonight of all nights, but he had a pretty damned good idea it centered on whatever he and Axel had walked in on after work. It had to have been at least two years since they'd whipped out any of their collector editions and, even then, playing the game was reserved for the holidays, but here they were, gathered round their oversized poker table and battling it out Godfather-style.

And Viv was riveted. Or at least she had been for the first few hours. In the last thirty minutes, her eyes had grown weighted and her carriage a little less rigid than when they'd settled in and started fighting over who got which player tokens. She wasn't giving up though. Hell, if anything her competitive streak was the main thing keeping her upright.

She snatched the dice off the game board and eyeballed the long stretch of nastiness ahead of her. One thing about Axel and his properties—he did *not* fuck around. If Viv didn't roll a nine or better she'd have to start selling shit off, and Jace had a pretty damned good idea that wouldn't sit too well with his Little Miss.

She shook the dice and prepared to roll.

Knox held up his hand. "Hold up."

Axel growled and leaned into the table, his accent a little thicker from all the Scotch and time spent around his mom. "Ignore the bloody dobber, Viv. Roll the dice."

Sylvie backhanded him in the shoulder. "Haud yer wheesht. The man's got a proposition for the lass."

Knox grinned at Viv, pinched his fingers together, and waggled them in front of his face. "I'mma gonna make you an offer you can't refuse."

Zeke perked up from the opposite side of the table, an appalled expression on his face. "Was that supposed to be a Sicilian accent?"

"I don't know," Beckett said as he counted his stash, "but I'm pretty sure Marlon Brando just rolled over in his grave."

Trevor chuckled and slunk down farther in his chair.

Knox frowned, flipped Zeke the bird, and shifted his attention back to Viv. "As I was saying…how about we make a deal."

Viv cocked her head. "What kind of deal?"

"You pay me protection and if you land on any of Axel's properties I'll cover the rent."

She scowled down at the board, scanned her neatly lined up money and pursed her lips. "Why?"

"Well, for starters, you're cute. I'm also a sucker for gray eyes, and your cookies don't suck."

Confusion pinched her face. "You're just doing it to be nice?"

"More like I'm betting you make it past Axel squeaky clean and pay me for nothing." He shrugged and leaned back in his chair. "Two hundred every time you go around the board. It's a win/win."

Hell yeah, it was. It was also one of the best avoidance answers he'd ever heard out of Knox because, at this point, if Viv hit *anyone's* property she was toast. Knox didn't give a shit about anything except not seeing a pretty girl lose, and damned if he didn't love his brother more than ever in that moment.

For a second, Viv got scary still and her mouth pressed together hard like she was reining in some serious shit. She got it together quick though and nodded her head. "Okay." She swallowed big, set the die aside and dug out two-hundred bucks. "Deal. You get my payday every time I pass go."

He took the money and waggled his eyebrows. "Pleasure doing business with you."

"Oh, up yer arse wi' it," Axel groused. "Yer just suckin' up ta Viv while ye can. Wait 'til she's back in the office and we'll see which of us she likes better."

Oh, yeah. He totally loved his brothers right now. Every fucking one of them.

Knox took his turn next and a five-minute barter session between him and Trevor ensued.

Vivienne scooted her seat back and stood, drawing all negotiations and side-chatter to a standstill. "Sorry." She ducked her head and stepped around her chair. Her voice when she spoke again cracked just the slightest bit. "Don't stop for me. I just need a quick break." She hurried from the room, angling for the main hallway instead of the half bath off the entertainment room.

Jace was on his feet before she'd disappeared from sight. "Mom, watch my money."

Ninette wiggled her fingers like she couldn't wait to do a little creative accounting. "With pleasure."

He glanced back at her on his way out long enough to hit her with a mock warning. "Just remember. If you spend too much of it, I won't have any to bail your ass out."

"Yeah, yeah." She shooed him out of the room. "Go check on your girl. I've got this."

The hallway stretched shadowed and quiet in front of him, only the muted laughter of his family and the faint strains of some bluesy country crooner drifting from the entertainment room behind him. The door to his suite stood open and the only light to guide his feet emanated from the closed bathroom door on the far side of the room. He rapped a knuckle against the door. "Viv?"

"Yeah, I'll be out in a minute."

Like hell she would. He might have suspected a crack in her voice before, but there was no missing the quaver threaded through the overdone chipper response. He eased the door open.

Braced with her good hand on the vanity and the other tucked tight against her waist, Viv stood with her head hung so her hair covered her face. Despite her attempts to hold it in, her shoulders shook with silent sobs.

He moved in behind her and slid his arms around her waist. "Which part was it that got you? The fact that he was looking out for you, or the fact that he tried to do it gentle?"

She huffed out a ragged half laugh, half whimper and dashed one hand against her cheek. "It wasn't just him. I mean, he was sweet. Charming. But so was Beckett. And Trevor. All of them."

He buried his face in her neck, pulled in her scent and savored the moment. The quiet sincerity of her words. "Turn around, sugar."

She sniffed, wiped her other cheek, and slowly did as he asked.

God, she was beautiful. Even with tearstained cheeks and lashes spiked with wetness, her gray eyes roiled with the beauty of a distant summer storm. "Tonight meant something to you."

"No." Another tear slipped free. "It meant everything. I've never had that. Not once. Friends yes, but not a family. I don't care if I never have another night like it as long as I live, tonight's been perfect."

He wiped the tear away and cupped the side of her face. She might not have grasped the full concept yet, but they'd cracked the door. Shown her a glimpse of what their life could be like. Would be like, once she finally let down her guard. "It won't be the last, sugar. That much I promise." He tucked her hair behind one ear. "Now, you wanna call it a night and get some rest, or do you want to head back out and let everyone know you're all right?"

"You think they know I lost it?"

Hell, yeah, they knew she'd lost it, but he wasn't about to point that out. Not yet, anyway. "What difference does it make? I keep tellin' you, we'll take you like you are. Snivels, cackles and any four-letter word you dare to try. Doesn't matter if you crawl out of bed with your panties in a twist and a wicked case of PMS, no one here's going to hang you for it. Might give you a wide berth for a day or two, but we'll still be here when shit evens out."

She peeked up from under her wet lashes and pouted in a way that said she had a hard time buying it. "Can we wait a few minutes until my eyes aren't red?"

He grinned at that, gripped her hips, and backed her against the vanity. "I'll do you one better. I'll kiss you until your eyes are heavy and your lips are swollen. Then they'll spend more time chuckling about what we've been up to instead of why you left in the first place. That work for you?"

Her giggle was sweet, still tinged with the aftermath of her crying jag, but free of the weight from before. She smoothed her hand above his sternum and cocked her head in a playful slant that came off twice as sexy with her vulnerability still on full display. "Yeah. I think that works for me just fine."

TWENTY-THREE

THE LAST OF Jace's brothers disappeared down Haven's long, winding drive, leaving only him, Viv and the quiet acreage to do what he had to do. Viv's little hybrid sat shiny and ready for action next to his Chevy in the circle drive, and her key lay anchor-heavy in his palm.

One week he'd had her safe and mostly to himself. Seven days to build a bond and show her how perfect she fit with his brothers and the girls. With him. But after Beck and Knox's assessment at rally today, he couldn't dodge reality anymore. Viv was safe and it was time to let her choose.

He pushed off the porch's cedar pillar and stuffed Viv's keys in his pocket. He'd give his mom and Sylvie props. As soon as they'd heard Viv had the all clear, they'd both bailed on a sudden and dire need for mani/pedis and an impromptu run for the grocery store.

Stalking into the house, he flipped off the TV Sylvie had left on in the entertainment room and headed to his study off his suite. The door stood ajar with one of the Star Wars reruns tuned low and filtering out into the hallway. He eased inside and shut the door behind him.

Viv glanced up from her laptop, checked her phone and dove back into her work, scowling at the screen. "You guys done already?"

Classic Vivienne concentration, a single-minded focus he'd learned was more the norm than the exception. Huge assignments that would stagger most people, she'd break down into manageable chunks the way a sous chef tackled dinner prep for an army. "Agenda was short today."

"No dastardly plans for world domination?"

"That's next week. This week's reserved for bunko and a knitting bee." His smart-assed quip earned him a wry pucker and saucy glare, but at least it got the scowl off her face. He moseyed around the desk, pulled her from the chair and took her place, pulling her into his lap. "You want to tell me why you're glaring daggers at the screen?"

"I can't get the banner layouts right." She swiped the touch pad and fiddled with the highlighted text.

The crimson background and fun lettering looked fine to him, although it was about the last style he'd have expected her to use. "What do you want them to look like?"

She motioned close to the screen, sectioning it out with two fingers. "You're supposed to make sure there's balance between the objects, and that the message can be assimilated quickly."

"Sugar, I asked what you wanted it to look like. Not what it's supposed to look like."

"Hmm." She furrowed her brow, cocked her head a bit and started shifting the elements.

Chuckling at her cautious response, he tugged her away from the keyboard and twisted her on his lap so her legs dangled over the arm. "Sweetheart, the only thing lacking with any of your work is *you*. You've got spunk. Let it out and follow what comes natural. Besides, it's five hundred bikers and their Harleys. I promise, we'll be more interested in a good time than ad flow."

"Well, there is that." She dropped her head on his shoulder and fiddled with his Haven tags. The pricey platinum pendants were a crazy idea Axel had come up with shortly after they'd pulled Zeke and Trevor into the group. Ever since, every one of the guys wore theirs come hell or high water. For some reason, Viv seemed fascinated by them, so he'd started wearing them on top of his shirt instead of beneath. Though most of the time when she touched them, she didn't look quite so distracted.

"Something wrong?"

Shaking her head, she sat up and checked her phone again. "Not really. I just haven't heard from Callie. It's been over a week."

"Considering the state she was in last time she called, I'd say that's a plus."

She shoved the phone back on the desk and nestled back against his chest. "What if something's wrong?"

The easiness that had developed between them in the last week was the best part of her being here. More often than not, she seemed to curl into him on instinct, so much trust and openness in the action it was a wonder he left the house at all. "Sugar, this thing between you and Callie's gotta stop. If you don't, one of you is going to end up hurt. Best rule of thumb in something like this—if nothing changes, nothing changes."

"How am I supposed to stop it?"

"The part you stop is yours. The rest is up to her. You can't fix this for her, Viv."

She huffed out a tired exhale and splayed her hand above his heart.

Damn, he hoped she didn't leave. Not now. Not when she'd finally started letting him in. But giving her the choice was the right thing to do.

He kissed the top of her head and covered her hand with his, giving it a gentle squeeze. "We need to talk."

Viv froze, tension gripping her for several seconds before she jerkily pushed upright. "Sure. Whatever."

Something in her tone knocked him sideways and put him on alert, her aloof and shuttered response shoving his original topic to the back of his mind. "Something else going on besides you worrying about your sister?"

"Not a worry, no."

"But there's something on your mind."

She shrugged as much as she could with her wounded shoulder just starting to mend. "More preparing than anything."

"For what?"

She stood, turned to face him, and leaned her ass against the desk, fisting her hands around the edge. "The talk."

How the hell could she know what the guys had decided? Hell, he'd just barely committed to telling her himself. "Not sure I follow."

"You rethinking things between us. You've been really good to me this week, and I know you feel bad about me getting hurt, but it's probably better if we face things head-on."

His thoughts sputtered, stalled out altogether, then lurched forward. "Let me see if I've got this right. You think I want to talk to you about us not being an us?"

"Usually, that's what comes after 'We need to talk.' And I don't blame you. I really don't—"

"'We need to talk' cues you straight into thinking I'm walking away from you?"

"Well, not just that, but everyone knows—"

"What else?"

"Huh?"

"What else made you think I was leading up to 'the talk'?"

She ducked her chin and studied the carpet, her face turning a pretty shade of pink. "You haven't... I mean, we've kissed but nothing else."

"Are we talking about sex?"

An answer might not have slipped past her lips, but the hard line of her mouth said plenty.

Un-fucking-believable. If the surprise turn in topics wasn't so damned frustrating and his bloodstream so amped up on adrenaline, he'd have laughed.

He gripped her hips and pulled her closer, centering her between his knees. "Only reason I haven't stripped you down and buried myself between your thighs, sugar, is because you earned a bullet stepping between me and a man with a gun. I might be a gruff, uncouth son of a bitch, but I'd never put my needs over yours. Not like that. It most certainly does *not* mean we're done."

Her gaze snapped back to his. "I thought..." She blinked a few times and tightened her grip on his shoulders. "I guess I thought you were losing interest and were waiting to let me down easy."

God, she was cute when she got flustered. Jumpy and tentative, but sweet and innocent. He stood, sucked in a calming breath and dragged a thumb along her cheekbone. "Sugar, my dick's had a perpetual semi since I set eyes on you and gets rock hard and ready for business if you so much as lick your lip. Trust me, I'd lock your ass up and work you over for hours if I thought your body was ready for it."

"Oh."

"Yeah. Oh." He cupped her face on each side and got up good and close. "Meant every word I said the night I brought you here, Viv. Whatever this is between us, I want more, and I'll kick down whatever hurdles stand between us to get it. Me giving you time to heal doesn't mean I don't want to fuck you until you scream."

Her lips parted on a tiny gasp.

"Now, any other jacked ideas you got cooking in that head of yours?"

She rolled her lower lip inward and nibbled on the edge. "Maybe."

Maybe? Really? He'd have to find more ways to keep those damned hamsters of hers occupied going forward. "Let's hear 'em."

She shook her head. "I don't want to talk about it right now."

"Oh, we're gonna talk about it." He picked her up and plunked her ass on the desk. "Spill it. Now."

That did it. She straightened up and hit him with a solid scowl. "Fine. The night you brought me here, you said you were holding back with me. That you were afraid you'd scare me off. Well, just so you know, I'm not a prude. I can take whatever you dish out, in or out of bed."

Son of a bitch. Viv pissed off was sexy as hell, but all that attitude paired with her throwing down on sex was a wet dream. The blood rushed to his dick so fast it was a wonder he didn't pass out on the spot. "Never said you were a prude, sugar. I said I was afraid to go too fast and dirty for fear I'd run you off."

"Well, maybe I want fast and dirty."

"Yeah?"

"Yeah."

He snatched her hand and pressed it over his raging erection. "You feel that?"

Oh, yeah. She felt it, whether she wanted to admit it or not. In the space of two seconds, all the fire she'd aimed at him shifted to full-on hunger, her lips loosening and her breath sawing in and out.

"That's what you do to me, sweetheart. Doesn't matter if you want slow and easy or fast and dirty. If you want it, you tell me and I'll deliver. What you *don't* do is get up in that head of yours or beat around the damned bush."

She gently squeezed his length through the denim, her eyes never straying from the bulge beneath her palm.

"You hear me?" he said.

Licking her lower lip, she lifted her gaze and stroked him tip to root. "Yeah."

He ground his cock into her touch, the noble and entirely unwanted task of giving her the choice to leave falling further and further on the priority list. Hell, right now the only priority he had was seeing how far his Little Miss was willing to fan the fire she'd started. His voice dropped an octave. "You need your man to give it to you?"

The air around them hung thick and heavy as an August night in Texas.

Viv nodded, slow and trance-like.

"Tell me how you want it, sugar."

Her voiced trembled, so quiet he barely heard it. "Dirty."

His cock jerked behind his jeans and the slow ache in his balls ramped to insistent need. Another hundred years on the planet and the worst case of dementia couldn't shake the memory she'd just given him. One perfect, carnal word spoken from those plump, pink lips. If Hugh Hefner could capture it with a camera, he'd increase his fortune tenfold. "How's your shoulder?"

"Zeke says I start physical therapy next week."

He slid her off the desk and pressed his raging cock against her soft belly. "I'd say that's a clean enough bill of health to give my girl what she wants." He dragged his thumb along her lower lip until they parted. He slipped it inside and she wrapped her mouth around it, her teeth gently scraping the edge.

"That right there." He pulled his thumb free and slicked the moisture along her mouth. "Want to see that sweet tongue of yours on my dick. Your pretty lips stretched around my cock."

"You didn't let me before."

"Because I was so damned close to coming, I'd have never made it." He aimed a pointed look at the floor between them. "Not going to stop you now, though."

Damned if the little minx didn't purse her mouth in a way that promised all kinds of innocent trouble. She held his stare and eased to her knees.

"Ah, Viv…" His voice wavered and his lungs emptied on a shaken hiss. Countless times he'd imagined seeing her like this, and in every scenario he'd been the one in control, the one guiding and coaxing her forward. Now reality was here and all he could do was burn in the hesitant power radiating off her.

She worked the buttons on his jeans and shimmied them and his briefs past his hips enough to free him. His cock jutted heavy and ready just inches from her lips. She traced her finger along one vein then gently coiled her hand around the base. Her warm breath fluttered against his skin. "Talk to me, Jace."

"Having a hard time thinking about anything past your mouth right now, sugar." He cupped the side of her face, so damned tempted to fist that wild hair of hers and pull her the rest of the way forward. "You tugged the tiger's tail and said you wanted to play." He flexed into her grip. "So let's play."

She grinned and pressed a lingering kiss at the base of his shaft. Pulling away enough to peek at him from beneath her lashes, she murmured against his skin. "It's not the tiger's tail I'm interested in."

Before he could so much as register the snarky comment, her tongue flicked out for a taste.

His breath seized and every muscle tightened, his whole being fixated on her tongue's wicked, leisurely path toward the tip. It was beautiful. One of the most erotic and intimate pictures he'd ever seen, her eyes closed as she savored and sampled every inch of him. With other women it always seemed a bit of a show, coy looks and smiles mixed with well-placed touches. This was a gift. Real participation and desire that resonated deep.

She tongued the ridge beneath his glans and opened her eyes, the usual light gray closer to a summer storm and glossy with need. "You wanted me to let go." She circled the tip. "I deserve the same from you."

Wet heat surrounded him, her soft lips gliding nearly to the base of his cock in one surge as her challenge ricocheted through his head. Let go? Hell, he was already in a fifty-thousand-foot free fall. What was left of his good intentions shattered into tiny splinters at the vision of her at his feet, worshiping every inch of him. No timidity, no shame, just absolute abandon. This was the woman he'd sensed buried deep, the hedonist begging for release.

He buried his fingers in her hair and fisted the wild mass at the back of her head, urging her into a deeper rhythm and rocking into her luscious mouth. "This what you wanted?"

A pretty mewl vibrated along his cock and her nails dug into his hip where she braced herself for balance.

He tightened his grip, not enough to hurt, but enough to heighten her senses. "Wanted the untamed man to push you where you want to go?"

Another moan, this one paired with a scorching silent plea from those big gray eyes.

Releasing one hand, he outlined her mouth stretched around his girth. "Get me to the edge, sugar. Right up to the peak. Want my dick so fucking hard and heavy by the time I slide inside you, I can't see straight."

She pulled away and licked the end of him, her shallow breath rasping against his slick flesh. "I want to taste you."

He covered her firm grip with his own and dragged the mushroomed head along her lower lip. "You want to have a night in charge, we can play that scenario out, but tonight is not that night." He guided himself between her lips and urged her back into motion with his fist in her hair. "Tonight, I'm coming inside you. Feeling your pussy grip my cock so hard I can't remember anything else the rest of the night."

She moaned around him and upped her efforts, bobbing up and down as though she couldn't get enough. The flat of her tongue rasped each ridge, and the end of him whispered against the back of her throat. He'd never last long like this, not with that ravenous look on her face and her hair tickling his thighs.

Relinquishing her grip on his hip, she cupped his tight sac and rolled him in her palm.

His muscles tightened and he damned near gave in, pulling her off him about a quarter of a second before she got the taste she wanted. "Naughty girl." He fisted himself to stave off the orgasm still churning in his balls and tried to suck in a decent breath. The second he thought he wouldn't change his mind and spill on her tongue anyway, he hefted her up and spun her around. Sliding his hands under her tank, he skimmed her torso until he cupped her breasts. He ground his hips against her ass, the denim harsh against his throbbing dick. "Get your shirt off."

She wiggled free of it, favoring her injured side, and tossed it to the floor.

Nuzzling behind her ear, he plumped her tight mounds and thumbed her nipples. "You getting shot sucks, but that bullet hole making you swear off bras is a nice side benefit." He licked the shell of her ear then blew across the wet line. "Now the jeans."

Unhooking her buttons and zipper took longer. Her head fell back on his shoulder and her fingers fumbled as he worked her breasts. When she'd pushed them and her panties to her knees, she gave up altogether and covered his hands with her own.

"Hu-uh," he said. "Want 'em all the way off. You want it dirty, then I want you naked and bent over my desk. Want to make sure I never walk in this room again without having that image burned into the back of my eyelids."

"Jace." She arched into his touch and tried to slide one hand down.

"Get 'em off, sugar, or I'll make you wait for it longer."

She huffed and shoved them the rest of the way off, kicking them to one side.

"Good girl." He tapped the inside of one foot with his boot. "Now spread your feet wider and bend over, chest flat against the desk."

"What about your clothes?"

He stroked the line of her spine from the small of her back to her neck and pressed her to the desk. "Feeling a little exposed? Indecent?"

A shiver rippled beneath his palm and goose bumps spread across her skin. She laid her check against the desk and closed her eyes, her answer coming out in a whisper. "Yes."

"Good." Sitting in the chair, he smoothed his hands over her ass and down the backs of her thighs, and damn near came from the visual. He ghosted his thumbs along the sides of her swollen pink labia and gently blew along the shiny, slick skin. "How about now?"

Her hips lifted in a none-too-subtle invitation and a low, grated groan filled the room. "Jace, please."

"Please what, sugar?" He slicked two fingers through her folds and coated her swollen clit with her wetness. "You want me to work you with my mouth or my cock?"

"Your cock." She wiggled as best she could, pressed against the desk. "Please."

Splaying his hands on the globes of her ass, he leaned

in and pulled in a deep breath, teasing her flesh with the barest brush of his lips. "Not sure I can now." He exhaled and licked the same path he'd made with his fingers. "Got your sweet pussy served up so pretty, don't think I can pass up a taste." He circled her clit with his tongue. "Think you'd be smart to hang on."

He struck, sucking the tight nub in his mouth and flicking it with his tongue.

Viv cried out and bucked against him, tremors wracking her legs as she fought to angle for more.

God, he loved the taste of her. A sharp nectar that lingered on his tongue. Over and over he worked the plump folds, teasing her entrance and stabbing inside. She was right. This woman wouldn't just take what he dished out, she'd demand it. Deserved everything he could give her and then some.

With one last lap of his tongue, he stood and held her in place with a fistful of hair. He plunged two fingers in her drenched core. "Gonna work you hard, sugar. You ready for that?"

She whimpered, but nodded her head in quick agreement.

He pulled his fingers free and spanked her ass. "Need an answer."

"Yes."

He mirrored the spank on her other cheek, smoothing the stings away as fast as he gave them. "Yes, what?"

"Work me hard."

Back and forth he alternated, tiny, stinging slaps on her reddening ass and teasing, short thrusts from his fingers, until both their labored breaths filled the office. His cock strained tall and hard against his belly, the flared head tight and desperate for her wet heat.

He shifted, dug a condom out of his pocket, and tore the package open with his teeth. Adrenaline coursed through his blood so thick and fast, it was a wonder he got the damned thing rolled on without fumbling. "You so much as feel a twinge in that shoulder and don't tell me, you're gonna find a side to me you don't like. We clear?"

"Crystal."

He laughed and gave her ass an extra smack. "See you're a smart-ass when you get fired up." He coated his cockhead in her wetness and lined himself up. "Let's see how you get when you explode."

He plunged to the root in one thrust, and his growl tangled with her cry of relief. Damn, but she was heaven. Ripe and tight, tiny flutters already rippling around his dick and building perfect pressure in his balls. He slid his hand under her torso and lifted her up, one arm slanted between her breasts with his hand around her neck, and the other anchored across her hip so he could hold her in place and finger her clit. "Need you there quick, babe. Find it and take me with you."

She let out an agonized moan and angled her hips to take more of him, her hands gripping his wrists for dear life. "Harder."

Something savage and primal took over, his hips slapping against hers and his tight balls tapping her swollen flesh. With each thrust, her breasts swayed and jiggled, the tiny points just begging for his lips. "Can't wait anymore, sweetheart. Time for you to fly." Before he could second-guess the action, he pinched her clit then gave it a stinging slap.

Viv threw her head against his shoulder and let out

a ragged wail, her walls clinching down on his cock so hard his lungs seized. "Jace!"

His cock jerked and flexed inside her, his own release jetting free so powerfully, he surged forward and nearly threw them both across the desk. He braced and rocked against her writhing ass. He couldn't think. Couldn't do anything beyond ride the clutch of her pussy and the fierce pulses ricocheting up and down his shaft.

Christ, she was perfect. Wild and sweet. Dirty and innocent. As if the universe had converged in some cosmic event and made the ideal woman just for him. After all he'd done, despite all his sins and imperfections, she was here. Bound to him in the most fundamental way a man could claim a woman. Somewhere, somehow, he must have done something right. Now all he had to do was find a way to make sure she didn't slip away.

Viv let out a tremulous breath and dropped her head forward. How Jace managed to hold her against him with the sweat coating her torso was a mystery, but she was sure glad he could. There wasn't a muscle anywhere on her willing to function beyond breathing, and she was awfully glad her wild hair covered her face, because she was pretty sure it screamed *Gobsmacked*.

He rolled his hips against her one last time and slipped free of her core, steadying her with hands at her hips before he dealt with the condom. Seconds later, he turned her and pulled her tight against him, his denim a delicious friction against her bare thighs and belly. "You okay?"

She nuzzled into the crook of his neck and savored the manly sunshine scent of him. "Okay is probably the wrong word. Boneless sounds good." She giggled and kissed him behind his ear. "Well, maybe not boneless. That makes me sound like a steak."

He chuckled low and swept her into his arms. "I do believe my girl's fuck drunk."

"Ha!" The sharp bark busted free as sure as it would've after three or four tequilas, more light and worry free than she'd been in...well, ever. "I think you may be right."

Carrying her into his adjoining bedroom, he flipped on a side light and laid her out in the center of the king-size bed. "How's the shoulder? Any pain?"

"There's only one part of me registering anything right now and it's not above my waist."

"The hotter you burn, the sassier you get." He crawled over her long enough to kiss the end of her nose then rolled so he lay beside her, one knee cocked in a casual, sexy pose. Funny, how he was completely dressed and she was buck naked, but didn't feel the least bit uncomfortable. "You okay with how things went down?"

"Hmm?"

He inched closer and smoothed his fingertips over her mound. "I'm asking if anything was too much for you."

She opened her mouth to fire off another smart-ass comment, but promptly shut it the second she locked on to Jace's deadly serious gaze. Was he out of his mind? She freaking loved it. For the first time in her life, she'd experienced the kind of passion she'd only fantasized about. Rough, raw, carnal bliss, and then some. Of course, the whole spanking and dirty talk thing might just have been him giving her what he sur-

mised she wanted. If she admitted how much she liked
it, he might think she was a freak.

Tell him the truth.

The thought zapped through her in a liberating
strike. Why couldn't she own it? If anyone would accept her like she was, it would be Jace. "I liked it."

His lips curled in a wicked but oh-so-gratifying grin,
and he drew slow tempting circles on the inside of her
thigh. "You screamed my name loud enough to carry
through the whole house. I'd say you more than liked it."

Damn. "You don't think your mom and Sylvie heard,
do you?"

His slow, easy laughter wrapped around her. "No
one here but us, sugar. Wouldn't give a shit if the whole
family was here, though. Fucking love the sound of my
name from your mouth." He slid his hand to her knee
and lifted her leg up and over his hip so her core was
exposed. Slow and soft, he brushed his fingers along
her sex. "Want to see my come here. Want you to feel
it when I mark you."

Her stomach flip-flopped and it was all she could
do not to squeeze her thighs around his questing touch.

"You got a problem with Zeke running tests?" he
said.

"That depends." Gone was her loopy tone, replaced
with something far more husky. "Are you comfortable
with Zeke doing a pelvic on me?"

He scowled and cupped her mound in a proprietary
way that might have pissed her off it hadn't come off so
defensive. "Scratch that. We'll get you a woman doctor.
The only man getting anywhere near your pussy is me."

She rolled her lips inward to fight back her smile.
Good to know she wasn't the only one rolling around

in the possessive neck of the woods. Probably best she got off the topic of sex before things got out of hand and he stood Axel up for the entire shift. "So, you want to run tests and change the gender of my gynecologist. Now that we're clear you're not out to break things off between us, what exactly did you want to talk to me about?"

She'd thought the change in topic might unwind some of the tension, but if anything, his scowl turned uglier. He tugged the comforter from underneath her legs and covered her up, not meeting her eyes. "The guys think you're safe. Beck and Knox have combed all the evidence, and they think I was the target, not you."

"Someone tried to kill you?"

He shoved his hair away from his face and reclined against the headboard. "It wasn't an accident. Got security cameras in the parking lot, and the man with the gun was aimed straight at me, so it was a hit."

"Why would someone want you dead?"

"Hell if I know. Got a lot of people I've pissed off over the years, but don't know any who'd want me to stop breathing." He shrugged and laced his fingers with hers. "Except maybe Hugo. Beck says he'd be shocked if Moreno would pull something so public, though."

"Then the club is the last place you need to be."

"Not gonna hide at Haven, sugar. I've got a job to do, and I'm going to do it like I always do. Security's been beefed up and everyone's on guard. Beckett's even called in a few of his contacts at DPD to make their presence a little more prevalent. Hopefully not the kind that goes with more arrests and ugly segments on the nightly news. Too much more bad press and even your PR mojo won't keep my customers coming in."

He pulled their joined hands up to his mouth and teased his lips across her knuckles, studying her over their joined fingers. His cropped beard tickled her skin and his warm breath radiated deep. Squeezing her hand, he lowered it to the bed and dug into the front pocket of his jeans. A second later, her keys dangled from his fingertips. "Axel brought it out for you. He parked it out front."

"I can go?"

The second the question came out, his face hardened and his chocolate eyes glimmered closer to black. His lips pressed together so hard they were nearly white. "I'd rather you stay, but it's your call."

God, it was tempting. The last seven days had been so easy, surrounded by people that accepted her no matter what mood she'd been in or how she'd presented herself. Even showing up to breakfast with no makeup in Jace's pajama bottoms with the waist rolled up too many times to count and an oversize T-shirt, they didn't blink.

And Jace…being around him centered her. Took the edge off all the should-dos and have-tos running around in her head, just by being close to him. Surrender would be so simple.

Jace's rumbling voice cut into her thoughts. "You're not staying, are you?"

"You have no idea how strong of a personality you are, do you?"

"Don't know much about my personality, but I'd heave a Mack Truck across the driveway with my own two hands and feet if it meant you staying here."

She giggled at the image and ran her fingers through the soft beard along his jawline. "What was your first business?"

"A little pub in lower Greenville called Trident. What about it?"

"The first time it turned a profit, how did that make you feel?"

"Greedy, which is exactly the reason I want you to stay here, so wherever your logic's headed isn't the strongest."

She pressed a finger over his lips to silence him. "But it felt good, right? Like you could hold your own?"

He nodded, though it was plenty obvious all kinds of retorts were building up in that head of his.

"You're huge, Jace. Larger than life. I need to know I can hold my own with you. That I'm not taking this path because it's easy and comfortable, but because I choose it. That I'm strong enough you won't swallow me up."

He lifted the hand she'd used to silence him and nipped the pad of her finger. "Not an ounce of weak in you, sugar. Afraid, maybe, but not weak."

She traced his lower lip. "There's a difference between you believing it and me believing it."

Cupping the side of her face, he leaned in, pressed a lingering kiss to her lips. "I'll give you that one," he murmured.

His cold, platinum Haven tags knocked against her knuckles where she touched his chest. She scooped them so they lay in her palm and traced the Haven emblem with her thumb. "You're lucky. Growing up with people you can count on, who support you no matter what, is precious. You have no idea what I'd have given to have that in my life."

His fingers tightened in her hair, and he cocked his head at a thoughtful angle. "You might not have had it growing up, but you can have it now. My family's yours if you accept them. I get you need time to figure it out on your own, but that doesn't mean I'll stop trying to reel you in." Slowly, he lifted the chain over his head and put it around her neck. "You keep these, and remember that."

"Jace, I can't take these."

"You can and you will." He kissed her forehead, pulled away and rolled to his feet, tucking his T-shirt into his jeans. "I've got to get to work. You feel the need to bail tonight, you do it early so you don't fall asleep driving home."

"Jace—"

"It's all right, sugar. I get it. I don't like it, but I get it." He anchored one arm beside her, tucked a stray strand of hair behind her ear and cradled her face. His gaze roamed her features as though locking every detail away for the very last time, and his lips pinched tight. When he spoke, his strained voice raked her from the inside out. "You take what time you need, then get your ass back to me."

Five seconds later he was gone, his powerful strides carrying him out the door without so much as a backward glance.

Surely taking some time to adjust and get her bearings was the smart move. No one in their right mind would dive into a healthy relationship this fast. Especially after everything she'd been through.

She clenched the tags above her heart and scrunched deeper into the pillows, the weight of her decision pressing on her heart. It might be the smart move, but it hurt like hell.

TWENTY-FOUR

Viv PUNCHED THE mute button on the TV's remote and tossed it to the couch cushions beside her. The vibrant graphics from the fast food ad illuminated her townhouse's otherwise dark living room and sent towering shadows up the vaulted ceiling.

Jace was right. Her decor was pretty, but it was about as homey as a hotel room. The neutral colors and clean lines added up to a whole lot of *meh*. On the bright side, she could make it almost five minutes down here without thinking about him. In her bed or her safe room, she was lucky if she could make it three consecutive seconds. Sleeping without him curled protectively around her was impossible.

Her phone's home screen glowed 10:07 p.m. Over twenty-four hours since she'd left Haven and not one call from Jace. She'd been so certain coming home was the right thing to do, a way to center herself and give her emotions some time to level out. Instead, it just seemed to spotlight all the good she'd left behind. She'd thought for sure he'd call at least once to check in, but the stupid phone had sat dark and dead all stinking day—except for the hundred times she'd checked it "just in case." Maybe her leaving had pissed him off and made him rethink what he wanted.

She dropped her head back on the cushion and let out a frustrated huff. The mental gymnastics were exhausting, bullshit insecurities colliding with what few reasonable thoughts her mind could pull together. For about the hundredth time since he'd draped them around her neck, Viv fisted his Haven tags and closed her eyes. The cold platinum dug into her palm and the Haven emblem burned as clear in her memory as it had the times she'd studied it in the light. The gift shouldn't mean so much. Heck, to most women it would seem almost juvenile. Something more expected in a high school soap opera. But the second the chain had settled around her neck, her whole world had tilted, the dreams of closeness and acceptance rattling up from long-locked emotional vaults she'd never imagined reopening.

My family's yours if you accept them.

There had to be a kicker. In her family there had always been a gotcha, an inevitable rug yanked from beneath her feet, or disappointment pitfall. She'd managed it. Adjusted her expectations and grew accustomed to the emotional bumps and bruises.

With Jace and his family, it wouldn't just be bumps and bruises. Their level of peace and support would put the altitude too high for minor injuries. Oh, no. She'd suffer all kinds of broken and bloody feelings if things ever went south. She wasn't even sure she'd survive the kind of hurt that went with loving Jace.

The TV brightness flashed behind her eyelids.

On the screen, blue and red police lights strobed in the latest news segment, and well-dressed patrons milled in a parking lot among some of DPD's finest.

Viv unmuted the volume and tugged her chenille blanket up to her shoulders just as the video cut to Paul Renner mid press conference. The graphic at the bottom of the screen read *House of Representatives Candidate Speaks Out.*

"This country is all about life, liberty and the pursuit of happiness, and I, for one, fully support those who reach for the American dream of building their own business. But when the safety of our citizens is in jeopardy, something must be done. The longer we allow businesses who condone or protect dangerous activities to flourish, the more the violence will escalate."

"Ugh." Viv punched the TV off with a harsh click of the remote and tossed it to the coffee table. What an idiot. How did people not see past that slimeball?

The same way they don't see past Jace.

And she'd been one of them.

Tossing the blanket aside, she padded to the kitchen, her bare feet slapping against the wood floors. Jace would sure get a kick out of these pajamas, white flannel bottoms with silver moons and stars, and a gray wifebeater that made her usual tanks look saintly. She snatched what was left of the bottle of red she'd started last night and poured a generous glass. God, she hoped she slept tonight. No way could she face Jace at Crossroads tomorrow without at least a few uninterrupted hours, assuming he didn't go back to pawning her off on Axel.

The phone rang midgulp, the polite ringtone she used to give a professional image grating against the otherwise blistering silence.

Jace.

Viv clunked her wineglass down and hurried to the couch, snatching it up so fast she nearly fumbled it.

Callie's contact picture shined up at Viv from the phone's screen. The image was four or five years old, her sister's innocent smile wide and happy, and her eyes clear and sober.

The warmth behind Viv's sternum withered and a heavy weight settled on her shoulders. She slid her thumb across the screen. "Hey, Callie."

Her sister's frantic voice whispered through the phone, and for once, her words weren't slurred together. "Vivie, you gotta help me. I'm in trouble."

"OUR ORGANIZATION SIMPLY cannot condone poor behavior from those receiving charitable funds. My recommendation is we adopt a zero tolerance stance on any actions taken by our award winners resulting in legal ramifications."

Jace fisted his hand beneath the table and fought the urge to coil the same amount of pressure around the new director's throat. For the last two hours, he'd listened to the charity's newest jackass lay out his new and improved plans for the organization, but this one he couldn't keep quiet on. "This organization is supposed to benefit troubled boys. The mission statement pretty much demands the benefactors, in fact, be troubled."

Aaron Davidson, aka new fearless leader and close associate to Paul Renner, sneered at him from the head of the long conference table. "I'd expect such a perspective out of you. Given the latest news reports, I'm not sure you're the best individual to offer advice on this issue."

"As long as my money's funding two-thirds of your scholarships, you'll listen or you'll lose the contributions. For repeat offenses, I've got no problem yanking money, but no one, and I mean no one, yanks themselves out of the gutter without a few slips. You'd know that if the soles of your Italian shoes ever got real-life grime on them." Jace shoved upright fast enough his chair legs grated against the marble floors. "It's late. You debate all you want, but you know where my head is on this."

He stalked from the room and down the long, sterile hallway. For years, they'd met at the downtown museum, and normally he'd take his time leaving to enjoy the private works kept in the back offices. This time they blurred past him, so damned much adrenaline coursing through his veins it was hard to walk. Sanctimonious assholes, every one of them.

Well, maybe not all of them. Evelyn and a few of the other women were good people, but men like Davidson rubbed him all kinds of wrong. They wouldn't know a hard time if it crawled up in their lap and sucked their damned dicks. Of course, he hadn't exactly gone in tonight in the best frame of mind. A full fucking day he'd waited and not one fucking call from Vivienne. He knew she was safe. In the week she'd been at Haven, Beck and Knox had wired her security up good and tight, and Danny was on watch, making sure she was really as safe as his brothers assured she'd be. Still, it was like she'd run home and locked him out of her head.

Well, he'd make sure she remembered who he was tomorrow. He'd meant every damned word he'd said to her over the last week, and like it or not, he'd show her how a real man got what he wanted.

"Mr. Kennedy."

Jace spun toward the feminine voice behind him.

Evelyn Frank hurried his way, her heels clicking out a quick tempo. She stopped just an arm's length away and pressed a hand against her chest while she caught her breath. "I'm sorry to hold you up."

The hairs on the back of his neck prickled to attention and his shoulders pushed back, instinctively bracing for whatever news lurked behind her uneasy smile. "Yeah, I'm ready to be done. What do you need?"

"Well." She glanced down the hall toward the meeting room. "Mr. Davidson thought it might be less disruptive if you provided your votes via proxy going forward. Of course, I'd be happy to relay agenda items and votes for consideration when needed."

"Less disruptive, huh?"

She ducked her chin and smoothed the front of her peach dress. "I'm sorry. I don't particularly care for the new direction thus far, but I do want your voice to be heard."

Damn, he was sick of this shit. Of Paul, and Davidson, and all the other pompous pricks who thought their shit didn't stink. They had no problem taking his money, but they wanted nothing to do with his voice or his ideas.

For the first time in more years than he could count, he didn't have a decent comeback. "Yeah. Whatever." He turned and strode down the hallway, leaving Evelyn locked in place.

He'd cleared the front doors and started down the steps to the parking lot when his phone vibrated in his pocket. Danny's name and number flashed across the screen. "Viv okay?"

"Don't know, but she's on the move."

TWENTY-FIVE

GOOSE BUMPS RIPPLED up Vivienne's arms. The cold, harsh landscape of the apartment complex before her was carved straight out of a Wes Craven flick—broken, silent and way too shadowed.

She put her car in park and zoomed in tighter on the app she'd used to track Callie. The blue dot pulsed a whole lot calmer than her heart, and was centered over the building to her left. It had to be right. All Callie had been able to give her was the apartment number B20, but that matched the faded white B painted on the side of the building.

Callie was out of her ever-loving mind coming here. Even drunk, Viv would've cottoned to the creep factor and run the opposite direction.

"You gotta hurry, Vivie. If they figure it out, it'll be bad." Beyond the apartment number and a whispered, *"I've got to go,"* that was all Callie had shared. No explanation on what might be figured out, or who Callie was in trouble with. Just the usual search and rescue call, and the utter confidence that Viv would march in, wave a magic wand and get them home safe and sound.

Viv killed the engine. The chill from the door handle matched the icy fear crawling down her spine.

You don't have to do this alone. Not anymore.

The second the thought rustled through her mind, she released the handle and reengaged the locks. Jace's tags clinked at the sharp movement, a ghost of blue from the dashboard lights reflecting off the matte platinum. She clutched them and let out a wobbly breath. The edges of her phone cut into her other palm, all but begging her to give in and ask for help. Jace would be mad as hell if he knew where she was, but he wouldn't hesitate to come.

To keep her safe.

Her heartbeat steadied and the nasty landscape seemed to sharpen in focus. He *would* keep her safe. Always had. She punched in her passcode and thumbed through her contacts, a comfortable warmth radiating through her chest.

The line rang once before Jace's gruff and deadly serious bark kicked through the earpiece. "Tell me your ass is still in the car."

"What?"

"Gotta call from Danny, said you're toolin' around near the fairgrounds, so my guess is you got an SOS from Callie. Tell me your ass is still in the car."

The warmth of seconds before blasted up to inferno and her checks burned. "You have someone watching me?"

"Told you, sugar. You mean something to me. That means I'm going to keep you safe, even if I'm gritting my teeth and keeping my distance. Don't care right now if that also means pissing you off."

She opened her mouth to bite back, but the words he'd given her boomeranged back through her head. His mom was right. She got to choose what kind of man she wanted with her in this life, and while Jace might be a high-handed, presumptuous cave dweller, he also cared enough to have her back. "I'm in the car."

"Good. Lock the doors and stay put until I get there."

"How long?"

"Ten tops. I'm halfway there already."

Definitely a presumptuous, cave-dwelling type. "Then think on this while you drive. I. Called. You."

She hung up before he could answer and let out a slow, steadying breath. On one hand, she wanted to curl up against him and show him how much it mattered that he cared. On the other, she wanted to choke the knuckle-dragging ape.

Hard not to understand his protective streak though, not after what he'd been through. At nine years old, she'd spent the bulk of her time playing with Barbies and My Little Pony. He'd been blasted with a cold, adult reality and killed a man. How could it not shape his life?

A loud crash sounded across the dark walkway followed by a masculine shout. Another followed it, this one a woman's. A gunshot ricocheted between the buildings and a scream rang right behind it.

Callie.

Viv punched the locks and jumped out of her car, leaving the door wide open.

Hard footsteps pounded against concrete somewhere in front of her.

Following the sound, Viv jogged into the shadows and rounded the corner.

Callie sprinted her direction, a man with slightly balding black hair right behind her with a gun in one hand.

"Callie!" Viv reached for her sister and tried to guide her the right direction, but Callie stumbled and pulled Viv down with her.

A hand clamped around Viv's ankle and dragged her against the cold concrete, her sweatshirt snagging so the cold gray stone scraped her bare back.

Callie scrambled to her feet and took off, screaming

toward the parking lot as the man leveled a nasty-looking gun in Viv's face. "You get your girl and my drugs back or your face won't stay pretty long."

The words were barely out of his mouth before his head reefed back and an even-nastier-looking gun pressed against his temple, Jace towering over the man like a God out for vengeance. "Your fucking head's gonna have a hole in it before that happens. Now get that gun out of my woman's face."

Jace tightened his grip on the son of a bitch's hair and dug the gun's muzzle deeper in his temple. Whoever he was, he was on something, his trigger finger way too jumpy for Jace's tastes. "I'm twitchy as hell and looking for a good excuse to get bloody. Drop the fucking gun."

The man's heavy breaths came out in short puffs against the cool winter night, and his eyes darted around the walkway as though looking for help. When all he found were shadows, he tossed his piece to the concrete and held up his hands.

Jace tugged the man off his knees and shoved him away from Viv, snatching the discarded gun and stuffing in his jacket pocket. "Get to the car, sugar."

The thug sneered at Viv over his shoulder. "Hope your friend doesn't mean too much. Know lots of people in her crowd. I'll find her sooner or later. She doesn't have my stash, or money, she pays in blood."

"Jace," Viv whispered behind him, way too much fear and desperation in the sound for something barely heard.

He never should have let Viv leave Haven. Hell, at this rate, he was gonna lock Callie up, too. "Then I guess I'd be better served to put you down now and make sure she doesn't pay at all."

"You think I give a shit?" the man said. "I don't get my hands on that stash, or let my man know it's been handled, I'm dead either way."

Vivienne inched in tight behind him, her hand creeping under his jacket to fist his T-shirt at the waist.

Jace loosened his stance but kept his gun ready for business. "Who's your boss?"

The man gauged the distance between Jace and the nearest safe zone. "You really think I'm gonna spill with some jackass I don't know?"

"I think if you want help getting that target off your back, you'd better."

"Yeah, who the hell are you?"

"Doesn't matter. You don't want to spill, that's your deal. You're the one who seems to be short enough product to get you killed." Jace urged Viv toward the parking lot, keeping his gun steady.

The man lurched forward as if to stop them, but threw up his hands and froze when Jace firmed his aim and braced to fire. "Moreno."

And the hits just keep coming. At least Hugo liked cash more than grudges. "Call your boss. Tell him someone will make contact and handle the payoff."

"That's not gonna buy me shit."

"It's what I'm offering. He'll get the call before morning, but if the girl so much as gets a splinter before or after, Moreno will be the least of your problems."

Fisting his hands, the man scowled and took two steps back. "Twenty-four hours. You don't make contact, I start tracking." He stormed off into the shadows, never looking back.

Jace backed up, staring into the darkness and nudging Viv toward the parking lot. "Which part of, 'stay in the car,' didn't you understand?"

"I heard a gunshot."

"Which is why you should have stayed put." Only when their feet hit asphalt did Jace turn and practically drag her toward his truck parked cock-eyed in the middle of the lot with the door still open.

Viv reared back and dug in her heels, her eyes trained dead ahead on Danny rooted right next to her car with a similar hold on Callie. "You left me." As fast as she'd stopped, Viv jumped back in motion and stormed her sister. In under four paces she was nose to nose. "I went after you, and you left me there with a gun in my face. That's what I get for helping you out? Again?"

"Vivie, it wasn't like that, I—"

"Enough." Jace held out his hand, palm up. "Keys."

"I'm fine," Viv said.

"Wasn't asking how you were. I want your keys before our pumped-up friend comes back with more assholes. Now, give me the damned keys."

Viv got as close to a snarl as he'd ever seen her, eyes still locked on Callie, and slammed them in his palm. "Fine."

Jace pulled her house key off the ring, tossed the rest to Danny, and spun Viv by the shoulders. "Take Viv's ride and get Callie to the compound. I want every damned detail out of Callie by the time I get there." He jerked open the truck door and all but pushed Viv in. By the time he climbed in his own side, she'd buckled up tight, but glared daggers out the windshield.

"She left me."

"Told you how it is with people like Callie. Nothing changes, nothing changes." He revved the engine and flicked the headlights to bright. Not a soul stirred behind the black and broken windows ahead.

Viv clenched a fist near her sternum, her breath huffing like a marathon runner, trying to act normal, but failing bad.

"You hurt?"

"Not on the outside." She snapped to attention when he veered on the highway, and scanned the side streets around them. "Where are we going?"

"I'm taking you home."

Four solid minutes she glared out the windshield, her gaze so stern it was a wonder the glass didn't shatter. She still didn't lower the fist from her chest. Either she was puzzling seriously big shit together in that head of hers, or she was plotting to cut off his nuts. Maybe both.

I. Called. You.

Hardly anything else had taken up space in his head since she'd uttered the words, their impact freight-training deep in his gut over and over again.

He pulled up in front of her house and shoved the gearshift into park.

The locks snapped opened.

Nothing.

Maybe she was in shock. Not an unreasonable response considering she'd gotten up close and personal with the wrong end of a gun. Christ, just visualizing the scene again made him want to punch something, or hurl, and he'd been on the opposite side.

He hopped out and strode to the other side. Popping open the door, he unlatched her seat belt and held out his hand. "Come on, sugar. Let's get you inside."

She flinched as though the words, or his voice,

snapped her out of a trance. Her gaze lifted to meet his then shifted to her front door behind him.

"Gonna ask you again. You okay?"

Uncurling her fist, she rubbed her palm over her heart. No, not her heart. His tags.

She shifted so fast, he had to jump back to keep from getting plowed with a knee to the nuts. "Give me the key."

He handed it over, and she jumped from the cab and stomped to the door.

A sick, nasty churn started up in his stomach, and a fine sheen of sweat coated his back and neck. This was bad. Bad as in deadly storm brewing and "I'm done" kind of bad.

Fuck.

Yeah, he'd been pissed. What man in his right mind wouldn't be, seeing his woman with a gun in her face? He scrambled for arguments, reasons she'd understand, but all his head could process was the cold, powerless fear clambering up his throat.

She threw the door wide and let out a sharp whistle.

Ruger was already there, the back half of his body wagging to make up for his stubbed tail and nudging Viv's hand.

She snapped and pointed to the truck, shutting the door and locking it in one quick flick of her wrist. Yanking open the back door, she motioned Ruger up in the back cab and slammed it behind him.

"Viv, what the fu—"

"You made a mistake tonight. This isn't home." She swallowed so big he felt it in his own throat, and her eyes widened with such vulnerability he nearly hit his knees. She palmed his tags and squared her shoulders. "My home's with you. I choose you."

TWENTY-SIX

VIV HAD A lot to learn about family. In the span of minutes, her own blood had left her to face an armed man alone, and the man she'd dubbed as trouble had not only thrown himself between her and a gun, but been willing to spill blood to keep her safe. Yeah, she had a lot to learn.

Jace pulled into the old, affluent neighborhood he'd taken her to weeks before, the sprawling houses on either side of the street dark but for the discreetly placed landscape and porch lights. A full moon slipped in and out between the tree canopy overhead, and stars sprinkled the winter sky.

Punching a gate controller on his visor, he slowed and pulled into the compound's circle drive, two hot rods, another truck, a Jeep, and her Honda turning the space into a poorly planned parking lot.

An almost maniacal giggle wrangled up from her belly, shaking her shoulders so hard it jarred her wound.

Jace put the truck in park and cupped the back of her neck. "I like that laugh a whole lot more than the silent bit, but damned if I know what there is to laugh about."

"I'm an idiot." She shook her head. The grand home with its ivory stucco walls and wrought iron accents glared the same judgment she'd given Jace all those days ago back down at her. "The first time I saw this place, I never considered it could be yours. I assumed it belonged to someone different. Someone in a suit with a pedigree and a sterling education."

"Yeah, well, one out of three ain't bad."

Her heart clenched and her cheeks burned. "Like I said. I'm an idiot."

He guided her face toward his. "You've got your own demons, sugar. Shit that taints your past like all the rest of us."

"But I—"

"Doesn't matter." He kissed her forehead and sucked in a deep breath that sounded a whole lot like relief. "You see me now," he muttered against her skin. "That's all I want."

Pulling away, she cupped his face. His beard prickled against her palms, soft despite the harsh appearance it lent his face. The moon reflected off his nearly black eyes and accented the stark scar at the corner. "I see you. I see it all, even the parts you hide from everyone else."

"Viv..." His eyes locked onto her lips and his warm breath fluttered across her face.

Safe. With him she'd always be safe, or as safe as any person could be with another. She dragged her thumb across his lips, her own tingling with the need for contact. Closing the distance, she pressed her mouth to his, the contact no less powerful now than it had been the first time she'd tasted him. Their lips and tongues tangled, a perfect dance that flowed natural and wild between them. If fire had a flavor, this was it. Bold. Fearless. So damned consuming, it pressed in on every side and swallowed her whole. No more waiting. No more second-guessing everything. Jace was hers, and she'd claw anyone or anything that tried to keep her away.

He pulled away and pressed his forehead to hers. "Jesus, sugar."

God, she loved his voice, especially like it was now. Deep and rumbling so low it resonated across her skin.

Sitting up, he opened his door. "You hold that thought. I gotta deal with Callie's shit before I get more company than I want."

She jumped to the patchwork tile drive, slammed her door shut, and opened the crew cab for Ruger. As soon as Jace rounded the back of the truck, she started digging. "What does 'deal with it' mean?"

"It means Hugo's gonna want payment for the stunt your girl pulled." He guided her to the front door with a hand at the small of her back. "Seeing as how he's already pissed I pushed him out of a steady income stream at my clubs, patience won't be high on his list."

Viv halted just shy of the front door. "You mean pay for what she stole?"

"They're not inclined to give that shit away. They also tend to send a stout message with those who steal from them."

"You can't pay for her."

"You choose me?"

Viv froze. "Yes."

"You see me?"

"Yes."

His lips curled for a grin guaranteed to make ninety-nine-point-nine percent of the female population drop their panties on sight. "Right. So, you're mine. Callie's yours. That makes her family and I deal with family." He threw the door open and guided her across the threshold. "Though you may not like the way I deal after about ten more minutes."

"What's that…" Viv's forward movement trailed off along with her thoughts. Zeke hunkered in front of Callie on the couch in the center of the room, checking her over. Danny stood sentry beside her with his arms crossed and a scowl that promised he'd take her down in a heartbeat if she tried to bolt. What she hadn't expected was the rest of the crowd gathered off to one side, Beckett, Trevor and Knox each nursing a different high-end beer. Though with the knot of cars out front, she probably should have reasoned they'd all be there.

Jace grabbed her hand and ambled to his brothers, Zeke and Danny following close behind. "You talk to Axel?"

"Yep," Knox said. "Too close to closing time to head this way, but said he'd be here as soon as he wraps up. You've got his proxy."

Pulling a toothpick from his pocket, Jace popped it in his mouth and focused on Zeke. "How bad is she?"

"Bruise on her face looks worse than it is," Zeke said. "Another goose egg on the back of her head to match the one from New Year's Eve, and a probable cracked rib. Considering the stunt she pulled, she's lucky the tally's that small."

Jace zeroed in on Danny. "You get details?"

"She rode shotgun on a deal there last Wednesday, saw where they stashed their X, and decided a little industrious activity would generate enough cash to pay her bills."

"So where's the cash?"

"Gone. She threw a party Friday night, woke up with what was left of the stash and the money gone, and thought a repeat visit was a great idea. My guess, she's in for fifty large."

Viv's breath rushed out and, for a second, the little bit of dinner she'd managed to eat almost flew out with it. "Fifty thousand dollars?"

Still on the couch where they'd left her, Callie sat with her face averted and her knee jiggling in a nervous cadence. Her hair looked as though it hadn't seen a brush in at least two days, and her jeans and tie-dyed T-shirt probably hadn't had attention in twice that.

Trevor shook his head and rubbed the back of his neck. "Man, she doesn't go half-assed, does she?"

"So, pay it." Knox shoved a chunk of dirty blond hair out of his face in the hot, absent-minded professor way she'd grown to appreciate over the last week, and chin lifted toward Jace's tags hanging around Viv's neck. "You marked her, so she's family, and Haven covers family debts. Get in and out, and Moreno's not out a penny."

Beckett crossed his arms, his big biceps straining the arms of his T-shirt. His voice rumbled about half volume compared to the rest of the men. "It's not that simple. Hugo needs money *and* a message. Word gets out he's giving a pass to lost product, he'll lose face and start finding himself short across the board. Not to mention he's gonna want to use this to get back into Crossroads."

"No." Every head whipped Viv's direction. For the last week, she'd been quiet around the men, opting for small talk and ignoring the details when they dove into business. But she'd be damned if Callie ended up being the reason Jace was out money, or ended up with more headaches at Crossroads. "I'll find a way to pay him off, but he can't get back into Crossroads. Jace has worked too hard to get him out."

The brothers and Danny all looked between each other as if they weren't entirely sure what to say.

Jace, on the other hand, twirled his toothpick with his tongue and grinned. "You're cute when you get wound up." He tugged her in front of him and pulled her in close enough his beard tickled her temple. "Hugo's not getting back in my club, and you're not paying a penny. We'll handle this."

"But—"

"No buts. We've got this." Jace lowered his voice and focused on Zeke. "You got a place we can dry Callie out while we clear things up?"

"Might have to hop a few states and call in a favor, but it can happen quiet."

"Detox?" She'd tried for the last year to get Callie to get help, but her sister wouldn't hear of it. "What if she won't agree?"

"Sugar, your sister's got two choices. Find a way to pay Hugo back, or send a message via her corpse to anyone stupid enough to steal from Hugo again. The only means she's got to pay him back right now is me, and I'm wrapping that payback up with one big string— treatment. She might act crazy, but I guarantee you, she's smart enough to know she won't last a day with Hugo's guys on the hunt. So, which do you think she's gonna choose?"

All the blood in Viv's head free-fell toward her feet and she swayed, bumping into Jace behind her. Out of the corner of her eye, Callie sat hunched over and picking her nails. "He'd really kill her?"

"In a heartbeat. She knows that or she wouldn't have run the way she did."

Viv crossed her arms tight and fought back a shiver.

Nothing like learning your sister hadn't just left you to fend for herself, but did it knowing Viv wouldn't come out breathing on the other end.

"Hey." Jace craned enough to study her face. "It's over. Or it will be in a few more hours." Straightening, he jerked his chin toward Callie and directed his comments to his brothers. "We need her stashed someplace Hugo's men can't find her. The compound's too obvious."

Danny spun into action. "I got her."

"Hold up." Jace motioned Danny back and traded a lot of silent eyeballing between the rest of the brothers.

Each dipped their chin in a silent acknowledgement, boyish but sneaky grins mirrored on every one of them. Clearly, if she was going to hold her own in this family, she had a lot of nonverbal translation to get up to speed on.

"Good," Jace said as though they'd debated out loud. "Zeke, start working on detox for Callie. Knox and Trev, track down Hugo and set up a meet. Me, Danny and Beck will handle drop-off." He pinned Danny with a hard stare. "You up for this?"

Danny's head snapped back. He hesitated long enough to meet each man's gaze, then straightened to full height and squared his shoulders, his slack mouth spreading to a rowdy smile. "Hell, yeah."

"That's the answer I wanted." Jace smacked Danny on the back and guided Viv toward the couch. "One more head-to-head and we can get this shit put to bed."

All the men but Danny peeled off.

Callie glanced at Jace, Danny and Viv headed her way then jerked her head the other direction and scowled at the villa's massive stone entrance.

Jace halted in front of her and crossed his arms, his take-no-shit attitude in full force. "Look at me."

Her sister's knee jiggling started back up and she tucked both hands under each leg.

Jace's voice dropped to a scary growl. "Only gonna give you this chance once, and I want your eyes while I do it."

Whipping her face to Jace, the jiggling stopped. "I need to go."

"You need to listen," he bit back. "You and I both know you're in a hell of a fix. Because you're Viv's sister, I'm willing to bail your ass out of hot water. In exchange, you agree to detox at a place well out of sight of Hugo's reach and straighten your shit."

"I don't need your help."

"If you want to keep breathing, you do. The way I hear it, you're in for at least fifty grand for the X you stole. Now, unless you've got about three times that floating around, the odds of you coming out from any altercation with his men is slim and none."

"I just need to find the X."

"See, that's what you don't get. Hugo's going to want to send a message to you and any other idiot fool enough to steal from him. So you don't just need what you stole, you need more. You get me?"

For the first time since Viv had walked in, the tension and anger in Callie's too-thin frame eked out, leaving nothing but stark fear and realization in its place.

"I'm giving you one shot," Jace said. "One. After that, you're on your own. No more late-night rescue calls. No more bailouts. No more anything. And if you think me fronting what you owe plus the hefty penalty is going to make Hugo disappear long-term, let me share this. Hugo's boys are dedicated twisted fucks with long memories who get off on making statements. If you're smart, you'll take this deal. If you love your sister at all, you'll see to keeping her happy by not draggin' her through your daily hell anymore."

Callie lifted her head, her tear-filled eyes aimed at Viv. "I'm fine. I've just been out having a good time. Going to parties—"

"I'm done, Callie." The second the words slipped out, the pressure bearing down on Viv's shoulders eased so much she thought she'd float off the ground.

Jace stared at Viv, his harsh face showing zero leniency, but his eyes screamed of pride and encouragement. He was right. If nothing changed, nothing changed.

"This is your last chance," Viv said. "I love you, but I won't keep doing this anymore. I won't let you hurt me or anyone else I—"

Viv flinched and snapped her mouth shut, the words she'd nearly let slip free still burning on her tongue. There were only four people in the room, but it felt like a crowd of thousands looked down on her, the bulk of the weight coming from Jace in her periphery.

Swallowing around the thick knot in her throat, she tucked her hands in the front pocket of her sweatshirt and prayed her near miss hadn't been as obvious as it felt. She turned to leave, the need for distance and time to recalibrate leaving her flustered and disoriented. "Jace is right. The decision's yours, but it's the last intervention you'll get."

Thirty-six years Jace had walked this earth, partying with all kinds of wild people and dabbling in substances he shouldn't have, but the rush burning through his veins in that moment beat the sum total of them all, hands down.

The words. They'd been right there on the tip of her tongue. Damn near airborne. He still couldn't decide if he was glad she'd choked them back, or pissed she'd clammed up. To hear those words on her lips, he'd trade just about anything, but then he'd end up acting like a whipped pup in front of his brothers and he'd never live it down.

Across the room, Viv stared out the wall of windows overlooking the pool. The night skies on the other side made a perfect backdrop and reflected her troubled frown in the glass. It might have only been twenty feet away, but it might as well have been Omaha.

He zeroed in on Callie. "No fuckin' around. Are you in, or out?"

Callie sniffled and dashed away a tear with the back of her hand. "I really don't need—"

"It's a yes or no answer. Viv said her piece and she's backin' my play. Now which is it? In or out?"

Callie aimed pleading eyes Viv's direction, but Viv kept her eyes trained on the backyard. "I'm in."

"Smart choice." He eyeballed Danny and jerked his head toward the front door, and his soon-to-be new brother hustled Callie out of the house.

The door snicked shut, and quiet settled thick and riddled with energy.

Viv's gaze slid to his in the reflection, her pretty gray eyes so big and vulnerable, it was all he could do not cart her upstairs and tell the rest of the world to go to hell. She'd want him to ignore it. Shit, she'd probably sent at least ten prayers up asking for exactly that, but he was done with things in between them, even the unspoken ones.

He ambled her direction and slipped his arms around her waist, never breaking her stare in the window. Nuzzling her ear, he drew in her crisp, bright scent, letting it settle deep in his lungs. "You scared?"

"She's my sister, of course I'm scared."

"Wasn't talking about your sister." He tucked his hands in her sweatshirt pocket and covered her tiny fists. "Nothing to be afraid of with us, Viv. Not about how you feel or the words that come with it."

She twisted and peered up at him, her eyes glossy with unshed tears. "I don't want to talk about this."

"Give me one good reason."

Viv swallowed huge and glared back out at the pool. "People leave. One way or another, they leave, and I'm not ready for that with you. Not yet."

His arms tightened around her, and a nasty growl lodged in the back of his throat. Christ, her family had done a number on her. His might be all kinds of weird and ten leagues beyond socially acceptable, but they'd never once not been there for him. Eventually, she'd learn what that acceptance and support looked like, but for right now, the best he could do was hold steady and let her adjust.

"I'm not going anywhere, sugar. Might have gotten hotheaded once, but I learned my lesson and mean to prove it. What you've got to get is where you've been and where we're headed are two different places. When you get that, you let me know." He turned her in his arms, tilted her face up to his and brushed a soft kiss against her lips. "I'll give you those words. When you're ready, you let me know and I'll go first."

TWENTY-SEVEN

Viv woke with Ruger's hundred-pound, muscled body curled and wedged behind her knees the same as always, but the room was dark. Pitch dark.

Jace's room.

Even after the week she'd stayed at Haven, she still couldn't get used to the blackout blinds he kept over the balcony sliding glass door. Both of her townhouse rooms were loaded with windows so she woke up naturally with the sun, but here a person could sleep from sunup to sundown and never have a clue what time of day it was.

Still, something wasn't right. She reached across the bed and met only cool, soft sheets. Twisting the best she could with Ruger pinning her legs under the bedcovers, she propped up on an elbow and flipped the bedside lamp.

Jace's side of the bed wasn't just empty, but unruffled, the sheets and comforter barely disturbed by her almost motionless sleep. But that couldn't be right. When he'd dropped her and Ruger off at two in the morning, he'd promised he'd come straight back.

She pried her legs free and fumbled for her phone on the nightstand.

10:20 a.m.

Wow. A solid eight hours, and she still felt like she could handle another two at least. Not surprising, though. With the lack of sleep the night before, and the come-to-Jesus with Callie, her body was probably due for more than its share of downtime.

Or you just finally made your mind up and surrendered to what felt right all along.

Well, wasn't that a harpoon strike from her conscience. Now that she thought about it, she hadn't felt this relaxed since she'd woken up floating on morphine. The lack of mental gymnastics tumbling around in her head didn't suck either.

She'd still like to know where the heck Jace was.

Thumbing up her contacts, she punched his number and padded to the bathroom.

Ruger yawned and plunked his chin back down on the bed, watching her from between his paws.

"This is Jace. You know what to do." Clipped, gruff and to the point, just like everything else about the man.

Viv punched the end button before the beep kicked in and stood stymied in the middle of the bathroom. She couldn't remember the last time Jace didn't pick up when she called. If he'd ever headed into a meeting where he couldn't talk to her, he always called or texted her in advance. Calling up her messages, she found a fat zero there, too.

Are you okay? Give me a call when you can.

She hesitated with her thumb over the send button. Surely that wasn't too needy. Concern was reasonable when a man didn't come home like he said he would, wasn't it?

"Oh, for crying out loud." She hit send and tossed her phone to the counter. No more overthinking things, at least not for today. What she needed was a long, hot shower, and a frat-boy-sized breakfast.

Thirty minutes later, she strolled toward the kitchen with Ruger at her heels. The sweats she'd swiped from Jace's closet required enough rollovers at the waist it was almost laughable, and his tank hung halfway down her thighs, but they were comfy. In hindsight, she should've at least packed a few things before she loaded Ruger in Jace's truck and declared her path forward, but she'd been too caught up in the moment to think further ahead than five seconds. Though, maybe it was good she hadn't. At this point, she wasn't too sure if she was moving in for good, or just doing a back-and-forth, dual living arrangement.

God, where was Jace? A little conversation right now would sure help, because the longer her head went unsupervised, the more her warm-and-fuzzy fizzled.

The house was quiet, more so than normal. Midday sunlight slanted from the living room windows, and the steady hum of the washing machine's spin cycle droned in the background. Usually, she'd at least register the steady back and forth chatter between Ninette and Sylvie, but today all her senses caught was a trace of coffee and cigarette smoke. She rounded the arched stone wall that separated the main living room from the vast kitchen and dining area.

Ninette sat perched on a stool at the breakfast bar and stared into her coffee cup, one heel anchored on the stool rung and her elbow propped on the granite countertop. Smoke curled in a lazy ribbon from the tip of the cigarette wedged between her fingers toward the vaulted wood beam ceilings. Either she was deep enough in thought she hadn't heard Viv and Ruger's approach, or she was pissed off at Viv for leaving and was dishing out the silent treatment.

Either way, Viv would have to face things sooner or later, but she wasn't doing it without caffeine. "Good morning."

Ninette snapped her head up, took in Viv and the dog, and lifted an eyebrow. "You're back."

Distracted *and* pissed. Excellent. "Of course, I'm back. I'm nervous, not stupid. When I make my choices, I prefer to do them with a clear head. Your son has a talent for persuasion."

Ninette smirked and tried to hide it by sipping her coffee.

Pretending she hadn't noticed and didn't care, Viv opened the side door off the kitchen, let Ruger out for his morning business, and beelined for the Keurig.

"You get nervous a lot?" Ninette said. It was a fair question, though the idea of anyone, even a woman as fierce as Ninette, looking out for Jace seemed funny.

Viv ambled to the opposite side of the bar and leaned one hip against it. If she'd ever wondered which parent Jace learned the killer death glare from, she had her answer now because Ninette aimed hers dead center on Viv. "Jace is the kind of man I want with me."

The glare softened to cautious understanding.

"But I have no idea what I'm doing," Viv said.

Ninette's booming laugh filled the kitchen and echoed off the high ceiling, vibrant and full of life. "None of us do, honey. The best we can do is wing it and hang on for the ride."

"True." Viv checked her phone again. "Speaking of the man I want with me, have you talked to him? He said he'd come home last night and he's not answering his phone."

As quick as her laugher appeared, her sour expression slipped back in place. She looked away and took a healthy puff off her cigarette before snuffing it out. "Probably tied up at work. It happens. Got to let him do his thing." She snatched her coffee cup and strode to the sink.

"What's wrong?"

"Nothing wrong." Nice words, but they came way too quick and without a bit of eye contact, which was all wrong for Ninette. Just like Jace, neither of them said anything without full visual contact, particularly when it was important.

Ninette tucked the mug in the dishwasher and wiped her hands on a dishtowel. "Me and Sylvie are headed into town to run some errands for the boys. Probably best you do your work here today and give Jace a chance to get home. Let me know if you need anything in town." Another three seconds and she was gone, striding toward the wing of the house where she and Sylvie had obnoxious-sized suites. Both were decked out with what they called "unnecessary, but kick-ass amenities" installed by their overindulgent sons.

Viv paced to the windows overlooking the backyard.

Ruger ran hell for leather across the yard after Sylvie's little cairn terrier, Max, both of them with their tongues lagging to one side. The Toto look-alike dog might've been a sixth of Ruger's size, but in his head he was a giant, always provoking Ruger in one way or another.

Surely everything was okay. Jace had promised there wouldn't be anything else between them. Not once in their confrontation with Callie or his conversations with his brothers had he kept her segregated. So, why did her stomach feel like she'd stepped into the opening of a horror film?

No, everything was fine. He'd call her if it wasn't, and poking and prodding him all day with repeat phone calls would only put her in the annoying girlfriend category. No way was she going down that path.

She freshened up her coffee and wandered to Jace's study, leaving Ruger and Max to their sunny day. Logging into Jace's laptop, she dove into the event details of the week. Banners, caterers, scheduling and publicity. It sucked her in and buffeted her morning worries.

Hours later, her phone rang, 5:05 p.m. and a number she didn't recognize displayed on the home screen. "This is Vivienne Moore."

"Vivienne! I'm so happy I caught you. This is Evelyn Frank from Creative Souls. We met at the art auction a couple of weeks ago?"

"Yes, I remember you. How did the tally from the fundraiser turn out?"

"Fantastic. We drew an extra ten thousand in contributions this year and sold all of the artwork. Unfortunately, our scholarship announcement event isn't going quite as smoothly. I was hoping you might be able to help me out of a bind."

Viv barely stifled the squee that ripped up her throat and shoved to her feet so she could pace. Thankfully, her response came off a whole lot more professional than the giddy two-year-old happy dancing in her head. "Oh, how so?"

"I think I mentioned our usual planner has a somewhat challenging personal life. She contacted me over the weekend and said she's had some issues bubble up that won't allow her to finish what she's set in place. Re-

ally, everything's already scheduled, we just need someone to step in and keep things moving until event day."

"And when is that?"

"This Saturday. The venue is the same, so you already have some idea of how we utilize the space, and
it's a luncheon so the total event time will be limited to
two or three hours. I know it's short notice, but I was
hoping you might be able to lend us a hand."

Five days with the footwork already done would be
a cake walk, especially if their planner had done the
same level of planning for the luncheon Viv observed
at the dinner and auction. She punched up her calendar
on the laptop. "It looks like Saturday's free for a luncheon, but I've got several planning meetings for other
big events scheduled throughout this week. If you can
allow some flexibility where those are concerned, I
think we can make it work."

"Excellent! We've got several people you can leverage into long-term contacts, and with you stepping in
to save the day at the last minute, it will make an even
stronger impression. It'll be a win-win for both of us."

No kidding. If the crowd at the dinner and auction
was any indication, she'd be rubbing shoulders with
some of Dallas's social elite. Between Jace's business
connections and this event, she'd be able to grow her
client base across all income brackets. "How soon can
you get me contacts and existing information?"

"I've got it all gathered up and ready to send, including a compensation package for your time this week.
Shall I use the address on your card?"

"Please. I'll need a little time to review it and then
I'll contact you back with next steps. Sound good?"

"That's perfect. I'll talk to you soon."

Viv ended the call and rubbed her thumb along the phone's edge. As gift-horse opportunities went, this was huge. Definitely something worth touting on her resume if all went well.

She scrolled through the list to Jace's name and hit send, her blood humming with a champagne tingle.

"This is Jace. You know what to do." Jace's terse voice and the impersonal beep that followed dashed a little of her giddiness and breathed more life into the unease that had plagued her all morning.

"Hey, it's me. I'm sorry to call you again, but I just got the best offer from Evelyn at Creative Souls. They want my help for the scholarship luncheon next weekend. Isn't that great?"

Silence ricocheted back at her.

She clenched her hand and braced her knuckles on the desk. "Anyway, I was excited and wanted to share the news. I know it's silly, but I'm kind of worried about you. Call me back so I know you're okay."

Ending the call, she dropped the phone on the desk and plunked into Jace's big leather chair. When Jace had dropped her off, he'd acted like dealing with Hugo wouldn't be a big deal. More of an inconvenience than a worry. But what if it was a big deal? What if he'd gone off to handle Callie's mess and ended up in trouble? Damn, but she wished he'd call her back, or at least shoot her a quick text.

The study door opened and Ninette leaned into the doorjamb, one hand on her hip. The brooding frown she'd sported before was gone, replaced with an almost frightening determination.

Viv plastered on the best smile she could. "You and Sylvie have a good trip?"

"I lied, we didn't go. You a news watcher?"

Viv's head snapped back. "Why would you lie?"

"Never mind that. Time for you to take a break and catch a little TV." She opened the door wider and jerked her head toward the hallway. "Come on."

Fear wrapped icy fingers around Viv's neck and gripped tight. Rounding the desk, she hurried after Ninette, the edgy discomfort she'd tried to ignore all day blasting past denial and urging her forward at a near jog.

Ninette was already halfway down the hallway headed toward the entertainment room. She spared a glance over one shoulder. "Beck said I was supposed to keep my mouth shut, which I think is shit, but they didn't say anything about the TV staying off."

"Jace Kennedy, owner of several Dallas and Fort Worth nightclubs, is in the news again today, though this time his troubles are of a more personal nature than the woes his club has endured of late."

Vivienne dropped down in the middle of the leather sectional, Sylvie and Ninette on either side of her.

The eager beaver newscaster stood outside the downtown Dallas Police Department and aimed her best concerned citizen expression at the camera. The late-afternoon sun cast her in a picture-perfect frame she'd be able to use in resume segments for years to come.

"Early this morning, police arrested Kennedy, a colleague by the name of Daniel Parker, and a man suspected of being part of a well-known drug ring, in what was reported to be a sizable drug bust. Kennedy and his cohort were found in possession of cash in excess of one hundred thousand dollars, purported to be pay-

ment for illegal substances. Authorities were forced to
drop all charges and release Kennedy when they were
unable to produce evidence to support their claims.
The arrest comes behind a string of violence and drug-
related arrests at many of Kennedy's clubs—a point
local politician Paul Renner was quick to comment on
late this morning."

"Son of a bitch." Viv shot to her feet and snatched
the remote from beside Ninette, muting the sound before Paul's whiny voice could tack on to her escalating
temper. "Where is he? I just called and he's not answering his phone."

"Kinda hard to answer from jail."

Viv spun at Jace's ironic retort from the doorway
behind her.

He leaned over the couch and kissed his mom on the
forehead. "I see you take instruction real well."

"She's got backbone. She can take it," Ninette said.

Beckett sauntered into the room and Jace ambled
around the sectional headed straight for Viv, an apologetic smile on his face that didn't quite match the fatigue
on his face. Between the two, Viv wasn't sure whether
to slap him, or kiss him until he couldn't see straight.

"Wasn't worried about her spine," Jace said to his
mom, still aimed toward Viv. "Was worried about that
overactive mind and soft heart of hers. Think maybe
you might factor that in with your undercut next time?"

The second his arms wrapped around her, all the
tension she'd battled since waking up scattered. "You
should have told me," she said in his ear. "You said
nothing else between us."

"And what? Have you worried all day when I knew
I'd be fine?"

Vivienne pulled away enough to stare up at him. "How would you feel if I kept something like that from you?"

His lips twitched and he ducked his head to hide what she was sure ended up being a full-on grin.

Sylvie piped up from the couch with a well-timed intervention. "How'd ye manage to miss all the fun, Beck?"

"Stayed on the outskirts in case Hugo did something stupid. Me waylaying the cops that swept in is the only reason Moreno didn't end up cuffed like Jace."

"You helped Moreno before Jace?" Ninette said.

Jace turned to his mother. "It was a smart move. Got us a little good will with Hugo. Besides, I had Danny."

"Where is he?" Viv said.

Jace lowered his voice and cupped the back of her neck. "Danny's not Haven. Not yet. Last night was a test run, but he's fine. On his way to Louisiana with some clothes for Callie."

"Hell of a test run in my book." Beckett dropped into the corner of the sectional and threw a booted foot up on the cushion beside him. "The rest of the guys learn how he stepped up to take the fall for you, bein' a brother will be a done deal."

"How'd you get busted in the first place?" Ninette punctuated her question with a flick of her lighter and fired up a fresh cigarette, one of almost a carton if the giant ashtray on the coffee table was any indication.

Jace glanced at Beck, the first hint of worry he'd been unable to cover since his one-on-one with Callie at the compound. "Had to be a vice tail on Hugo. They probably saw a chance to make a big nab and took it." He focused on Viv. "I've got great lawyers and nothing but a stack of money to pin me with. I explained the whole thing was just a simple business deal, me reimbursing a club patron for damages to his ride while on my property."

"They didn't mention that part on the news."

"Why the hell would they do that?" Sylvie said. "It ruins the story."

True. Media outlets might aim to be fair and equitable in the way they covered the news, but they still had to turn a profit like everyone else.

Viv edged closer to Jace. The last thing he needed after a night like he'd had was a lecture, but no way was she dropping her point, no matter how uncomfortable it made everyone else. "You can't hide things like that from me. It's not right. Nothing between us means *nothing.*"

The weariness in his features shifted, the eyes of a patient and confident hunter staring back at her. He palmed the side of her face, tracing her cheekbone with his thumb. "So you're all in. Ready to lay everything out there?"

Shit. She'd stepped right into that one, and in front of an audience, too. She rolled her lips between her teeth and tried to ignore the three sets of very focused gazes aimed their direction. "You went to jail dealing with crap my sister created. I'd say I have an interest."

Jace chuckled and pulled her closer, kissing the top of her head. "I knew you'd shoot straight to guilt. That's why I told everyone to keep their mouths shut until I could be here in person to fight that reaction."

"Well, guilt is kind of a valid response, don't you think? You don't need any more bad publicity and wouldn't have had it in the first place if it hadn't been for Callie."

"It's over, sugar. Done. I told your sister it's the only pass she's getting. Now…" Jace ducked down, put a shoulder to her stomach, and stood with her dangling over his back.

"Jace!" She braced one hand at the small of his back and tried to push herself upright. "Put me down!"

Ninette, Sylvie and Beck all laughed at the two of them, Beck shaking his head as if Jace's behavior was par for the course.

Jace smacked her ass and strolled toward the hallway. "No way in hell. I've had a shit night and need some shut-eye. The least you can do is help your man get to sleep."

Sylvie's boisterous whoop rang out behind them. "Ha! I'm no' thinkin' sleep's the top on his agenda."

Ignoring her, Jace strode toward his suite, his booted footsteps muted by the thick crimson rug.

"Seriously, Jace. Put me—" Before she could finish her demand, the world spun and Jace caught her by the back of her head and back, buffeting her fall against his massive bed. "Down," she finished on a breathy whisper.

Jace held himself above her, knees on either side of her thighs and his forearms braced beside her head. "Missed you."

Any arguments, playful or real, died on her lips. With the curtains drawn nearly closed, only a sliver of late-afternoon sunshine cut through the room's darkness, but even in the shadows the stark vulnerability on his face wiped everything but right here and now from her thoughts. She smoothed her fingers through his beard along his jaw, too tongue-tied by the solemnity in his gaze to speak.

"Meant what I said in there," he said. "I asked them to keep quiet so I could be the one to combat you feeling guilty."

"I believe you."

He hesitated a moment. "Appreciate that, sugar, but you asked for everything, so you need something else." He studied her, his gaze shifting to absorb every nuance on her face. "I also didn't want them to tell you without me here because I was afraid you'd run. Being in that cell, knowing you were with me—that you chose me— was the best damned thing and the worst terror all at once. I just got you back here and I wanted a fighting chance to make sure you *stayed* here."

Her heart clenched and her hands trembled against his chest. She'd done that. Made him doubt her feelings for him by putting distance between them every time things got too deep or too frightening. Taking the time to evaluate moving in was one thing, a reasonable time to make a purposeful step, but there were plenty of other times she'd been too prone to bolt. Heck she wouldn't have even given him a chance to begin with if he hadn't been so determined and found a way to back her into their dates.

And then she wouldn't have this. This moment. This man.

She swallowed huge, the task ten times more difficult with the fist-sized knot in her throat. He'd been brave enough to admit his mistakes. After the shooting he'd looked her square in the eye and owned how he'd reacted too quickly. Too harshly. Surely she could do the same.

"I give you my vow." The words came out shaky. Far less confident than the ones he'd given to her, but no less heartfelt. "I might have tried to bolt in the past, but I won't do it again. I'll wait and think things through. I'll talk to you and hear what you have to say first."

His mouth curved in a slow, sexy smile. "Yeah?"

"Yeah."

He cupped the side of her face, his thumb trailing soft against her cheekbone. "Prettiest promise anyone's ever given me."

"I won't break it. Not any more than the one you made me."

He brushed his lips against hers, whisper soft, and gave her back her own words. "I believe you." Resting his forehead against hers, he closed his eyes and let out a relieved but weary sigh.

Wrapping her arms around him, she smoothed her hands along his back, savoring his heat and the comfort of his presence. "You're tired."

He lifted his head, that smart-ass grin of his slipping back into place. "Not the best idea to catnap in a holding cell, sugar. Haven't had any shut-eye, and what little sleep I've had since you left Saturday hasn't been for shit."

"Then let me take care of you."

One eyebrow cocked high. "That plan include you naked and next to me while I'm lights out?"

"How about you take a long, hot shower first? I'll get you something to eat while you're in there, and *then* you can go lights out with me next to you."

He gave her more of his weight and one of those low, sexy growls rumbled past his lips. "How about you shower with me? Then more than the shower will be long and hot, and we can get to you being naked faster."

She giggled, wrapped her legs around his waist, and tangled her fingers in his hair. "You're incorrigible."

"You like it?"

She more than liked it. She craved it. Craved *him* and every sweet, passionate and tumultuous moment that came with being with him. "What's not to like? Even better, you're all mine."

TWENTY-EIGHT

For the fourth time in under twenty minutes, Jace backtracked through the specs on a new joint venture and started up from page one. Usually, the numbers drew him in deep enough the rest of the world disappeared for hours, but today, not so much. For that matter, not yesterday either. All his mind seemed capable of processing was Viv. The things he wanted to show her. All the experiences he could give her. Every place and way he wanted to claim her. Having her three doors away through the workday made focus practically impossible.

He shucked the report to the side of his desk and reclined back in his chair, one foot on the edge of his desk and his hands behind his head. Two o'clock was too early for Scotch, even by his standards. Maybe he should look into a separate office space for Viv, or renovate one of the unused suites at Haven into an office for her. Then again, if he did that, he'd miss those short-skirt views from the passenger seat as they rode in together each day.

Hell no, he wasn't separating them. Maybe the better answer was to put her desk in here with his. Or, better yet, just have her work sitting on his lap.

He rubbed his eyes and tried to clear his head.

A knock sounded on his door and Viv peeked around the corner. "You busy?"

Not the kind of busy he needed to be, as in buried balls deep the way he'd been this morning. "Just working through some reports."

She stepped farther into the room, her jacket on and her briefcase and purse hanging off each shoulder. "You mind if I borrow your truck again? I need to run by the museum and double-check a few of the layouts for the luncheon this Saturday."

The luncheon. Man, she'd been so damned happy the last few days, totally pumped on the idea she'd landed a gig on her own and was doing something to help the charity he worked with. The perpetual grin on her face was enough to make a man want to trail around after her like a lost puppy.

He stood, opened the top desk drawer, and snatched the keys Ivan had delivered earlier that morning. "Can you drive a stick?"

Viv leaned her hip against the doorframe and pursed her lips. "Not since high school. After mom bailed, the bar didn't have anyone else to call when dad was too drunk to see straight, so I got a crash course with his beat-up GTO."

"Well then, this one should be a piece of cake." He dangled the keys in front of her. "You crawling in my cab shows way too much leg when I'm not there to fight off the gnats."

She twisted the key fob so the gold, black, and red shield with the horse in the middle faced her. "You trust me with the Porsche?"

"Trust you with a hell of a lot more than a car, sugar." He coiled an arm around her waist and pulled her to him. "Figured I'd keep it here so you have something to drive when we're working. You get in a bind, give me a call and I'll come get you."

"You sure? I was going to stop by my place and pick up a few things."

"Yeah, about that." For two days she'd tiptoed around their living arrangements instead of outright saying what was on her mind, and he was done with it. He tightened his hold and braced for impact. "No need for you to pack anything else. I'm sending a crew to pack up your clothes. If there's something else you want brought to Haven, make a list and they'll pack it up, too."

"Um, don't you want to talk about that first?"

"Been waiting for you to cross that bridge, but you didn't, so I just did. You want security while we figure out how this dance works, then you keep the townhouse. Rent it out if you want, and pocket the cash."

"I can't do that, I've got a mortgage."

"Not anymore you don't."

"What?"

"Your mortgage doesn't exist anymore. It's paid in full as of yesterday afternoon."

"Jace!" She straightened as tall as her five-foot-two frame would allow and got up in his face. "You can't just pay the note on someone's home without talking about it first."

"I can and I did." He nuzzled the spot behind her ear that always seemed to make her moan, and lowered his voice. "Though I'll admit Knox helped."

She tilted her head to give him better access and groaned exactly like he'd hoped.

"We can go over this as many times as it takes until you get it," he said against her skin, dragging slow kisses along her neck. "You chose me. I take care of what's mine." Pulling back, he met her eyes. "Now, no matter what happens to me, you've got a safe place no one can take from you. Besides, I want you with me at Haven."

She dug the heels of her hands into his shoulders and pushed away as much as she could manage with his un-yielding hold. "It's not right, Jace. You can't come in and pay off my debt. You already took a huge hit be-cause of Callie. How am I ever supposed to feel like I'm giving equal?"

"I see we also need to sit down and take a good hard look at my books. I cast my finances wide and deep. The bars aren't all I've got my fingers in, and neither your townhouse or Callie's fuckup will make even a blip in my bottom line. They're both done, so you may as well suck it up and start figuring out what to move and where it's going."

"Without a discussion."

"Yep. And this equal shit? Family doesn't do tit for tat, and you're way more than family. How's that for clarity?"

She screwed her mouth up to one side, gauged his face for two or three seconds and shrugged one shoul-der. "I don't know where I'll put my clothes. Your clos-et's full."

Praise Jesus, score one for the home team. One thing about Viv, she knew when to battle and when to roll over. She also had enough spunk she'd probably circle around for another skirmish before she accepted their new reality, but he'd be ready. "I'll give you the whole damned thing if you'll get more Levi's and lose some of the suits."

"I can't meet clients in jeans."

"Then keep the skirts." He skimmed his hand over her ass and down her thigh enough to slip beneath the one she had on and started inching it up. "I'll admit, they've got their perks."

She wrestled free and wiggled the skirt back down, a playful scowl on her face the whole time. "You're going to sex me to death."

"You got a better way to go?"

Her lips twitched as she hefted her briefcase back up on her shoulder. "We're not finished talking about the mortgage."

"Talk all you want, sugar, but it's done." He palmed her ass and smacked it. "Now go before I break the seal on office sex."

With a happy squeal, she hustled down the hallway and waved just before she headed down the stairs.

Hell, yeah, this was the life. Viv happy and bright, gaining her confidence, and shining all that goodness on him. He'd get those words from her. One way or another, he'd earn them and he'd never let her regret it.

Situated back behind his desk, he dove into his reports, determined to knock out his backlog so the night was free and clear for Viv.

An hour in, Shelly poked her head around Jace's door. "Hey, the lady from the charity is out front to see you. Evelyn Frank?"

His new proxy. Honest to God, if Evelyn hadn't offered the job to Viv when she did, he'd have yanked his funds from the organization and sent the scholarship winners to school himself. For all he knew, that's why she'd made the call to Viv. In the four years he'd worked with Creative Souls, Evelyn had gotten to know him pretty damned well. Enough to know he wouldn't keep shelling out nearly three hundred grand a year if the board started jacking with the mission statement. "You sure she's here for me? Viv's picked up a deal for them, too."

"Nope, she asked for you."

He sighed and locked up his computer. "Tell her I'll be there in a minute."

Shelly ducked back down the hallway, and Jace followed more slowly behind her. It wasn't Evelyn's fault Renner's newest lackey was a dick. And whether she'd hired Viv as a mercenary maneuver or not, the connections would help grow Viv's business without his input, something he understood her needing better than most. He'd be an idiot to screw things up for Viv by rattling cages now.

Jace wandered through the main section of the club, the lingering scent of cleaning materials overpowering the remnants of last night's so-so Tuesday night. The dance floor and surrounding booths sat quiet and almost completely shadowed, but if he bothered to check, he'd find every corner as shiny and new as the day he opened for business. He paid a mint for the crew that maintained Crossroads, but one of the things that kept his customers coming back was the place never got old. Not literally or figuratively.

Evelyn stood outlined in the doorway, the lobby lights behind her streaming enough to show her neck craned for a better look at the mysteries that lay beyond.

"Don't get too tied up on the dance floor," Jace said, still shrouded in the shadows. "It's pretty run-of-the-mill as far as bars go."

Evelyn spun and pressed a shaky hand to her sternum, a guilty smile flickering into place. "Jace. You startled me." She fiddled with the draped neckline of her designer red dress, accidentally nudging the long gold chain around her neck with her perfectly manicured nails. "I've never been here before, but have heard so much I couldn't resist taking a peek."

"I'll give you the whole tour if you want. The better sections run along either side, contemporary for the Millennial crowd, retro for the Gen Xers, and a pub for the folks who don't identify with a label."

Her face brightened as though she couldn't wait to accept, then flashed to a flustered, almost regretful grimace. "I'd love to, but I need to get back to the office as quickly as I can. Things are a bit hectic with the luncheon only a few days away."

So, she was on a mission for Davidson. It had to suck being the top dog's pawn. "All right, then. Let's have it."

"Yes, well..." She studied the tops of her conservative shoes, coughed and straightened up, meeting his gaze head-on. "The board wanted me to check in on something. Or, I guess I should say, see if there was any validity to some rumors they'd heard."

Guess he called that one. "And the rumor is?"

"I'm not sure you're aware, but I contacted your date from the gala and hired her to handle the final details for our scholarship luncheon this Saturday. Our planner had some personal issues that took her away at the last minute and we needed someone to handle the details."

He started to answer, but his gut checked the action, and he clamped his lips shut.

Evelyn's cheeks turned a delicate pink, and she fiddled with the latch of her designer purse, a nervous tell he was pretty sure she wasn't even aware of. "Some of the board members are wondering how deeply the two of you are involved. More to the point, they're wondering if I made an error in bringing her in to handle the event. Given the…err…mishap you had with the police the other day and all the problems with your clubs, they're not sure she's the right person for the job."

Son of a bitch. Guess that answered whether Evelyn had hired Viv as a slick tactic to keep Jace's money. Good news for Viv that she'd nailed it herself, but shit news in the realm of claiming her publicly.

"I told them not to jump to conclusions," Evelyn added quickly. "That I'd check it out myself and report back."

"Good of you to do that." How he uttered the blasé statement with the acid unloading in his belly was a damned miracle. Even pretending Viv wasn't his made him want to cut something. Didn't matter if it was only the three days until the event was over or three hours. Sure, Viv would understand if he told the truth, but losing this gig would suck all the happiness she'd been throwing around the last two days right out of her. No way was he doing that to her. Not now.

He shook his head and powered on all the finesse he could manage. "Nothing between me and Viv besides the work she's doing for the club. I needed a date, and she needed contacts. Sounds like it worked out for everyone."

Evelyn studied him a second or two. She might run in more refined circles than Jace cared for, but she was still a smart damned woman, one who knew chemistry when she saw it. Her eyes narrowed tighter for just a moment and she nodded. "I assumed that was the case. I'll be sure to share that information with Mr. Davidson and let Viv finish what she's set out to do."

"Appreciate it."

She turned and started toward the main entrance, but stopped a few steps in. "For what it's worth, this will be my last year with the board."

Jace pulled a much needed toothpick from his pocket and tucked it between his lips. "Odds are good it's my last, too." He just hoped his reputation didn't jack the whole deal up for Viv.

VIVIENNE NUDGED THE kitchen door shut with her hip and padded barefoot under the porte cochere to the four-car garage on the other side. It was one of two garages at Haven, the other with eight slots to match the overload of testosterone housed under the mansion's roof.

On the other side of the closed garage door, a heavy metal object clattered against the concrete.

Jace's voice wasn't loud, but it sure wasn't muted. "Cock sucking, no good son of a bitch."

Viv barely got the door opened without spilling either the crystal tumbler filled to the brim with Scotch for Jace or her red wine. No small feat considering how hard she giggled through the whole fiasco. "Whatever you're doing under there, it doesn't sound like it's going well."

Jace rolled out from beneath a classic, but beat-up-looking black Camaro. His faded jeans were ripped in a few places, and his black T-shirt should've been tossed a few years ago, but the way it stretched across his chest made her palms itch for contact.

He grunted as he stood. "You're late getting home." It came out as more of an accusation than a statement, his eyes hooded and all the more sinister with only the spotlight under the car brightening the garage. He snatched a rag off the hood and wiped his hands, prowling her direction.

Man, Ninette hadn't been joking. His mood was so thick it was hard to breathe, let alone meet his hard stare. "I had to juggle details for the speaker on Saturday." She handed him his Scotch. "Your mom said you've been a bear all afternoon and to come bearing gifts."

He set the drink on the workbench beside her with a careless thunk, never taking his eyes off her, and repeated the process with her wine. Coiling his hand around the back of her neck, he pulled her in close and backed her toward the wall. He grumbled against her lips. "Need this more."

His mouth slanted across hers with a vengeance, not angry so much as tense. Or was it needy? In the time she'd known him, he'd given her soft, sexy and downright dirty, but this was desperate. Deliciously dangerous and heady.

She relaxed into him, every muscle uncoiling and instinctively surrendering to his strength, letting him take control and crushing the details and worries of work to nothingness.

Her shoulders met the garage wall, Jace a solid mass of unyielding muscle against her front. He plundered her mouth, taking as much as he demanded. Coaxing her with carnal sweeps of his tongue she felt to the very tips of her toes. This wasn't about sex, or any prelude to it. This was about connection. A consuming, carnal fire that branded her from the inside out. As if he needed to claim her as much as he needed air.

He pulled away and stared down at her, his breath coming short and fast.

Viv palmed the back of his neck and tried to catch her own breath, her body demanding more even as her mind insisted words were more important. "You okay?"

Dragging his thumb across her well-kissed lower lip, he let out a slow exhale and rested his forehead against hers. "Gettin' there." He traced her jawline in idle strokes for long, quiet seconds and then eased back. "You got troubles with the thing Saturday?"

A long, tired sigh slipped out before she could catch it. "Not troubles so much as difficult people. The reps for our speaker felt it necessary to review every aspect of the luncheon and had a long list of requisite accommodations."

"Since when does Dean Haddock have a list of accommodations?"

Viv shook her head then rested it against the wall behind her. "Not Dean Haddock. Not anymore. It seems SMU had a conflict and had to yank the dean for a different engagement. Paul Renner's taking his place and his campaign team is making the most of it. You'd think he'd have to actually win the House election before his folks got to throw demands around."

Jace went rigid, the hand that had been absently massaging her uninjured shoulder clamping down in a firm grip. "Paul there today?"

"No." Her heart kathumped three speeds faster than normal, and the image of a rabbit bumbling into a panther's line of sight came to mind. "Is there a problem?"

He pressed against her, any distance he'd allowed between their bodies when he'd ended the kiss eradicated. His warm breath ghosted against her face, and he wrapped his arms around her, fisting his hand in her hair. "I don't trust him. Especially with you."

Surely he wasn't thinking of what she'd said after the gala. She'd explained that. Not once, but twice. "Do you trust me?"

Jace's gaze roamed her face, taking everything in. "I trust you with everything, sugar, but Paul's got a grudge where I'm concerned. He's done some crazy shit to try and even the score for things that went down in college. I can't help but wonder if he'd be willing to take his anger out on someone I care about."

"What kind of grudge?"

Jace studied her, his lips pressed tight and eyes sparking with anger. "I met him in law school. Most of the kids there were well off, even the ones on scholarships. A few of us were from rougher backgrounds and working to make things better for ourselves. Paul built connections with a handful of folks like me and ran a scam. Tried to fleece them out of their scholarship cash. I saw it coming, turned the tables, and left him red-faced and short on cash."

"Well, that's not so bad."

"No." Jace grinned, ducked his head, and rubbed the back of his neck. "Probably wouldn't have been a big deal if the college bigwigs hadn't gotten wind of it. They don't take too kindly to people who monkey with their income streams and scholarships fill their coffers more than you think. The ordeal ended up costing Paul's family a load of cash and trouble to placate the dean, and Paul still got the boot."

"So? How's that warrant him riding your ass now?"

"Money. His family put him in restraints and said he wasn't getting anything more than an allowance if he didn't prove he was worthy to inherit. The threat of losing a three-hundred-million-dollar estate is enough to make a lot of men do stupid shit. Rumor has it, him winning this election would get that collar out from around his neck."

Viv ran a finger down the side of his neck, his pulse strong and steady. "I bet turning the tables on him felt good."

Jace's mouth quirked and he leaned in close. "Didn't suck." He kissed her again, this time more tender than before, so rich with emotion it vibrated through her until her blood sang.

When he lifted his head, she wrapped him up tight and buried her face in his neck. "I'll be careful with him. I'll get through this and won't have to deal with him anymore."

Jace's arms tightened around her.

Vivienne pulled back to meet his eyes. "Is something else wrong?"

For the first few seconds, he scrutinized her, pensive and pressing his fingers deeper against her scalp. "I promised you there wouldn't be anything else between us, but sometimes a man needs to take care of things the way he sees fit. Need you to give me a few days, and then I'll tell you everything you need to know."

TWENTY-NINE

MIDAFTERNOON SUNSHINE SLANTED through the museum's windowed lobby, showcasing Viv's last-minute work in tidy detail. The white and stainless steel motif she'd selected for the furnishings had generated more than a few raised eyebrows, but then the volunteers had unveiled the scholarship winners' colorful artwork, and suddenly everyone was on board with the idea. Without competing colors or emphasis, the bold and vibrant works of their up-and-coming beneficiaries took center stage and generated a debut gallery feel to the event.

Evelyn had called it a stroke of genius. Viv chalked it up to Jace. Bit by bit, his constant encouragement had fashioned a key for her creativity, one that popped the locks on ideas she'd dismissed as asinine, and fueled her long-stifled instincts. The more she listened, the bolder her ideas blossomed, her textbook teachings resuming their place as guideposts instead of infallible rules that must be obeyed.

Striding through the wide lobby, she rechecked all the items from her clipboard. Chairs, press section, podium, sound system, brochures and catering, everything in its proper place and ready for action.

Perfect.

She pulled her phone from her pocket—2:37 p.m. With no more details to check on for tomorrow's luncheon all she'd do the rest of the afternoon if she stuck around here would be fidget, waiting for her time alone with Jace tonight. So what if she cut out before five and got a jump start on prettying herself up for her date?

Aftershocks from Jace's goodbye kiss on the front porch this morning rippled through her, bolstered by the devilish parting shot he'd added as she got in her car.

"Got the whole place to ourselves tonight, sugar. I suggest you delegate and save your energy for when you get home."

Her cheeks stretched on a huge smile. Yeah, like that wouldn't sabotage a girl's work ethic. Maybe she'd pay Jace back in kind and text him about the clean bill of health her doctor had sent over this morning. Odds were good he'd storm the museum and cart her back to Haven whether she was ready to leave or not. Especially since he'd already earned a green light from Zeke three days ago.

At least he'd acted a little more like himself this morning. He'd still been guarded and tight-lipped, refusing to share what had been on his mind all week, but some of the gruffness was gone. Maybe she could sex a conversation out of him. A sneak attack while his guard was down and his tongue was loose.

However it came about, Jace was due for his own come-to-Jesus talk. He might think he was helping by keeping her in the dark, but if he knew how many insane alternate ideas she plugged the darkness with, he'd probably spill every secret he'd ever learned.

"Vivienne!"

Viv snapped her head up and turned, Evelyn's chipper voice still bouncing off the marble floors and soaring ceilings. "I thought you were gone already."

Evelyn's coral suit and ivory camisole was a nearly

perfect contrast to their surroundings. Come to think of it, every time Viv had seen Evelyn, she always came color coordinated to the event with not so much as a hair out of place. She'd probably choke if she saw Viv's preferred after-work attire.

Flicking her hand toward the kitchens, Evelyn hurried Viv's direction, her designer shoes clacking a rapid rhythm the whole way. "The caterer caught me on the way out. You can never reach them when you need them, but they're always quick to find you when it's time for a payment. I'm ready to head out now, though. Do you need anything from me before I go?"

"No, I think we've got everything in place. All we do now is execute."

"Excellent." Evelyn unfolded her cashmere camel coat from one arm and shook it out. "I'm so glad this is almost over. I was ready for a change even before the new president's nonsense about you and Jace, but that whole bit was the last straw for me. It's time for something new."

Viv's heart kicked so hard she nearly fumbled her clipboard. "What nonsense about me and Jace?"

"Oh, it turned out to be nothing. Mr. Davidson heard you were intimate with Jace and, with all the bad press, insisted we find someone else to finish the event. Frankly, I'm surprised Jace has put up with all the social jabs they've given him lately. You'd think a charity would do whatever it took to keep their major contributor, not cut every tie but the finances."

"Wait, what do you mean, 'cut every tie but the finances'?"

Evelyn scowled and finished buttoning her coat. "The idiots basically kicked him off the board, saying they couldn't afford to have someone with such a jaded reputation providing guidance for the organization's future. Fools. I'll be shocked if he stays with them after tomorrow's announcement. It will take them months to find a replacement, but they'll do it without me."

She tossed her scarf over one shoulder, patted Viv's shoulder and winked. "Not to worry, though. You won't be affected. I went to see Jace myself and he insisted you two barely knew each other, so that's what I told the board. My advice, gobble up all the contacts you can, and make the most of it." She waved over one shoulder and hustled to the front door. "See you tomorrow."

He insisted you two barely knew each other.

Over and over it looped in Vivienne's head, a crush of emotions pile driving her all at once and nearly knocking her legs out from under her. She couldn't believe it. Wouldn't. Not after all he'd shown her. Jace was many things, but duplicitous wasn't one of them. At least not in a fashion that would ever hurt her.

Beyond the wall of windows, Evelyn hurried to her Lexus SUV, the strong winter winds tossing her sleek bob and tailored coat to one side. Evelyn was a smart woman. Observant, but discreet. No way would she have written off a relationship between Viv and Jace so easily, not after sitting next to them for most of the charity auction. And the timing alongside Jace's odd behavior the last few days was suspicious.

Something was up. Big-time. Something big enough he'd been willing to deny what burned between them. With one last glance around the lobby, she tucked her phone in her pocket and headed for her coat in the kitchen. Now all she had to do was figure out why.

THIRTY

SEVEN O'CLOCK. JACE yanked his watch off his wrist and tossed it to the nightstand. The heavy metal thudded against the wood and slid toward the edge, nearly taking his Scotch along with it. Three hours he'd tried to reach Vivienne. Three itchy, tense hours he'd spent imagining every worst case scenario before she'd finally texted back with a terse, I'm fine. Be home soon.

Soon. What the hell did "soon" mean? Thirty minutes? Two hours? Tomorrow? He snatched his drink and stomped to the balcony off his room. He should've put a tail on her, at least until he was sure the bit with Hugo was put to rest. Payoff or not, Hugo still couldn't be ruled out as the one who'd tried to take Jace out. After how much Jace had laid down to bail out Callie, the leap to figuring out how valuable Viv was to Jace wouldn't take Hugo long either.

Ruger padded alongside him and nudged his hand. For the last hour, the dog had barely left his side, whether out of worry, or man-to-man commiseration, Jace wasn't sure.

He dropped into one of the cushioned Adirondack chairs and glared up at the night sky. The spring stint had taken a nosedive in the last few weeks and reminded everyone it was still January. His heavy breaths fogged against the chill with each exhale, but at least the cold damped some of the fire beneath his skin.

Headlights swept the side of the house and the purr of his Porsche idled for a minute before the evening's quiet took over.

Thank God.

The muscles in his shoulders unwound enough he could move without feeling like he'd shatter in a million pieces, but his stomach wouldn't release. Something was up. His instincts practically screamed it. No way would Viv go radio silence without an explanation if something hadn't gone down.

Probably Paul. If he had any inkling what Viv meant to Jace, he'd pull any trick he could to screw things up.

A chime sounded from deeper in the house and Ruger took off at a sprint.

Keep your seat and your cool. If she was anything like him, the worst thing he could do was push. Prod, maybe, but not push. She'd evened out the last week. Found her place and her own footing between them. If she had a grudge, she'd tell him.

Maybe.

Fuck, where the hell was she?

A few minutes later, Ruger's happy panting sounded from the open door behind him.

A heavy swoosh sounded on the bed, her coat he'd guess by the weight of it.

Ruger's nails clipped on the wood deck before he pranced into view, his body wiggling with happy relief. He sat between the two chairs with his tongue lolling out to one side and stared up at Viv, still out of sight behind him.

Man, Jace understood that look. Perfect adoration and not an ounce of shame for it.

Viv strolled into view, her conservative black pantsuit and heels no more rumpled than she'd been when she'd left this morning, but her movements heavy with fatigue. Or trouble. Hard to tell which yet. She set a tumbler of Scotch on the table between them, eased into her chair, and patted her leg.

Ruger inched forward and laid his head on her lap so she could rub behind his ears.

Scotch. Not wine like she usually drank. Shit was definitely *not* good.

To hell with it. "Something buggin' you?"

Viv slowly nodded, her eyes locked on the crescent moon.

"I take it that something has to do with us?"

Again, with the sinister and silent agreement. Her fingers never broke the easy strokes on the back of Ruger's neck, but everything else about her said detonation was imminent.

The night's chill hit him all at once and mingled with a clammy, sick sweat along the back of his neck. He gripped one armrest hard enough the tips of his fingers went numb. A proactive approach might be best. Maybe cart her down to the basement and lock her up so she couldn't run. "You think it might be better if we talk instead of you disappearing off the face of the Earth and scaring me and your family?"

She twisted, the inquisitive fire behind her gray gaze turning the night's chill sweltering. "You've been angry the last few days. I want to talk about that."

Oh, hell no. That was the last thing they needed to talk about. In eighteen hours, the whole damned thing would be over anyway. Surely he could stall her for that long. "I told you I couldn't talk about that yet. I will. Soon. I need you to trust me."

She held his gaze, the same laser-like expression his mom had used on him when he'd done something stupid as a kid. The kind of look that turned a man inside out and almost compelled him to spill his shit. She sucked in a long, patience-buffering inhalation, and dragged her finger under Ruger's collar. "What would you do for me, Jace?"

"Anything. No limit." He straightened in his chair and set his drink beside hers. Intuition prickled with a foreign twist he couldn't interpret. "Someone hurt you? Paul?"

She cocked her head and picked up her drink. The sip she took was huge, even by his standards, but she gulped it down without so much as a grimace. Standing, she set the drink aside, crossed her arms, and studied the horizon. "Being in the dark hurts me. I'm diving into a relationship with a man who admittedly doesn't tell me everything, but insists I trust him anyway. Who's told me things I want to believe so much it hurts, but will devastate me if I find out it's all a lie."

She turned and nailed him the rawest expression he'd ever seen. "Do you know how hard it is to walk through the dark and not imagine all the trapdoors and booby traps along the way? I could barely navigate relationships with men I felt nothing more than appreciation for. Negotiating that terrain blind with someone who shakes me to the core is scary as hell."

For the first time since his calls went unanswered, his worry settled. Something had tripped her, for sure, but whatever did it wasn't the root issue. This was about trust. Building it. Understanding it, and giving her something to hold on to. "It's scary because you've got no practice." He stood and prowled toward her. He pulled her against him, his hands anchored just above her ass and in her hair so she couldn't look away. "What you don't get yet is that scary place you're stumbling through's not the dark. It's shelter. My shelter. No matter what it takes—money, time, words, or blood—I'll give it to keep you safe. Sometimes that means me keeping my silence."

"So, I'm just supposed to trust you? Cross my fingers and hope I don't stumble? Give me a reason, just one, why I shouldn't insist to know what's going on."

For the umpteenth time in a handful of days, the words he'd tucked away for when the time was right surged upright. Well, fuck it. She might be pissed he didn't wait longer, but he wasn't leaving her unarmed against her doubts. Not anymore. "I'll give you one. A big one you can hang on to no matter what happens." He cradled her face in both hands and leaned in close, willing his words to sink deep. "When I said I'd give blood to keep you safe, I meant mine. My life, if that's what it took. And scared or not, I think you know, a man wouldn't give up his life for a woman he didn't love."

Viv tightened her grip on Jace's shoulders and fought to keep her legs under her. His words slammed against her defenses and razed every barrier she'd ever built to their very foundation. Tears welled so fast they spilled down her cheeks before she could choke them back. A vicious pressure built behind her sternum, a mix of joy and utter terror sending her heartbeat on a wild ride. "Jace."

"You don't have to be afraid. And you're damn sure not alone." Slow and easy, he ghosted his lips over hers. A dark, yet beautiful angel coaxing her toward surrender. "Give it to me, sweetheart. Whatever's brought this on and weighting you down, let go and let me carry it."

She whimpered, and his mouth slanted over hers, catching the vulnerable sound with his kiss. His fingers tangled in her hair at the back of her head, holding her captive for his feasting lips and tongue. Strength and warmth surrounded her, a liberating presence that urged long-clipped wings she hadn't even known existed to unfurl.

And Jace would be there. Soaring beside her. Blazing paths in front of her. Always ready to dip and catch her if she fell. That was shelter. The safety and certainty she'd always wanted.

Pushing against his shoulders, she pried herself from his fervid mouth, her breath huffing short and heavy. Her lips tingled at the loss of contact. "I know you talked to Evelyn."

His features hardened and fear flashed across his face. "Whatever she said, you have to let me—"

"It doesn't matter." She smoothed her fingertips through the soft whiskers along his jawline. "I don't know why you said what you did, but I know it was for me. I suspected it right after she told me, but couldn't imagine why you'd say it. I drove for hours trying to figure out how to bring it up."

"I love you, Vivienne."

Her heart thudded to a stop then jolted to top speed. Nothing could sound as sweet as those words on Jace's lips. They burned through her, rumbling and beautiful as thunder. Forceful and intoxicating.

"I knew it the night I saw you at The Den," he said before she could catch her breath. "I didn't want to. Tried like hell to slake the interest somewhere else, to fight and hide it under curiosity and goodwill, but the truth is, you branded me in a second. I don't want to hide that mark, that piece of my soul you've cornered just for you, but I'd do it a thousand times over if it got you what you wanted."

"And you thought I wanted this gig."

"I know you did, sugar. Saw it in every saucy swing of your hips and the way you dug into the work. There's nothing wrong with you being pleased to score a win on your own. Me sucking up my pride for a few days was worth it to see you shine."

"I would've turned it down."

He smoothed a windswept strand of hair off her cheek and tucked it behind her ear. In that moment, the gruff, in-your-face man he showed the world disappeared, the love he'd confessed soft and gentle in his gaze. "I know you would have."

And there it was. Jace putting her needs before his. Blazing paths in front of her, even at his expense. She buried her fingers in his hair, the long strands tickling her forearms as she pulled him to her. Chilled wind snapped and whirled around her as if to faster spur the words pushing up the back of her throat. Her skin prickled with a heightened connection to the world around them.

Jace's stare never wavered, his easy smile and eyes filled with so much understanding and patience he seemed content to wait as long as she needed.

Her heart hammered in her throat. "I love you, too."

Quiet for such a declaration, barely audible over the wind, but the power it wielded inside rattled to her soul. The steady hum coursing through her catapulted to a resounding choir. She floated without leaving the ground, dancing with the weightless wonder of a feather on an evening breeze.

Jace cradled her face in his hands, eyes roving her features. "Won't let you regret that, Viv. As long as I breathe, I'll earn that gift." He closed his eyes and lowered his head, his nose sliding alongside hers as his warm exhale fluttered against her cheek.

"Jace." It was all she could get out, the knot of emotion in her throat too thick for words even if her mind was capable of generating rational thought.

His lips found hers. Teasing, lingering kisses that transformed her fears and euphoria to something else. Something desperate and wild.

"Need to feel you, sugar." He nipped her lower lip. "Need you under me."

No way would she argue with that idea, the promise of his weight and the way his muscled body moved against hers prodding her heartbeat faster. "Yes."

He cupped her ass and picked her up, his low, triumphant growl filling the cold darkness.

She curled her legs around his hips and clenched her hands around his neck, never breaking her lips from his.

Behind them, Ruger padded into the bedroom.

Jace reached back, thumbed her pumps off her feet, and lowered them both to the bed.

Ruger braced his front two paws on the edge of the bed as though considering whether he should or shouldn't take the leap, but Jace beat him to it, barely lifted his mouth from hers. "Ruger, *bett*."

Dropping to the ground with a pathetic whimper, Ruger padded to the insanely expensive dog bed Jace had brought home the night before.

Vivienne smiled against Jace's mouth and slipped

her hands beneath his T-shirt. That was another thing about Jace. He might've focused on uncovering parts of her she'd hidden away, but not once had he tried to change her. Without so much as a flinch, he'd not just accepted everything about her life, but made himself a part of it. She splayed her hands over his pecs, savoring his warm skin and exotic scent. "He hates that bed."

"Not sharing you. Not tonight." He levered her up enough to slip her suit jacket off and tossed it to the floor. Her ivory silk tank sailed right behind it. He hesitated at the sight of his tags framed by coral lace and nestled inside her cleavage. Cupping her breasts through the thin material, he dragged his thumbs across her beaded nipples and teased his lips over the exposed swells. "Gotta say, those look a lot better on you than they ever did on me."

"That's a matter of opinion. I liked them on you better. It gave me an excuse to touch you." God, she loved his mouth against her skin, the velvety glide and the way his beard rasped soft behind it. How his breath warmed her flesh but sent delicious shivers skating down her back. No drug could compare to this. No high or thrill-seeking adrenaline rush was capable of inducing this sweet, floating bliss.

"Sugar, one thing you don't need is an excuse to touch me." He licked beneath the lace edge, nudging the fabric lower as he worked the clasp behind her. "Ever." The fastener slipped free and he eased the bra away, his solemn stare locked on her exposed breasts as his thumbs teased the sensitive underside. "Never get tired of unwrapping you." He palmed them both and circled one peak with his tongue. "Never."

Scorching, wet heat surrounded her, glorious zings

of pleasure darting between her legs as he suckled her deep. Burying her fingers in his hair, she cocked her knees and flexed into the persistent ache building at her core.

His hips settled deeper between her thighs so his jeans-covered cock rode rough against her clit, but it wasn't enough. She needed more. Nothing between them but skin and heat. She shoved his T-shirt up to his shoulders. "Clothes, Jace."

He jerked away long enough for her to wrench the shirt over his head and latched onto the other nipple, plumping the breast he'd left behind in his hot palm.

She arched into his touch, reveling in his possessive grip and the slick heat of his mouth. His cheeks hollowed with each pull and his warm exhalations buffeted her skin. The image alone was enough to send her nearly to the peak, his dark features against her pale skin as wicked as the sensations he played on her body.

Sliding her hand between them, she palmed his shaft, so hard and ready, her sex spasmed in anticipation. She tugged the fastenings, but couldn't gain the leverage she needed to slip them free. "Baby, I need you."

He sat back on his heels and unhooked her pants. Tugging them past her hips, he backed off the bed and slid them free, studying every inch of her in a leisurely glide that left her wet and aching. He focused on the matching thong he'd left behind. "Christ, Viv." He braced one arm beside her hip and dragged his finger over the lace, down the center of her mound, and between her legs. "Drenched all the way through."

She rolled her hips and moaned, covering his hand with hers to increase the pressure. "Stop teasing, Jace."

"No teasing, sugar." He peeled the lace away and

straightened beside the bed, yanking open his jeans. "Tonight you get it all. Anything you want." He shoved them past his hips and his cock sprang free, thick and straining toward his belly.

Anything. Be whoever she wanted. Ask for whatever she needed, and he wouldn't judge. She parted her knees, the muscles at her core fluttering with a need only he could fulfill. "Anything?"

He kicked his jeans aside and froze, eyes riveted on her offering. "Anything."

Emboldened, she widened her legs further and trailed her fingers across her mound. "You said you wanted to take me bare."

His gaze shot to hers.

She dipped lower and circled her entrance, imagining his engorged head prodding there instead. "That's what I want."

His presence surged larger than life. No man had ever looked at her like that before. Hungry. Reverent. Wild and untamed. He crawled onto the bed, dark skin stretched taut across well-defined muscles. A predator. A dark lord stalking his conquest. An animal staking his claim.

Kneeling between her spread thighs, he fisted his beautiful cock and pumped, shameless and magnificent. "You sure?"

Oh, she was sure all right. Every day since he'd proudly brandished the results of Zeke's tests showing him cleared for action, she'd harassed her doctor for her own results. She nodded and sucked in a jagged breath. "I've been on the pill for years and I'm clean. I got the paperwork back this morning."

Slow and sexy, he inhaled deep, his gaze lingering

on her busy fingers at her clit before lifting his eyes to hers. He pried the hand she'd fisted in the comforter free and kissed her palm. His eyes slid shut as though offering a silent prayer. "Gonna take care of you, Viv."

The intensity swirled bigger, an all-consuming compulsion to feel him over her, around her, inside her. "Jace, please."

Keeping her one hand captive, he cupped her mound with the other, plying his fingers alongside hers and delving through her wetness. He guided her drenched fingers to his lips and licked. "Gonna make sure you never take those words away from me."

He laced their fingers together and leaned over her, their joined hands pressed on either side of her head. His rigid cock lay heavy atop her mound, a pearl of pre-come glistening at the tip. "Gonna mark you the way you marked me."

Ripples fired low in her belly and her hips surged upward, the greedy ache between her legs swelling to match her pulse. She closed her eyes and pushed against his hands as if that might somehow spur him faster. "Damn it, Jace. Please."

"Easy." His hands didn't budge, easily pinning her in place as he dragged his hips backward. He rocked his shaft along her clit, the prominent veins ravaging the tiny bundle of nerves with each slow, purposeful stroke.

A strangled sob slipped free, frustration and pleasure mingling for a mindless desperation. "I'm so close."

Shifting farther, his cockhead slipped between her folds and he prodded her weeping entrance. "This what you want?"

"Yes. Please."

He notched himself inside. "Look at me, sweetheart."

She pried open her eyes. His dark, fathomless gaze locked on to hers, so powerful in its intensity it swallowed her soul, surrounding her in warmth and endless shelter. Inch by inch, he eased inside. Stretching her. Filling her. Claiming her. "Jace."

He rolled his hips and increased his rhythm. A slow and beautiful crescendo that took him faster and faster, his long strokes plunging tip to root. Hunger licked through her, a ravenous and mercenary urge pushing her to consume everything he offered and demand more. "Feel it, sugar. Ride it."

She couldn't *not* feel. In that moment, sensation was all that existed. The tender push and pull of his flared head inside her. The slap of his sac against her ass with each thrust. The slick wetness as he pistoned deep. This was passion. Bright, bold and furious. Unique to the man claiming her. Taking her to the peak.

Pressure swelled and erupted red hot, the clench and release of her pussy around his shaft rippling out in all directions. She couldn't breathe. Couldn't think beyond the frantic pulses at her core and the ecstasy racing through her veins.

Above her, Jace shifted, driving deeper. His hair hung long around his face, his gaze locked on his thick rod spearing deep.

She wrapped her legs around his waist and dug her heels into his flanks. "I want it." She dug her nails into his shoulders and bucked against his savage thrusts. "Let me feel you come inside me."

He slammed to the hilt and his head dropped back, his throat corded and strained as a guttural roar broke free. His cock jerked and pulsed inside her, her walls contracting around him in a welcoming grip, milking him with greedy, almost violent clasps.

Two people, connected in one moment by something so much more than flesh. By something she'd never dreamed existed. It was perfect. Worth fighting for. Worth believing in and dying for.

Easing against her, he gave her his weight, rolling his hips and bracing his forearms on either side of her. A peaceful openness marked his features. No worries. No agendas or barriers. Only pure, undiluted emotion. Raw and vulnerable. His rasped voice rolled through her with the lure of distant thunder. "Love you, Viv."

She cradled his face. His hair lay damp beneath her palms and a thin layer of sweat slicked between their undulating hips. This man was hers. Despite her fears and uncertainty, he'd hung on and helped her find not just herself, but a whole new layer of strength. "I love you too, Jace."

He trailed slow, lingering kisses across her brow, her nose, her cheeks. "You good?"

She ground her hips against his, reveling in the feel of his release and the intimacy that came with it. "Better than good." She splayed her hand above his sternum and his heart pounded a heavy, but steady beat beneath her palm. She couldn't go through with tomorrow. Not after this. Not after what they'd done to him and what he'd done for her. "Jace?"

"Mmm?" He nuzzled her neck and kissed behind her ear.

"I'm going to call Evelyn and tell her she'll have to handle tomorrow on her own."

She felt him smile against her skin and his body shook on a chuckle. He lifted his head and grinned down at her. "No, sugar. You're gonna go, kick that luncheon's ass and tuck their check in your pocket. Then you're going to come home to me and we're gonna do this all over again."

"But—"

"You feel that?" He rolled his hips as if to make a point. "Doesn't matter what anyone thinks. Or what they *think* they know. You're mine. I know it. You know it. Our family knows it. Soon enough, we'll make sure everyone else knows it, too."

THIRTY-ONE

MORE LAID-BACK THAN he'd felt in years, Jace punched the gas on his Silverado and took the Highway 75 on-ramp at top speed. Midmorning sun beamed bold and beautiful across the outlet malls and restaurants lined thick on either side of him, the parking lots bustling with people out for stress-relief in the form of good old-fashioned capitalism.

He cranked Shaman's Harvest up a notch and leaned his elbow onto the center console. The clock on the dash beamed a condescending 10:15 a.m. back at him, but even being late for rally couldn't shake his good mood. Christ, the last time he remembered feeling this light was back when he and Axel were eight and spent their summer pedaling wherever their pawn store bikes took them.

Viv loved him.

Every time the thought swept through him it put a goofy smile on his face and knocked his discipline a little further off track. At this rate, his brothers wouldn't just yank his man card. They'd clear a space in the pantry for Viv to can and store his nuts. Fuck if he cared though. Those sweet little sounds she'd made as he'd pumped inside her, and the way she'd curled up against him after, made whatever they dished out worth it.

Maybe she'd be up for a hop to Vegas and a Haven-style elopement. Nothing said, "Let me spoil you rotten for the rest of your life," like a ride to Sin City on a private Gulfstream. Then again, going with her gut was still new to Viv. *I do* might be too much for her cautious nature just yet.

He'd get her there. One way or another, she'd take his name, no matter what it took to convince her. Hell, persuading her was half the fun.

The music trailed off and the Bluetooth ringtone filled the cab. Overlaying the navigation screen, Axel's name was plastered next to the telephone graphic.

Let the pussy-whipped comments begin.

Jace punched the answer button and switched lanes, goosing the engine up to eighty. "Yeah, I'm on my way."

A beat of silence. "How far out?"

"Twenty tops. The guys all there?"

Another awkward pause. "We got a problem, brother. Been waitin' to tell you when you got here, but Knox just called with more info. I'm not thinkin' it's wise to wait anymore."

The morning's peace evaporated in an instant. The sun, so full of warmth and promise seconds before, turned harsh and unforgiving, and the morning chill lanced to the bone. "Talk."

"Got the guy who shot Viv."

Jace fisted the steering wheel hard enough it groaned beneath the pressure and his mind lasered to a killing focus. "How'd you get him?"

"Knox got a hit on facial recognition with the cleaning crew about four this morning. He and Beck busted the nasty scunner layin' some serious accelerant on the far side of the club. My guess, if they hadn't caught the alert, we wouldn't have had a club to come to this morning."

"Where is he?"

"Got him tied up at one of Trev's hangars. He's not going anywhere soon. Probably wishes like hell he was dead after Beck worked him over."

"He got a boss, or am I only gutting him?"

Another voice sounded in the background, Trevor given the drawl behind it. A second later Axel was back. "Viv with you?"

"She's at the scholarship luncheon. Said she'd come by the club between one and two. Now who the fuck's this guy working for?"

"Shite." Movement rattled through the line, Axel moving and doing it quickly. "The museum, right?"

The hairs on the back of Jace's neck prickled, and the muscles in his chest tightened to the point he could barely draw a breath. "Axel, stop dicking around. Who the fuck is this guy working for?"

A loud *kachunck* rattled. The back emergency door he and Axel always used going in and out of the club. "Need you to reroute to Viv. Trev and I will meet you there."

Jace shifted to the far lane and gunned the engine further. "Axel—"

"Our boy Moreno got a new partner in crime," Axel said. "Got a contact from someone with a mutual interest in seeing you take a financial *and* a personal hit. Moreno provided the resource, his new partner provided the funding."

"Who's the third?"

Axel hesitated. "It's Paul."

The tires droned against the pavement, an irritating white noise that plucked his escalating temper like a foolhardy gnat. Paul. Motherfucking Paul.

Jace swung into the HOV lane. "You got proof?"

"Rock solid. The dozy cunt didn't bother to use a burner. Knox got bank transactions and traced call records linking directly back to Paul's accounts. Remember those two reporters Knox helped out last year on credit card hackers? Well, as of ten minutes ago, the evidence was wrapped up all tidy with a bow and shipped straight to them. Paul's political career is toast."

The buildings and concrete sound walls lining the highway streamed into one steady blur. Jace's body burned from the inside out, muscles coiled and ready for release. "His career's not going to make a shit by the time I'm done with him."

"Jace."

"That son of a bitch put a bullet in my woman."

"Jace." Axel's voice lowered, a calm and steady thread buffeting the cold, murderous storm raging through him. "Brother, listen to me. You want to hurt Paul, you take away his easy life. Take away the cameras and the money, and let him live with nothing. Vengeance in blood is too easy."

"I want him."

"And Viv wants you." He paused long enough to let it sink in. "Use your head, brother. Viv's a fine lass, but you can't hold her from a cell."

Vivienne. She'd bled because of him and his past. Could have been yanked out of his life entirely if she'd stepped so much as an inch farther in front of him.

"Jace. Talk to me."

The first of four downtown exit signs flew by on his right. Five more minutes. Five minutes and he'd take care of Paul once and for all. He ended the call and answered to the empty cab. "I'm done talking."

THE MUSEUM LOBBY thrummed with low, steady chatter from the catering staff and intermittent checks of the sound system. All around Vivienne, various event contractors scurried to handle last-minute details so they could collect their checks and get on with their weekend.

This was the good part. Watching puzzle pieces snap into place and surveying the big picture while her awareness prickled, focused and ready to intercept the inevitable curveball. Nothing was better.

Usually.

Today, she may as well have been in another state. No matter how many times she rechecked her lists, she couldn't find her groove, too many of her thoughts still tangled in Jace and last night.

Being here was wrong. No matter how many times Jace had assured her finishing was the right thing, it still felt like a betrayal. Sure, she'd pocket a few contacts, but at this point did she really want them? If what Evelyn said yesterday was true, the board had all but flayed the skin off Jace's back, but left him carting the bulk of their financial load.

He only did it for you.

Her stomach twisted, and she clenched her clipboard hard enough her knuckles burned. He'd have never taken their crap if she hadn't been part of the equation. She'd poked and prodded him for more information about the charity's actions, but he'd clammed up entirely saying it didn't matter.

It did matter. A lot. How could she stand here and cater to these people after everything he'd given her?

On autopilot, she paced toward the kitchen and scanned the assembly area set aside for reporters.

They'd had to double the area when word had gotten out Paul would be their guest speaker, although why anyone would want to broadcast any more of his whiny diatribes she couldn't fathom. Nothing fresh or creative ever came from his mouth. Since announcing his candidacy, all she'd ever heard were personal attacks on Jace and Paul's competitors with a dash of righteous crusades thrown in for fun.

Quick, sharp heel strikes echoed through the lobby and Evelyn's voice rang out behind her. "Vivienne!"

Viv turned to find her quasi boss bustling as quick as her legs could carry her without breaking into a full jog. Her cheeks were flushed and an excited sparkle gleamed in her pale blue eyes. She snatched Viv's arm as soon as she came into range and redirected her back to the front of the lobby. "I know you've got a lot on your plate, but Paul just arrived and Mrs. Renner is with him. If you're out to build your business, she's a name you want on the top."

"Paul's married?"

"Paul's mother." She dipped closer and scanned to make sure no one was in close enough range to overhear. "She's too hoity-toity to stay for the whole event, so if you want to meet her, now's your chance."

A commotion sounded from up ahead of them and flashbulbs went off.

"Oh, dear." Evelyn's hand clamped tighter on her arm. "The press is already here."

They were indeed. Lined up for a prime view of the podium were the three main network affiliates, held in check only by the black velvet stanchion rope separating the media queue from the contributing guests.

"It's fine. I'll handle it if they get out of hand." Actually, she'd like to give the sharks a boatload of bait and leave Paul floundering in a feeding frenzy. That wouldn't work to the charity's advantage though, and idiot board or not, the mission was still an important one for Jace.

She slowed her steps, forcing Evelyn to do the same, and pasted on a professional smile.

Ahead, Mrs. Renner motioned toward the podium and spoke to a younger man and woman hovering to one side of her. Somehow, she'd imagined Paul's mother would be the height of sophistication with a plastic-surgery-perfect face. But the woman barking orders ran closer to Queen Elizabeth, minus the matronly hats and about twenty pounds.

Paul turned as she drifted into hearing distance. As usual, he sported a black custom-cut suit with a classic politician's white shirt and blue tie. "Ah, Vivienne." He draped an arm around her shoulder and pulled her close. "Mother, you remember the event planner I mentioned over dinner last night. Vivienne Moore, meet my mother, Patricia Renner."

Flashbulbs fired in Viv's periphery and a shiver snaked down her spine. God help her if any of those hit the press. She didn't doubt Jace would believe her if she told him there was nothing to it, but Paul might still end up one arm shy of what he had today.

She stepped forward and offered her hand to Mrs. Renner, discreetly divesting herself of Paul's touch. "Mrs. Renner, it's good to meet you. Evelyn's said lovely things about your philanthropic work."

Oh, how the lies and bullshit rolled off her tongue. Normally, she'd breathe through it and remind herself of her goals. How the platitudes and niceties were necessary in her line of work. But were they? Really? What if she worked with people whose egos weren't so important they required constant stroking? Or, even better, her clients were people she respected and could learn from? Who was it that deemed the social elite better and wiser?

Patricia's droning, Charlie Brown teacher voice broke through Viv's meandering thoughts. "Tell me, what other clients are you working with right now?"

Her thoughts tumbled and sputtered in a chaotic mess, and her heart lurched. She opened her mouth to answer, but nothing came out. Time crashed around her in a blinding light with the force of a stampeding buffalo.

"I think you've caught our girl off guard, Mother." Paul palmed the small of her back. "You don't need to be shy with us, Vivienne. You've certainly shown your ability to work without a net this week. What other projects will be keeping you busy this year?"

Within earshot, the press looked on. Some had their phones mashed between their ear and shoulder, jotting notes on binders, and others simply held their phones in the best position to capture anything and everything that was said. Off to one side, a photojournalist stepped over to better bring Viv into the picture.

She licked her desert-dry lips and smoothed a hand down the front of her classic black sheath dress. "I have a wide variety of clients at the moment. Many are small business engagements, though there are a few charity drives intermingled."

A bullshit answer. Cheap and cowardly. And here she'd mentally flayed Paul for failing to make a stand in his politics. She couldn't even hold her own and show pride in a simple conversation.

"Well." Mrs. Renner folded her hands in front of her waist. "I'm sure we could do our part to help your small little business grow in thanks for helping us on such short notice."

Her "small little business." Man, the comparison to Queen Elizabeth had been closer than she'd thought. Viv was a little surprised Patricia hadn't paired the statement with a condescending pat on the head.

Paul motioned to the stadium. "My mother had a few suggestions we'd like to see incorporated, if you don't mind."

"Actually, I do mind." Viv straightened a good two inches taller and squared her shoulders. Small little business indeed. "We've taken significant care to place the event elements so all the focus is drawn to our scholarship winners' art." She faced Mrs. Renner deadon. "I'd also like to clarify. The people I'm working for are wonderful—a cutting-edge technology company, an aviation firm, security experts and several entertainment venues. There are a few investment companies as well. My main partner introduced me to most of them. Perhaps you've heard of him. His name is Jace Kennedy."

Reporters who'd only halfway been paying attention to the conversation went on point and jostled for better position. Flashes from a handful of cameras snapped in a riotous rhythm.

Paul pinned Evelyn with an ugly glare and his voice dropped to barely audible levels. "You said they were through."

Evelyn fiddled with the V-line neck of her cobalt blue

dress, but her eyes sparked with a bit of defiance. "Well, I didn't dig too far, and Viv was willing to dive in, so..."

Mrs. Renner raked Vivienne with a disdainful glower. "No wonder you were hesitant to claim affiliation. Jace Kennedy's a thug, and the people who do business for him are no better."

"Really?" Viv increased her voice so the reporters could clearly hear. "The way I hear it, it's your son who's fond of dirty deals, not Jace."

Behind the front line reporters, assistants scrambled to hand over notepads and microphones.

Patricia bristled and snapped to the peak of her barely five-foot frame, shooing Evelyn away with a dismissive wave. Her words shook with whispered fury. "Unless you have the means necessary to protect yourself in a libel suit, I suggest you hold your accusations."

"It's a bit more than accusations, isn't it? I mean, no one can prove you bought off UNLV's dean to hide Paul's scams, but I'd bet the college covered their ass and kept a public record on why Paul was expelled."

"Ma'am, are you alleging wrongdoing by Councilman Renner?"

"Can you elaborate on your claims?"

"Explain the connection with UNLV."

Questions fired from the reporters faster than she could register them all, each leaning over the rope and angling for her attention. Paul's bodyguards swept in tighter, forming an intimidating barricade between their little group and the agitated media.

Paul gripped her upper arm and steered her back two steps, protective for all outward appearances, but his eyes snapped with thick, gut-churning rage. He murmured low enough he couldn't be heard over the crowd.

"You're a foolish woman. I'd thought you'd be smart enough to learn your lesson with Jace and take advantage of a fresh start."

Undaunted, Paul pinned her with a deadly stare and slid his hand so it lay directly over her wound. He smiled and squeezed.

Viv whimpered and tried to break free, but Paul's fingers dug deep, honing-in almost dead center to where the bullet had ripped through her flesh. "Bad things happen to foolish people, Ms. Moore. I suggest you learn that and recant your nasty lies before things get out of hand."

Jace's voice cut above the crowd's chaotic roar from over her shoulder before Paul's words fully died off. "Things are already out of hand. Now get your fucking hand off my woman."

THIRTY-TWO

JACE YANKED VIV away from Paul and into his arms. Her heartbeat thrashed against his chest and her breaths came short and rapid, but she was safe. Safe and surrounded by what looked like a press op gone wrong.

Every one of the men and women clambered for position, their voices shouting for even a flicker of acknowledgment.

Paul pasted on his politician's smile and ambled closer to the press, hands up in a placating motion. "If everyone would please relax just a moment, we'll take a few questions in an orderly fashion. This is simply a misunderstanding."

Beside Paul, Mrs. Renner shifted uncomfortably, her facing burning a livid red.

"Councilman Renner, can you elaborate on your relationship to the lady behind you and her claims you were expelled from UNLV?"

Jace slipped his hands beneath Viv's hair and cupped the back of her neck. Beneath his palm, her skin was cool and clammy. "You want to tell me what the hell they're talking about?"

Before Viv could answer, Paul's holier-than-thou voice carried over the throng. "Ms. Moore was assisting us with today's event and unfortunately fell victim to a disgruntled colleague from my past. It was all a misunderstanding."

Viv spun in Jace's arms and faced the crowd. Despite her tiny stature, the air around her snapped with the fury of a giant. "I didn't misunderstand anything. If you'll check UNLV's records, you'll find Paul Renner was discharged from the university for attempting to swindle scholarship and student loan funds from fellow students."

A commotion sounded near the main lobby entrance, a separate news team scrambling in with cameras pointed their direction.

Paul tagged the crew rushing into the fray and stepped back with a small nod. "I believe we'll address these accusations in a more appropriate venue after authorities have had an opportunity to investigate further."

You want to hurt Paul, you take away his easy life. Take away the cameras and the money and let him live with nothing.

Jace shifted Viv behind him and stepped into Paul's line of retreat. "I'm thinking those authorities might like direct contact with the people who almost lost their money. I'd guess their lives are in a much different place ten years later and not nearly as swayed by threats to keep their silence."

Before Paul could reroute, or fire an answer, a woman from the newest team shouted and thrust a microphone between the wall of guards. "Councilman Renner, we received evidence from a trustworthy source today tying you to an individual known to work with Hugo Moreno."

The bustling room stilled, all attention shifting to the reporter who'd posed the question.

Paul smoothed his tie into place and tucked one hand in his pocket. If it hadn't been for the shaky smile that went with it, the unruffled stance might have worked. "I assure you, I have no ties of any kind to Mr. Moreno, nor any of his associates."

"Sir, the files sent to us today show intermittent, large deposits into the account of Carlos Santoia, a man arrested for possession with intent to distribute and photographed on numerous occasions with Mr. Moreno. Each of the deposits occurred just twenty-four hours prior to very public arrests for dangerous and illegal substances at Crossroads. The latest deposit was recorded yesterday morning in the amount of ten thousand dollars. Last night, Mr. Santoia was recorded in the act of attempted arson."

"The information is fabricated." Paul glanced at his mother beside him and visibly flinched at the furious scowl she aimed back at him. "Once researched by authorities, I'm sure the root of this unscrupulous information will be uncovered."

"In addition to the deposits, there are also phone records indicating your direct communications with Mr. Santoia. Do you claim those were falsified as well?"

"Of course. This is nothing more than Mr. Kennedy seeking retribution for negative media coverage."

"Sir, these reports came from outside Mr. Kennedy's realm and from a source who's skilled in tracking white-collar crime. Do you have history with Mr. Kennedy that would justify his falsifying such evidence?"

Mrs. Renner's expression hardened and Paul's lackluster smile slipped. She motioned the two young assistants behind her toward the back entrance and marched away without a word.

Paul stared at his mother bustling away and his face blanched. Even when he faced the crowd, his eyes seemed distant and unfocused. "I'm sorry, I won't be able to address your questions at this time." He spun and strode after his mother, his bodyguards tight on his heels.

Jace turned to follow, but Viv gripped his arm. "Jace." She burrowed against his chest and wrapped her arms around his neck. "Let it go."

He pulled in a deep breath, praying for something—anything—to quash the mushrooming need to eviscerate the narcissistic bastard. Viv's fresh, sunny scent surrounded him like an answered prayer.

Viv's a fine lass, but you can't hold her from a cell.

Axel was right on that score, and any retribution sure as hell couldn't be divvied out with reporters and cameramen scampering at every exit. He'd no more had the thought, than he sensed his brothers behind him.

Trevor rounded to one side of Jace and Axel on the other. "What the bloody hell happened here?"

Jace gripped Viv by each shoulder and edged her back enough he could see her eyes. "Kind of like to know that myself."

Viv ducked her head for a second, fingers plucking his T-shirt at one shoulder. "I lost my temper." She looked up and rolled her lips inward, genuine remorse flooding her mystic gray eyes. "I know I shouldn't have said anything, but Mrs. Renner called you a thug, and I lost it."

Trevor hung his head and pinched the bridge of his nose, his torso shaking on a chuckle, but Axel's hardy, baritone laughter sang through the lobby without a care for who heard it. "Damn, you're a feisty lass." He slapped Jace on the shoulder. "And here we were foolish enough to think she'd be left all alone with the big bad wolf. I take it that last bit we walked in on had something to do with Knox's tidy package?"

Jace nodded. "Ended up being twice as bad with Viv's little preshow warm-up."

"He was behind the shooting, wasn't he?" Viv asked.

Trevor glanced over his shoulder and scanned as though gauging who might be able to hear. "That and everything else. We can't drop evidence on the shooting without bringing you and Zeke into it, but we can damn sure nail him on the drugs and arson."

"It's still not enough." Twice now Jace had lived through the gut-grinding panic of closing in on Viv in a nasty situation. No way in hell was he letting a third happen if he could help it. "That son of a bitch needs to pay for what he's done."

"He will." Viv laid her hand over his heart and cocked her head at a cheeky angle. "And if it's all the same to you, I'd find it a whole lot more satisfying if you let karma be the one to collect. Besides, all of this year's shows are in reruns now, and Sylvie and Ninette have been looking for their next popcorn fix. I can't imagine they'd find anything more entertaining than watching Paul dodge reporters and squirm on the stand."

His brothers' laughter roared full force on either side of him, and Viv beamed a beautiful, mischievous smile up at him.

Christ, he was blessed. All the shit Viv had gone through because of him, and she could still lift him up. Absolve him and unwind his fury with a simple quip and a saucy smirk.

He pulled her to him, kissed her forehead and guided her toward the back exit. "We'll see."

THIRTY-THREE

THIS WAS THE LIFE. Safe, tucked up tight next to Jace on the black leather chaise, and surrounded by lighthearted family chatter. The laid-back type of night at home Viv had dreamed of as a kid but never had.

The entertainment room was packed, all the brothers stretched out on the sectional, or on the floor with piles of pillows behind them. As usual, Sylvie and Ninette sat perched in their primo, center seats, feet propped up on the coffee table with a bowl of popcorn between them. The only thing missing was Callie.

Man, but she owed Jace for his intervention. Even more to Zeke who'd gotten Callie in a ninety-day treatment center. The best of the best, he'd called it. A place that didn't just detox and introduce them to twelve-step programs, then send them out the front door, but actually worked beside them in the early days. After talking with her on the phone this afternoon, she believed it. It'd been years since she'd talked to Callie without the topic centering around a drink, a crisis, or the next party, but today had been different. Her voice had been clear and bright and her thoughts genuine and heartfelt. Especially the shaky, "*I love you, Vivie,*" she'd shared before they'd disconnected.

"Mmm!" Ninette waved toward the TV and swallowed down her mouthful of popcorn. "Here it is."

"*The political climate in the race for U.S. House of*

Representatives turned frigid today for front-runner Councilman Renner after a white-collar crime investigative source leaked evidence tying Renner to one of Texas's most notable drug lords."

Knox chimed from his spot on the floor and smacked Beckett on the shoulder. "Ya hear that? 'White-collar crime investigative source.' I like the sound of that."

"Why?" Beck said. "It's just refined speak for hacker."

"Haud yer wheesht. Ye'll make me miss the good parts." Sylvie fisted another handful of popcorn.

Axel chuckled from the corner seat beside her. "Never mind you've recorded and watched the bloody five and six o'clock stories three times already."

"Yeah, but it never gets old." Ninette nudged Zeke in his spot beside her. "Turn it up."

"Bank transactions and call logs tie sizable deposits to one of Hugo Moreno's colleagues and are suspiciously timed with well-publicized arrests at Dallas's local club, Crossroads. Recordings were also submitted showing a foiled arson attempt committed in the early hours this morning with a corresponding deposit from Renner's accounts a day prior. Renner's campaign office has been unavailable for comment, however, family matriarch Patricia Renner appeared briefly outside their palatial ranch on the outskirts of Dallas earlier this evening."

The video cut to Paul's mother, stiff-backed and obviously wrung out, standing outside the front door of a home Viv would have expected in *Gone With the Wind*. An older man nearly a foot taller stood slightly behind Patricia, a supportive hand placed on her shoulder. She unfolded a sheet of paper and delivered her comments in a monotone, almost beaten voice.

"*The Renner Family wishes to address the accusations made against Paul Renner this morning in hopes that requests for comments and interviews by the media will cease and desist, and that attention will be refocused in a proper direction.*

"*This family does not condone, or approve of, affiliation with individuals tied to illegal activity, nor do we approve of malicious endeavors to undercut private citizens through fair means or foul. While we hope that the claims against Paul prove to be unfounded, we wish to make it clear that we have no participation in the alleged actions, nor will we be a part of the investigation or resolution. Regretfully, this will be a trial Paul faces on his own. We ask that you respect our family's privacy, and allow us this time of adjustment.*"

"Damn." Trevor scratched the back of his neck and bunched his long, surfer-god blond hair on the top of his head. "Tried, convicted and publicly hung in under twelve hours by his own family. That's harsh."

"Guess that answers whether or not he's back in the will," Beck tacked on.

"Not harsh enough." The gentle tug of Jace's fingers as he combed through Viv's curls belied the angry bite in his voice.

Viv splayed her hand over Jace's chest. His heart thumped slow and steady beneath her palm, as constant and vital as the space he'd claimed in her life. Over and over, she and the guys had tried to rein Jace in since they returned home.

Axel had even gone so far as to tell him his dick had made him stupid. The altercation had almost started a true brotherly tussle, until Axel had slapped his chest with both hands and held out his arms at each side. "Go ahead, you wallaper. You always did swing like a pussy."

Somehow, Axel's in-your-face approach had punched through, and Jace had shaken his head and laughed it off. Of course, the Scotch Viv had promptly handed him hadn't hurt either.

"Do you think the guys would mind if we went to bed early?" she asked where only Jace could hear.

Like the run-in with Axel, Jace's mood swung a one-eighty and his eyes lit with an indulgent gleam. "Don't really care what they think if it means getting in bed with you." He lifted her hand off his chest, kissed the inside of her wrist, then pried himself out of the chaise. "We're out for the night."

"Ah, ye fuckin' killjoys." Axel jabbed his mom with an elbow, his brogue twice as thick around his mom. "Didnae I tell ye they'd be all googly-woogly and cut short our fun?"

"Leave 'em be, lad." Sylvie waved Jace and Vivienne off and grabbed more popcorn. "Beckett's brought the first three *Fast and Furious* movies, and we're not stopping until they're done."

Jace helped Viv out of the chaise and paused next to Trevor. "You get that thing I needed taken care of?"

"Yep. Next two weekends are good. You get the okay, I'll handle everyone's schedules."

With one short nod, Jace guided her out of the room with a hand at her back.

"What was that all about?" Viv threaded her fingers with his as they strolled down the hallway to the back part of the house and Jace's suite.

"Planning."

Great. Even getting Jace out from in front of the TV and away from repeat images of Paul's sanctimonious mug wasn't enough to pull him out of his caveman responses. "Planning what?"

Inside their room, he shut the door behind them and ambled to the bed. He tossed the accent pillows and the shams to one side. "Making sure something doesn't happen again."

She grabbed his wrist midway pulling back the covers. "Jace, you have to let this thing with Paul go. I'm fine. The press has everything they need to make sure he learns his lesson. His life will be a living hell for months."

He sat on the edge of the bed and pulled her between his legs. Starting at the top, he slid free the buttons on her favorite chambray shirt. "Wasn't talking about that." He slid the soft, worn fabric over her shoulders and sucked in a long, steadying breath as he appreciated her bared breasts. He trailed the backs of his fingers up and over her sternum, then ghosted his thumb across her wound. "Though I'd like Paul's life to be a hell of a lot longer than a few months."

Goose bumps scattered along her skin and her breasts grew heavy and hungry for his touch. Part of her wanted to drop it and do whatever it took to make him give her more, but then that was probably what he wanted. "Then what are you planning?"

For long, palpably rich moments, he studied her, his palms smoothing up her arms and over her shoulders instead of where she craved them. "It piss you off I didn't claim you with Evelyn?"

A tingle wiggled down her spine, an alert for something big barreling her direction. "Yes."

"You want me to be able to do it again?"

"You do and it'll take a lot more than an apology and great sex to make it up to me."

His lips quirked to a wicked smile. "Great, huh?"

"Well, it didn't suck." She slid her hands under his T-shirt and guided it up and over his head. "It still wouldn't buy you another get out of jail card if you pulled that mistake twice."

Before his T-shirt hit the floor, he pulled her astride him and rolled her to her back, pinning her to the mattress. "Then make sure I can't ever do it again." His dark hair hung loose around his stern face, his rich, nearly black eyes so intense it stole her breath. "Marry me."

The world around her froze, sound and time screeching to a halt while her mind scrambled to catch up. "What?"

"Marry me." He cupped the side of her face and skimmed his thumb along her cheekbone. "Take my name so everyone knows you're mine."

Marriage. With Jace. To have this closeness, this connection, to someone long-term. The concept powered through her head, rippling across details and roadblocks faster than she could process them all. "But we haven't even talked about that. About what we want from life. About what long-term looks like. Or kids. I don't even know if you want kids."

"I want you. I want my family. I want an easy life where I can be myself and love the people around me without worry. If that includes kids, I'll be thrilled. If it doesn't, I'll share my love with other kids the way

I've done all along. Everything else is just details. Now, say yes."

"But what if—"

He silenced her with his lips, bold, coaxing strokes from his tongue lulling her adrenaline-laced panic into a slow, pulsing burn. Bit by bit her muscles uncoiled, her body surrendering to the moment and the future he offered. Slowly, he pulled away. "Say yes. Don't overthink it. Just take the leap and let me catch you."

Tingles scampered up her neck and across her shoulders, and soft, wispy flutters spiraled through her belly. His scent and weight blanketed her, so symbolic of the anchor he'd proven to be in her life. The ferocity in his gaze promised so much more than words ever could. "This is crazy."

"Is that a yes?"

God, she was insane. Bungee jumping whacko insane. A giggle bubbled out of nowhere and she smiled so big her cheeks hurt. She buried her fingers in his hair and hung on tight, her breath huffing marathon fast. "Yes, it's a yes."

"Good choice." His mouth lifted in a satisfied grin. "Though if you'd said no, I'd have made it my mission to persuade you."

He would've, too. Since the first night she'd met him, he'd never stopped pursuing her. Never failed in his protection of her. Some women might find it stifling, a step beyond contemporary boundaries, but for her it was constant and sweet. A solemn vow from her rough and tumble, take-me-as-I-am man. "I'm finding I like the way you persuade me, Jace Kennedy."

"That's good, sugar, 'cause you're in for a lifetime of it." He framed her face, the raw emotion and sincerity she'd felt in his kiss bared in his dark eyes. "Whatever the future gives us, however that happens and whatever it looks like, I'll be here. Whatever it takes."

EPILOGUE

GOOD FOOD, LOUD music and his family all around him. Or more accurately, his family and his wife. Jace braced his booted foot on the rung of Axel's chair beside him and kicked back in his chair. Even through the music's pounding bass, Viv's happy hoots and shouts hit Jace loud and clear from his table to one side of the dance floor. Her Levi's and black tank were way more sedate than the other women preening through the Bellagio's trendy bar, but not a one of them held a candle to Viv.

Damn, but the woman could move, her hands cocked above her head, eyes closed and head swaying with that wild hair of her loose on either side. And those hips. If she kept that shit up much longer, their post-wedding party was going to be mighty damned short.

Trevor rounded the table on his way back from the bar and waved at Sylvie and Ninette, both dancing off all the excited energy they'd built prepping for Viv's surprise getaway. "Man, you're one lucky bastard."

"Don't I know it." Jace took the beer Trev offered and tipped the top in salute. "Appreciate you working out the trip."

"You had him at 'Vegas,' and you know it," Knox said.

Beckett shook his head and swirled his Jack and Coke. "Still can't believe you bit the bullet, Jace. I love the hell out of Viv, but married? We're talking no more variety, bro."

"I don't know, man." Zeke cocked his head for a better look at the girls, still going strong. "I think it's good. It feels good having another woman in the family."

"Och, there's another lad dancing with trouble. Before you know it, you'll be standing for the priest and statin' your own vows." Axel sat up in his chair and dropped his voice to a gravelly rumble, his face a scowling imitation of Jace at the ceremony. "'And under no circumstances will I beat, maim, or spill blood in the name of vengeance for Vivienne, particularly where Paul is concerned.'"

"I still can't believe she made you say that," Knox said to Jace.

Jace could. Viv had prodded, pouted and threatened to back out of the wedding until he'd sullenly agreed. Though she'd been right. The media and Paul's family disowning him had done a pretty damned effective job of trashing his life. "Told her I'd do what it took. It made her happy, so I said it."

Beck snickered over the rim of his drink. "Plenty of loopholes in that wording, too."

"Exactly," Trevor said.

The song shifted to something new, and a rush of women flocked the floor, crowding out the freeform dancers for a line dance.

Sylvie and Ninette whooped and sashayed toward the bar, eyeballing their fair share of men on the way.

Viv ambled to the table, one hand piling her hair on top of her head and the other fanning her face. She scanned the rest of the men at the table. "Seriously? I'd thought you guys would have a whole string of women lined up by now. Don't tell me this marriage business has you guys gun-shy?"

"Not us, lass." Axel curled his arm around her waist on her way past and pulled her into his lap. "We're takin' notes from our fearless leader and his fetching bride so we know how to find our own paragon of virtue."

Viv's laughter rang loud and full, so at ease with his brothers Jace's chest tightened as though a giant fisted his heart. She was perfect. For him. For their family.

Jace nudged Axel's chair with his boot. "Stop pawing my wife, you mangy Scot. Pretty sure those vows meant she only gets to sit in my lap."

Axel scoffed and smacked Viv on the ass as she pried herself out of his bear hug. "Bloody killjoy. And if anyone's mangy, it's you. I know my Armani from Hugo Boss." He rubbed his hand across his chest, the weighted glow of his fifth or sixth Scotch shining in his eyes. "Never underestimate the power of cashmere on a lass."

The whole table broke out in a chorus of chortles, Knox and Beckett extolling some of Axel's more colorful wardrobe phases.

Viv straddled Jace's lap and circled her arms around his neck, the bold and colorful woman he'd sensed in her from the beginning shining bright. Her cheeks were pink and her smile satisfyingly peaceful. "You sure they're having a good time?"

"You worried about your boys?"

"Well, I don't want them bored. This is supposed to be a party."

"Sugar, it's only ten o'clock and we're in Vegas. They're just getting warmed up. Trust me." He pulled her left arm free and studied her wrist, smoothing his thumb along the edge of her new tattoo. He still couldn't believe she'd gotten Haven's ink. The edges were still red, but the artwork was off the charts badass. Designed like a metal cuff, she'd taken their emblem and made it her own. "Feel okay?"

She shrugged and wrapped him back up. "A nuisance more than anything." Her eyes glittered and she winked. "Nothing to knock me off my wedding night game."

Oh, yeah. His woman was out of her cage and living large. He cupped her hips and pulled her in tighter. "My old lady need attention?"

Her lips hovered just inches from his, curled in a pretty smirk. "I'm all hot and sweaty."

"Bet I can get you sweatier."

"But the guys—"

"Will deal just fine. Now, are we leaving, or staying?"

She bit her lip, and her smile answered about two seconds before she did. "We're leaving."

"Good choice." Jace stood, taking her with him then lowering her feet to the floor.

"Where the hell are you two going?" Knox shouted.

"Gotta consummate my marriage."

"You did that two seconds after you said 'I do' and left with Viv over your shoulder. The bloody reverend didn't know whether to laugh or call the cops."

Like he'd ever get enough of Viv. An hour or a hundred years from now, he'd still fight to keep his place beside her.

Jace slapped Axel on the shoulder, and nodded to the rest of his brothers, pulling Viv tight against his side. "A man has a job to do, he makes sure it gets done right."

* * * * *

If you fell in love with the Haven Brotherhood in
ROUGH & TUMBLE...
You're going to fall even harder in WILD & SWEET...
Read on for a sneak preview
from Zeke and Gabrielle's story.

ONE

FRIDAY NIGHTS WERE such an irony. With no social life, Gabrielle Parker could stay up as late as she wanted and sleep to obscene hours the next day, but there was never anything worth burning the midnight oil to watch. On the bright side, she'd logged a few more of hours of overtime at the garage. Fixing clunker engines that should have been scrapped years ago might not compare to a hot date, but one more paycheck and that computer she'd been saving for was a done deal.

She dodged a nasty pothole on the dark country road and steered her custom '71 Chevy C-10 truck into her tiny subdivision. God, she loved where she lived. Big yards, a beautiful lake not more than three hundred feet beyond her backyard, no fences, and down-to-earth people. Dallas and its suburbs might be caught up in everything new and flashy, but Elk Run clung to its sixties and seventies charm. In fact, it was the only neighborhood in Rockwall or around Lake Ray Hubbard that hadn't sold out. There sure wasn't any waterfront property left. In the last ten years, all the land around the lake had either been gobbled up by big conglomerates for their huge money-making enterprises, or fancy schmancy neighborhoods lined with jaw-dropping McMansions.

Rounding the wide curve at the end of the one-street edition, her headlights swept her single-story, ranch-style home. The simple rectangle layout with its shallow, gray asphalt roof and buttery-yellow siding probably wouldn't appeal to other people her age, but she wouldn't trade it for anything. She could do without the empty driveway though. Her brother's missing car was no surprise. After all, Danny had a thriving social life, but in the two years since their dad had died and left them the house they grew up in, she still hadn't gotten used to coming home without Pop's car being in the third empty space.

She slammed the shifter into Park, killed the engine, and snatched her purse off the bench seat. Maybe Danny being out on the town was a good thing. No older brother meant no one giving her grief over her movie selection. She could *Pretty Woman* it up all night and no one would be the wiser. Or maybe tonight she'd splurge and give *Troy* a go. Hard to say no to Brad Pitt in his heyday.

Two steps past the gleaming indigo hood of her truck, she stopped dead in her tracks. Mrs. Wallaby's porch light wasn't on. She could have sworn she'd left it on this morning when she went over to feed her vacationing neighbor's cat, but then she'd also been running thirty minutes late for work and hadn't had her first cup of coffee. With that combination, she was lucky she'd made it to the garage with jeans on.

Keys jingling in the otherwise quiet spring night, Gabe cut across the three-quarter-acre lot to her neighbor's house. Now was as good of a time as any to pick up the mail and make sure Astrid had enough to eat. The sky was deep sapphire velvet with not one cloud to mar it. People in the city didn't have a clue what they were missing on a night like this. Fancy skylines and close conveniences might be nice every now and then, but no way would she trade it for the starry goodness overhead.

She thumbed through Mrs. Wallaby's mail on her way to the front stoop, sorting out the weekend sale circulars and bills. Unlocking and opening the front door, she flipped the hallway light on, let the storm door swing shut behind her, and ambled through the short entry.

"Astrid?"

She'd made it halfway through the living room before the darkness registered. In the corner, the lamp she definitely remembered flipping on before she'd left this morning sat dark on the end table next to the couch. And where the heck was Astrid? The only time she no-showed at mealtime was when strangers came to visit.

The fine hairs on the back of her neck and arms lifted and a shudder trickled down her spine. The house was pure quiet. No breeze, no settling creaks, or humming from the air conditioner. Just dark. Eerie, too-quiet dark.

She dropped the mail on the coffee table and slid her phone out of her jeans pocket. No reason to freak out. Mrs. Wallaby probably just sent one of her grandkids out to check on the house and they'd accidentally trapped Astrid in a bedroom. It sure wouldn't be the first time the skitzy cat had found herself in such a bind.

Punching the main button on her phone for a quick check-in with her neighbor, the home screen flashed a blinding white. Before she could blink her eyes back into focus, quick-moving, heavy footsteps pounded from the hallway behind her and a bulky, shadowed form lumbered toward where she stood. For one freeze-frame moment, his remarkable gaze locked onto hers, spotlighted by the phone's soft glow. Before she could dodge out of the way, he shoved her hard to one side. Her boot snagged on the coffee table, and the right side of her torso slammed crosswise against the marble top.

Son of a freaking gun. That hurt.

The screen door slammed, and the rumbling echo of her crash course with Mrs. Wallaby's anvil-sturdy furniture still resonated through the house, but no more footsteps. And thank God for that, because her side felt like it had gone head-to-head with an engine block. Rather like a stubbed toe times ten thousand while some unseen force squeezed her lungs in a vise grip.

She pushed to her back and yelped into the darkness. Okay, so moving wasn't a super bright idea. Neither was breathing. But staying here was even higher on the stupid scale. Yeah, the house was quiet now, but only an idiot hung around in the dark after a run-in with a thug, and she was definitely not an idiot.

Bracing her ribs with one arm, she sucked in a very limited breath and forced herself upright. An ugly grunt croaked up the back of her throat and a cold sweat broke out across her forehead and neck. For about five seconds, she wasn't even sure staying vertical was a maintainable goal. If she couldn't see with her own eyes that Mrs. Wallaby's table was still whole and hearty posttumble, she'd have sworn a sliver of the marble had broken off and buried itself between her ribs.

She shook her head and clamped tighter to her phone. She staggered to the sliding glass door that led to the backyard just in case the shady linebacker was still out front and flipped the lock. Putting her weight into opening the door, she tottered out into the night as fast as her protesting ribs would tolerate and dialed 911.

Two hours since Zeke Dugan had walked away from his last trauma case, and he still couldn't unwind. After three twelve-hour emergency shifts in a row, his body might be on board with a direct trip home and a whole lot of shut eye, but his psyche was still jonesed up from blood, guts, and gunshot wounds.

Punching the locks on his Z28, he strode to the private rear entrance of Trevor's new bar, The Den. Not a snowball's chance in hell he'd have brought his custom '69 hot rod to Deep Ellum if he'd had to park it out front, but safe in the private back lot with Beckett's security cameras overhead, only an idiot would mess with his baby.

The crowd's low and happy rumble hit the second he pulled the door wide. Barely nine o'clock on a Friday night and the place was already packed, which went to prove that Jace and Axel weren't the only two Haven brothers who could launch an entertainment venue. Any businessman who could draw the Deep Ellum crowd before eleven or midnight was a genius.

Zeke chin-lifted to the little brunette bartender he'd referred from his own days slogging drinks while he worked through med school. "Hey, Vicky. Guys busy?"

"Only if you call Trevor gloating over his full house with Jace and Axel busy." She motioned to the adjacent room through the wide arch, never breaking stride on the order she was working. "They're laying down roots in their usual booth. You want a Bohemia Weiss?"

"Yep. No hurry."

She grinned. "You sure? You look like you need a shot of something with more punch."

Oh, hell no. "You forget my Mr. Hyde side?"

Her smile died, and this time she nearly fumbled a

shot glass. Of course she hadn't forgotten. Zeke's hair-trigger temper had intervened in the form of unforgiving fists and zero conscience when a bunch of frat boys thought it was a good idea to not take no for an answer where she was concerned. It was a wonder he hadn't gone to jail. But then again, that was the night he'd met Jace and Axel. If it weren't for them heading off the cops, he'd still be tending bar, but with a record, instead of living his dream as a trauma doc.

Her expression softened, understanding and grateful all at once. "I haven't seen that side of you in years, but if it's high-end Brazilian beer you want, then that's what you'll get."

"Appreciate it." He ambled to the opposite side of the bar, weaving through the forest of square tables and laughing patrons. Trev had wanted a place where people could hang out as regulars but with a trendy vibe. He'd absolutely nailed it. Rock and movie memorabilia from the last forty years adorned exposed red brick and ivory mortar walls, but the bar along back had literally been flown in from Kilkenny, Ireland. If a Hard Rock bar got it on with an Old-World Irish pub, The Den would be their out-of-control offspring.

Crossing into the second room, the whole atmosphere shifted. Tiny white lights like the ones that went on Christmas trees were strategically placed on the ceiling so they didn't look strategically placed, and every seating area had its own style. Sixties to ultra-modern, tables or booths, it didn't matter. Every spot gave a nod to a different trend.

Not surprisingly, more of the women hung out in this room, which was also why The Brotherhood had its own reserved spot in the back. No one sat there but brothers or those they'd claimed for their own. Ever.

Jace, Axel, and Trevor all marked his arrival about three steps into the room and offered everything from a raised beer to shit-eating grins in the way of greeting. The tension he'd been carrying around all night eked out of him. This was what he needed. If anyone could help him get to the bottom of whatever was eating him, it was his brothers.

He jogged up the three steps to the raised, semi-enclosed space and rounded the table for a chair with primo viewing. "No Viv tonight?" he said to Jace.

Jace finished off his Scotch and slid the empty out where their waitress could see he needed a fresh one. "Got a gig she's working tonight. Some of Trev's old buddies."

Axel snickered. "Not thinkin' managing a male dance review falls under your new wife's definition of hardship."

"Whoa," Zeke said. "Been a while since you've been in touch with your old crew." In fact, Trev studiously avoided all reminders of his brief stint shucking clothes for drooling women.

Trevor raised his beer and eyeballed Jace over the rim. "I'm actually surprised Jace didn't put up a fuss when I told Viv what the guys needed. They might not go full monty on stage, but backstage it's a damned free-for-all."

Jace stretched one arm along the back of the vacant chair next to him and smirked. "So long as they don't touch and I'm the one burning off the sexual frustration after, I don't care if they drop trou the second she walks in the back door. Besides, Viv worked up is a thing of beauty."

"Ach, Christ," Axel said. "There he goes again. Rubbin' his good fortune in everyone's face."

Their waitress sauntered up the steps, hips swinging and long, uber-platinum blond hair hanging loose to her shoulders. The impact would have been a knockout if the smile on her face didn't feel so calculated. "Vicky sent your refreshes. Scotch for Axel and Jace, Bud for Trevor, and Bohemia Weiss for Zeke."

Impressive. Zeke didn't recognize the woman so she had to be fairly new. Either Vicky had prepped her good before sending her in with refreshes, or she was a woman with drive. The question was whether the drive was healthy ambition or geared toward snagging a sugar daddy.

Trevor finished off his beer and slid it to the waitress. "Thanks, Lannie. Don't worry about us for a while. If we need you, we'll flag you down."

So she was after a sugar daddy. Too bad. Good help willing to learn and grow in a place like this would be a godsend to Trevor with all his success.

"You sure? I don't mind checking back."

"We're good, darlin'." Pure calm, cool Trevor. The bastard never lost his head, not even when it came to leveling justice via his fists.

Disappointment penetrated those vibrant, but all too worldly green eyes of hers a second before she spun and sashayed down the steps.

"She's a persistent lass," Axel said.

Trev pushed back on the hind legs of his chair and rested the butt of his beer bottle on his thigh. "A little too much for my taste. Never seen a woman scope out and target customers with big cash to spend faster than Lannie."

"You sure she's not a plant?" Jace said. "Never know who might be out for info."

Trevor shrugged and took a swig of his beer. "Knox ran a check. Wouldn't hurt to have him take another go though."

"Where the hell are he and Beckett anyway?" Zeke said. "I thought they were coming out tonight?"

"Knox is knee-deep in some hacking case. Beckett had a last minute call from some socialite out in Fort Worth in need of a security detail," Jace said.

Axel snickered and sipped his Scotch. "Bloody bastard never could say no to a pretty face."

"More like a pretty paycheck," Trevor said. "Beck said she's got good long-term client potential with low risk."

"Damn. I wanted to hear how Danny was doing with Beckett's crew." Zeke had been the one to introduce Danny Parker to the brothers almost two years ago. If things kept going the way they were, he was all but one vote away from being the next addition to the family.

"Not a bad word to be heard," Axel said. "According to Beckett, the man's taken to security and protection like an adolescent boy to *Playboy*."

Not surprising. Danny's future had damned near gone to hell in a handbasket his senior year in college, breaking into high-end homes and stealing what he needed for a blossoming drug habit. According to Danny, it was his dad and a serious come-to-Jesus one-on-one that had knocked some sense into the young kid. "Knox ever finish the deeper dive on Danny's background?"

"Not much more than what we uncovered when you first brought him in," Axel said. "Still working at the body shop you found him at when he's not working with Becket. No major changes in relationships. His mom's still stacking up minor drug offenses, though how the hell she's dodging them I'll never figure out."

"She a looker?" Trevor asked.

"Haven't seen a picture, but Knox has," Jace said. "Said she doesn't look a thing like Danny, but probably held her own about twenty years ago."

Zeke turned his bottle on the tabletop, widening the circle of condensation around it. "She going to be a problem?"

"Don't think so," Jace said. "Knox found trails where Danny's given her money, but no evidence it's more than him making sure she keeps her distance. From what we can tell, there is absolutely no love lost between mom and the rest of the clan."

"He's got a sister, right?" Trevor said.

Jace nodded. "Yep. Gabrielle."

"Gabe." All heads shifted to Zeke. "He calls her Gabe. Says all the guys do."

"You met the lass?"

Zeke shook his head. "No. Been by there a few times and have seen her truck out in the drive, but she's always locked up in the bedroom when I'm there. Got a sweet ride. Another one of Danny's custom jobs, a '71 Chevy C-10 with a highboy conversion."

"A woman with a custom truck." Trevor shook his head and knocked back more of his beer.

"Not surprising really, if you think about it," Zeke said. "She grew up with men. Danny said their dad kicked her mom out when Gabe was little. Add to that, she works with men all day as a mechanic. Danny says she's a really good one too."

Jace planted an elbow on the table and ran his thumb through the beard along his jawline. "Well, she must spend a lot of time there, because she hasn't got much of a social life. Knox said she didn't have one damned social media account active. No records. No tickets. Hell, all he could find in the way of pictures was her driver's license. For a twenty-four-year-old in today's world, she's an anomaly."

"Any idea how we find out more about her?" Zeke said.

Trevor tipped his head to the wide arch that fed in from the main room. "We could just ask him."

Sure enough, Danny ambled into the room hand in hand with a tiny little brunette with super short hair and a biker vibe. His customary wool skully was in place, this one navy blue instead of his usual gray or black. His black hair hung way past his shoulders. Blended with his dark skin, most people chalked him up as Native American on first glance, but given what Danny had shared about his dad, he'd guess his ancestry ran closer to India.

"I don't know." Zeke tapped the side of his beer with his thumb. "Any time Gabe's come up in conversation, he's gotten tight-lipped. I get the feeling he's sensitive where she's concerned."

"Protective." Axel twisted enough to get a better view of Danny, now introducing himself to his lady's friends. "Not a bad characteristic in my book."

As if he felt the four sets of eyes on him, Danny turned and locked gazes with the rest of them.

Jace waved him over.

Danny gawked, obviously surprised by the summons. Considering no one but brothers, Viv, or the moms ever sat at their table, the shock was understandable. Even the women he'd all but forgotten around him seemed a bit stunned.

Still, he didn't hesitate. If Jace's invite made him uneasy, he didn't show it, making his way through the casual sitting areas like he traversed the path every day.

Before he hit the top stair, Zeke stood and held out his hand. "Hey, man. Didn't expect to see you here tonight."

Danny clasped his outstretched palm. "Didn't exactly plan on it, but..." He motioned over his shoulder where the pixie-headed brunette still waited with her friends. "Sometimes you go where goodness leads, yeah?"

He shook hands with the guys and took a chair with his back facing the crowd. Not a bad move considering how many curious eyes were pinned on him. Trevor dove in first, making small talk and asking about Danny's gigs with Beckett.

Axel leaned in and rested his forearm on the table. "You thinkin' Beck's line of work is something you might be interested in long term? Or are you more interested in building your custom work?"

Danny's eyes widened. "Hadn't really thought that far ahead. Can't really pull custom work alone. Not without a bigger pipeline."

"If Zeke's ride is any indication, you got a serious gift." Jace dipped his chin. "If it's something you enjoy doing, then you should do it."

A ringtone sounded and Danny grimaced. He slid his phone out of his back pocket, checked the home screen, and frowned. For about two seconds, it looked like he'd answer it, but he sent the call to voice mail instead and sat the phone face up on the table. "Sorry."

Before anyone could answer, the phone lit up again.

"This ain't a job interview," Jace said. "You need to take the call, take it. That seat won't combust while you're gone."

Danny picked up the phone, scanned the men at the table, and stood. "Yeah, it's my sister. Give me a minute."

As soon as he hit the bottom step, Jace mirrored Axel opposite him and crossed his arms on the table. His gravelly voice was only loud enough those at the table could hear. "Well, that could prove a timely opening."

"Timely, or altogether wrong." Zeke jerked his head to where Danny was standing not fifteen feet away. Danny's stare was hard and locked on some distant spot against the far wall, one hand planted on his hip and tension radiating off him hotter than a late August afternoon in Texas. "Whatever she wants, it doesn't look good."

Zeke had no more finished his sentence then Danny hustled back up to the table. "Hey, guys. I hate to do this, but—"

"There a problem?" Jace said.

"You could say that. My sister's hurt. Had some asshole tackle her while she was checking on a neighbor's house."

The buzz Zeke had fought to unplug since he'd walked out of Baylor's level one trauma center ratcheted back into top gear. "Hurt how?"

Danny shook his head. "I don't know. Not bad enough she couldn't call me herself, but bad enough I could hear paramedics in the background givin' her shit for not taking treatment."

"It's bad enough she called paramedics?" Zeke said.

"Not her. The cops. Sounds like she walked in on

a break-in next door." He met each man's eyes one at a time, but did it with an urgency that said he'd put his sister's needs before his own without a backward glance. "I gotta go."

Zeke stood. "We'll take my car. I got my stuff in the back."

"Man, I can't ask you to do that. It's all the way out in Rockwall."

Rounding the table, Zeke slapped Danny on the back. "I know where you live. My ride was practically reborn in your garage, remember?"

"Ah, the legendary birthing place of badass hot rods and our fearless doc in action." Axel stood and chin-lifted to Jace. "This I gotta see. You in?"

Jace threw back the rest of his Scotch, plunked the tumbler on the table, and followed his lead. "I hear Rockwall's a happening place on the weekends. Can't miss this."

Trevor grinned and rose slow from his chair. "Have a feeling I'm gonna regret missing this, but I got a business to run. Y'all have fun."

Danny stood rooted in place, his gaze shuttling between the three of them.

Axel motioned him down the stairs. "Your sister needs you, and we're following you two. Get a move on."

God, the look on Danny's face was priceless, the lingering worry for his sister mingled with the disbelief he had not one, but three men at his back when he needed it. Zeke slapped him on the shoulder and jerked his head toward the back parking lot. "You heard the man. Let's do this."

TWO

Just over the I-30 bridge, Zeke downshifted and took the first exit on the far side of Lake Ray Hubbard.

The engine protested the unwelcome yank on its reins with a throaty growl and startled Danny out his silent study of the passing scenery. "Sorry, man. I should have been giving directions."

"Might have only been to your place a few times, but it's kind of hard to forget." The subdivision was basically just one long street lined with small, old-school craftsman and ranch-style homes that looked as good now as they had thirty or forty years ago. Even better were the huge yards and scenic views. Just driving into the neighborhood was like entering a utopian time warp. "So tell me what we're walking into."

"Don't know much," Danny said. "Just know Gabe went to check on one of the neighbor's houses and got knocked around by someone who'd broken in. She called the cops, then me."

"You catch anything the paramedics said to her?"

"Couldn't hear them over her growlin' at them to stay the hell away from her."

Yelling was good. It was when people were too out of it to give a shit, or couldn't talk at all that spelled trouble. "She say where she got banged up?"

"Nope, but she's not too talkative. Not in situations like this. Tends to clam up." Danny rested his elbow on the passenger door and shoved his skull cap back an inch. "She sounded like she hurt, though. Kind of like she was holding her breath. If you knew Gabe, you'd know that means it's probably bad."

"When you say she tends to clam up, what's that mean?"

For a second or two, Zeke thought Danny had zoned on him again, his gaze locked on the businesses and homes streaming by outside. "She doesn't do so good with people. One on one she's okay once she gets to know you. It's the getting to know you part that's tough. She comes off a little rough. Standoffish. Most people figure she's a bitch."

"Is she?"

Danny twisted to make eye contact. "Gabe? Ah, hell no. She's about as sweet as you'll ever find. She just locks up around strangers. People think it's because she wants nothing to do with 'em, but the truth is, she can't cope."

"She's an introvert?"

Danny shrugged and straightened in his seat. "We thought that was the deal at first. Or that she was really shy. Then some shit went down in middle school and high school. Dad took her to a shrink, and he said she had some kind of anxiety thing. Something to do with social settings."

"Social Anxiety Disorder?"

"Yeah, that sounds right."

Well, that explained why Knox couldn't find a social footprint for her. "The doc give her anything for the diagnosis? Any meds to help her out?"

"He offered, but she wouldn't take 'em. Said she didn't want drugs controlling her."

Man, he hated hearing things like that. It wasn't an uncommon response, but it was damned unfortunate considering the right script could open up a whole new world for people like her. "You don't talk about her much. What's she like?"

Danny huffed out a near silent chuckle. "Like I said. Sweet. Got a great eye for art. Takes care of the whole damned neighborhood like they're her blood." He opened his mouth, closed it, and frowned.

"What? Her having a heart and taking care of the people around her sounds like a good thing."

Danny shook his head. "Taking care of the neighbors isn't the bad part. What sucks is they're the only friends she's got."

"How's that bad?"

"Because there's not one of them under the age of sixty-five. She's twenty-four years old. Most women her age are on the phone, ringing up their girlfriends non-stop, and out chasing men. Gabe's got no girlfriends. Only had two boyfriends I know of, and those lasted about a week each."

Now that was intriguing, especially considering how Danny had no problem jumping into social situations and making friends with even the nastiest personalities. "You think something happened to trigger it? Something in school maybe?"

"I don't know. Maybe. She tried to fit in with the girls at school a few times, but none stuck. The last time I heard her mention people from school, she was twelve. Came home in tears and wouldn't go to school for two days after that. Dad didn't have a clue what the hell to do, so he bought her a camera. She's been wrapped up with her art ever since."

"Photography?"

"Sort of. More like graphic art, but she takes the pictures and then makes it into something else. You have to see it to understand."

Rounding a wide curve in the old road, the Camaro's headlights swept the painted Elk Run subdivision sign up ahead. Unlike the fancy rock and iron-work entrances that marked the high-end neighborhoods farther down, Elk Run's reminded Zeke of public campsites and state boundary lines alongside the highway. They'd barely made the turn into the neighborhood before the blue and red spinning lights from the cruisers and ambulance ahead whisked through the Camaro's interior.

"Damn." Danny leaned forward a little in his seat. "She didn't tell me it was this bad."

"Probably looks worse than it is." Zeke paralleled against the curb closest to the ambulance, and the headlights from Jace's Silverado slid into the spot behind them. "Why don't you head on in to check on Gabe, and I'll see what the paramedics know. I'll meet you inside."

He'd barely got his car out of gear before Danny jumped out, rounded the hood, and jogged to the house's main entrance. After grabbing his gear from the trunk, he met up with the two-man ambulance crew before they could get their rig in reverse. "Gabrielle ever accept treatment?"

"Sorry, man. We can't talk treatment without a release."

"Right. Let me put this a different way. I'm a doc and a friend of the family. How did she present?"

The driver glanced over at his partner, who promptly shrugged as if to say he didn't have a clue. He looked back at Zeke. "You taking responsibility?"

"Absolutely."

The guy huffed and rubbed the top of his head. "She's a stubborn one. Never did let us do an assessment, but given the way she's holding her torso and the shallow breaths, I'd say she's got contusions and cracked or broken ribs."

"Anything else? Focus? Dizziness? Pupils?"

"Looked okay as far as we could tell. Hung around as long as our boss would let us, but if she's not up for help, we've got no reason to stay."

Zeke nodded to them both, waved, and stepped back so they could back out. "Thanks. Appreciate it."

Jace and Axel strolled up on either side of him, but it was Jace who spoke. "What's our play on this?"

"If we're as close to bringing Danny in as I think we are, then I vote we treat him like we would a brother."

Axel grinned, slid one hand in his designer slacks, and moseyed toward the cluster of cops gathered in front of the house. "Take control it is, then."

Jace chuckled and prowled alongside him. For about a millisecond, Zeke pitied Rockwall's finest. The founding members of The Haven Brotherhood were notorious for sending the best of law enforcement on a merry dance. In under five minutes, they'd have this crew eating out of their hands.

Zeke jogged up the steps to the front stoop where a uniformed rookie stood watch. Before the kid could put up much of an argument, Zeke slid through the open front door and into the main living room. Two steps in, he froze.

The woman beside Danny had her head down, her hair obscuring her face, but the differences between them even without her facial features showing were night and day. Where Danny was even with Zeke at six foot three, Gabe couldn't be much over five foot. And she was tiny. A honey-blonde faery hidden behind a deceptively rough exterior of faded jeans, flannel shirt, and steel-toed boots.

Danny's escalating voice punched through Zeke's dumbfounded haze. "What the fuck do you mean there's nothing you can do? She's hurt. She gave you a description. Find the motherfucker and make his ass pay."

Before the cop could consider putting the cuffs on his belt to good use, Zeke stepped in. "Hey, Danny. How about you let me see how your sister's doing?" He offered his hand to the cop on Gabe's other side, opened his mouth to speak, and damned near swallowed his tongue.

Oh, yeah. Gabe was a living breathing faery, complete with pale blue eyes, a heart-shaped face, and pouty, full lips. No man could look at her mouth and not crave at least a taste.

"I'm Dr. Dugan." He forced his attention away from Gabe and focused on the irritated cop. "I'm a friend of the family. I think if we can make sure Gabe's okay, everybody's stress level might even out. You got everything you need from her for now?"

The cop shook the hand offered and nodded, more than a little relief dancing behind his tired eyes. "What we don't have now, we can follow up on tomorrow." He cast a curt glare Danny's direction then a tight smile at Gabe. "You think of anything else, don't hesitate to use the number I gave you."

If she heard anything the cop said, or noted his swift departure, she didn't show it, keeping her gaze locked on Zeke. Her breaths were definitely shallow, and not once had she loosened the arm she had wrapped around her torso. The other arm she kept tucked tight to her side. The light in the room wasn't much, but her pupils looked normal.

She inched behind Danny and sucked in a short, sharp gasp. "I'm fine."

God, she was cute. Kind of like a cornered, feral kitten who couldn't decide whether to bolt for the closest hiding spot, or come out clawing. Even glaring daggers at him it was all he could do to hold back a chuckle. "That's what the paramedics said you told them, too. The problem is, your brother's about to go vigilante on a bunch of guys with badges because he's worried about you. He'd probably let that shit go a whole lot faster if someone who actually knew what they were talking about made that call."

"For the love of God, Gabe," Danny said. "Zeke's a trauma doc. He drove all the way out here, so just let him check you out."

The arm she held wrapped around her torso tightened and, while it was a subtle move, she flinched. Not a good sign if such a minute shift caused her pain.

"Give me five minutes," he said. "You might be right and just have a strain. If that's the case, you can give Danny a hard time for making a fuss."

She bit her lower lip, and his gut tensed as sure as he'd taken a physical punch.

Funny. Under normal circumstances, he could outwait the most stubborn patient, but standing there in front of her, an almost lethal tension burned through his muscles. Like his whole damned life teetered on the tip of a fiber optic point and could topple into hell or float to heaven depending on how she answered.

Her gaze shuttled from Danny to Zeke. "Five minutes."

Wow, Danny hadn't overexaggerated. People really could get the wrong impression from his sister's hard exterior, but the fear behind her eyes said the limit was more about what she could tolerate when it came to strangers.

"Five minutes," he agreed. He could have done it in three, but he'd take the extra bonus. Then he'd figure out how to make the leap from stranger to someone worthy of coaxing the wild and sweet kitten from her corner.

GABE WAS OUT of her ever lovin' mind. Saying she could make it five minutes around Danny's friend without coming off like a complete idiot was like saying she could tap dance for ten thousand people. If he'd been some average, ordinary Joe, *maybe* she could have pulled it off, but this guy—this doctor—was too beautiful for words. Olive skin, storm-gray eyes, and dark chocolate hair cut in one of those short *GQ* model styles that was just long enough a woman could run her fingers through it.

Or hang on for dear life while he kissed her with those killer lips.

Danny prowled to the wide window that spanned the front of the living room. They were down to just one cop car now, but the red and blue lights on top of it still spun their dizzy routine. "I'll go follow up on Mrs. Wallaby's house. Make sure she's locked up."

"No." She twisted to stop him, and a sharp jolt pierced straight through her chest. Scrunching her eyes, she held her breath and prayed the pain would ebb a little faster than it had the last two times she'd made such an ill-advised move. She wasn't stupid. Whatever injury she'd earned was way worse than anything else she'd had before, and if she hadn't seen the whopping huge ambulance bill Mr. Decker down the street had earned after his heart attack, she might have let the paramedics take a look.

Big, strong hands curled around her shoulders. Not Danny's, though. She opened her eyes and got a load of Zeke's up close and personal goodness. Talk about effective pain relief. Her whole damned body purred on idle, soaking in everything about him, stabbing pains be damned. You couldn't really say he had a beard. More like well-trimmed morning stubble that accented a strong, square jawline. His nose made her think of marauding Vikings, but up close his lips made her full-on stupid.

Zeke loosened his grip on her shoulders and smoothed his big hands to her upper arms. "Steady now?"

Steady was debatable, but she wasn't thinking about the ache anymore. More like one hundred percent focused on the warmth of his touch through her soft flannel button-down. "Yeah."

"Good." He locked gazes with Danny over her shoulder. "How about you stick with us for right now? Axel and Jace have things out there under control."

"Yeah, man. Absolutely. Whatever she needs."

Zeke studied her a second longer, released his hold on her arms, and jerked his head toward the bedrooms down the hall behind him. "How about we check you where we don't run the risk of an audience?"

He turned and led the way before she could muster any kind of argument. Careful not to jar her torso, she

followed him down the hallway, Danny close beside
her with a sturdy hand at her back. The stage-fright
sensation that came with strangers wasn't surprising
after battling it for years, but her response to Zeke was
different. Even Jimmy Franklin in high school didn't
have this kind of impact on her, and he'd muddled her
mind enough to talk her into giving up her virginity in
the backseat of his mother's Honda.

Zeke Dugan was a whole different beast. Everything
about him was bold and powerful. Even the way he
walked commanded attention. For a doc, he was pretty
dressed down, his faded Levi's molding lean hips and
grip-worthy backside. His pale blue T-shirt was simple
too, but stretched across his torso in a way that promised
lean, defined muscles underneath. Everything about
him exuded confidence. A man comfortable taking control even in unfamiliar surroundings.

Without his powerful scrutiny bearing down on her,
her thoughts boomeranged back to Zeke's comment
and the shitty committee that inevitably piped up with
any unknown or stressful situation stomped up to their
pulpit.

You don't know this man.

Unknown equals unsafe.

Too many people, all of them looking at you.

Judging you.

She tried to ignore the surging chorus and muttered
to Danny, "Who're Axel and Jace? I don't want them
in Mrs. Wallaby's house."

"They're friends." Danny kept his easy stride. "Good
people. If Mrs. Wallaby was here, she'd have Axel set up
with chocolate cake inside of five minutes, so let it go."

Easy for him to say. He wasn't the one her neighbor

had entrusted with her house, and she couldn't afford to let one of the few people she could actually talk to down. For years, Mrs. Wallaby had been the closest thing to a mother she'd had.

Instead of taking a left to Danny's room, Zeke stepped into hers, flipped on her light, and stood to one side of the door. He motioned her toward the bed. "You want to sit or stand?"

"Stand," she said. Then tucked on an awkward, "please." Yep. No way was she getting anywhere near a bed with this guy. She couldn't even manage decent manners, let alone conversation, and he wasn't even in touch distance yet. And was that a foreign accent? At first she'd thought he sounded like someone from the East Coast, but for a second there, his words had an almost Latin lilt to them.

"Not a problem." He shut the door like he was in a physician's exam room instead of surrounded by her very private haven. "Danny, can you get the blinds?"

He's only here as a favor to your brother.

No man like this guy would ever be interested in you anyway.

If you let him look too close, he'll see the real you.

Before she could panic and bolt, he was in front of her, the expression on his face all business. His long strong fingers cupped the sides of her face along her jawline and guided her head side to side, then front to back as if checking mobility. "Danny said you fell?"

She tried to mute the negative thoughts in her head and nodded, though his firm grip didn't allow for much. "Whoever it was pushed me over."

"You landed on the floor?"

"No, on the coffee table."

"That thing?" Danny said. "I've seen cinder blocks with more give."

The quip drew a grin from Zeke and the lightheadedness Gabe had struggled with grew a whole lot more pronounced. "Pretty sturdy stuff, huh?" He checked her eyes. "Did you hit your head?"

"I don't think so."

"No loss of consciousness?"

"No."

"Dizziness?"

"Does not being able to breathe count?"

It came out huskier than she'd intended, and she blanked her face to try and cover it.

Instead of garnering distance with her disaffected expression as she had when she'd used it in high school, Zeke nailed her with a blisteringly hot smile. Her heart jolted hard enough to give her shrieking ribs a run for their money. "Yeah, that counts."

"Okay, then dizzy." See? Not so bad. She'd answered his questions and only came across as a borderline bitch. Not too bad considering the circumstances. Until he reached for the unbuttoned edges of her flannel shirt and edged it off her shoulders.

Gabe jerked away and gasped at the sudden movement, tightening her arm around her chest.

Zeke froze, but kept his hold on her shirt. His voice was low and calm. Professional and soothing. "I need to see, *gatinha*. Danny's here. You're safe."

God, she was an idiot. Of course, it wasn't personal. He was a doctor and did this kind of crap every day. Heck, she'd probably never see him again after tonight anyway. She nodded and focused on the far wall. Colors from her latest art projects tucked into her many photo boards blurred together. Soft pink flowers, bold blue skies, and sage-green grass. "It's Gabe, not *gatinha*."

"I know what your name is." Even without looking, she could hear the smile in his voice.

"Then who's *gatinha*?" The soft flannel skimmed over her shoulders and down her arms, leaving tiny goose bumps in its wake. The fabric *swooshed* in an airy heap to the bed behind her.

"Not a who. A what. You see if you can figure it out while I check your ribs." He urged her to drop the arm she still had wrapped around her middle and lifted the hem of her tank. The cotton tickled her bare flesh on the way up, and his breath drifted light and teasing across her belly as he crouched beside her.

She tried to block him out, to imagine she was some-place else, but his scent was all around her. Not over-powering cologne like some men favored, but a barely there hint of something summery and warm. Like a re-ally high-priced body wash with a seriously powerful, yet sensual undercurrent.

He pressed in one particular spot on her side, and she hissed. "This where you made impact?"

Despite the painful contact, her cheeks burned as though someone had taken a blow torch to them and her heart fluttered in an out-of-control beat. "I think so."

"You'll have some pretty bruises for sure." He straightened and stood perpendicular to her injured side, placing one hand over her sternum and the other directly opposite on her spine. "I'm going to push my hands together, and I want you to show me where it hurts, okay?"

She nodded, almost eager for something to take her mind off all the other sensations battering through her.

In all of a second, she changed her mind, the slow pressure between his hands sending a brutal stab through her chest. She pointed to where it hurt. "Here."

Instantly, he let go and stepped back, reaching for the high-end messenger bag he'd brought with him. The stethoscope he pulled free sent a wave of relief through her. This routine she was familiar with. With the ear tips in place, he stepped in close and placed the flat disc above her heart. "Just breathe normal."

Yeah, like anything in her life had been normal for the last hour. Breathing had been a crapshoot since she'd landed on the coffee table. Next to him, it was twice as hard.

He shifted and slid the disc under the back of her tank. "Take a deep breath."

She shook her head. "It hurts."

His hand at her shoulder squeezed in a comforting grip. "Just do your best."

Her best wasn't much and sent a fresh wave of discomfort coursing through her torso.

Stepping back, he dropped the stethoscope around his neck, trailed his gaze along her shoulders and arms, and frowned. "You cold?"

More like strung out on sensory overload and in desperate need of a beer. "A little."

He snatched her flannel off the bed and held it out so she could slide it on without too much torque on her ribs. When he'd helped guide the edges up and over her shoulders, he turned her to face the end of the bed, sat on the edge so he was on eye level with her, and loosely clasped his hands between his wide legs. "I'm about ninety-nine percent sure you've got two, maybe three, cracked ribs. If that's the case, treatment is minimal and easy for you to handle on your own. The problem is, I'm worried about your breathing. Broken ribs on their own aren't a huge issue, but if they puncture a lung it can cause problems fast."

Danny edged in closer to her and smoothed his hand down her back. "How do we know if that's a problem?"

"I need an X-ray."

"No hospitals." She scowled up at Danny beside her. "I just got my bills paid off, and I'm not racking up more if I can take care of it on my own."

"I said you could take care of the ribs on your own," Zeke said. "Lungs are a whole different matter. We're talking the difference between you having a few weeks of rough sleep, versus you not waking up." He zeroed in on Danny. "She needs an X-ray."

Danny stepped back and motioned to the door. "Okay, let's go."

"No."

"Gabe, don't be a dumb ass," Danny said. "It's an X-ray, not a fucking transplant."

"Yeah, well, the last time we walked into a hospital, Dad never came back out." She clamped her lips up tight and averted her face. Great. Now she was a loon and a wimp.

Warmth and the delicious pressure of Zeke's fingers encircled her wrist. "What if I told you there's a place I can take you and it won't cost you a dime? A stand-alone place without a ton of people."

"Like an urgent care?"

"Sort of, but without all the crowds. We'll take X-rays, see what the damage is, and go from there. But trust me, lungs are not something you want to mess with. Better to play it safe."

A firm, but polite knock sounded on the door. Danny opened it but kept one hand on the knob, only leaving a two-foot gap between the edge and the jamb. Her brother's Goliath frame blocked whoever was on the other side. "Hey, Jace."

A deep rumbling voice issued from the hallway. "Everyone's pulling out. Beckett's got a crew coming by to do their own check of Wallaby's house."

"Who's Beckett?" She shifted closer to Danny so she could put a face with the voice.

Danny stepped away at the same time, revealing yet another seriously hot guy with one hand propped on the door frame. So this was Jace. She'd heard Danny mention the name a time or two, but never imagined he'd look like this. He wasn't *GQ* hot like Zeke. More like old-school rock-star hot, complete with shoulder-length dark hair and a full beard/mustache combination. She'd bet he had at least one custom Harley lined up in his garage to go with his faded jeans and well-worn leather jacket. He even had the dirty growling voice and the wicked, all too assessing stare to go with the image. "How you holdin' up, sugar?"

Gabe ducked her head, her sturdy boots the visual equivalent of a lifeline.

"Best guess is two or three cracked ribs," Zeke answered for her, "but I need X-rays to rule out pneumothorax."

Quiet stretched in the tiny room. Even without looking up, she had a good feeling there was a lot of silent macho man eyeballing going on.

Zeke broke it with a firm, "I want to take her to Sanctuary."

That got her attention. She looked up in time to see Jace's grin flatline.

Jace studied her, considered Danny for another second, then focused on Zeke. "You sure?"

"What's Sanctuary?" she asked.

Zeke stayed focused on Jace. "Not safe to let it go without checking and she's not comfortable in a public place."

Funny how he'd zeroed in on the real stickler instead of the cost aspect of her not wanting medical treatment. The care and concern probably should have been a comfort, but the fact that he'd figured out what a freak she was only made her feel two more shades of stupid. "I'm fine."

Jace pulled a toothpick from his pocket, tucked it under his tongue, and scanned Gabe head to toe. "Sugar, if my brother's willing to put his ass out there and take you to Sanctuary, then I doubt the word *fine* is anywhere in his diagnosis." He dipped his head toward Zeke, an unspoken and indefinable meaning behind the look so intense it sent a shiver dancing down her spine. He turned and sauntered down the hallway. "Let's huddle with Axel, and we'll head out."

THREE

ONLY AN INDUSTRIAL grade exterior light marked Sanctuary's heavily secured, yet nondescript entrance, but Zeke could have navigated his way there in his sleep. From the outside, it was little more than a standalone warehouse nestled alongside a whole string of storage buildings. The inside was a whole different ballgame, one he and his brothers leveraged for a variety of favors when the right opportunities presented themselves.

He parked his hot rod just outside the main door, and Danny swung Gabe's truck in right beside him. Thankfully, Jace and Axel had agreed to let him handle the thing with Gabe solo. Neither of them were too thrilled with the fact he'd mentioned Sanctuary in front of Gabe, but once he'd reminded them how close Danny was to being family, they'd dropped their argument and headed back to work. It didn't hurt that Zeke had come up with the idea of playing the mini emergency facility off as a private medical care operation to cover what really went down inside.

Punching the automated locks Danny had added to the car, Zeke ambled to Gabe's truck and held the passenger door wide while Danny helped Gabe out of the raised cab. "The ride hurt too bad on the way over?"

Gabe didn't look at him, but shook her head. Understandable considering the night she'd had and the pain she wrestled.

"We'll get this over with as quick as we can, then Danny can pick you up some pain killers on the way home." He flipped the locks on the building's front door and deactivated the high-end security system inside the entrance. When Beck had insisted on the fingerprint scanner on top of the standard key code, Zeke had argued they were going overboard on precautions. Then Beck had pointed out the total cost of the assets hidden inside, and Zeke had conceded overkill might not be a bad deterrent. Especially considering the type of people he treated here.

He flipped the light switches and the rows of commercial fluorescents overhead hummed their eager greeting. Two emergency gurneys were centered on the industrial tile floor with focal lights mounted above them. Racks stocked with all the basic emergency gear he could ask for lined both side walls, while huge monitors and Knox's state-of-the-art computers were mounted along the front.

Danny paced to the center of the room and gaped at all the equipment. "Man, this is cool."

"Where are we?" Gabe didn't seem nearly as impressed, holding her spot by the door just as tightly as she kept that arm of hers coiled around her waist.

Zeke shrugged and fired up the main computers. "It's not as big of a deal as it looks. Just self-insurance taken to the extreme."

"Self-insurance." The way Gabe said it made it more of an openly skeptic statement of disbelief than a question.

"Yep. Some people would rather fork over insurance premiums for their own setup and guarantee privacy. Not to mention, there's no wait time."

"And you know people like this?"

"I know a few." Most of them were men with a dirty background and zero interest in getting anywhere near a public facility with records and a friendliness for cops. Not to mention, they were usually plugged up with bullet holes or knife wounds when they came through Sanctuary's doors.

He motioned to the dark, isolated room off to one side. "Danny, do me a favor. Turn on the light in there and help Gabe have a seat."

The two shuffled off in the direction indicated while he dug through the cabinets in search of a hospital gown. He could have sworn he'd ordered some when they first tricked out the facility, but damned if he could find them now. Then again, modesty wasn't something he normally had to deal with behind these walls.

To hell with it. He gave up looking and headed in with Danny and Gabe. If her color was any indication, she needed pain relief and quiet a whole lot more than she needed standard protocol. One look at her, tense and obviously shaken as she perched on the edge of a metal chair, and the same protective impulse he'd battled when he'd touched her back at her house roared full bore. "Okay, *gatinha*. I'm just going to snap some pictures, take a look at what's going on, and we'll see if we can't get you home. But first, we've got a tactical hurdle to leap."

She frowned at him then glanced at Danny. "What kind of hurdle?"

He nodded in the general direction of her torso. "My machine doesn't play nice with metal. I might not be a woman, but even I know pretzling into or out of a bra is a trick even without a broken rib. With one, it's going to be impossible. So who do you want to help you out of it? Danny, or me?"

In all of two seconds, her cheeks flamed a bold red and her already shallow breaths turned even threadier. "I can do it."

Zeke lifted a brow. "You willing to risk hurting yourself more in the process?"

Unlike Danny, who had an unbelievable poker face when he chose to use it, every thought and emotion Gabe processed burned bright and beautiful across her face. Embarrassment. Fear. Confusion and acceptance. It kind of made him want to see a whole lot of other expressions on her face. Like the fleeting glimpse of pleasure he'd caught when his fingertips first touched her skin.

"You won't look?" she said.

He fudged as much as he could. "I promise I'll give you all the privacy I can, but you've got to remember, this is an everyday thing for me."

She bit her lip and stared down at the floor. "Then I'd rather have you."

"Thank God," Danny said, twisting for the door and fiddling with his skully like he always did when he was antsy.

Zeke held out his hand and pulled Gabe to her feet. "Danny, why don't you wait in my office across the hall? It shouldn't take us more than five minutes once we get her situated."

Seemingly happy to have dodged an awkward moment with his little sister, Danny hightailed it out of the room and shut the door behind him.

Zeke stood behind Gabe and edged her flannel shirt off her shoulders with as much indifference as possible.

It was a hell of a lot harder the second time knowing what was hidden underneath. Unlike her brother, Gabe's skin was closer to cream, only a hint of golden goodness taking the edge of what could have made her seem pale. And it was soft. Soft, taut, and stretched over easy, lithe curves that made him want to touch her in ways that would make Danny want to shoot him on sight.

He eased the hem of her tank up.

Her hands closed over his, stopping him in his tracks.

"It's okay. I'm just lifting it enough you can slide your arms out. We'll get the bra off and get the tank back in place. The cotton will be fine for the X-rays."

For a few seconds all she did was stand there, locked in place. More than anything, he wanted to move in closer and give her comfort. Tactile, lingering comfort.

She swallowed so big, it looked like it hurt, then she nodded and released his hands. "Okay."

Moving as quickly as he dared, he lifted the shirt up, thankful for how the stretchy fabric allowed her to slip her arms out with minimum distress. He didn't give her time to process what came next, flipping the clasp on her bra.

Her gasp ricocheted through the room and made his dick twitch with a whole lot of ideas on how he could illicit the same sound.

God, he was an asshole. A patient was standing in front of him, hurting and mortified, and he was entertaining how many ways he could get his hands all over her. He slid the straps off her shoulders and tugged the tank back down so she could maneuver her arms back in. "See? All done."

Before she could answer, he strode around her, folding up her innocent white bra as he went, and laid it in the chair next to her purse. His mind conjured up a whole slew of images to go with that plain scrap of fabric, none of them decent or acceptable given the circumstances. He ground his teeth together and forced his thoughts back to the task at hand. "Okay, let's see what's going on with your ribs."

The process went relatively quick and easy. Or easy for him, anyway. To her credit, she muscled through the difficult times when the shots required she lift her arms up and out of the way, but shook with fatigue by the time it was over. He guided her back to her chair and paused by the closed door. "You want help putting that back on, or can you handle freewheeling it on the way home?"

Another appealing flush rushed up her neck and she stuffed the bra deep in the hippy-style hobo bag. "I'm good."

Yeah, she was. Tough in a way that put most of his patients to shame. And yet, she was still the kind of soft and sweet you wanted to see curled up next to you. Definitely a feral kitten.

He opened the door and found Danny anchored on the other side, his arms crossed and his mouth pinched in a hard line. "You done?"

"Yep. Give me five and we'll know what's up."

Reality was more like three minutes, the result pretty much what he'd expected—two clean, nondisplaced fractures and no sign of damage to the lung. Good news for her as far as risk went, so long as she didn't push matters in the early healing process. He grabbed an RX pad, powered down his computer, and flipped the lights.

Gabe's semi-whispered words drifted into the intersecting hallway. "Don't you think it's weird he's got access to his own mini hospital?"

Zeke hesitated outside the X-ray room door.

"It's not a hospital, Gabe." Danny didn't seem as interested in hiding his commentary. His deep voice traveled crystal clear. "It's like an Urgent Care. You can find one of those on every damned corner anymore. And no, it's not weird. You know how rich people are. Enough money and connections and you don't have to wait or deal with the riffraff. So what if it helped you out this time?"

"It's just weird. How do you know those guys aren't into illegal things?"

"Trust me. The brothers are many things, but the one thing you can count on is them doing the right thing. Always."

"That's the other thing. Why do you keep calling them brothers?"

"Because they are."

"They don't look a thing alike. No way they're family."

"Blood ain't everything, Gabe. Let it go."

Danny wasn't wrong on that score. In the ten years he'd known Jace, Axel, and the rest of the guys, he'd had more of a family than he ever did growing up. Not that his parents didn't try, they were just usually too beat after trying to make a living to have much energy left for a little kid.

Gabe kept up with her arguments, her suspicious nature undoubtedly something he should be more concerned about, especially with Danny having one foot in the brotherhood. Instead, all he could focus on was her voice. Soft and sweet as a fluffy kitten even if she was talking ninety miles an hour. Which was kind of funny when he thought about how limited her words had been throughout the rest of her ordeal.

A shaky vulnerability crept into her voice. "What happens if they're not as good as you think they are and something happens to you? You're all I've got left."

"Jesus, I'm not in high school anymore, Gabe. I haven't done anything like that in years."

Well, not entirely true. Zeke knew damned good and well Danny had done at least three sizable B&Es to pay off his dad's mortgage. But Gabe had gotten to keep the house she'd grown up in.

"I'm not Mom," Danny said. "I know you missed her growing up, but I'm not going anywhere. Not by choice or by accident. The brothers are just guys like me who found a way to make their mark on the world. They're helping me find my way."

"How? Doing what?"

Danny hesitated.

Zeke straightened off the wall he'd leaned into and rounded the entry. Keeping his head down, he scribbled out a prescription, hoping his preoccupation would cover the timing of his arrival. "Well, the good news is your lungs are solid. On the downside, you've got two fractured ribs."

"How do you treat that?" Danny said.

Zeke halted in front of the two of them and focused on Gabe. "Not much I can do. In the old days, they'd wrap the chest to alleviate the pain and support movement. Some folks still do, but I don't advise it. The most important thing you can do is take big, deep breaths several times a day. If I wrap your ribs it'll make deep breathing hard to do."

"What about work?" she said.

"Danny says you're a mechanic, right?"

She nodded.

"Yeah, engines aren't going to be on your short list for at least three to four weeks."

"I can't be off work for four weeks."

Danny squeezed her shoulder. "Mike's cool. He'll work you out some kind of deal."

"If he doesn't, let me know," Zeke said. "My brothers have all kinds of businesses. I'd bet at least one of them needs some short-term help that wouldn't put too much strain on your ribs." He handed her the script. "These ought to help with pain until you can shift over to ibuprofen. For at least two or three nights, I want you to be sure and take them at night so your breathing stays steady while you sleep."

She carefully tugged the paper from between his fingers and scowled down at it. "You don't have drugs here?"

And there were those cute claws. Funny how all they did was make him want to provoke her a little more. "This is a medical facility. Not a pharmacy. Besides, uncontrolled narcotics are against the law. I've got a license to protect."

Talk about a complete load of shit. He had enough narcotics to cover all kinds of injuries locked up nice and tight in storage, but no way was he clueing her into that after what he'd overhead. He stepped back and motioned Danny to the door. "Why don't you get her home so she can rest? There's a twenty-four-hour pharmacy just up the street, and those should be pretty cheap generic."

Danny helped Gabe to her feet. "Aren't you coming?"

"Nope, gotta clean up and turn everything off." Reaching into his back pocket, he pulled out his billfold and snagged a business card. He handed it to Gabe. "If the pain gets worse or you're worried about anything at all, call me at that number. I don't sleep much so don't worry about what time it is."

Danny stretched out his hand. "Thanks, man. I can't tell you how much I appreciate you helping us out."

Zeke shook the hand offered and slapped Danny on the back. "Wasn't a problem. Happy I could help." He made it until Danny and Gabe reached the main door before he gave in to pure impulse. "Hey, *gatinha*."

She kept her torso ruler straight, but craned her neck toward him.

"Whether you call or not, I'm stopping by in a few days to check on you."

Gabe frowned.

Danny smiled huge and almost smacked Gabe on the shoulder, but stopped a few inches before he made contact. "See? Told you the brothers were awesome."

An unapologetic snort drifted back to him a second before the door shut, leaving him alone in the sterile room.

Awesome was debatable. Dancing into dangerous territory was more like it. But for the first time in months, that constant buzz beneath his skin was quiet, and he had a pretty good idea tangling with the little kitten was the cause.

Don't miss the next steamy
Haven Brotherhood romance
WILD & SWEET
Available in ebook and audio April 2017 from
Rhenna Morgan and Carina Press
Wherever Carina Press ebooks are sold
www.CarinaPress.com

ACKNOWLEDGMENTS

ONE OF THE best parts of writing is sitting down with subject matter experts to explore new ideas and professions. Jace's story gave me the opportunity to visit with one of the best and most personable doctors I know. My utmost gratitude to Dr. H. Dwight Hardy III for his time and patience answering my *very* long list of questions... not to mention his constant care throughout the years. If only all docs could be like him.

I'd also like to thank Angela James for her enthusiasm and support in launching The Haven Brotherhood. As with most of my characters, Jace and his brothers are near and dear to my heart, so having Angela as my editor and their champion is both a blessing and an honor.

Finally, a never-ending thank-you to Cori Deyoe, Juliette Cross, Kyra Jacobs, Audrey Carlan, Dena Garson and, of course, my family. In the ups and downs of the publishing world, they are my anchors. I *might* be able to struggle through the process without them, but I'd be frayed beyond repair in the end, and it wouldn't be nearly as much fun.

ABOUT THE AUTHOR

RHENNA MORGAN IS A happily-ever-after addict—hot men, smart women and scorching chemistry required. A triple-A personality with a thing for lists and an almost frightening iPhone cover collection, Rhenna's a mom to two beautiful little girls and married to an extremely patient husband who's mastered the art of hiding the exasperated eye roll.

When she's not neck deep in writing, she's probably driving with the windows down and the music up loud, plotting her next hero and heroine's adventure. (Though trolling online for man-candy inspiration on Pinterest comes in a close second.)

She'd love to share her antics and bizarre sense of humor with you and get to know you a little better in the process. You can sign up for her newsletter and gain access to exclusive snippets, upcoming releases, fun giveaways and social media outlets at *www.rhennamorgan.com*.

If you enjoyed ROUGH & TUMBLE, she hopes you'll share the love with a review at your favorite online bookstore.